DATE DUE

AMUNDA PUBL

Eureka

ANTHONY QUINN

Eureka

JONATHAN CAPE
LONDON

1 3 5 7 9 10 8 6 4 2

Jonathan Cape, an imprint of Vintage Publishing,
20 Vauxhall Bridge Road,
London SW1V 2SA

Jonathan Cape is part of the Penguin Random House group of companies
whose addresses can be found at global.penguinrandomhouse.com.

Penguin
Random House
UK

First published by Jonathan Cape in 2017

penguin.co.uk/vintage

A CIP catalogue record for this book is available from the British Library

ISBN 9781910702529 (Hardback edition)
ISBN 9781910702536 (Trade paperback edition)

Lines from 'Provide, Provide' are taken from *The Poetry of Robert Frost*
by Robert Frost, published by Jonathan Cape. Reprinted by permission of
The Random House Group Ltd

The song 'Surabaya Johnny' is from the musical *Happy End*, written
by Kurt Weill, Elisabeth Hauptmann and Bertolt Brecht

The lyrics from the song 'This Bitter Earth' are by Clyde Lovern Otis

Typeset at 12.25/13.75 pt Fournier MT by Jouve (UK), Milton Keynes

Printed and bound by Clays Ltd, St Ives PLC

Penguin Random House is committed to a sustainable future
for our business, our readers and our planet. This book is made
from Forest Stewardship Council® certified paper.

For Dan Franklin

Believe me, there are certain mysteries, certain secrets in my own work which even I don't understand, nor do I try to do so . . . Mysteries have to be respected if they are to retain their power. Art disturbs: science reassures.

Georges Braque

I

EUREKA!

Nat had been staring at the word for an age. He had typed it upon sitting down first thing this morning, and it had squatted there at the top of the page, alone and unbudging, ever since. *Eureka.* From the Greek, *I have found it.* The irony of that wasn't lost on him. Not only had he not found it, he barely knew where to start looking. And yet the word had seemed to him such a promising one, bristling with scholarly pride, an intellectual yahoo. *Eureka.* He must have first heard it, like everyone else, at school: Archimedes seeing the water rise as he lowered himself into his bath and suddenly understanding that the volume of water displaced must be equal to the volume of the part of his body he had submerged, which in turn would solve the problem of measuring the volume of irregular objects. 'Eureka!' he supposedly cried. Or, as the class wag had translated it: 'This bath water's too bloody hot.'

For want of something else, he typed:

A screenplay by Nathaniel Fane

Nat had once been an instinctive writer, and trusted his gift to the extent that he could simply turn up at his desk in the morning and start clattering away, his fingers a blur over the typewriter. The reassuring metallic rat-a-tat-tat of the keys would carry him through to lunch, and even if he didn't get it right straight away – who on earth did? – the words kept pouring out of him. By the end of the day he would have ten or twelve pages of dialogue. Now every tall white sheet of A4 loomed like an Everest.

He had written his first screenplay eight years earlier, a racy romantic comedy called *The Hot Number*, which had won him an Academy Award. His name, already well known in British drama, became a fixture in showbiz gossip columns. Film producers sought him out; society people fawned over him. 'Nat Fame', the rhyme he had cultivated from youth, had become his cherished sobriquet.

Early success proved, as it so often does, a false friend. He had written a number of screenplays since; only two of them had been produced. The last one, *Square in the Circle*, was strafed by villainously bad reviews, and went up in flames. He was paid, of course, but it didn't much salve his pride. Nor did it keep his name where he wanted it, front and centre in the public consciousness. His latest enterprise was to adapt for the screen a story by Henry James. The immediate task had been to find a new title – the producers had what they called a problem with *The Figure in the Carpet*. There wasn't much support for the word 'figure'. And they all hated 'carpet'. When he proposed *Eureka* they didn't seem very enthused by that, either. A Greek what? asked Berk Cosenza, the moneyman from New York. Nat was in a room of blank-faced executives; only when he half recalled an account of some king using the eureka theory to determine the purity of gold in his crown did Berk lift his head and squint in his direction. *Gold?* he said. Nat wasn't sure of the details, but having caught the scent of interest he quickly pressed his tiny sponge of information for all it was worth.

It had nearly run dry when Berk began to nod his head. He held up his palms straight and spread an imaginary line through the air. 'Eureka,' he said. A couple of others echoed the word in cautious approval. Nat, wise to the shifting currents of favour, returned an expression intended to suggest that this stroke of inspiration was entirely down to Berk's genius. He had got his title.

And two weeks later that was all he had got. He rose from his desk, yawned and lit a cigarette, standing in the wonky parallelogram of sunlight laid across the carpet. From his window he could see the parapet of the Royal Academy, his next-door neighbour. Nat had lived at Albany for six years, though he had recently moved to a larger set on the top floor; he liked to think of himself going up in the world. He had spent a fortune redecorating the flat, replacing the patterned, swagged look with a lot of chic black-and-white Italian furniture. He'd had the carpets ripped up and the toffee-coloured parquet beneath lacquered to a high gleam, and into the bedroom had imported a huge polar-bear skin. On this he liked to loll and imagine himself borne aloft, like Hannibal on his elephant. Mirrored glass was inlaid everywhere, for the way it made the light dance in the room. The kitchen, where he never prepared anything more than an omelette, was an angular symphony in marble and steel. The expense was not in vain, either. *Queen* had done a photo shoot of the set when they came to interview him.

He pulled up the sash window and listened to the hum of traffic that wafted over the rooftops from Piccadilly. A morning's mooching had driven him to distraction. His typewriter waited – the conscience in the room. Could he justify sloping out for an hour or so? It was the writer's dilemma: you become so sick of your own company, and yet you daren't be too long away from it. He picked up his sweater from the back of the chair and slung it over his shoulders, Riviera-style. He gave himself a quick dousing of L'Heure Bleue, and set out.

In the Albany courtyard he lingered for a moment, enjoying the monkish quiet. It still seemed remarkable to him that such tranquillity existed with central London right on the doorstep. So: back or front? The building's Janus-faced aspect was another thing he delighted in. Leave by the front entrance and you were absorbed into the soothing gentility of St James, with its clubs and galleries and tailors. Slip out the back door and a right turn would pull you into the venereal embrace of Soho and its lovely squalor.

He chose the front way. The problem of *Eureka* might be more easily resolved by immersion in the smart neighbourhood Henry James preferred. Here on Jermyn Street he could imagine the rattle of carriage wheels and the rustle of crinolines familiar to the citizens of *fin-de-siècle* London. Except they were doing away with all that: the producers wanted it to be a present-day version of the story. So, out with the frock coats and opera hats, in with the brocade suits and kipper ties. The plot remained the same. Two friends revere an ageing novelist, Hugh Vereker. The narrator, a critic, writes an article about Vereker's latest book; shortly afterwards he happens to meet the author himself, who suavely but firmly dismisses the efforts of the critic – of every critic – to locate the essential 'secret' of his work, 'the string the pearls were strung on, the buried treasure, the figure in the carpet'. The other friend, George, on hearing this, takes up the challenge and rereads Vereker's books in search of their elusive secret. The attempt to unravel it becomes an increasingly fractious contest between them.

Having read it again, Nat felt that something had shifted in his understanding. Now the veils and screens of its intellectual puzzle seemed merely a decoy, a diversion from the central drama of the story, which was the unresolved triangle between George, his fiancée Gwen and the narrator, Chas. Was it actually a romance, disguised as a literary teaser? Or the other way round? He would have to decide, and sooner rather than later. The studio wanted the first draft in six weeks' time.

At the little newsagent's on Bury Street he bought twenty Peter Stuyvesant and a stack of magazines, which he carted into Wilton's and laid to one side of his luncheon table: they still called it luncheon here. With a plate of oysters before him he riffled through *Town*, *Esquire*, the *New Yorker*. By the time he was finishing his sole meunière he had polished off *Playboy*, *Queen*, the *Statesman*, *Vogue* and *Paris Match*. He read impatiently, pecking at titbits and quickly discarding them. Nothing properly held his attention in this restless mood; he would get halfway through an article and abandon it, bored. It was only while he was idling through that day's *Chronicle* that he found something that made him sit up in his chair.

> The German film director Reiner Werther Kloss was the toast of the Parisian beau monde this week. His film *The Private Life of Hanna K*, about a fragile romance between a French maquisard and a German woman during the war, has been a box-office smash in France. It was marked by a gala dinner in his honour last night at the Palais-Royal. Kloss, 33, wunderkind of the new German cinema, behaved on the occasion with perfect affability and good manners.

At a press conference he thanked his hosts and said that he continued to be honoured everywhere but in his own land. 'Maybe film directors are today's prophets,' he joked. He added that he looked forward to working on his next film, an adaptation of the Henry James story 'The Figure in the Carpet'. 'It's a strange piece, something I've wanted to do for years,' he said in his quiet voice. 'It is about the mysterious conundrum of art, this story — about the way writing torments and obsesses us, can lure us into madness. Sonja [Zertz, leading lady in three of his pictures] will star, also Vere Summerhill, one of the great British actors.' It is understood that the film will be a modernised version of the story, set mainly in London and Italy. Can Henry James be brought up to date? 'Of course, he's a modern,' the director replied. 'He used also words like "fag end" and "dudes". That's up to date. We have someone writing the screenplay at the moment, so we should be ready to shoot it this summer. I have the greatest hopes for this film.'

Nat snapped the paper shut in a spasm of irritation. He and Reiner Werther Kloss had yet to meet, it was true, but that was no excuse for the director to sound quite so offhand about the script. He had 'someone' writing the screenplay, did he? Just fancy. Would it have killed him to identify that 'someone' as the award-winning screenwriter Nathaniel Fane?

He prickled as he thought of his consequence in the world slipping. There was no stock on the market more irrational than the stock of artistic popularity. His was on a downward plunge, it seemed. He had never minded disobliging references to himself in the papers, so long as they were accompanied by a photograph and his name was spelt correctly. What he couldn't bear, what absolutely put a crimp on his day, was being anonymous, reduced to a mere 'someone', an also-ran. He would ask Penny, his agent, to contact the *Chronicle* – casually – giving notice that, further to yesterday's news item, etc., Nat Fane would be writing the screenplay of Reiner Werther Kloss's next film. Just that. Readers had to be kept informed, after all.

The bill was shocking, as it always was at Wilton's. He paid and left, wondering where he might go to escape his oubliette of insignificance. A place where he might be spotted, pointed at, talked about. Outside, the March afternoon was mild, the sky clouded and sunless. He was near his club, the Nines, on Dover Street, but dropping in there would hardly buff up his diminished lustre; at this hour it was unlikely anyone would be around, and if there were they'd probably be asleep. He sauntered on, until he came to Brown's, and decided that he fancied tea in the hotel's lounge. This too proved a disappointment, a room whose air was dead but for the tinkle of china and the genteel murmur of a couple of elderly ladies who'd been there since 1951. He sank down onto a sofa, ordered a pot of Earl Grey and asked the waitress to bring him some newspapers, so as to check where else his name was being ignored.

Another thing nagged him about the Kloss piece, the remark the director had made about the themes inherent in 'The Figure in the Carpet'. He'd got the stuff about writing as a torment and an obsession. But what was this about 'luring us into madness'? Where on earth was *that* in James's story? Perhaps the German's imperfect command of English had misled him; perhaps he hadn't meant to say that, or else he had been misquoted.

He had returned from the gents and was pouring himself another cup of milkless tea when he noticed something odd. His wallet, parked on the table, looked conspicuously slimmer. It had been plumped with a wodge of ten-pound notes – now there was just one. He looked about the room, mystified more than outraged. The two old ladies were still blahing away; a couple of American tourists had just settled in across the room – non-starters as suspects. His visit to the loo had lasted all of three minutes, maybe four, so whoever it was must have been quick about it. He supposed it might have been some light-fingered opportunist happening to pass by, but the lounge was so somnolent at this hour even that seemed unlikely. It was why he had thought it perfectly safe to leave on the table in the first place.

The waitress, catching his eye, approached him with an obliging smile. She wore a cap and white pinafore over black. He wasn't going to make a fuss, but beckoned her forward conspiratorially.

'Miss, did you happen to see anyone hovering about this table a moment ago? I ask because my wallet appears to have been relieved of about, ooh, a hundred pounds.'

The girl's eyes widened in alarm. 'You mean' – she dropped her voice to a scandalised half-whisper – '*stolen*?'

'That is exactly what I mean.' Close up, she was almost cartoonish in her prettiness: heart-shaped face, button-nosed, violet-coloured eyes framed by long, dark lashes. The pancake make-up was as thickly applied as an actress's. Beneath it, her expression looked pained to the point of tearfulness.

'Oh, how awful! But I'm sorry, I – I didn't see anyone.'

Nat clicked his tongue gently and glanced about the room again, though he sensed the uselessness of further scrutiny. 'I've heard of "daylight robbery" yet never quite believed in it. So there's a lesson. I suppose I should – would you be good enough to fetch your manager for me?'

She paused for a moment, sympathy still in her voice but a distant concern crinkling her eyes. 'I'm not sure he's here at the moment,' she said. Then she gestured at the violated wallet. 'Did they really take . . . everything?'

Nat stared at her, and chuckled. 'Well, they left me a tip. A tenner. But I'd been expecting to keep the lot.' When she still stood there, he adapted his tone to something more businesslike. 'Perhaps you could find someone else in authority.'

The girl gave an obedient nod, and withdrew. Stupid of him, really; he'd only taken it out of his pocket because he didn't like the thing spoiling the line of his suit. But it was just money after all, it wasn't valuable stuff, not like the time they'd burgled the flat in Onslow Square, taken all the jewellery and peed on the carpets. That was horrible, barbarous . . .

Of a sudden he understood, and quickly rose from the sofa. He crossed the room and turned down the staff corridor where he'd seen her disappear. A liveried waiter halted, about to stop him – then didn't. He walked on through the clanging kitchen and its steaming miasma, past white-coated staff too busy or indifferent to notice him. Instinct had taken over and directed his steps out into a service yard, where he found his waitress alone, leaning against a wall. Her cap was off, exposing a prim bun of mid-brown hair. She had just taken out a cigarette when she saw him, her face stiffening with surprise.

'Hello again,' said Nat, moving in close and producing his packet of Stuyvesant. 'So sorry to interrupt your break. Here, have one of mine.'

The girl, faltering, said, 'You're not supposed to – it's for staff only . . .'

'Oh, I'm sure we can bend the rules just this once. And you did say your manager wasn't around.' He beamed charmingly at her, still holding the proffered smoke. With a twitch of reluctance she took one, and averted her gaze.

'Do you have a match?' he asked.

As she reached into her pocket Nat took a step forward and seized her wrist. She gasped in surprise, and tried to pull away, but his grip was as strong as whipcord.

'Get off me,' she hissed, eyes daggered at him. 'I'll scream and have the police on you.'

Nat smiled. 'Really? Go on then, let's hear it.'

She still fought against his grip, but from the panicked shiftiness in her eyes it was clear she wasn't going to scream after all. Reddening with the exertion she muttered, 'You big bully.'

'Oh, don't be like that, we were getting on so well,' said Nat, who now pulled her wrist away and inserted his other hand into her pocket. He felt around for a moment, ignoring her outraged protests, and deep in the skirt's folds found what he'd been looking for: a wad of ten-pound notes. He held it up for her inspection.

'That's mine,' she said sulkily. 'Savings.'

Nat half bleated a laugh. 'Of course. Which you always carry on your person. Well, you mentioned the police – let's have them decide which of us it belongs to.'

He began to strong-arm her towards the door, and felt her struggling intensify. She pulled against his hand. 'Wait, wait. Please – don't turn me in. I only took it because I knew you could afford it.'

Nat stopped, and cocked his head. Her innocence, so convincing a few minutes ago, had been but a mask. 'How d'you know I can afford it?'

She gave him an unillusioned once-over. 'You're Nathaniel Fane, aren't you? The writer.'

Nothing could have been better calculated to mollify his bruised vanity. He knew it, and almost laughed at himself for succumbing. He let the manacle of his hand loosen on her wrist. 'I suppose you've seen me on the telly.'

She protruded her lip in casual affirmation. 'I saw a couple of your plays. When I was at RADA.'

'Ah. Enjoy them?'

She pulled a considering expression. 'They were fine.'

Nat, despite himself, burst out laughing. 'Now isn't *that* the faintest praise!' He scrutinised her. 'RADA ... At least your training hasn't gone to waste. That little display of fellow feeling back in the lounge was masterly. You looked fit to bawl. It had me fooled – for a minute.'

She narrowed her eyes. 'What gave it away?'

'Ha. It was the moment when you looked at the wallet and asked if they'd "really" taken everything. The *really* was the tell – it suggested, implicitly, that you knew the thief had left something in there. A tenner, in fact.' He paused for a moment. 'So: you do this for a living?'

'What, thieving?' Her tone was offended.

'I meant waitressing.'

She nodded heavily. 'It pays the rent, just about.'

'And the stage?'

'I've done the odd thing. Some club theatre. Nothing *you'd* have seen.'

Nat raised his eyebrows. 'You've no idea what kind of things I've seen.' He glanced at his watch. 'I'm a bit too busy to go chasing after a policeman. Consider this a reprieve, but I'd advise you not to make a habit of it. Others may not be so lenient.'

She held his gaze for a grateful moment. 'Thanks.'

He was moving off when he thought of something, and halted. 'By the way, why *didn't* you take the lot?'

She shrugged. 'I couldn't leave you without a bean. That would've been cruel.'

For a moment he thought she was joking, but her expression wore no trace of humour. He gave a little shake of his head as he exited the yard. The Good Thief, he mused. He might be able to make something of that.

Back at home he prepared for the evening with a bath, from which he emerged without Archimedean enlightenment, but soothed at least, and cleansed. As he dressed he listened to his favourite long-player of the moment, a series of duets by Coltrane and Johnny Hartman, whose velvety voice sounded almost like a tenor sax itself. How anyone could sing 'Lush Life' and stay in tune was beyond him. He made a phone call to check that he was still expected, then packed an overnight bag with a change of clothes, a bottle of '59 Latour and a couple of magazines he hadn't yet read. He briefly wondered if his hostess would provide the necessary, and, deciding not to leave it to chance, packed two Venetian carnival masks and his riding crop.

Before he left he hovered at the typewriter, contemplating his title. Was *EUREKA!* quite right? It had been nagging away at him. Opening his bottle of Tipp-Ex he carefully blanked out the screamer, so that it now read

EUREKA

He allowed himself a satisfied nod, as if he had just concluded a proper day's work.

EXT. NEWSPAPER BUILDING ('THE MIDDLE'), LONDON — DAY.
Camera, fairly high, watches as a young man, CHARLES PALLINGHAM (CHAS), *walks through crowds on Fleet Street and enters the building. We see him through the glass doors talking to a woman on reception, who points him in the direction of the lift.*

INT. LIFT — DAY.
CHAS *in the lift next to a pretty girl, to whom he gives the eye. The girl gives him an ambiguous once-over. Lift stops, opens and another man enters: he and the girl know one another and share a few moments of whispered flirtation.* CHAS *tries not to look crestfallen.*

INT. NEWSROOM — DAY.
The room is bustling with staffers preparing to put the late edition to bed. CHAS *weaves between them, nosily taking it all in. Camera tracks behind him and we see, through an open door, an editor in his office. He spots* CHAS, *and though he's on the phone he beckons him in with a fond smile.*

INT. OFFICE — DAY.
Books everywhere. The literary editor's domain. GEORGE CORVICK *still on the phone.*

> GEORGE
>
> . . . Call it our little secret. Yeah, OK . . . bye. (*Rings off.*) Chas, my boy! I knew I could count on you.

> CHAS
>
> A friend in need —

> GEORGE
>
> — is a pain in the neck, I know. Have a seat.

CHAS *sits down.* GEORGE *rummages in a stack of books until he finds the novel he's looking for. He slides it across the table.* CHAS *examines it with a frown.*

> CHAS
>
> Vereker. His new one? I thought *you*'d be doing this.

> GEORGE
>
> And so I would, only I've been 'called away'. To Paris.

> CHAS
>
> Oh?

> GEORGE
> (*affably*)
>
> So we need a thousand words on it by Tuesday.

> CHAS
>
> Right. I feel honoured . . .

GEORGE

You ought to! You're the one chap, other
than myself, I can trust to nail Vereker
down.

CHAS
(*nodding*)
You mean, greatest novelist of his generation, that sort of thing –

GEORGE

No, no, none of that good-better-best stuff.
That's for prize marrows, not for senior
novelists. I want a review that brings out
the *sense* of . . .

CHAS

The 'sense' of . . . what?

GEORGE

My dear boy, that's what I want *you* to
say!

CHAS
(*uncertainly*)
I'll do my best. So – Paris?

GEORGE

A mission of mercy. You know Gwendolen
Erme?

CHAS

The novelist? *Down Deep*?

GEORGE

That's her. We've got to know each other
a bit. She's in Paris with her mother,
who's been taken ill. Telephoned me in

tears, so I thought I should ride to the rescue.

CHAS
You think the mother will rally on seeing you?

GEORGE
(*laughing*)
Oh, you're a wag! I've a feeling Mrs Erme may not be long for this world, in which event I should be on hand to comfort her only daughter.

CHAS
You're that keen?

GEORGE
She's a catch. But I may have to wait it out.

CHAS
Good luck.

He stands, picks up the book, and GEORGE *comes round to shake hands.*

GEORGE
See you on my return. And thanks again. (*He nods at the book.*) I know you'll get it.

CHAS
The sense of it.

GEORGE
Precisely.

CHAS *leaves the office, watched from behind by* GEORGE.

2

Billie, tired from work, descended the steps at Frederick Street to find Monty on top of the bin, gnawing on some unidentifiable bit of food. His fur, whose shade, depending on the light, changed from carroty to marmalade and then to ginger, had a somewhat oily aspect this evening. When she lifted him off she noticed a graze across his face where another cat must have swiped him.

'Have you been fighting again?' she asked.

Monty looked away, as if he didn't want to talk about it. She unlocked the door and the cat traipsed in after her. She put a shilling in the meter and looked through the post while she brewed a pot of tea in the kitchen: circulars, a couple of things for Jeff and a letter for her, which she opened.

> Dear Miss Cantrip,
>   Thank you for your application of 15 March. I regret to inform you that the vacancy has already been filled. We will, however, keep your name on our books and contact you should another position come up in future . . .

She sighed, ripped the letter in half and tossed it in the bin. She searched the shelf for a mug, but all three were in the sink, amid a heap of dirty plates and dishes. It was almost a point of honour to Jeff that he never did any washing-up, or any other sort of cleaning. He affected not to notice the mess, and scoffed at her for caring, though when he first moved into the flat he had been quick to remark on how run-down the neighbourhood was. Billie had done her best to brighten the place and keep it tidy. This week she had put a little vase of primulas on the kitchen table, and decorated the windowsill with an arrangement of her mother's painted clay pots. The walls were covered with Jeff's stuff and her posters of Impressionist favourites. In the bedroom she had hung purple velvet curtains that puddled on the floor, and put down a paisley rug, though it was hardly more than an offcut of carpet. She would tie a silk scarf over the lampshade to lend a touch of Continental raffishness. The cramped confines of the bathroom, however, seemed beyond remedy, and lines of clothes hung over the tub like flayed skins, wrinkled and somehow imploring.

She washed the dishes, and dried one of the mugs for her tea, which she carried into the bedroom. Carefully sliding a single out of its sleeve she put it on the Dansette's turntable and dropped the needle on its revolving edge. It was the Beatles' new one, which she had played so many times the night before that Jeff had eventually stormed in and shouted at her. It was a double A-side, which meant that both songs were supposed to be as important as each other. She wasn't sure about 'Strawberry Fields Forever', with its woozy key changes and its glistening, secretive air of possession, though, oddly, it had caught Jeff's interest. Having disdained pop for as long as she'd known him, he condescended to stay in the room while this one was playing. But it was 'Penny Lane' that had grabbed Billie. She had never really heard a pop song that made the noticing of everyday life its point – barbers, bankers, fire engines, rain, blue suburban skies – going like a flurry of bright snapshots, one after another. It was jaunty and sad at the same time. She lay back on the bed, entranced. Here came her favourite bit, about the nurse who, though she feels she's in a play, 'she is anyway' – another of the song's riddles, the way it seemed both real and yet a dream. She loved that; she loved all of it.

She had just put it on again when the phone rang. It was Nell.

'Are you all right, darling? What's that noise?'

Billie leaned down to the Dansette and cut the music. 'Beatles' new one – just bought it.'

'Ooh yes, *I* like that one!' cried Nell, her voice rasping from the day's cigarettes. 'I saw them on telly the other night. Isn't Paul gorgeous?'

'I prefer George.'

'Hmm. Trust you to go for the moody one. So did you hear from the agency?'

She cushioned her head against the pillow. 'Yeah. It's already gone, but they said they'd keep my name on file, blah blah . . .'

'*Oh!* I'm sorry, love. How disappointing. Though being a secretary to that bitch might not be such a marvellous thing anyway.'

'I s'pose.'

'Why don't you come over? I'm just putting a macaroni cheese in the oven.'

Billie glanced at her watch; it was tempting, she had to admit. Her mum was a good cook, and at her kitchen table she would be certain of a sympathetic ear.

'I can't, Mum, sorry. Jeff's going to be home any minute. He'll want some dinner.'

'He could make something for himself,' she said bluntly. When this provoked no response Nell let out a deep sigh. They couldn't keep having this argument. 'Well, shall I see you at the weekend?'

'Yeah. See a film, maybe.' They then had a little debate as to whether Billie would go up to her house in Kentish Town or else meet in the West End. Without anything being said she knew Nell would prefer not to come to the flat and have to talk to Jeff. A few minutes later, they said their goodbyes. At the threshold of the bedroom Monty stared at her, expectant. She went to the fridge and poured out a saucerful of milk, which he began slowly to lap.

Billie had begun to wonder about her mother. She'd noticed Nell ringing her more often these days, rather plaintive for her company. After two failed marriages, she had been living on her own for about five years. Her first husband, Johnny, she'd met when they were at the Slade; their seven-year marriage had produced two daughters, very few paintings and a legacy of bitter recrimination. Johnny, hopeless and alcoholic, had died of liver failure in an Earls Court bedsit when Billie was eleven. Roy, her second, was an itinerant Irishman who had been one of their lodgers, not an alcoholic but an ill-tempered gambler, inclined to bullying. They had weathered a few storms, including a long period when it emerged that he'd been stealing from her (his betting habit had run away with him). She stuck it out and endured the knocks until the day Roy lashed out not at her but at Billie, whose head happened to be nearest to him. Nell threw him out, though not before she delivered a smack to *his* head. The guilt she felt over these misalliances was expressed in a disproportionate wariness of her daughters' boy-friends; she didn't want them making the same mistakes.

Billie was listening to 'Penny Lane' for perhaps the twelfth time – even Monty looked a bit sick of it – when she heard the key scrape in the lock. She cut the record short, jumped off the bed and went out to greet him. It was hard to tell whether Jeff was in a good mood or not these days. The set of his mouth was lugubrious, and his shoulders stooped in a way common to people who didn't enjoy being tall. He wore his brown hair mid-length with sideburns, all the Edwardian rage, but had recently shaved off the Beatles moustache, to her relief. His cool, unkempt look – hipster pants, suede jacket – was offset by a wide navy tie whose artlessness rather touched her; it meant he had manners enough to smarten up for his round of the galleries. Jeff made collages which he spent hours hawking about. The result of today's enter-prise she awaited with something close to dread.

'How did it go?'

Jeff glanced at her as he sat down at the kitchen table and yanked off his tie. He put his Rizlas and tobacco on the table, ready to roll up. 'Huh,' he began. 'The new ones I was trying to flog?'

'Yes?' She was uncomfortably holding her breath.

'Mapleton's want to take them – all six.'

She covered her sharp intake of breath with an exuberant whoop. 'Jeff! That's absolutely – oh, congratulations!'

Jeff allowed himself a wry smirk as he lit his rollie. Billie plumped down on his lap and kissed him. She felt a tremendous surge of relief, and behind it surprise, for secretly she had doubted that his collages were any good. They seemed to her dark and brooding and ungainly; a bit like Jeff. But here was affirmation of his talent.

'So Mapleton loved them?' she asked, once she'd recovered herself.

'He wasn't there. It was the manager I dealt with.'

'Does he have the say-so?'

'Yeah, yeah, it's all above board. He said he'd get a cheque to me sometime next week.'

'How much?' she asked nervously.

He tucked in his chin. 'Never you mind. But enough to treat you to a "slap-up meal" as they say in the *Beano*. So get your coat.'

'What, now? I was going to do us some fish.'

'Are you saying you don't want to celebrate? After what I've been through?'

'No. I mean yes,' Billie said quickly, 'let's go out.'

What he had 'been through' was rejection; nothing out of the ordinary for an artist, though few were as prickly as Jeff. Whenever a gallery turned down his work he would go into a long sulk, railing against what he saw as a conspiracy to deny him his due. Billie did her best to assuage his injured feelings, but it was a struggle: Jeff clung to his legend of being neglected, wronged, sold short. It was his perverse badge of victimhood. As they ambled along the Gray's Inn Road he talked with an enthusiasm she'd hardly known in him before. Thanks to this he could probably afford to rent his own studio, another step, he reckoned, in his mission to be taken 'seriously'.

Billie hesitantly suggested he should wait before making that kind of investment. Their finances were still quite precarious, and a room, even round here, wouldn't come cheap.

'You might show a little faith in me,' Jeff replied, with a short irritated laugh. 'This game's hard enough without your nearest and dearest reminding you how poor you are.'

'That wasn't what I said. All I mean is that there are bills to pay before we can risk the extra expense of a studio.'

Jeff scowled at this, and fell silent until they reached the Italian on Caledonian Road. Once they'd been seated at a little window table and had a carafe of red brought over his good mood returned, and he became voluble about his new patrons and their amazing commitment to him. As he continued Billie wondered at his almost childlike self-absorption, his ability to talk, exclusively and without interruption, about the all-consuming struggle of Being Jeff. Perhaps what had prevented her from noticing it early on was her utter besottedness with him. But she did notice it now.

They had met when she was at drama school and he was lecturing part-time at an art college. They had had to be secretive about it at the start because Jeff was already in a long-term relationship with an older woman, Gloria, a painter who rivalled Jeff in her self-absorption – and eclipsed him in her liking for a tantrum. Billie had heard enough about her to know that this was a woman who would not go quietly. Jeff kept putting off the day he'd 'drop the bomb', possibly out of fear, until Gloria eventually found out for herself and stormed round to Billie's digs. Jeff, who happened to be there, took the brunt of it, but Billie caught a few verbal side-swipes during the encounter. 'So this is the little cunt I've been tossed over for,' she hissed, on first clapping eyes on her. A russet-haired fiend in beads and hooped earrings, she looked Billie up and down. 'I'm surprised – I thought at least she'd have a pair of tits.'

For months afterwards the volcano of her rage bubbled and spat, sometimes down the phone, sometimes in personal visits to the street, when she would sit in her car and wait for one of them to come out. Jeff finally had to get the police onto her. At the time it had rather impressed Billie that he was prepared to ride it out for her sake; he later said that she, Billie, was the only woman alive he could have done it for. It had brought them closer, knowing that together they'd stared Medusa in the eye and not been turned to stone.

That was two and a half years ago. Since then, she had come to realise that Jeff was no picnic either. Neither of them had made much professional headway since their college days, but Jeff took his professional setbacks very personally. The abrasive manner he adopted with those who might help him was unfortunate. Billie felt his dissatisfaction as an atmosphere in the flat, like the fug of his roll-ups; it was hard not to inhale it. Now, perhaps, his luck was turning. She took a long swig of the wine and tried to concentrate.

'Anyway,' Jeff said, refocusing his gaze, 'what else is happening?'

This was her cue to talk about something other than him. 'Oh, I had a letter from the agency. The job's gone, I'm afraid.'

Jeff frowned. 'The secretarial thing? Would have been a waste of time anyway.'

'Not completely. It would be something to tide me over while I wait. And better paid than what I'm doing now.'

'No need to worry about that. With Mapleton's cash we'll be sitting pretty.'

Billie smiled, but felt cautious. 'I know, that's great, but I want to be earning my own money.'

'Running around after that old bitch?'

'Funny. That's what my mum called her.'

'Takes one to know one,' Jeff muttered.

'That's not very kind,' said Billie, bristling. 'If you made a bit more of an effort with her —'

'Look, she can't stand me, so what's the point in trying? I can't help it if she's bitter.'

Billie, hearing this, paused for a moment. 'If she is bitter, she's got reason to be. People — men — have let her down, quite badly. Doesn't mean she's a bitch. You could be nicer. If not for her sake, you could do it for me.'

Jeff raised his face heavenwards in a show of long-suffering disbelief. 'God, what is this? I have one bit of good fortune that I'd like to celebrate, and instead we end up having to talk about your mother. Are you determined to put a downer on this evening?'

She looked away. There were all sorts of things she could say to him at this moment — truthful, hurtful things — but she took it as her unspoken role in life to keep the peace. She paused for a few moments while the waiter filled their glasses, then she changed the subject, coaxing him round, smoothing the creases.

They met at their usual corner of Leicester Square. Billie, preoccupied with the film listings in *What's On*, looked up as Nell approached.

'Hello, darling,' she cried, bending to kiss her daughter and trailing a scent of Je Reviens, white spirit and Player's Medium Navy Cut. She still had a sweat rag in her hair and paint flecks on her hands. She wore a close-fitting black jumper with holes at the elbows and a pair of blue slacks. Nell, in her mid-forties, hadn't lost her looks, though Billie wondered if a little more attention to her grooming might enhance her romantic prospects. Like a taxi, her mother roamed about with her light 'on'.

'Right, there are two here I like the sound of,' said Billie, tapping the magazine. 'There's *Blow-Up*, or *Accident*.'

Nell pulled a comical frown. 'They sound lovely. Sure there isn't one called *Catastrophe*?'

'Dirk Bogarde's one of yours, isn't he?'

'Hmm, I've gone off him a bit,' said Nell, as if there had been some personal falling-out. 'Didn't like him in the one where he was a servant.'

Billie, who knew about these things, said, 'OK, then, *Blow-Up* it is.'

Inside, a muffled aroma of dust and burnt coffee hung about the dark. Motes danced in the projector's thick wand of light. They had arrived in time for the adverts, which always encouraged her mother to comment – a little too loudly – on the hollowness of a slogan or a woman's outfit or some other absurdity that tickled her. Billie thought this chuntering might be related to her loneliness – Nell, working on her own all day, perhaps just needed to hear herself speak – but it embarrassed and vexed her nonetheless. She sensed others around them listening, and judging. A couple of film trailers followed, one of them featuring Terence Stamp.

Nell gave vent to a breathy erotic moan. 'God, he's gorgeous, isne?'

'*Mum*. Shh.'

Billie felt bad for this prissy reprimand, and worse when, from the corner of her eye, Nell turned meekly towards her and whispered, 'Sorry.'

A hush descended, the lights dimmed, and the sombre black certificate flashed up the title with its thrilling 'X' rating. Now she was safe to lose herself, tilt her gaze and soak up the colour and sound pouring off this giant aquarium of light. At her side Nell settled into her seat. They waited together like votaries at the altar of a dark and all-powerful cult.

'What I'd like to know is –'

'Christ, Mum! I've sat through exams that asked me fewer questions than you just did in there.'

Billie, exasperated, was stalking through the foyer, Nell lagging a few paces behind. Afternoon had turned to evening since they'd been inside, and street lamps blotched the square in amber. The smoke from a chestnut stall briefly blinded them.

'Well, I'm sorry but I just couldn't make head nor tail of it.'

'Yeah, I gathered.'

Still feeling guilty for shushing her before the lights went down, Billie had been prepared to put up with a few of Nell's interruptions. They started out quite simple ('Who's he? Who's she?') before bewilderment properly took hold and every knight's-move of the plot, such as it was, prompted another urgent query. That Billie herself hadn't altogether grasped what was going on put a fine point on her irritation. After a while she had leaned over and hissed in her mother's ear, '*I'll tell you afterwards,*' which at least had the desired effect of shutting her up. It didn't stop her fidgeting, though, or muttering beneath her breath.

I've got to find her a boyfriend, thought Billie.

She slowed her pace to allow her mother to catch up. 'Let's go and get something to eat,' she said, trying to soften her tone. Tucked behind the other side of Charing Cross Road was a little wood-panelled bistro, Chez Solange, where they ordered croquemonsieurs and beer. Billie, feeling calmer with a drink in front of her, looked across at Nell, blithely munching on her food. It was like being with a child. She took a deep breath.

'OK. I'm ready for your questions.'

Nell gave a demurring 'huh' in reply. 'You don't have to humour me, you know. I'm only your mother after all.'

'Don't be like that.'

Nell waited a moment, then said, 'All right. The photographer, did he — had he discovered a murder in that park?'

'Yes. No. Maybe.'

'Oh well, that clears it up.'

'It's ambiguous. That's the whole point. You're never sure what's real and what's imagined. I thought we were in for a thriller when he blew up those photographs and started to piece the clues together.'

'Yes, I enjoyed that bit,' said Nell thoughtfully. 'That, and the wind rustling the leaves, when he's in the park.'

'It built up this sort of intrigue. But nothing follows from it. His studio gets burgled and then he just goes swinging round London, getting stoned, going to the club. It was like two different films happening at once.'

Nell nodded, though bafflement still clouded her face. 'Mm . . . but what was it really *about*? What were we meant to think?'

Billie sighed, looking off into the distance. 'I dunno. I suppose it's about . . . illusion. Not being able to connect with anything. With anyone.'

'Me laddo seemed to be connecting all right during that orgy. And Vanessa. Though I'm surprised they were allowed to show her fanny.'

'I think that was Jane Birkin. Vanessa only showed her top.'

Nell protruded her lower lip in a conceding way. Billie could tell she hadn't really satisfied her curiosity. She sometimes read the film crits in the *Observer*, when Jeff bought it; but they didn't seem that clued-up either, and quite often they gave the plot away, which she didn't like.

'I don't think you should get worked up about what it means. The important thing is whether it's entertained you.'

'But if you're sitting there scratching your head . . .'

'Doesn't matter. You can like something – love it, even – without "getting" it, can't you? It's not always about a thing making sense, it's about the effect it's having on you. You're an artist – you must see that?'

'My things are quite straightforward. I look at a jug of flowers, or a garden through a window, and try to paint it.'

The restaurant was filling up with a Saturday-night crowd, young couples in the main. Something was going on fashion-wise, Billie noticed. A girl and a boy were standing side by side at the bar in front of them, both wearing paisley shirts, jeans, both with the same brown hair down to the shoulders. They were nearly identical! Nell had ordered more drinks, keen to eke out the evening until she must get the 24 back to Kentish Town and let herself into an empty house.

In a changed tone she said, 'Talking of painting, how's Jeff?'

She must be in a chipper mood to volunteer that, thought Billie. 'He's fine. Actually he had some good news this week. A gallery – you know Mapleton's? – they bought six of his . . . things.'

'Oh. That must have pleased him. They're *great*. Mapleton's, I mean.' This last unsubtly implied that the same could not be said of Jeff's collages.

Billie continued, with a lightness she didn't feel, 'Yes, it's quite a relief. I don't think he could have taken much more rejection.'

Nell half laughed. 'It's like Van Gogh – an occupational hazard.'

'I know that. Anyway, he deserved a bit of luck.' She paused, wondering if she should risk it. 'He thinks – he says – he's going to use the money to rent a studio.'

Nell pulled a doubtful expression. 'Really? I thought he'd got a place.'

'No, he used a friend's until they sold up. And my flat, well, you know how small that is.'

'But can he afford it on top of the rent he pays?'

Billie didn't want to get into a discussion about Jeff's finances, which were chaotic. He had run through a small inheritance years before they met and had contrived to lose his only reliable job – lecturing – through sloppiness (he'd kept missing his own classes).

Her brief hesitation caused Nell to sharpen her gaze. 'He *does* pay you his half of the rent?'

'Whenever he can.'

'Oh, Billie, you're going to . . .' She shook her head. *Be ripped off just like me* was the unspoken warning.

'We get by. And this could be the start of something. I don't – I don't want to discourage him. His confidence has been low.'

'Then maybe he should do something else, because it's a tough living. You need a thick skin. Nobody asks us to paint, you do it cos you must. Helps to have talent, mind.' That was her mother: she could switch from virtual child to flinty grown-up in an instant.

'Jeff's got talent,' Billie said with indignant loyalty, though in her heart she lacked conviction. Nell responded with her most philosophical shrug. The maddening thing was that she had earned the right to talk like this. Even when she was being robbed or abused by some man, or had failed to sell a painting for months, she kept the home together with cleaning jobs, secretarial work or a bit of modelling. She had gritted her teeth and 'got on with it', making sure Billie and her older sister were clothed and fed and at school on time. Nell had made some terrible choices in her life, but as a mother she had never let anyone down.

After dinner they walked up Charing Cross Road to wait at the bus stop. The West End traffic honked and growled on its way to who-knew-where. They talked a little about Billie's next move, now that she'd been turned down for the secretarial job.

'I sometimes think I should jack the whole thing in, try something else. What you were saying about a thick skin . . . I'm not sure I could cope even if I made it.'

Nell put a gentle arm around her. 'Course you will. It's just you have to wait for the break. Waiting's the hardest part. In the meantime, here.' She thrust a ten-shilling note into Billie's hand.

'Oh, Mum, don't.' It was irritating, because she could do with it.

'How else should I spend my money?'

Billie smiled. 'You could treat yourself to a new jumper,' she said, fingering the hole at her elbow.

Nell gave her a playful slap. 'I don't need smart clothes. Who would I be trying to impress, anyway?'

It was lightly said, but the tentative yearning behind the question caused Billie a tiny jolt of unhappiness. Then a bus rumbled into view, which spared her the trouble of having to supply an answer.

INT. DRAWING ROOM OF BRIDGES, A COUNTRY HOUSE —
DAY.
*About twenty guests at leisure after lunch,
reading, playing cards.* CHAS *is among them,
closely watching an older man talking to
their young hostess,* JANE. *This man is the
novelist* HUGH VEREKER. *Moments later she escorts
him across the room to introduce him to* CHAS.

                    JANE
  Hugh, this is my friend Charles Pallingham.

VEREKER *and* CHAS *shake hands and trade
greetings.*

  Chas writes for the papers. About books.

                  VEREKER
  Ah. Read anything good lately?

                    CHAS
  As a matter of fact I've just finished
  your latest -

                    JANE
  Already? But it's only published this week.

                    CHAS
  I had an early copy.

JANE

Actually there's an unsigned review of it
in the *Middle*. Have you seen it, Hugh?

VEREKER

I don't believe I have . . .

JANE *hurries off, leaving the men together
for a moment.*

CHAS

I wonder, do you get nervous around
publication?

VEREKER

Not any more. It's a pleasant surprise
nowadays to meet young people who've even
heard of me.

CHAS
(*shyly*)
As a matter of fact, um –

JANE
(*interrupting*)
Here it is! 'Melancholy roar of an English
lion.' Shall I read it you?

VEREKER, *laughing, plucks the newspaper out
of her hands.* CHAS *watches him with an eager
eye.*

VEREKER

I'll take it upstairs with me, if I may –
I'd rather do my suffering in private. See
you at dinner.

He nods to them. Exits.

28

                    CHAS
How tantalising. I was really hoping to
see his reaction.

                    JANE
Oh, why? It's not a bad review he's got.

                    CHAS
I know. I wrote it.

                    JANE
You did? Oh . . . You're a sly one. Why
didn't you tell him?

                    CHAS
I was about to, but - fate intervened.

                    JANE
Golly! Chas, just think of it, reading your
little piece.

CHAS *shrugs, with a sense of his review's
diminished lustre discernible in his face.*

INT. DINING ROOM, CANDLELIT — NIGHT.
*Camera pans along a dinner table, where
about twenty-five people sit in evening dress.
Stops at* CHAS, *seated between strangers,
looking uncomfortable. Opposite him is* JANE,
*vivacious, beautiful, commanding. Time passes,
and while pudding is being served* JANE *snags
the attention of* VEREKER, *who sits across
from her, and two seats away from* CHAS.

                    JANE
Did you get to read the *Middle*'s verdict
then, Hugh?

                    VEREKER
Yes, it was fine. You know, the usual
twaddle.

JANE's gaze shifts naughtily to CHAS, who
looks embarrassed, and keeps silent. At his
side, an earnest young woman, MAUD, picks
up on the conversation.

                    MAUD
So it doesn't do your book justice, Mr Vereker?

                    VEREKER
Oh, it's a charming piece. All I mean is,
the reviewer doesn't see –

CUT TO: A dish is passed in front of him,
momentarily interrupting the talk.

                    MAUD
Doesn't see what?

                    VEREKER
Doesn't see anything, I'm afraid.

                    MAUD
Oh dear. What a clot!

                    VEREKER
                 (laughing)
No, not a bit. Nobody does. I don't blame him.

                    MAUD
            (solemnly turning to CHAS)
Nobody sees anything.

                    CHAS
I've often thought so.

30

Across the table JANE *smirks at him, being the only other person in the room who knows the identity of the 'clot'.*

EXT. LAWN — NIGHT.
House guests milling about on the lawn, lit from the long French windows. CHAS, *saying goodnight to a couple, makes his way towards the house.* VEREKER, *spotting him, breaks off from his little group to hail him.* CHAS, *reluctantly, stops to talk.*

> VEREKER
>
> Charles? Please. I wanted to apologise. I gather I most unwittingly wounded you at dinner. Jane told me you wrote that notice in the *Middle*.

> CHAS
>
> Oh, don't worry. No bones broken - I think.

> VEREKER
>
> I feel awful about it. Really. Will you do me the honour of sharing a drink before you dash off?

CHAS, *hesitant, is mollified by his charm, and perhaps flattered by his attention. He nods agreement.*

INT. SMOKING ROOM — NIGHT.
CHAS *and* VEREKER *sit in matching wingback armchairs. The lights are low, the mood conspiratorial.*

VEREKER

It's the strangest thing. I don't usually read newspaper reviews, and I wouldn't have done today if Jane hadn't ambushed me. The truth is, whether they're good or bad – and yours was exceptionally good – they have all, I should say, comprehensively missed the point.

CHAS

Ah. So what do you consider the, um, point?

VEREKER

I suppose I mean the particular thing I've written my books for. (*He pauses.*) There is in my work an idea that governs the whole and gives it meaning. It's a little trick of mine, from book to book. It animates every page, every line. I call it a trick, but really – putting modesty aside – it's an exquisite scheme.

CHAS

And no critic has spotted it?

VEREKER

Not one! Nor will they. I've given them clues – right there, plain as your face – and still they stumble about in the dark. So it has become, by default, my secret.

CHAS

Which I dare say you rather enjoy . . .

VEREKER
(*smiling*)
I confess I do. I almost live to see if
it will ever be detected. But I needn't
worry - it won't.

CHAS
That makes me determined to discover it.
You say it informs every line. Is it a
kind of esoteric message?

VEREKER
It can't be expressed in journalese, I'm afraid.

CHAS
Journalese is all I have.

VEREKER
And fiction is all I have. We each choose
our own.

CHAS
Well, at least tell me this: is the secret
something in the style or something in the
thought?

VEREKER
I must away to my bed, dear boy. Don't
bother about it.

He rises to his feet, extending his hand.
CHAS *rises too, and they shake.*

CHAS
I wouldn't bother - except that you've
made it seem so very enthralling. Is it
something . . . beautiful?

VEREKER

The loveliest thing in the world. Goodnight, then.

VEREKER *walks away, but stops at the door
and turns to find* CHAS *looking after him
in puzzlement. He smiles, and waves a finger.* 'Give it up - give it up!'
  He exits, leaving CHAS *alone, gazing into
the distance.*

3

Nat angled the Silver Cloud through the slender funnel of the mews entrance and parked. His agent's offices were round the corner on Wimpole Street. He could have come on foot – it was only a ten-minute stroll – but arriving by car felt more appropriate to his status as a client. 'I've got the Roller outside on a meter' was a sentence he relished delivering. It tickled him to think how much he loved this car, the long sleekness of it, the purring throb of the engine beneath him, the way other vehicles seemed to defer to it on the road, moving out of its path. All hail to thee, Fane of Albany! The one ant at the picnic was the appearance of an identical motor in Antonioni's latest, *Blow-Up*. Now people would assume that he was trying to emulate David Hemmings, looking oh-so-cool in his white jeans and shirt unbuttoned down to here as he piloted his Rolls around London. Nat had bought his a year before, but sensed he would still look like the copycat.

In the foyer of Penelope Rolfe Management he flashed a smile at a couple of dolly birds clicking by, their outfits and make-up as vividly coloured as a kingfisher. Their smiles in return inclined Nat to wonder if they had the smallest idea who he was. The corridor leading to Penny's office displayed framed posters of her clients' plays and movies. He always felt reassured to see his own, an American promo for *The Hot Number*, flamboyantly signed in marker pen by himself. Six years ago, improbably. Through the open door Penny, on the phone as ever, silently beckoned him forward with her bejewelled hand.

'Let's keep that our little secret,' she said, winding up with her invisible interlocutor and unloosing a cackle at their reply. 'All right, my love, bye-bye.'

Penny cradled the receiver and spread her palms in beatific

welcome. She was wearing one of her paisley turbans and a sky-blue star-printed jersey dress ('Biba, darling'). Her face, tanned and shielded by the huge tinted lenses of her spectacles, gave her a faintly mythological aspect: half agent, half owl.

'What little secret would that be?' said Nat, planting himself in a customised white-leather swivel chair.

'Hnnh?'

'You said on the phone, just now, about a secret.'

'Well, it wouldn't *be* one if I told you.' Her eyebrows arched saucily. 'So I have news. Herr Kloss – Reiner – will be in town next week, very eager to meet you, can't wait to read the script. Which is . . . ?'

'Showing all the symptoms of genius; I need merely to keep the patient comfortable.' He thought it prudent not to admit he'd only written twelve pages. Film was a procrastinator's business, in any case: they wouldn't respect him if he delivered on time. 'Did you hear back from the *Chronicle*?'

'Yes, they said their correspondent didn't mention your name in the Paris article for one good reason – she wasn't told you were writing the script.'

'She?'

'Yes, a staff writer. I made a note of her name . . . Freya Wyley.'

'Freya?! Good heavens, of all the –'

'You know her?'

He did, very well. They had been friends since Oxford, more than twenty years now, and would meet whenever she was in London. She was a restless spirit, so it wasn't easy to keep track of her. Last he'd heard she was on secondment in Paris, which would explain her being at Reiner's press conference. According to Penny, she had been trying to get an interview for the *Chronicle*, but Reiner was proving uncooperative.

'He's right to be wary,' said Nat. 'Freya Wyley isn't someone to tangle with. She's sharp as a briar.'

'She ever get her claws into you?'

Nat allowed himself a wistful smile. 'No. Though not for my want of trying.'

Penny's gaze crinkled in confusion. 'You mean . . .'

He shook his head, pricked by an unbidden memory of a night

they had once spent together, years back, her in tiny black knickers, holding a Martini and laughing at the highwayman's mask he wore. He'd loved that helpless laugh, the way she threw her head back so you could see the inside of her mouth. If ever there had been in his life The One That Got Away, it was Freya. Penny was still staring at him.

'It was nothing – a passing fancy,' he said, and coughed to announce a change of subject. 'Have you talked money with them yet?'

'I've *arsked* for twenty,' Penny drawled. 'They'll probably go in at ten, so fifteen might be realistic.'

'If fifteen is realism it may be time for me to switch to romance,' said Nat, curling his lip.

Penny gave a disapproving tut to this response. He had to realise, she said, he'd been out of the game for a while. You were only as good as your last script, and *his* last couple had been flops. Fifteen grand would be good money, in the circumstances. They talked about percentages and the fee he could expect if they didn't complete on *Eureka*.

'It'll get done, though,' Penny said. 'Reiner needs a hit as much as you do.'

'What? He's just won a prize for *Hanna K.*'

'He made that three years ago. There's been one since that got destroyed in a warehouse fire – turns out the negative wasn't insured. Very fishy.'

'How did I not know this?'

'It was hushed up, darling. Story like that comes out it could make things very difficult; backers get nervous, the studio gets cold feet. Reiner's a lucky boy – they managed to bury it.'

Nat was quietly impressed by Penny's worldliness. He had doubted her judgement on occasion – she praised mediocrity and disdained anything with a whiff of experiment – but when it came to insider gossip she could be relied upon to serve up the goods, piping hot. The idea that Reiner Werther Kloss had got his fingers burnt was rather amusing. Penny in the meantime had switched to her brusque *femme d'affaires* tone.

'Leave the money to me. You just get that script done. When we meet next week it's important that you show him you're someone who's dynamic, who's go-ahead. I know that might be a stretch.'

Nat laughed. 'Your confidence in me is touching.'

'Well, I thought at least you'd have a draft to show me. What've you been doing all this time?'

By a saving coincidence a secretary chose that moment to tap at the door and tell Penny her next appointment was here. Nat, rising from his seat, had been spared an inquisition, though Penny continued her pep talk as she escorted him down the corridor. She'd heard that Reiner was quite the taskmaster on set ('You know what those Germans are like') and wouldn't put up with slackers. This wasn't just any old job.

'Fortunately I'm not just any old writer,' said Nat crisply.

Back in the foyer it was busier than before; clients were flopped on sofas, chatting to one another, waiting their turn. All this hopefulness, this hunger, he thought; it was almost poignant. Penny had called to one of the seated throng, who rose and came towards them. Nat did a double take as she passed him. He'd seen that face before – under a waitress's cap at Brown's.

'Um, hello?'

The girl, taken by surprise, stared at him.

'You've met?' said Penny, frowning from one to the other.

'I believe we have, just the once. Though I didn't catch your name.'

'It's Billie,' she said quietly, feeling her heart go like a greyhound.

Nat inclined his head graciously, but his smile was devilish. 'I seem to recall you were in . . . accounts?'

Billie felt herself blush, but Penny, oblivious to the teasing, put in: 'Don't be daft, Nat, Billie's going to be one of our best young actresses.'

'Of course! My mistake. I remember your performance.'

'Oh, you've seen her then?' asked Penny, interested now.

'Indeed I have. She quite *stole* the show.' Nat, seeing the girl's mortification, decided to take pity. 'Look after her, Penny. She's got talent, this one.'

He said his goodbyes, and strolled out. Billie, who had managed a wan smile in thanks, felt her breathing slowly calm to normal.

He had spared her. Penny was gassing on about something, but Billie was too hysterical with relief to listen to it.

Nat swung the car east along Wigmore Street. The morning was warm enough to have the hood down. A little breeze ruffled his hair. He was still thinking about the girl – *Billie*, indeed – and the coincidence of their having the same agent. Naughty of him, really, to put her through that but at least he hadn't given her away in front of Penny. After their little confrontation at the hotel he was probably the last person in the world she'd thought, or hoped, to meet again; but London was like that, throwing people together.

She looked different from the first time. More nuance in the planes and angles of her face. He supposed she was twenty-two, twenty-three, maybe. No, he wouldn't dream of it. He'd been out with actresses before; a long time ago he'd even married one. He and Pandora had met at Oxford, and trod the boards together: they still talked somewhere, surely, of their Beatrice and Benedick at the Playhouse, and their last-night *coup de théâtre* when they surprised everyone, including the director, by swapping roles. He'd secretly thought his Beatrice was in a superior class to her Benedick, but let that go. After university they had got together in London and within a year were hitched. They were too young, of course, and too alike, being ambitious, attention-seeking and wildly competitive. Her career in the West End had taken off while he was still trundling along the runway. He winced to think of her 'luminous' performance as Juliet at the Criterion; his own, as Tybalt, was mauled by the critics. Following another disaster, as Octavian in *Antony and Cleopatra*, Nat retired from acting, though he could never forget the humiliation. Pandora went off to New York; he went off to write plays; the marriage went off the boil.

Aside from the conflict of temperaments, there had been the problem of his very particular sexual predilections. He had made clear to Pandy from the outset that he enjoyed spanking and being spanked, preferably with a cane or crop, though an open hand would do at a pinch. It always intrigued him to see the effect this disclosure had. Certain women he had tried to initiate into the practice made no attempt to disguise their revulsion; others had given it a go, as one might an alarming dish on a foreign menu, then decided it wasn't their thing. Pandy had taken to it in a combative spirit, as he might have guessed, leaving both of them black and blue for a while. Yet it became apparent that spanking was not, for her, anything to do with pleasure; she had willed herself into the habit for his sake, and once the bloom of love had withered, she partook of it with mechanical forbearance. Nat, sorrowful, began seeking partners for his purposes elsewhere; he suspected that his wife had already had recourse to her own. Those terrible rows, though, and the tantrums! Even there they had competed with one another, to be meaner, madder. When they finally separated someone enquired as to which of them would get custody of the anecdotes.

Cruising to the end of Goodge Street he laughed out loud, remembering. He held the wheel lightly in one hand, while with the other he drummed out a little tattoo on his fingertips. He noticed one or two admiring glances from passers-by as he dawdled at the lights. Everyone loved you in a Roller. His journey had become aimless, which was fine; the car gave him a dreamy sense of cushioned escape. As he did a circuit of Russell Square he saw that they were pulling down the old Imperial Hotel. Great dusty gaps yawned through scaffolding while the remains of the terracotta brickwork made a last stand, mortified by their denuding. Nat didn't much care. He had no feeling for Victorian architecture and its fussy self-importance; he liked Georgian solidity and the clean, austere lines of modernism, and dismissed almost everything in between. The Imperial did have some history, though. Freya had once told him about a murder committed there in the thirties – one of the 'tiepin' killings – and it had also hosted the occasion of his first London lunch with Jimmy Erskine, theatre critic, bon viveur and an early champion of Nat's. It must have been '48 or '49, just after he came down from Oxford. He'd dined out on the story of Jimmy halfway through lunch leaning across the table to ask, sotto voce, 'Are you absolutely *sure* you're not homosexual?'

Poor old Jimmy. Another Victorian relic gone. He had lived to a great age – though after bestriding the London theatre scene for nearly half a century he had been in mournful decline. The *Chronicle* had put him out to grass and most of his books were out of print. His final volume of memoirs, *Ecce Homo*, had been published to no fanfare at all. Freya had written a fond profile of him in his grumpy anecdotage, and Nat had rounded up various well-wishers and theatrical bores for a dinner to mark his eighty-fifth birthday. About three years ago he had spotted Jimmy dining with his faithful secretary-servant George in the Ivy and had sent over a bottle of champagne. Jimmy had dispatched a note in return, two words, shakily written: *non vintage?!* At the end of lunch he had watched the old man being helped to rise on a pair of sticks and totter out with agonising slowness. At the time he thought that he might never see him again.

He was right. Jimmy died the day after Churchill, in January '65, thus ensuring that his final curtain attracted even less notice than it ordinarily would have done. The obituaries dribbled out, brief, respectful, lukewarm. It struck Nat that barely anyone appeared to remember who he was. At his memorial service at St Martin-in-the-Fields the organist played Chopin, Elgar and the slow movement from the 'Emperor' concerto. Nat delivered a generous and tender eulogy, but he was privately dismayed that so few were there to hear it. Jimmy had outlived many of his contemporaries, but it was still a paltry attendance for someone who had been a legend of hectic sociability. Later, he wondered whether he had been mourning the man or the evanescence of stardom itself, the blaze before the inevitable dissolve. As Jimmy used to say, *Tout passe, tout casse, tout lasse.*

Nat had never paid for a prostitute and did not consider himself a swinger. He had once stumbled upon an orgy, but had held back from participating. His own preferences in sexual theatre were for one or two women, in a variety of submissive and dominant permutations. He wanted sex to be a game of pleasure, wherein fantasies were a democratic enactment, each partner submitting to the other in equal degree. It still puzzled him that people should recoil from spanking, or think it perverted, for he saw it himself as innocent as the swish of a badminton racket.

This evening he had a date with Naomi, a woman he'd met about six months ago through an ad in the personal columns of *Gent*, a favourite magazine. It read: 'Pliant girl seeks strict diet of fun and games.' Nat had scented a submissive, and wrote to her, suggesting they went on 'a diet' together. He signed himself Citizen Cane. Some weeks later he received a terse reply: 'Send for me.' A phone number was appended. They met at a club in Soho. Naomi turned out to be grey-eyed, well dressed, witty, and divorced. *Just like me*, thought Nat delightedly. They drank Negronis. When he asked her how she envisaged the rest of the evening, she replied, 'Back to your place for a good hiding.' Without further ado they repaired to Albany.

Since then they had fallen into a semi-relationship, meeting for intensive and exhausting sessions of spanking, usually followed by sex. Their fantasies seemed to match one another's exactly, and they varied their role-playing in combinations of master and maid, priest and acolyte, doctor and patient, teacher and pupil. Naomi, a dancer by profession, had amazing stamina. Quite a lot of the fun, for Nat, was talking about it afterwards. Did she prefer to be struck by a cane or a hairbrush? How did she like that whip across her bum? Had he gone too hard – or not hard enough? Only later did it occur to him to ask her whether she had had other replies to her advert in *Gent*. Oh yes, she said, about three hundred, all told. Seeing the shocked expression on his face she admitted she'd only replied to a handful. A handful being . . . how many? She shrugged: five or six. And those respondents, it seemed, were all occasional performers in her bedroom. Though he rebuked himself for his jealousy, he felt let down.

Naomi tried to reason with him. He saw other women, didn't he? Nat replied that he did not, at least not in the way she meant. But she'd been there when another woman was in bed with them! she protested. Yes, but they were mere bit players to be shared, he wouldn't dream of seeing another woman outside of her company. So she was supposed to be monogamous, was that it? He shook his head sadly, no; it was just that he had assumed he was enough for her. Naomi was quiet for a few moments, before she asked how would it be if one of her fellers joined them for a night together? But there was no way on earth Nat would go for that.

Things between them had not been quite right since. Though he hadn't returned to the conversation, he tormented himself with images of her being pleasured by a faceless half-dozen others. Naomi must have picked up these tremblings of disquiet because this evening she turned up at his door with a young friend of hers Nat hadn't met before. Melissa, tall and slender, greeted him with a crooked smile. She wore a white cotton blouse with a yoke collar and a gauzy chiffon skirt that showed her long legs to advantage. While his guests settled themselves on the velvet couch Nat mixed them each a Tom Collins. He found it difficult not to stare at Melissa, twiddling her straight blonde hair. Her prettiness was distracting, and faintly unreal.

'And how do you ladies know one another?'

'I met Naomi when she was at the agency,' said Melissa in a girly voice that irritated him.

'Mel's a full-time model,' Naomi supplied. 'She's got the best legs since Cyd Charisse.'

'Funny, that's exactly what they said about mine, too,' said Nat.

Mel looked at him and frowned. 'Naomi says you're a writer.'

'I'm afraid I can't deny it.'

'What sort of writer?'

Nat gave a little sigh of resignation. 'Oh, the disreputable, indolent, early-to-decay sort.'

'He writes plays,' said Naomi with a sidelong look, 'and film scripts. *Square in the Circle*, came out a couple of years ago?'

'I didn't see that,' said Mel.

'Nor did anyone else,' he snapped. 'Now, shall we get on with the business of the evening?'

He was aware of being brusque, unable to hide his annoyance that Naomi had brought along a stranger without asking him. She had obviously intended this to be a peace offering after the revelations about her other men, but Nat saw it as bad timing, and a deplorable lapse of taste. Nothing he could do about it now; it would be ungrateful, not to say ungentlemanly, to throw the package out. In the bedroom he and Naomi took the roles of a duke and duchess who are offended by the drunken behaviour of their housemaid, a part Mel had evidently prepared for, stripping down to reveal a pair of loose Victorian knickers with a slit at the back. Ordering Mel — renamed 'Maud' in their playlet — to assume the position, he gave her twelve stingers with a cane, watching as her buttocks crimsoned after each stroke. Her whimpers of pain excited him, somewhat against his will.

The game changed when he announced that the duchess too was to be chastised for having wasted his money on a new dress. Now Melissa watched as Nat produced a whip and roughly pulled down Naomi's knickers. He delivered twelve savage strokes to her backside, making her count each one aloud. As she lay there, exhausted and panting, Nat felt a spark of malice leap within him; seizing hold of her hair as if it were a bridle, he dealt her another half-dozen cracks until he saw a thread of blood open on her flesh. She had stopped counting by the time he had finished. Fagged with his exertions, and slick with sweat, he collapsed across the bed.

'Fucking *hell*,' Naomi gasped, wincing as she touched one tenderised buttock to find the tips of her fingers red. Mel, he noticed, was agog at his display of brutishness. 'What's got into you?'

'As one sadomasochist said to the other,' said Nat with a half-laugh. 'Did I not mention there'd be whips?'

'You know what I'm talking about. You don't grab my hair, ever.'

He had been expecting an argument, but this was a surprise. What was it about women and their hair? You could thrash them till they bled and not get a peep of protest – but dare touch their precious locks and they'd turn on you, snarling. Mel was standing over him, swishing the cane like some Regency buck practising his swordplay. Well, he'd earned this one for sure.

'Start counting,' she said, her arm raised. The instant before the cane descended he was shaken by a quiver of ecstatic apprehension. The point of the experience for him resided in exactly this anticipation, and in the warmth afterwards. Pain, from the impact of hand or whip, was no part of his thrill; it was simply the price demanded for the pleasure that preceded and followed it. Mel was dealing it out with interest, grunting like a weightlifter with the repeated effort of her swing. He had counted to sixteen or thereabouts before she quit, then Naomi took over. Whatever grievance she had been harbouring towards him she more than repaid, wielding the cane across his backside with vigour and purpose. Nat couldn't help thinking of Molesworth in the headmaster's study at St Custard's (*Kane descend whack gosh oo gosh oo gosh*) and let slip a giggle. Pausing for an offended moment, Naomi seemed to redouble her efforts, cursing as she thwacked him, so carried away that at one point the cane flew out of her sweating hand. She took it up, wiped it down and continued.

By the time she came to a halt, Nat's flesh was on fire. They lay there spent, lungs heaving, unable even to speak. Melissa conducted a cooing inspection of their striped hindquarters. Nat palpated his stinging arse: he would usually have been ready to have sex at this stage, but he could raise no part of himself upright. For a while he dozed, half listening to the girls chat away. When he came round the air was thick with the burnt-rubber odour of cannabis. Naomi, resting on her elbow, was drawing on a fat spliff.

Something had happened in that last hour, some new territory had been staked out between them; he wasn't sure if it was for good or ill. They hadn't hurt one another with such fierce intent before. Was he in deeper with her than he knew? The last time he had become possessive of a woman it had ended very badly. She turned to catch him looking at her, and handed him the joint.

He dragged on it and let the smoke plume down his nose. In a faraway voice he said, 'So we beat on, canes against the buttocks, borne back ceaselessly into the past.'

Mel wrinkled her nose. 'What d'you mean?'

'Oh, just my little misquote. *The Great Gatsby.*'

'Who's he? A magician?'

Nat stopped, mid-puff, and stared at her innocent face. 'My God, you're not even joking. Are you acquainted with the world of literature?'

'Don't be patronising,' said Naomi. 'We haven't all had a university education.'

'University's got nothing to do with it.' He turned back to Mel. '*The Great Gatsby* is a novel by F. Scott Fitzgerald. You've not heard of him either? Tell me, my dear, have you ever read a book – I mean, other than the phone book?'

Mel, not sure whether she was being teased or told off, said, 'When I was at school I read *The Lion, the Witch and the Wardrobe.*'

'Right. Anything else in the – what – ten years since?'

'Nat, shut up,' said Naomi. 'What's it to you? Not being a reader doesn't make you a bad person.'

'No, merely an ignorant one.'

Mel made a little moue of objection but said nothing. It was Naomi who had girded herself for a counter-attack. 'Don't worry, love, despite all his airs and graces he's no great shakes himself. You should see what the papers say about him.'

Nat, wrong-footed, spluttered out a laugh. 'What on earth d'you mean by that?'

'I'd rather not embarrass you with it,' she said with a dismissive glance.

'No, please, do tell. I read the papers avidly and see little of good or bad about myself.' He half thought she was bluffing; the remark could simply be a malicious stab in the dark, but he had to make sure.

Naomi gave a sly laugh and rolled off the bed. She began to dress. 'Matter of fact it was in yesterday's *Standard*. You didn't see it?' He hadn't, nor had his agent told him about it, which was ominous in itself. He shook his head, impatient for her to continue. 'Oh, just a paragraph about the state of your career. I wouldn't have noticed it but for the photo of you at the top. Well, that and the headline.'

Nat waited. It seemed she was going to draw the moment out. 'And the headline was?'

She paused in the middle of rolling up a stocking, distantly seeking out the exact words. '"British theatre's youngest living has-been".'

'Oh dear,' said Mel, sympathetic in spite of being insulted.

Nat, stung, tried to recall the names he knew at the *Standard*. Which viperous scribe had spat that poison? If he did have an enemy there he was at present unaware of it. Yet he'd also flinched at Naomi's relish in reporting the slight. It was as though she'd been waiting for the moment to make her thrust. He'd thought of her as a pal, a sexual playmate, maybe even a potential girlfriend, but the tone of voice she'd used just then had nothing of affection in it. Maybe she was still brooding over his recent violation. Melissa, following Naomi's lead, had also started to get dressed. Nat felt the night slipping away from him.

'Ladies, there's no need to rush off. Forgive my offence –'

'Which offence d'you mean?' said Naomi. When he hesitated she shook her head. 'You don't get it, do you? Poncing around like everybody should know you . . . You're so full of yourself you don't even notice how rude you are. Instead of listening to people you talk over them. If they don't suck up to you and acclaim your "greatness" you despise them. When I first met you I thought your conceit was an act. But it's not, it's who you are. And it's a drag.'

Nat was so taken aback by this sudden broadening of her assault that he was, for the first time he could recall in years, lost for words. The girls were both in their clothes by the time he managed to order his thoughts and find his voice.

'I had no inkling of quite how wretched a specimen I must appear. My faults must be grave indeed for you to speak so uninhibitedly. It's true, I was trained from a very young age to be a show-off. My mother thought me a genius! So I decided that people should take me at the same estimation, and for the most part they have done. This should not excuse my conduct. One cannot reach the age of thirty-seven and still be blaming the parents. But it may begin to explain it, and I hope that you, in time, may pardon it.'

He let his head drop in humble submission. They had listened, Naomi for her part stonily impassive; Melissa, who had perhaps never heard such a *mea culpa*, looked only bemused. They exchanged glances, and finally Naomi said to him, in an even voice, 'Well, then. Would you mind calling a taxi for us?'

Nat, somewhat deflated, said quietly, 'Of course.'

He was on his way to the phone when Naomi called after him, 'By the way, Nat, you could turn over a new leaf by being honest. I happen to know you're forty this year.'

INT. BEDROOM — DAY.

A montage of CHAS at work on the novels of VEREKER, stacked on the bedside table. Camera cranes above him as he lies on his bed, reading; the passage of time is indicated by his changing position, the white coverlet of his bed a clock face, and CHAS's dark-clothed body the clock hands. So he begins (1) at twelve o'clock, head against the headboard, knees pulled up, book in his lap; (2) at quarter to three, lying sideways across the bed; (3) at six o'clock, head now at the foot of the bed; (4) at quarter to nine, sideways, head on the other side; (5) back to twelve, only now face down, exhausted, book splayed on the pillow (we can see the author's name on the cover).

Montage is repeated, in reverse direction. Occasional close-up of CHAS's face, passing through stages of absorption, amusement, wonder, deep enquiry, frowning concentration and bewilderment. We have the impression of him nagging away at VEREKER's novels, trying to winkle out their unifying 'secret'.

Montage is repeated once more, music more insistent and anxious now, as CHAS reads on. Finally, he is back where he started,

48

head leaning against the headboard, his expression blank. Music slows to a halt. CHAS, *face on, thoughtful, holding a book in his hand, throws it directly at the camera, where it spreadeagles with a 'splat!'*

INT. THE MITRE TAVERN — DAY.
Lunchtime crowd in the pub. CHAS *and* GEORGE *sit together at the bar.*

                    CHAS
So you're back. Mission accomplished?

                    GEORGE
No chance. Gwen's mother is back too.

                    CHAS
I thought she was at death's door!

                    GEORGE
She was, until I arrived. Then she rose from her bed and walked - like Lazarus.

                    CHAS
Gwendolen must be relieved, though. And you've earned points for dashing over there and helping them home.

                    GEORGE
Yeah, but I'm back to square one. No use in my popping the question while the mother's alive - Gwen won't just leave her.

                    CHAS
The dutiful daughter. Well, it's a good test of your loyalty -

GEORGE

Mm, enough of the domestic travails - I want to know about *Vereker*. I can't believe you just ran into him!

CHAS

Jane knows everyone. I got lucky.

GEORGE

What did he say about your review?

CHAS

Funny you should ask. He said I got nowhere near to it -

GEORGE

He's right there -

CHAS

- but nor has anybody else, according to him. You see, there's something in his work, a sort of buried treasure, that has eluded every critic who's written about him.

GEORGE

I knew it! That day you came to the office, remember, I told you there was something about his work, some sense -

CHAS
(*ironically*)
I remember. The 'sense'. Which I failed to identify.

GEORGE

So what is it, then, this thing? Is it a point of style, a philosophical motif, what?

50

CHAS

Damned if I know.

GEORGE

But . . . you must have asked him?

CHAS

Of course I did. And he took great delight
in refusing to tell me.

GEORGE

Oh! So it's like that. (*He pauses.*) In that
case, I must go digging for this 'treasure' myself.

CHAS

He told me not to bother, it'll never be
found.

GEORGE

I bet he did. Hoarding his little secret!
Well, if that isn't a challenge to the
enquiring mind I don't know what is.

4

Rue Montalembert, Paris
17 April 1967

Dear Nat,

I gather from your agent that you weren't best pleased
about my failing to mention you in that little item I wrote
about Reiner Werther Kloss. 'He'd like it known that it
isn't just "someone" writing the screenplay, it's Nathaniel
Fane, award-winning playwright.' Ooh! Rapped knuckles.
All I'd say in my defence is that I <u>did</u> ask who the
screenwriter was and nobody at the press conference seemed
to know. But you may not want to hear that either.

Kloss is an odd fish, by the way; very articulate, not
without charm, but ticking to a different beat from everyone
else. He reminded me a little of my brother, one moment
solemn and self-possessed, the next minute laughing like
a hyena. He has the most amazing smile. I managed to
corner him for two minutes outside, but he turned down
my request for an interview. Maybe you could help there.

I'm coming back, sooner than planned, probably this
Saturday.

Love &c
Freya

PS How's the car?!

Freya had caught the boat train back from Dover and arrived at
Canonbury Square so early the milkman was still on his rounds. She
bought a pint from him. Unlocking her front door she found a scree

of accumulated post resisting her push. Once in the hallway she paused a moment, taking in the still, stale breath of the house, its apparent indifference hiding a shy welcome. In the three months she'd been away the trapped light of the interior had wrought subtle alterations, thinning out some colours – or the memory of them – while intensifying others. Her footsteps through the rooms felt tentative, as though she were a visitor, not an owner. This strangeness would wear off in the next hour, so she had to make the most of it.

In the bedroom a navy jumper she had forgotten to pack hung over the armchair. On her bedside table a novel she had been reading waited, a bookmark planted halfway in like a promissory note. In the wardrobe, one half of it denuded, wire hangers shivered. The cheval mirror, starved of change all these weeks, was surprised at the return of movement in its gaze. Up the next flight of stairs the mood of the rooms grew haughtier: where had she been all this time? The second-floor back was Nancy's old bedroom. When Freya had bought the house five years ago Nancy, her best friend, had moved in, intending to lodge for a couple of months while she sorted things out after her divorce. She ended up staying nearly three years, moving on just before she got married again.

Her departure had left a void in the house. It wasn't only Nancy's physical presence she missed; a lightness of spirit had vanished along with her books and clothes and perfume and hair clips. If they were both working at home there would be breaks for tea and cake, or a passing chat on the stairs. A guest staying with them had listened to their typewriters clacking away one morning and pronounced them the heirs of Vera Brittain and Winifred Holtby. Now there was a poignancy in the sound of her solitary typing, like a songbird that had lost its mate.

Restless, she had sought distraction abroad. She had always fancied the idea of foreign correspondent, and her editors at the *Chronicle* – with whom she was often at loggerheads – were only too pleased to have a productive but difficult employee at a safe distance. She had gone first to New York for six months, returned to London in the summer of 1966, and left again after a month for a secondment in Paris. She had lived on the top floor of an apartment building on the Rue Montalembert. The noise of traffic this high up was muffled to a murmur. Her next-door neighbour was a retired diplomat whom she would nod to whenever their paths crossed outside the iron-wrought cage of the lift. She kept the volume of her Dansette respectfully low, guessing he wouldn't be a fan of Sonny Rollins and Dexter Gordon.

And there, save for Christmas at her mother's in Sussex, she had stayed. She liked the city, its wide leafy boulevards and gregarious nightlife, and singlehood didn't oppress her the way it had in London. She buzzed about the place on a scooter, Belmondo-style, scattering the grubby pigeons as she mounted the pavement to park. It was the scooter that had started it all, really. She had been out late one night at a dinner party on Avenue Foch and was rather liking the man with the dark, willingly amused eyes sitting next to her. His name was Didier Laurent, and he worked at Reuters. They happened to leave at the same time; with the last metro gone, she wondered how he would get home. When it turned out he lived a few streets away from her she offered him a lift. He laughed in surprise when she returned a minute later astride the scooter and told him to 'hop on'. But he did so, and they razzed merrily through the midnight streets back to the seventh.

Wind-blown on arrival at his place on Rue de Lille she took up his offer of a nightcap. She could hear *Revolver* playing on the hi-fi as they climbed the stairs. In the living room a dark-haired woman lay on the couch, smoking, and with an inward sigh Freya realised a good-looking man like Didier would naturally have a good-looking girlfriend at home. He introduced her as Claire, his sister, and she breathed again. They drank Armagnac. Claire, two years older than Didier, was a violin teacher and played part-time in a band. Shy at first, she opened up once they began talking about music and Freya let slip that she played the piano. Across the room she could sense Didier watching her, wondering. She was wondering, too. When he was on the scooter he'd held his arms around her waist, but lightly; maybe that had been enough.

He called her the following week, and they met for a drink at a bar on the Rue du Bac. In the early-evening light his face seemed softer, less defined, and out of his office suit he looked younger, too. The squarish heavy spectacles he wore she assumed were an *hommage* to Yves Saint Laurent; no, he corrected her, to Michael Caine in *The Ipcress File*. It transpired Didier was quite the film fiend, and for a while they talked about recent stuff they'd seen – Truffaut, Polanski, Bergman. He became animated, though, when the subject turned to Reiner Werther Kloss, a young German director whose latest, *The Private Life of Hanna K*, he called a masterpiece. She watched his face as he explained, and felt herself warming to him, as she did to people driven by passions and who talked about them as though they really mattered. As she'd got older she'd noticed how some of her friends affected a cool indifference to things, and the affectation somehow became what they were: she saw it as a warning. A journalist couldn't afford to be starry-eyed, of course, you needed a streak of scepticism for the job. But there was much to be said for someone who had the right fire.

Much to be said for Didier altogether, she thought, as they progressed from bar to bistro, and the conversation took a promising sideways turn into personal matters. His parents were both academics at the Sorbonne, high-flyers, and consequently he had spent much of his youth surrounded by *grands intellectuels*. He considered them a narcissistic breed, and had pulled away from their narrow milieu into journalism. His sister had already resisted the parental path by choosing to play music. They had both lived away from Paris for a while, surviving on low-paid jobs, determined to be independent. Freya asked him whether their choices had made them all that different from M. and Mme Laurent. Didier wasn't sure, though his parents were too self-involved to care either way. He said this with a smile.

They ended up back at her place, smoked some dope, and he stayed the night. Over the following weeks they got to know one another, going for meals or to the cinema just off the Rue Saint-André des Arts. At first she had thought that age might be a stumbling block – she was eight years older than him – but if he wasn't going to make an issue of it there seemed no reason why she should. She met his friends, who seemed to number as many women as men: it struck her as an unusual ratio. In her experience the British male, and especially the British male journalist, tended to pal up with his own sex; women were regarded as either girl-friend fodder or background decoration. She was even taken to meet the parents, Paul and Odette, at a lunch in their high-ceilinged, book-clotted apartment overlooking the Seine. To Freya they were less intimidating than she had been led to believe; indeed, they were charming in their welcome, and quite ready to tease one another's academic ostentation.

At the end of lunch Didier had to dash off on a work assignment, so Freya walked back home with Claire. It was the first time they had been alone together. Quiet in company, Claire was more at ease one to one, and amused Freya with a drollery she had perhaps not registered against Didier's louder personality. Up close she could see the resemblance between brother and sister, in the fine-contoured face, sallow skin and lively dark eyes, yet there was a difference of effect that made them an interesting pair. Claire was a refined, recessive version of Didier, a watercolour to his bold oils. Back at Rue de Lille they listened to music for a while, and Claire talked about her band, who played 'sort of rock'. Freya must have pulled a face at that, because Claire laughed and said, 'You would probably hate us.' No, no, Freya protested, I'd like to come and see you. Claire looked sceptical for a moment, then said she was calling her bluff: they were playing at a bar in the Marais next week, she'd put her name on the door. 'And Didier too?' she asked. 'No, just you,' Claire replied. 'He's sick of coming to see us.'

So she had gone, alone, taking a seat in the smoky cellar bar while a support act went through their droning, clangorous set. She found herself oddly nervous during the wait for Claire's band; perhaps she *would* hate them, after all; you could never tell. When four whippety mop-haired youths ambled onstage with Claire, in sleeveless T-shirt and jeans, and they broke into a mellow mid-tempo number laden with harmonies and reverb, she felt herself relax. It was derivative – they clearly wanted to be the Byrds – but they could play, and Claire's violin lifted the sound with plangent folky overtones. Her abstracted look of concentration as she bowed away was innocently beguiling. The songs were of a jangly texture that made them hard to differentiate, though the audience greeted each one as though they were cult favourites. The one surprise came at the end, when Claire, loitering in the shadows till now, discarded her violin and, without preamble, sang the closing number in a clear, sweet contralto. It got the loudest applause of the night.

Freya waited a few minutes before going in search of her. She was hovering at the door of the dressing room when Claire spotted her and hurried over, dark hair moist with sweat, then threw her arms around her. Her skin felt almost feverish to the touch. Yet her eyes glittered in delight, as if she hadn't seen Freya in years and this was a longed-for reunion. She wondered at first if Claire had taken something, but then it dawned on her that this 'high' was actually the disinhibiting after-effect of performance. 'I'm so glad you're here,' she kept saying, and Freya, laughing, said that she'd have come earlier if she'd known this was the welcome awaiting her. She was introduced to a couple of band members and their girlfriends, slumped on a sofa, but she could feel Claire's eagerness to get away, just the two of them.

When they set off through the Marais Claire unselfconsciously linked her arm through hers and chattered on about the gig; she always felt the exhilaration of it for hours, she said. They stopped at another bar where, over a bottle of wine, Claire became confiding, intense. She wanted to know what Freya thought of the song she'd performed at the end. It turned out she'd written it herself, it was about a break-up, and she solemnly recited the lyric again. Sensing her need for approval, Freya said that it had reminded her of Sylvie Vartan, even a bit of Dusty Springfield. Claire looked down, nodding, and after a pause said, 'So you mean it was not very original? Clichéd?' No, that's *not* what she meant, at all: just because a song reminded you of someone else's didn't mean it was derivative. Every song, even the greatest, looked back to an influence. But that argument found no favour with Claire, who fell to brooding, as if her talent had been undervalued. Freya, wondering how she could be so prickly, tried to restore the mood by asking questions about the band, how they had met, how long they had been playing together . . .

It was no use. Claire had withdrawn into herself, and though she still responded her answers came without her previous enthusiasm. Outside again, Freya felt annoyed; she couldn't get on with someone so thin-skinned, and she didn't know her well enough to have an argument about it. They had reached the door of her apartment block. Freya leaned in to deliver a conciliatory kiss goodnight, at which Claire seemed to wake up to their imminent parting – she'd been in a daydream, she said, though it had been more like a sulk. After a stiff little waltz of farewell she turned away down the street. Inside the darkened hallway Freya leafed through her post while she waited for the lift's cage to descend. She was wondering how she would describe their evening to Didier – perhaps to omit the sour ending – when a knuckle-tap at the door surprised her. Through the glass she saw Claire, her expression moodily contrite. She let her in. 'I wanted to say sorry,' Claire muttered. She hesitated a moment before cupping her hands around Freya's face and pulling it towards her. Freya, bemused, hadn't much time to react before Claire's mouth was urgently on her own. For a moment she thought it was an extravagant seal on her apology, but the kiss went on, their mouths locked together, and only with the whirring clunk of the lift's arrival did they draw apart.

They stared at one another through the murk, breathing hard. What had they just done? Freya stepped away and pulled back the folding metal door of the lift. She could smile and say goodnight, pretend that what had happened was a moment of madness, or even that it hadn't happened at all. The velvety darkness of the hall held them in weightless suspense. She could feel the ghostly imprint of her lips.

'You'd better come up,' she said, holding open the door.

By the time she saw Didier the next day she had rehearsed the tone of voice – breezy – in which she would tell the story of her evening with Claire. Most of it was true: they'd had a great time, the band was cool, Claire's song had brought the house down, they'd gone for a drink together afterwards and talked about all sorts. Didier listened with a half-smile, pleased that his girlfriend and his sister had got along well on their first outing. Exactly how well he could never know. Even as she was talking her mind's eye was saturated with Claire's face, with Claire's naked body in her bed.

Freya had slept with women on and off for years, had once even fallen in love, so her attraction to Claire was not a bolt from the blue. But it was confounding nonetheless. On the one hand, the physical resemblance between brother and sister made it feel like some Shakespearean comedy of misunderstanding, with herself as the blundering patsy to be pitied and then forgiven. On the other, the blood relation drastically compounded the betrayal: it was unpardonable; it cried out to heaven for vengeance. She experienced a sudden irrational fear that Didier might smell Claire on her, like an animal picking up the musky secretions of its kin. Of course he remained quite unaware, screwing the lid on her guilt a notch tighter. He was talking now, and she tried to attend to him. But it was *her* she was thinking of and their near-hallucinatory night of kisses and cries as grey light crept into the bedroom towards dawn.

In the morning, side by side, Freya had given in to curiosity and asked Claire about her sudden prickliness at the bar – all she'd done was to make an innocent and quite flattering remark about her song. Claire looked penitent at this; she admitted her sulk had been more or less wilful. She had felt overwhelmingly attracted to Freya and, realising the danger ahead, had decided to retreat before it was too late. She thought the best tactic was to start an argument and thus torpedo any chance of deepening intimacy. But Freya had refused to take the bait – she wouldn't fight. 'Rather uncharacteristic of me,' she said wryly. Of course, Claire said, she saw how monstrous it would be of her to make a pass, and how embarrassing if Freya should recoil. As for Didier finding out, she shuddered just to think of it. And yet it was more complicated than that, for guilt wasn't her sole motivation. She had seen what she wanted *and therefore had to find a way of impeding it*. But why? Because the heart's desire was only worth achieving if you had to struggle for it, Claire said. Her mother, who had been in analysis for years, could probably explain it – she couldn't.

At the time Freya had thought Claire's psychological games-playing merely perverse. In retrospect she ought to have seen it as a warning. In the days following she made sure that Didier stayed at her place lest they ran into one another at Rue de Lille. She told herself it was an error, a spontaneous and foolhardy misadventure in love. She had been reckless, but she had got away with it. When Didier mentioned a dinner at a friend's to which Claire had also been invited, she made an excuse not to go. But for how long could she keep avoiding her without him suspecting something?

As chance would have it an old friend of their parents was now in town and Paul and Odette were throwing a little soirée at their place for him: a refusal was out of the question. Nearly three weeks had passed since the fateful encounter, time enough perhaps for the dust to settle, though there wasn't an hour when Freya had been able to stop thinking about it.

Chez Odette and Paul was already packed when she arrived. Down a corridor she saw Claire deeply engaged in conversation with a professorial type – it was an older crowd, a mixture of academics and writers, equal parts *chic* and *sérieux*, with a few students keeping up the end for youth and dishevelment. Didier fetched her a drink and she loitered in his wake, happy to play second fiddle among strangers. The main room, murmurish at first, grew louder and merrier as the serving staff kept the drinks topped up. Freya had got stuck with a severely bespectacled philosophy graduate whose talk was probing the limits of her French when Claire appeared without warning at her side. She was wearing a beautiful short silk dress in crimson and gold. Her make-up seemed more vampish than usual, especially around her dark eyes, and Freya wondered if it had been applied for her sake or the party's. Having greeted the philosopher with emphatic courtesy she said, 'May I take Freya off for a moment? There's something I must show her!'

At which she grasped Freya by the hand and led her through the press of bodies and along another corridor where the party thinned out. She opened a door at the end and ushered her inside. It was a bedroom, where guests' coats had been piled on the bed. She closed the door and with a snake-quick movement pressed Freya against it.

'Are you angry with me? Why haven't you phoned?' Her gaze seemed to accuse and implore at once.

'No, I'm not angry, just confused. And worried as hell that Didi may find out. I didn't trust myself to phone you, to be honest.'

'Has he said anything to you?'

'No . . . You?'

Claire bugged her eyes. 'He asked me whether we'd argued, because you hadn't been round. I think he knows something's not right.'

This is madness, thought Freya. I have cheated on a good and decent man with his own sister. If Didier found out, there could be no future for them. Even if he forgave her, it was over. Claire was someone who needed to play games.

'What are you thinking?' said Claire, searching her face for clues.

Freya shook her head. 'I hardly know. Except that this . . . this is all fucked up.'

'You blame me for seducing you. Don't you?'

'What?' she said with a snort of irritation. 'Of course not. It takes two to tango, as the song goes.'

'Ah, as I thought. You *are* angry,' said Claire, averting her eyes.

'I will be if you say that again. Stop playing the victim, for God's sake. All I'm trying to do is think straight – don't make it more difficult.'

Chastened, Claire backed away from her and perched on the foot of the bed. Freya moved to the window, which overlooked the sluggish grey ribbon of the Seine, studded here and there by a gleaming boat. A granular blue light lay over the evening like gauze, the shade of the city's romance with itself. *I love Paris in the springtime* . . . She had expressed puzzlement at Claire's habit of wilfully obstructing her own desire, and yet hadn't she done exactly that with Didier? She had discerned something secure in him, and out of perversity, or stupidity, had sabotaged it.

She dragged herself away from the view back to Claire.

'You said – just before – you had something to show me?'

Claire looked intently at her, and then half smiled. Still on the edge of the bed she used her fingertips to slowly, soundlessly slide her dress above her waist, concertinaing the slithery silk. She wore nothing beneath. The white of her limbs seemed to glow in the thinning light. With her gaze still on hers she wriggled backwards onto the bed, opening her legs as she did, and as Freya reached out to brush the inside of her thigh she knew that perversity and stupidity had been only bit players in her undoing: what had really brought her low was this, hot-eyed desire, the touch of flesh on flesh. Lying across the piled coats on the bed she inhaled their owners' mingled scents of perfume and cigarettes, and suddenly she was a student again, rollicking in a strange room while a party went on outside the locked door. The forgotten thrill of youthful insouciance was irresistible. Beneath her stirring hand she felt Claire's breathing gather and quicken, urging them both on in frantic pursuit of the moment: her cheeks were flushed as she threw back her head and gasped in abandon, and shuddered.

They lay there for some minutes, listening to Claire's heaving breath return to normal. 'So *that* was what you had to show me,' said Freya, and they laughed together, as if they had agreed on something. They were listening to the party at a distance, an occasional laugh or passing footstep, and thought nothing of it. Then voices came much closer, right outside the door. Freya realised the danger of fooling around in a place people would be using as a cloakroom – but at least they had locked the door.

At that moment the door opened and Claire's mother Odette stood on the threshold. Her face almost went into spasm as she saw them there, Claire's naked lower half still on show. Behind Odette a guest peered interestedly around her shoulder. *Oh fuck*, thought Freya, leaping up like a scalded cat, but Claire took her time, pulling down her dress before she rolled off the bed. In a mildly reproving tone she said, *'J'aurais préféré que tu frappes à la porte, Maman.'* Only then did it occur to Freya that this had once been Claire's bedroom. Her mother's expression passed rapidly from open-mouthed disbelief to a basilisk glare, though she said nothing: the sight of her daughter in a post-coital languor had reduced even her, an unsurprisable bohemian, to silence. She had been there for no more than ten seconds before she slammed the door shut on them.

In the shocked echo of it Freya stood before Claire. She had seen her lock the door – only, she hadn't. Claire insisted that she had, or at least she had 'meant to'. Not that it mattered.

'What? Odette practically caught us in the act – she'll be telling Didier right now.'

'No, she won't,' Claire said calmly. 'That's not how we behave. She'll be furious with me, of course, but we'll talk later when she's calmed down. I can promise you she won't tell Didier.'

Freya stared at her. 'But she still knows! And so does that person who was with her.'

Claire shrugged. 'My mother will hush it up. Darling, you don't understand how things work here. Discretion is the element we live in. It's how we've always lived. You think my parents have never strayed? Ha! I'm telling you, in their circles it would be more unusual if they *hadn't*.'

Freya was shaking her head slowly. 'All the same, I bet they never cheated with their siblings' lovers.'

'Don't upset yourself. Come over here and sit down.'

Freya smoothed down her rumpled clothes. She picked up her coat — conveniently at hand — and went over to kiss Claire, who grabbed at her wrist. 'Don't go,' she said. 'Nothing's changed!' Freya waited until she unloosed her grip. She straightened and moved to the door. Claire's eyes were still on her when she looked back. It was horrible, sickening, to have to creep away after what they'd just done. But she knew she couldn't stay there another minute.

The next morning she quit her apartment and moved to a small hotel while she made arrangements with the *Chronicle* and settled accounts. She got her deposit back on the hired scooter. She left no forwarding address at Rue Montalembert lest Claire or Didier decided to try and find her. *On your mark, get set / Get out of town.* Cole Porter again; a song for every occasion. Within the week she was on her way back to London.

INT. HALLWAY OF CHAS'S FLAT — MORNING.
CHAS, *in his dressing gown, walks along the hallway to pick up the morning's post. One letter, addressed to him in a copperplate Edwardian hand, he examines with a frown, and opens to read.*

> VEREKER(*V.O.*)
> My dear Charles — I much enjoyed meeting you at Jane's last weekend. But I fear I may have saddled you with a burden. I have never before told anyone about my little secret, and hardly know what I was thinking when I mentioned it to you. Now that I have, I find my pleasure in it somewhat spoiled. Perhaps the whole point of the thing happened to be that it *was* a secret. You'll think me crazy, but would you be a good fellow and not repeat what I said?
> With my best regards — Hugh Vereker.

CUT TO: *Camera on CHAS's face, grimacing with anxiety. Pensive, he turns back down the hall and up the stairs.*

EXT. STREET — AFTERNOON.
A cab pulls up at the kerb and CHAS gets out in front of a tall Georgian terrace in

64

Kensington. He pays the driver and, with a worried glance up at the house, climbs the steps to knock on the door. After some moments VEREKER *answers his knock.*

INT. HALLWAY — AFTERNOON.
VEREKER *laughs merrily on seeing* CHAS'S *uneasy expression. He invites him inside.*

> VEREKER
> You look like someone who's up before the beak!

> CHAS
> As well I might. I'm afraid I've been indiscreet - I'm so very sorry, Mr Vereker.

> VEREKER
> Call me Hugh. Calm yourself - it can't be all that bad.

He nods towards a living room and leads the way.

INT. LIVING ROOM — AFTERNOON.
A modestly but tastefully furnished room with long windows overlooking a leafy square. VEREKER *stands with his back to the chimney piece while* CHAS, *in an air of contrition, sits on a chesterfield facing him.*

> CHAS
> I got your letter this morning but - too late. I've already told someone.

                    VEREKER
Ah . . .

                    CHAS
You must think me such a waggle-tongue.
It's my friend George Corvick — the one
who commissioned that review for the *Middle* — and what's worse, I'm sure he's gone
and told someone else. A woman. They'll
try to figure it out together.

                    VEREKER
Never mind. You weren't to know. *Mea culpa* —
I ought to have been more circumspect.

                    CHAS
I swear to you I won't tell anyone else.
But I think George will be the very devil
to shake off. He half suspected there was
some mystery about your work from the
start.

                    VEREKER
Did he now? Corvick, you say . . . And the
woman?

                    CHAS
Gwendolen Erme. A novelist. The two of
them are very close. I dare say they'll
one day be —

                    VEREKER
Married? Hmm. That may help them.

                    CHAS
To discover the secret? How?

                    VEREKER
We must give them time. To be honest, I still
don't envisage anyone getting to the bottom
of it, even a writer. Especially a writer.

                    CHAS
It's funny, but the more you talk about
it the more eager I am to hunt it down.
I sense that it requires some imaginative
leap on the reader's part -

                    VEREKER
                   (smiling)
- 'and with one bound he had grasped it!'

                    CHAS
You're teasing me. You don't think I'm up
to it, do you?

                    VEREKER
I think you're a clever chap who should
look elsewhere for adventure. This one's
not for you.

                    CHAS
Maybe. I've chased hopeless causes before.
But I wouldn't underestimate my friend.
He's much cleverer than me, and he knows
your work inside out. If there's one man
who could winkle out the secret, this -
what? - figure in the carpet, it's George.

                    VEREKER
Ha! I rather like that.

                    CHAS
The idea of it being discovered?

VEREKER

No, no, that won't happen. I mean the
phrase you just used - 'the figure in the
carpet'. I once thought of it as a string
that my pearls were strung on.

CHAS

As in 'pearls before swine'?

VEREKER
(*laughing*)
I haven't such a low opinion of my readers, Charles. As a matter of fact I've
always considered them quite a discerning
bunch. That's why I'm surprised none of
them has ever spotted it - the 'figure'.

CHAS

Can you be sure - no one?

VEREKER

In forty years of writing I've received a
fair bit of post from readers, and I've
never picked up so much as a sniff.

CHAS

All the more reason I must apply myself.

VEREKER

Give it up, dear boy.

Camera fixes on VEREKER's *face, kindly, wistful, and expressive of a farewell.*

EXT. DOORSTEP — AFTERNOON.

The front door has been closed. CHAS *stands at the bottom of the steps for a moment, looking up at the sky, lost. Then he snaps out of it, looks at his watch and walks away.*

5

Cutting down Vigo Street into Soho Nat stopped at a flower seller's and bought a small carnation for his buttonhole. The antique foppery of the gesture appealed to him. 'I am the only person of the smallest importance in London at present who wears a buttonhole' – he recalled the line from *An Ideal Husband*. He was also wearing his white suit, intending to make a splash at lunch, though it was high-risk attire for a bustling Italian restaurant now he thought about it: one careless waiter and you'd be traipsing off with an actual splash to the dry-cleaner's. The Rolls was in for a service, otherwise he would have driven the half-mile to Romilly Street.

He was in a good mood. The April air had a benign, rinsed feel, and the sky wore a fetching shade of denim, patched here and there by cotton-wool clouds. That morning's post had brought a letter from Freya, which put a spring in his step. The dear girl was coming back to town sooner than planned, though she didn't say why. The week's other good news was that Penny had got him eighteen grand for the *Eureka* screenplay plus a percentage, more than he'd dared hope for. At least someone still believed in his talent.

Catching his reflection in the wide plate-glass window of a shop he halted and primped his hair. He was preparing for his entrance; the window was his mirror in the wings. Given his love of performance, of being a performer, it was still a source of wonder to him that he'd never made it as an actor. He had once believed it his destiny. At Oxford he had blazed across student stages like a micrometeorite, his lithe, quicksilver movement and confiding gestures mesmerising the uptilted faces in the stalls. The cheers he would get! He was talked about as the young pretender to

Olivier. Even Freya, no pushover, thought he had something, and wrote a glowing profile of him when she was briefly at *Cherwell*. He still had the cutting and from time to time would take it out to peruse. In the piece they had used one of his more pretentious claims to theatrical greatness as a pull-quote: 'Irving is the Father. Olivier is the Son. And I am the Holy Ghost.'

The silly boast proved truer than he could have guessed. After his bright start he all but vanished amid the icy altitudes of the West End. Where he had once enchanted and provoked his fellow students he could find no purchase on the affections of London theatregoers, and the harder he tried the more shrill and desperate he became. He never really understood why. Freya had once suggested that his natural tendency to perform in company, to be always 'on', had exhausted his vitality as an actor – he had nothing left to give onstage. He thought it might have been his ambition to direct that had undone him. Required to coach performance in others he somehow mislaid his own spontaneity. He seldom fluffed a line, and yet the words no longer sounded natural in his mouth. In the end he had to concede defeat. He missed it, though, all the same.

He was continuing on his way when ahead of him on the pavement he saw the tall, tousled figure of Ossian Blackler approaching. Nat fixed his gaze on the middle distance, hoping he wouldn't be noticed. They hadn't seen one another in a few years, during which time Ossie had become exasperatingly famous. A painter and printmaker, he had long outsold his contemporaries; nowadays several of his pictures hung in the Tate. Nat could hardly bear to admit that his desire to remain friends was in inverse proportion to Ossie's burgeoning celebrity.

'Hey.'

Nat froze, and turned a surprised face. 'Ossie? Good Lord!'

'Were you just trying to avoid me?' Ossie's saturnine brow was poised to take offence.

'What? Of course not. I was miles away. How *are* you?' Nat felt his heart sink even as he asked the question. Ossie was hopeless at small talk.

He ignored his enquiry; he was staring, almost glowering, at Nat's white suit. 'What's with the outfit?'

'Oh, just off to lunch. At the Trat.'

'Bit fancy for the Trat, isn't it? Who's the company? Princess Margaret?'

Ossie's drab work shirt and jacket – the favoured duds of bohemian Soho – seemed to rebuke Nat's flamboyance.

'Actually I'm meeting Reiner Werther Kloss. We're making a film together.'

'Oh yeah. Saw something of his once. Queer, I heard.'

'I believe he is that way inclined. He's also something of a wunderkind in the German cinema.'

Ossie frowned for a moment before unleashing one of his manic machine-gun laughs – *ha ha ha ha ha* – each *ha* humourlessly enunciated. '"Wunderkind",' he said in echo, as though Nat couldn't possibly be serious.

'He's got talent, whatever designation you'd prefer,' he said defensively.

'Someone told me they saw you driving a Roller about. Sounds like you're doing all right.'

'You had one, didn't you, a few years back? When you came to dinner at Onslow Square.'

Ossie nodded vaguely. 'Yeah. I sold it. High maintenance.' For a moment Nat wondered if he was hard up, but Ossie soon doused that spark of hope. 'I got an Aston Martin instead. Bit like a toy – but fun.'

'Seeing anyone at the moment?' Nat's voice seemed strangulated in his throat. He dreaded to hear of Ossie's latest conquest, but at least it steered them off the subject of prosperity.

'I've forsworn girlfriends for a while, they're just . . .'

'High maintenance?' Nat offered.

Ossie didn't hear the joke. 'So long as I get my end away I'm not bothered.' He had never set great store by charm. Nat sighed and glanced at his watch.

'I'd better cut along, dear boy.'

Ossie gave a lift to his chin, a sign of farewell. Nat had moved off when he was suddenly called back. 'Oh, yeah. They're putting on a retrospective for me. You should come along.'

'Right. Whereabouts?'

'Royal Academy,' he said without flourish, and walked off.

It was Ossie's habit – Freya had first pointed it out – never to say hello or goodbye. Nat glanced back at his retreating figure. He had tossed out that last bit of news with enviable nonchalance. In anyone else you would have suspected an act, but Ossie seemed genuinely indifferent. Perhaps his old friend Jerry Dicks had it right. 'Ossie has only two passions in life: painting and fucking.' But could you be an artist and *not* care about status? Nat himself was eaten up with anxious striving, with his own place in the pecking order, to the point that he could not separate achievement from success, though he knew them to be quite different things. It was maddening to be so competitive, but there was no helping it.

He was pleased to find himself the last to arrive at the Trattoria Terrazza, already abuzz with Thursday's lunch crowd. Mario, the owner, greeted him with a dip of the head that was at once familiar and deferential, then coaxed him towards his other guests. Penny saw him first, and waved. She was seated at twelve o'clock on the round table, flanked on one side by Berk Cosenza, the American producer, and a slim, lynx-eyed beauty he recognised as Sonja Zertz, Reiner's leading lady. On Penny's other side sat a plump, fidgety man in horn-rimmed spectacles who was introduced as Arno, Reiner's editor; next to him was Ronnie Stiles, a pretty-boy cockney actor who was lined up to play the narrator figure, Chas. To Ronnie's right was a diminutive, lightly bearded youth who wore a Chinese worker's cap, a dark blue sailor jacket and an air of quiet concentration; he was in the middle of showing his companions the trick of lighting a matchstick with his thumb. On seeing Nat he smiled with his eyes, as though to say 'I'll be with you in a minute', then focused on his match trick. He was evidently one of Reiner's entourage of gofers. So where was the man himself?

He took the seat next to the youth, who for an encore repeated the trick with both thumbs. As each matchstick flared simultaneously, the others – led by Penny – laughed their appreciation and cried 'Bravo!' Nat, feeling obliged to join in, presumed this was the apprentice's warm-up while they waited for the master to appear. When the applause died away the youth turned to him and said in a soft, faintly accented voice, 'Hello, I am very pleased to meet you. Reiner Werther Kloss.'

Nat almost fell off his chair in surprise. 'Ah, I see – um, Nathaniel Fane. Nat.'

'Yes, I know,' replied Reiner, fixing his gaze intently upon him. 'I greatly admired your work on *The Hot Number*. It – *was ist der?* – it hit my funny bone.'

'Not painfully, I hope,' said Nat, still trying to take in the fact that this unexceptional stripling was actually a hotshot film-maker. 'I had no idea you were so . . . youthful.'

Reiner shrugged modestly. 'I'm thirty-three. I have no magical elixir.'

A purring voice on his right interrupted them. 'You are not so very old yourself,' said Sonja. 'What – thirty-five, thirty-six?'

'Thirty-seven,' smiled Nat, avoiding Penny's eye.

'Which makes me, like, Grandma Moses,' said Berk from across the table. 'Let's order some food, I'm starvin' Marvin.'

They consulted their tasselled menus while Berk chuntered on about the great restaurants 'back home'. Heavyset, his muscle all gone to fat, Berk wore the expensive, too-tight clothes of an ex-prizefighter: an open-necked paisley shirt beneath a seersucker jacket. Sweat beaded on his brow, and he kept swiping it away with a huge white handkerchief. Whenever someone mentioned a favourite Italian in London he would immediately top it with a better place he knew round the corner from their offices in New York, run by a mama who rolled her own pasta, or 'paahsta' as he called it. Sonja, having listened, gave a long blink, as if trying to forget what she'd just heard, and turned to face Nat. Her low-lidded gaze and the half-smile on her lips suggested someone readier to be amused than instructed. Her cocked head invited him to speak.

'Your first time in London?' he asked.

'I visited, years ago, on a school trip. I remember going to the zoo and laughing at the monkeys. London was quite a – there were a lot of ruined buildings, empty spaces.'

Thanks to the efforts of your air force, dear, mused Nat, who only said, 'It looked quite shabby after the war.'

'You had the air raids of course,' said Sonja, as though she'd overheard his thoughts. 'But you repaid us.' Her smile was an ironic twitch.

'You come from . . .'

'Stuttgart. The bombers destroyed the old town in 1944,' she said levelly.

'But now we're all friends,' Nat said, his palms opened in conciliation. 'Perhaps I could show you a few places you may have missed as a schoolgirl.'

'Perhaps you could,' she said in a playful echo. The slight lisp of her accent and the fleeting image of her as a schoolgirl brought a warmth to his loins.

While the waiter took their orders Nat had the chance to scrutinise Reiner. His face was somewhat pudgy, which the beard partially concealed. Beneath his sailor jacket he wore what looked like a football jersey, proudly blazoned with the team's crest. What with the clothes and the match trick and the formal politeness he could have been a teenage boy out on a birthday treat. This didn't sort with the style of any film director he had ever met before. Or any adult, come to that. Reiner was conversing in German with Sonja over some item on the menu when he suddenly caught Nat staring at him.

'I was, um, just admiring your jersey. A football club?'

Reiner opened his jacket to display the crest. 'Bayern München. This is a shirt once worn by Franz Beckenbauer. You know him?'

'Not intimately,' Nat admitted.

'Reiner loves Bayern more than anything,' said Arno down the table. 'Watches them all the time. I think he'd rather be a footballer than a film-maker.'

Reiner, with a giggle, explained that he used to play as a teenager for his local side, Bad Wörishofen. He was quick and strong, a useful defender, and good enough to be invited for a trial at Bayern, but it didn't happen. 'I argued with the manager – a fool – and when the team was picked to play in front of the scouts he kept me on the bench. We were losing 5–0 or something, and still he would not put me on to play. So that was an end to the dream. But I had my revenge.'

Nat leaned forward, inviting him to explain further, but Ronnie Stiles chose this moment to interrupt. 'I had trials as a kid at West Ham. I wanted to be Geoff Hurst – famous England player, Reiner, he scored a hat-trick –'

Reiner held up a silencing hand. 'Yes, yes, the World Cup final, I was thinking you would mention that.'

'Champions!' Ronnie crowed insufferably.

At that moment the food started to arrive and Berk, clearing his throat, held up his glass to the company. Nat groaned inwardly. Why did Americans always feel it necessary to dominate the table?

'Friends, if I may, let me make a toast on this *vurry* special occasion. I am truly blessed to have around me such dynamic and talented people. Excited? Who wouldn't be excited! Here's to us, and to the success of this picture. To *Eureka*!'

They all echoed the name and clinked glasses. Nat took a sip of his Chianti and turned to Reiner. 'So what made you want to make this? Are you a passionate Jamesian?'

'Passionate? Maybe. I read James when I was a student, that age at which we are most responsive. I read many of the short stories, some I loved, some I thought "huh". But "The Figure in the Carpet" was the one that nagged and nagged at me. It is a story about obsessive people. All my films are about that.'

Nat nodded slowly. 'Yes, of course. The pursuit of meaning becomes –'

'An obsession!' Reiner's eyes suddenly glittered with delight. 'These two young men, neither of them exceptional, but intelligent and curious, become absorbed in a quest for truth. They both admire the great novels of Vereker, only to learn from the man himself that they contain a secret – are in fact entirely constructed upon this secret – which nobody has ever unlocked. What can it possibly be? For weeks and months they puzzle over it, argue about it, lose sleep because of it. The thing becomes their fantasy, their Holy Grail, until – fateful day – one of them believes he has got it.'

At that, Reiner paused dramatically, with a gesture of a conductor bringing his orchestra to attention. 'And there is the brilliance of James. He has contrived to make their suspense also the reader's. We are tantalised, mystified, by the very same thing. What is the figure in the carpet? The difference is, unlike the characters in the story, *we have absolutely no clue as to what Vereker's novels are about*! We have not a single sentence, a single *word*, of his prose on which to judge him. His books are entirely notional.'

'Does it matter?' asked Nat.

'Of course not! Why do we need to know? The tension lies not in the actual secret but in its effect upon the three main characters. It is not the solving of a mystery that excites people; it is the dramatic withholding of it. Think of "Rosebud" in *Citizen Kane*, the last word on a dying man's lips. What did he mean by it? It puzzles the audience, this word, it creates a mood of suspense. But then it emerges that Rosebud is simply the name painted on a child's sled. Is the picture better or worse for this revelation? Well. The human instinct is to investigate, to solve the enigma. But great art defies our urge to know, because it thrives upon what is insoluble, and inexplicable.'

'I take the point,' said Nat, 'but such withholding may alienate your audience. You cannot toy with their feelings indefinitely. How elusive does one dare to be? Take Antonioni, for example. His films are one riddle after another, but I'm not sure they're wonderful entertainment.'

Reiner nodded as one who had anticipated this argument. 'The trick, you see, is to engross, but not to explain. Most films have a conventional ending – the boy gets the girl, the soldier makes it home, the detective catches the killer. But the great film' – he held up a solemn finger – 'the great film confounds rather than reassures. James wrote, "Our doubt is our passion and our passion is our task." Give the audience a happy ending and they will forget it by the next week. But give them an *ambiguous* one and they will talk about your film for weeks, maybe for years.'

Nat, somewhat confounded himself, said, 'An interesting theory. It makes me wonder why you didn't adapt the story yourself.'

'I only write in German. For my first British film I wanted a native writer, one who is able to compress those long, long sentences of James into speakable dialogue.'

'That makes me anxious not to disappoint you.'

Reiner stared at him. 'How could you disappoint me? You are Nathaniel Fane!'

There was no resisting such flattery; it made Nat want to roll on his back and waggle his paws in the air. He contented himself with a modest chuckle that at once disowned and embraced Reiner's words. Across the table Berk had been monitoring their conversation.

'How it's going, Nat? You got something we can read yet?'

Nat didn't flinch. 'It's coming along. Just needs a bit of tweaking here and there.'

'You know we start shooting in four weeks. The actors will need a script to look at.'

'Sonja is a quick study,' said Reiner, smiling across at her, 'and I'm sure Mr Stiles here is very capable of learning his lines at short notice.'

'Meat and drink, Reiner,' said Ronnie through a mouthful of spaghetti. 'I learnt me entire part in *Mafeking* over a weekend. In an officer-class accent an' all.' Nat would come to learn that Ronnie flashed his hard-nut Stepney origins on the slightest pretext.

'So there's no need to panic,' said Sonja to Berk. 'You know that on *Casablanca* they didn't have a finished script even while they were shooting. The cast would be handed their lines on the morning they were due in front of the camera.'

'Ha ha, right, and look what a piece of shit *that* turned out to be,' said Berk, looking around the table. It turned out that they didn't even have a full cast yet.

'Which parts?' asked Penny, suddenly alert.

'George Corvick. Sellers has dropped out. We've got Alec Madden coming in to audition next week.'

'Oh, Alec's great,' Ronnie piped up. 'We shared a flat once. And a bird, too, I seem to recall.'

'Charming,' said Penny.

'Also, we're still looking for a Lady Jane.'

'She's just plain "Jane" in my screenplay,' said Nat. 'It was only James's Anglophile snobbishness that inclined him to give everyone titles.'

Penny, quick to press her case, said, 'I know Isabel Duncannon is free at the moment. She was wonderful as Perdita at the Vic.'

'Per what?' said Berk.

'*Winter's Tale*, darling. Shakespeare.'

It was agreed that they would look into Miss Duncannon's availability. In the meantime Berk announced that another backer had just come in, so the rest of the money for *Eureka* was now secured. Another toast! When someone asked him who it was, Berk replied that the backer probably wouldn't want his name out there: he was the type who valued his privacy. Nat, intrigued, saw that a little digging would be required.

'May I ask whether this benefactor is one of your countrymen, Berk?'

'Matter of fact he's one of yours,' replied Berk. 'He's a businessman here in London, has pretty good connections, and deep pockets. I'm happy to say he's pledged nearly a quarter of the budget up front.'

Nat sat up. A quarter? That would be a hefty commitment, and a risky one given the personnel involved. Reiner and Sonja were cultish names in the art-house cinemas of Europe, but they were untried and unknown here. Ronnie, on the way up after his role in the imperial epic *Mafeking*, was still rough around the edges. And an adaptation of a Henry James story, even with his own name attached as screenwriter, would hardly guarantee a safe return on one's money. No one else at the table seemed very bothered about who it might be, so Nat carried on the digging himself.

'When you say "good connections" . . . has he worked in films before?'

'Uh-uh. This is his first venture outside his . . .'

'Outside his what?'

'His area of expertise.'

Nat sensed Berk was enjoying this exercise in discretion, and that it might go on indefinitely. It was obvious to him that the more eager he became in his questions the more coy Berk would be in his answers.

He leaned back and sighed. 'Oh well. If you really can't tell me . . .'

Reiner, not interested in the subject, began to talk in German to Arno, and Berk, reluctant to see his purchase on Nat's attention slip, made an owning-up gesture. 'Strictly between us, it's Harold Pulver.'

Nat looked across the table at Penny, who said, 'Harry Pulver? Isn't he in prison?'

'Not when I spoke to him last week,' said Berk.

Nat only knew Harry Pulver's name through newspaper stories about his property empire, his volcanic temper and his run-ins with the law. An East End boy made good, he had been in and out of court for years on charges of racketeering, blackmail, fraud and tax evasion; his most recent infraction was an assault on a waiter who had annoyed him at a club in Mayfair.

'That poor man's still in hospital,' said Penny.

'Is he? According to what I read the guy provoked him.'

Reiner, tuning in again, said, 'Who is this man Pulver?'

'What they call a wrong 'un,' replied Nat. 'Berk, seriously – are you saying that this picture is being part financed by a gangster?'

'Whoa! Wait a *minute* there. The guy's no saint, granted, but he's not a . . .' He wouldn't repeat the unholy word. 'He's never been in prison, never been convicted of anything worse than speeding. I gather he's devoted to his mother –'

Nat burst into incredulous laughter. 'That clinches it! I give you *White Heat*. His not having a prison record is irrelevant, Berk. All it means is he's got a good lawyer.'

Berk shrugged. 'And a fuckin' great accountant by the sound of it, 'scuse my French. Don't rush to judgement, Nat. It's thanks to him we're gonna get this movie made.'

There was a brief silence as they absorbed this information. Then Arno said, 'But you did not invite Mr Pulver here, to meet us?'

'As you can imagine, he's a busy guy.'

Nat gave a sardonic snort. 'Probably out there right now crucifying somebody's granny. I hope you know what you're doing.'

Berk glared back at him. 'When you've been in this business as long as I have, you learn about people. Who you can trust, who you can't. Harold Pulver – he's a mensch.'

'What's in it for him? I don't peg him for a Henry James fan.'

'Me neither, but I do know he likes movies. Done some acting, in fact, few years back. Who knows, a non-speaking role might suit him.'

'As a waiter, perhaps?' said Nat.

Berk shook his head in disapproval, or perhaps it was only disappointment. Pudding arrived at that moment, and the conversation dispersed again. Ronnie began flirting with Sonja, who regarded him with the amused scorn of a queen with her jester. Berk lit a cigar the size of a dynamite stick; Arno swallowed a handful of pills for his indigestion. While they were finishing their coffee, Reiner ordered a glass of sambuca, repeated his match trick and set the clear liquid alight. The others watched as a bluish flame shimmered inside the glass; he stared at it dreamily for a moment, then tossed it down in one.

EXT. STREET — AFTERNOON.
An open-topped sports car is heading down
Park Lane. A close-up reveals the driver
to be GEORGE, *and his passenger,* CHAS. *They*
are talking animatedly to one another, occa-
sionally laughing, but we can hear only
soundtrack music, not their voices. Camera
pulls high over trees and the car shrinks
into the distance, though its vivid green
colour ensures that we don't lose sight of
it amid the other traffic.

EXT. STREET — AFTERNOON.
Music fades out. The car is now moving
down a quiet street in Chelsea. GEORGE *finds*
a parking space, but for a moment they
just sit there. Camera faces them through
the car windscreen.

                    GEORGE
  But you said you wanted to meet her.

                    CHAS
  I did. I do. Just a bit nervous.

                    GEORGE
  What on earth are you nervous about?

CHAS

Well, she's this important bluestocking
novelist, and I'm just a jobbing hack.
She'll probably despise me.

GEORGE
(laughing)
You nit! Gwen's not that type. She knows
all about you - reads your stuff, as a
matter of fact.

GEORGE *gets out of the car, and picks up a
bottle of wine from the back seat.* CHAS
*leans over to check his face in the rear-
view mirror.*

EXT. FRONT DOORSTEP — AFTERNOON.
GEORGE *has just rung the bell. He looks at*
CHAS *and smirks, handing him the bottle of
wine to take in.*

GEORGE
And by the way, she wears black stockings,
not blue.

He waggles his eyebrows suggestively, and
CHAS *laughs.*

INT. DINING ROOM — AFTERNOON.
GWEN *has just served lunch to her mother,*
GEORGE *and* CHAS, *who sits very straight-backed
at the table. The room is a throwback to
another era, old furniture, hunting prints
on the wall and the centrepiece a grand
portrait of a lady, possibly* MRS ERME *in her*

younger years. GEORGE *pours the wine, though* GWEN *holds a hand over her glass in refusal.*

MRS ERME

Well, Gwendolen likes *The Times*, and I used to read the *Telegraph* when Gerald was alive . . . but I do find the newspapers so lowering nowadays.

GEORGE

Oh, I do know what you mean, Mrs Erme. Charles and I only work for the *Middle* because we can't think of anything else to do. I suppose that's the definition of a journalist.

GWEN

That's rot, George. You love newspapers, and I'm sure Charles does, too.

CHAS

Well, George is a proper editor. I only write for the books pages.

MRS ERME

And do you make a *living* from that?

CHAS

With difficulty. I do other bits of free-lance writing.

GWEN

But you must enjoy it, surely, reading books all day. And you get to meet some interesting people, I've heard.

CHAS *glances at* GEORGE, *who waits for a moment before speaking.*

GEORGE

I believe Gwendolen is referring to a certain Mr Vereker.

MRS ERME

Vereker? I read one of his a while ago. A little recherché for my taste.

CHAS

You wouldn't be alone in that view.

GWEN

George told me you had quite a long talk with him.

CHAS
(*guardedly*)

Yes. I wrote a review of his new one, and we happened to meet at a friend's that week. He was very affable . . . I liked him.

GWEN

Even though he was pleased to tell you your review had completely missed the point?

CHAS

Well, me and every other critic. I think George has told you about -

GWEN

Yes, he has. In fact we've started a little project together. We're going to reread the entire Vereker oeuvre, book by book, in chronological order. It's the only way we're ever going to discover his 'little secret'.

                              CHAS
                         (*surprised*)
That's quite an undertaking. Twelve novels?

                             GEORGE
Thirteen. Plus two volumes of short stories.

                           MRS ERME
Good Lord! I feel exhausted just thinking
about it. What about your own work in the
meantime?

                             GWEN
It can wait. This can't. Our doubt is our
passion. We shall sift the evidence page by
page. It may be harder than we imagine –
but we shall solve this case if it kills us!

                           MRS ERME
You sound rather like Nancy Drew, dear.

                             GWEN
Ha! I've always dreamed of being a 'sleuth'.

                           MRS ERME
                  (*rising from the table*)
Well, if you'll excuse me, I'm going to
have a lie-down. Thank you, my darling.
Gentlemen –

She nods to both GEORGE *and* CHAS, *who stand
up in deference. She makes a shuffling exit
from the room.*

INT. LIVING ROOM — AFTERNOON.
A more relaxed mood now that MRS ERME *has
gone.* GEORGE *and* CHAS *are seated in*

armchairs, both intent upon the chessboard between them. GWEN *enters carrying a tray of coffee which she sets down on an adjacent table. Looking over* CHAS'S *shoulder she briefly surveys the state of the game.*

GWEN
Someone's looking vulnerable on his flank.

CHAS
I fear I've been, um, impetuous.

A pause while the two players stare at the board. GWEN *watches* CHAS *as she pours the coffee.*

GWEN
Not to divert you from the fray, Charles, but I wonder if I might ask you something?

CHAS
By all means.

GWEN
When Vereker said – I got this from George – that his 'secret' was apparent in every line he wrote, did he throw it down as a challenge? Or was he simply musing on its unfathomable nature? In other words, do you think he actually *wants* someone to find it?

CHAS
I've wondered about that myself. He no sooner told me about his secret than he warned me off trying to uncover it. 'Give it up,' he kept saying. Of course, there's another possibility . . .

GWEN

Which is?

She has been hovering at CHAS*'s shoulder;
now she walks round to sit on the arm of*
GEORGE*'s chair.*

CHAS

That there mightn't be a secret in there
at all. He could just be having us on.

GEORGE

Why would he want to do that?

CHAS

I don't know. To amuse himself?

GEORGE

He doesn't strike me as the whimsical type.
I mean, if Shakespeare had claimed there
was something cryptic in his work nobody
would have doubted him.

CHAS

Yes, but - Shakespeare! Would you really
attach the same credence to a claim of
Hugh Vereker's?

GEORGE

So you're suggesting he's deceitful?

CHAS

No, no - that's not what I mean. I just
don't know how you can be so sure that
there *is* some deep secret there.

GEORGE

Oh, but Chas, my boy, you must remember
that day we talked about Vereker in my
office. When I gave you the novel to review
I asked you to bring out the –

CHAS

'The sense', you said. Of course I remember. But I've no better idea of what you
meant then than I do now.

GEORGE, *his attention back on the board,*
moves a piece.

GEORGE

Check. Well, I was vague, granted. But I
did convey to you the possibility of something 'overlooked' in his work *before* you
met Vereker that weekend.

CHAS

This project of yours . . . Mightn't it be
easier for all concerned if I simply introduced you to him?

GWEN *gets up and comes back round to* CHAS's
side, her eyes on the game. CHAS *picks up*
his queen, hesitates, then moves it across
the board. GEORGE *looks at* GWEN, *whose*
expression is eager.

GEORGE

That might rather spoil the fun. One doesn't
wish to encounter the fox before one's had
a chance to run him to earth.

GWEN

Well –

GEORGE

Gwendolen and I disagree on this. She's dying to meet him. But she must play fair.

CUT TO: *He picks up a chessman and moves it decisively across the board.*

And that's checkmate.

INT. LIVING ROOM — LATER.
GEORGE *has briefly left the room.* GWEN *now occupies his seat, facing* CHAS, *who regards her with interest.*

GWEN

When will you next see him?

CHAS

Vereker? Oh, we're barely acquainted. Jane - Jane Burges - is his friend. That's how I met him.

GWEN *nods, looks thoughtful. She notices* CHAS'S *pack of cigarettes and holds them up enquiringly.*

GWEN

May I?

CHAS *feels for his matches, and quickly offers her a light.*

It's silly of me, I know, but I can't help thinking I must get to him. But George would go mad if he found I'd gone behind his back.

A beat, while CHAS *clears his throat.*

> CHAS
>
> Well, if you really - I could probably arrange something.

> GWEN
> *(coyly)*
>
> Charles, are you trying to make mischief?

> CHAS
> *(abashed)*
>
> No, I - I just thought if I could be of service . . .

> GWEN
>
> You heard what George said - I must 'play fair'.

> CHAS
>
> Yes. I'm terribly sorry. Forget I mentioned it.

At this moment GEORGE *returns to the room.* CHAS *fidgets in his chair.* GWEN *is a perfect sphinx.* GEORGE *looks from one to the other, smiling uncertainly.*

6

A perfect matutinal stillness reigned in Ennismore Gardens as Nat parked the Rolls beneath one of the plane trees. It was one of the oddities of London that you could turn off a roaring thoroughfare and find yourself somewhere as silent as a cobbled close. The stucco mansions lining the south and west sides of the square were preposterously grand; they could have been embassies, or discreet hotels for the untouchable rich. He shut the car door with a heavy clunk that almost echoed in the quiet.

He had come on a mission. At the end of lunch at the Trat, Berk had taken him aside for a moment – Nat had presumed it was to tell him off for calling Harold Pulver a gangster. He was wrong. It turned out that Vere Summerhill, lined up to play Hugh Vereker, was having cold feet about the project. The actor was an old friend of Nat's, though they hadn't seen one another in a while; Vere had spent much of the last decade working abroad.

'What's the problem?' said Nat, unconsciously picking up Berk's New York lingo.

'He says he's not sure about the script.'

'The script? What script? I'm in the middle of writing it.'

Berk gave a little wince. 'There's a rough outline. Of a script. I sent it to him.'

'A rough outline. Written by whom?'

'By me. It's more like a guide than a script.'

Nat tried to conceal his astonishment. As far as he knew Berk had never written anything longer than a memo. 'You've – are you telling me you've read Henry James?'

'I'm familiar with the background material. Look, I'm not claiming to be Joe Mankiewicz, but I had to give Vere something.'

'Hmm. The willies, by the sound of it,' said Nat. 'So what am I supposed to do?'

'Reassure him. Tell him how much this movie depends on him – no word of a lie, by the way.'

'What d'you mean by that?'

Berk sighed, dropping his gaze. 'Look, just between us, the only reason Reiner agreed to do this picture is Vere. He's nuts about the guy, has been ever since he was a kid and Vere was, you know, the next David Niven. It might be a queer thing for all I know.'

So that's why they hired me as screenwriter, thought Nat. It all went back to a cause célèbre of recent times. Vere, a leading man in the thirties and an R A F hero in the forties, had lived an apparently blameless bachelor life into his early-middle age. One night in the autumn of '53 he met two young naval ratings in a pub and went back home with them. The next day, after the men left his place, they got into a fight with two others and beat them up. It so happened one of the victims was a policeman. When the sailors were arrested the story of their night with 'that actor' came out, and the police cut them a deal. In return for dropping the assault charges the men would testify against Summerhill, claim that he had made advances and then 'overpowered' them – an unlikely contest, given the sailors' strapping physicality. Vere was hauled up on a charge of 'gross indecency', the first time the phrase had been used since the Wilde case in 1895. Nat had stood bail for him, which ensured his place in the older man's affections forever.

But Vere was convicted all the same: six months at Pentonville. On his release he found himself shunned by certain old confrères in the business. He did some stage work, which was well received, but he resented being broke and soon upped sticks for France, 'where they don't mind queers and ex-convicts so much'. In exile his reputation recovered; he picked modest, unshowy roles in a string of new wave films and to general surprise became sought after by a growing band of young directors. At Cannes he won an award for his performance as an artist dying of T B in *The Last of the Bassanos*. When De Sica named him in an interview as his favourite actor his stock took another leap. An international fashion house chose him as a model for their new range of sunglasses.

Almost by accident Vere had returned to what he was in the 1930s — a star.

So what, Nat wondered, had tempted him back to Blighty? It surely wasn't money. Vere could now run to an apartment overlooking Cap Ferrat. And this place wouldn't be cheap to rent either, he thought, looking up at the imperial facade of Ennismore Gardens. He pulled the ancient doorbell, and a buzzer sounded to admit him. A wrought-iron balustrade climbed away from the gloomy entrance hall. On the second-floor landing Vere had stepped out to greet him.

'Ah, the young pretender himself,' he smiled. The epithet dated from Nat's early days as an actor, though Vere couldn't have known the stab of pain it caused.

'Not so young any more, alas,' Nat replied with a laugh, shaking his hand.

Vere wore his sixty-odd years with the same ease he did his Riviera tan and his suavely cut suit. His dark hair was possibly dyed — the ex-matinee idol's vanity — but the lines on his face and the slight blurring of his features bespoke authority more than age. As he showed him around the rooms with their high cornicing and floor-to-ceiling windows, Nat listened with renewed envy to Vere's magnificent light drawl; even banalities were delivered with a musician's feel for cadence.

'You'll have tea, of course? It's the one thing I always miss when I'm away — the French can do weather and wine and perfume, but they've not a clue about *milk*.'

On the way through to the living room Nat couldn't help noticing the treasure on the walls; Vere had collected 'a few nice things' in the years since they'd last met. He spotted a Christopher Wood marine painting and a Paul Nash from the Western Front; there were sketches by Augustus John, Vaughan, Minton, a few Hockneys. On the chimney piece stood an exquisite small painting of a girl's head by Ossian Blackler. Nat studied it for a moment.

'I ran into Ossie recently, in Soho. Told me he's got a big show coming at the Royal Academy.'

'Yes, I read about that. How is he?'

'Same as ever. Congenitally incapable of charm. Not that it seems to have held him back.'

Vere was absently revolving the gold signet ring on his little finger. Nat, wondering for how long he could delay the inevitable, said brightly, 'So, back in London . . . for a long stay?'

'Oh, a little while. I've got a full MOT at Harley Street coming up.'

Nat stared at him. 'Nothing serious, I hope?'

He shook his head. 'I had a scare last year. Thought it might be cancer – but a false alarm.'

Vere picked up a gleaming silver box inlaid with ivory and offered Nat a cigarette. They both sparked up. Behind them came a brittle pitter-patter of feet: a blue-grey whippet trotted round the coffee table and folded himself on the sofa next to Vere. This, said Vere, was Mr Snooks, tickling and stroking his silky ears. The dog accepted the endearments before laying his head flat on the edge of the cushion. His sweet mournful eyes blinked at Nat.

'There's pathos in that gaze. He ought to go on the stage.'

'He's a little shy, old Snooks,' said Vere, favouring his pet with a grave smile. Rather like his owner, thought Nat, who sensed an ever more fugitive personality behind Vere's genial front. His stock-in-trade as an actor had been to project an outward poise from within a fervent romantic core. It had won him many hearts. But in life he seemed to have tamped down real feeling to the point of invisibility. His public ordeal – the revelation of his homosexuality and the trial that followed – had changed him forever. He had once confided to Nat that prison hadn't really bothered him: he had been toughened by the war. What he couldn't take was the catastrophic loss of dignity; that the press had been allowed to rummage about in his private life had sickened him. In consequence the portcullis had clanged down and whatever constituted his soul was hidden away from snoopers – and everyone else – for good. He was always friendly, always affable, always unknowable.

Nat took a deep breath. 'I heard from Berk that you're not altogether happy about the film.'

Vere sighed, and looked away. 'I'm sorry, dear boy. I just don't see what's there for me – I don't grasp this character at all.'

'Well, it's no wonder. You haven't read the script yet.'

'How so?'

'I'm still working on it. I had no idea Berk had sent this "outline" to you in the meantime.'

Vere rested his chin on steepled fingers. His next words came slowly, with a little wince. 'Darling, you know, I got through an awful lot of rubbish as a young actor. Cavaliers, courtiers, pirates, princes, whatever was offered. Most of it was damned good fun. But I never kidded myself that I was playing in anything other than rot.' He took a meditative drag on his cigarette. 'Well, the experience has taught me a couple of things. One – always get paid in sterling. Two – make sure your character is still standing by the last reel. If he dies any earlier it's not worth doing.'

'Good advice,' Nat said uncertainly.

'I've found it so,' agreed Vere. 'Which leaves me in a dilemma. Young Reiner couldn't have been more charming when we met, seemed to know all my work, even the stuff *I'd* forgotten. He told me something about this little story, about my character, "the eminent novelist". Made it sound intriguing. His people would send me a script, he said, so I waited, and waited. When it eventually arrived . . . *oh dear.* Henry James it was not. One would hardly have believed it worthy of *Jesse* James.'

'As I said, that's just some piece of junk Berk has thrown together. They ought never to have bothered you with it.'

'But can you really see me as this fellow?'

'Put aside any doubt on that score. You're one of the few actors alive who has it in him to play a literary genius.'

As soon as the words were out of his mouth Nat knew he'd overegged it. Why 'genius' when he could simply have said 'author'? You couldn't flatter someone so cloddishly and hope to get away with it. He risked a glance at Vere, who said quietly, 'Darling Nat. You have such an understanding of this business.'

Nat heaved an inward sigh of relief. Even Vere, civilised, unassuming Vere, had bought into the self-deluding myth of his profession: the actor was the almighty. But the cloud hadn't entirely lifted from the older man's brow.

'All the same,' he continued, 'there remains a difficulty.'

'Oh?'

Vere made a little gesture of regret. 'I decided to read the original story. This novelist – Vereker – he's a creature in the shadows. I don't think that's going to work, do you?'

Nat sensed Mr Snooks, the whippet, staring at him, a loyal

retainer awaiting satisfaction for his master. 'I think it does work. Vereker is the steady centre around whom the others satellite. So even when he's not there in person –'

'But that's my point. After those early scenes with Charles and Jane he simply evaporates. We hear of him through mere reports. One needs to have him on the screen, otherwise . . .'

There was a hint, albeit slyly veiled, of a threat. Vere would not be fobbed off. If he had twigged how keenly Reiner wanted him for the part then Nat didn't have much room to negotiate. So he plied him with assurances that the character of Hugh Vereker, far from evaporating, would be central to the dramatic design of *Eureka*. He flattered and cajoled and fudged the truth for a good ten minutes until Vere at last conceded that he 'might be able to get near the fellow' after all. My God, thought Nat, if he's this needy now what's he going to be like once the cameras start rolling?

Over another pot of tea and a cigarette the mood relaxed again, and Nat fanned out a few choice wafers of gossip he knew would please Vere. The actor had been out of England for so long Nat found himself in possession of far more material than he'd planned to draw upon. At some point Jimmy Erskine's name came up.

'You went to the funeral?' said Vere.

'I did. A pitiful turnout, I'm afraid.'

Vere shook his head sadly. 'Poor old fellow. You know, I always thought he'd led a charmed life. Everyone knew how much he liked the trade, including the police, and yet . . .' *And yet I was the one who went to prison for it*, was his unspoken remark.

'Luck of the devil, old Jimmy. Though it didn't last – he died alone.'

'Was there no one – at the end?' Vere asked.

'He had a chap who looked after him: George. But if you mean was there – no, nothing like that. Jimmy's boys were long gone.' Nat had an inkling that Vere would recoil at anything more explicit.

'I read his memoir, the second one. Of course there wasn't a word about what he'd got up to. Which reminds me. A publisher recently asked me whether I'd care to write an "honest account" of my case, the trial and prison and so on.'

'I suppose you turned him down flat.'

'*Au contraire*. I've got a few scores to settle with certain members of the judiciary – not to mention the police and the Home Secretary. It would also give me a chance to tip my hat to you.'

'Vere, you thanked me at the time. I don't require a public acknowledgement.'

'I'd like to, all the same. In fact I was hoping you might be able to help me. I can recall it well enough, but – *pace* Hugh Vereker – I'm not much of a writer. You could do something quite persuasive.' He tilted his head slightly. 'Perhaps it would be a chore. But I'd split the fee, if that made a difference.'

For a moment Nat was touched. 'Of course I'll help you. And there's no need to pay me.'

Vere smiled. 'And I must insist on paying you, dear boy. It would be the only way of ensuring its delivery.'

The address was a dusty little street of terraced houses round the back of King's Cross Station. Billie had walked here via the Caledonian Road, patrolled even at mid-morning by prostitutes, singly or in pairs, bobbing their heads down to the cars idling alongside. She followed a rag-and-bone man and his limping horse; they looked fagged out in the early-summer heat. In the distance she could see Jeff waiting. As she approached he raised his hand to waggle the keys.

'Isn't the landlord coming?' she asked.

Jeff frowned. 'Why should he bother? He's got my deposit.'

He turned and unlocked the front door. She followed him into an entrance hall, its ancient papered walls brownish and buckled from rising damp. A thin strip of carpet had been worn through to the boards. Billie sniffed the dismal bouquet of cooking odours left behind by a standing army of former tenants.

'Pongs a bit, doesn't it?'

Jeff steered his gaze upwards. 'I told you it was run-down. No one's cleaned here for yonks. Come on.'

Their footsteps scraped on the gritty staircase to the first floor. Disused gas brackets still clung to the walls. The landing window showed a cobbled backyard, weedy and cheerless.

'I suppose there's more light at the top, isn't there?'

'Maybe,' said Jeff doubtfully. 'I don't really remember. It looks different from when I first saw it.'

On reaching the third floor he got the other key out. This admitted them to a low-ceilinged attic room, where a diffident sunlight angled through the sash window. Billie tried the light switch – dead. The room had been looted of all fixtures; even the grate had been ripped from the fireplace. Billie sensed Jeff's mood begin to droop, so she put a bright note in her voice.

'It'll look cosy once it's decorated – and we could give these windows a clean,' she said, swiping down a grey cobweb with her finger. 'I can see you here, the artist in his garret . . .'

Jeff thrust his hands into his pockets and looked around distract-edly. Outside on a half-landing Billie found a toilet with a dingy washbasin. She turned a tap, which dribbled reluctantly. She glanced down at the lavatory bowl, half expecting to find something dread-ful, but it was empty.

'Running water, all mod cons out there,' she said, returning to the room. Jeff was standing at the window, hands still in his pockets.

'It looked bigger, somehow, when he was showing me round,' he said quietly.

'Jeff, you've always said how difficult it is to work at the flat, with my stuff in the way. But now look, you've got a place all to yourself. Think how much work you'll be able to get through!'

He sighed heavily. 'I'm not sure I *can* work here. It's so fucking grotty'.

Billie felt her shoulders slump. It *was* grotty, but he was so fucking miserable. They were silent for a minute.

'Well, you can only try,' she said. 'If it's not for you just give him a month's notice.'

Jeff puckered his mouth. 'A month? Some hope. I had to take the lease for *six*.'

She stared at him, aghast. 'Why did you agree to that? That's such a long –'

'The landlord said take it or leave it. Reckoned he'd got some-one else lined up if I didn't.'

Billie hardly dared ask her next question. The enthusiasm over his collages hadn't been mentioned for a few weeks, and she feared

Jeff's reaction to an enquiry. 'The gallery haven't paid you yet, have they?'

He shook his head. 'There's a hitch. Mapleton wants to reconsider, seems his deputy didn't know about a cash-flow problem or something.'

'But what's-his-name – he said he wanted the lot. He promised you, didn't he?'

'Of course he fucking promised!' Jeff cried impatiently. 'But so what? It looked like a sure thing and now it's not. Maybe *you* should call 'em up and demand they honour their agreement.'

'There's no need to be sarcastic, Jeff. I want this as much as you do.'

'Oh really? As much as I do?' His voice trembled with bitterness. 'I've waited for this break for years – literally, years. I've had to put up with so much shit, so much rejection, just hoping that one day *somebody* would get what I'm . . . doing. Finally, just when it looks like I've cracked it, they come back and tell me, "Well, we're not sure any more." Do you understand what that's like?'

'I imagine it's awful,' said Billie. She was only trying to be sympathetic, but he addressed her with such scowling, eye-rolling exasperation, that it felt as though she were somehow to blame for his setback. She could have told him about her own experience of rejection – the cycle of auditions, the hope of a call back, the lengthening silence – but she knew that Jeff would scorn it as an irrelevance. His suffering was his own, not to be trivialised by comparison with another's. He gazed morosely out of the window and began rolling a cigarette.

'I've paid the first month's rent,' he said presently. 'After that, who knows.'

Billie nodded. 'Well, if the worst comes to the worst, I'll just have to go on the game.'

Jeff, perhaps thinking he'd misheard, turned a frown on her. 'What?'

'Those girls who get into men's cars on the Cally Road – seems they're always in work, and I wouldn't have far to walk home. Earn a bit extra for us.'

She watched his expression, momentarily stunned, then horrified and disbelieving. Got him! She burst out laughing. 'Oh, Jeff, your face . . .'

Jeff straightened, a little annoyed to have been taken in. But then a smile twitched one side of his mouth. 'Daft cow,' he muttered, and joined her laughter with his own. She had rescued the mood, as she had to do quite often these days. It seemed to her you could divide people into two types. There were those she thought of as 'radiators', who gave out warmth and cheer and vitality. And then there were 'drains', their emotional negatives, who sucked the life out of everything. Even as she laughed, watched him shake his head, she felt under no illusion as to which category Jeff belonged.

Freya rubbed her eyes, itching from the dust. She had been hunkered down all afternoon in the *Chronicle*'s airless library, leafing through back issues of the paper. An acreage of yellowing newsprint sprawled over the desk. Her search had centred exclusively upon one name: Reiner Werther Kloss. She had followed his career off and on since his precocious debut *Rosa Luxemburg* seven years ago. As well as the papers, she had open *A Biographical Compendium of Film*, in its most recent (1965) edition.

> Kloss, Reiner Werther, b.Bad Wörishofen, 1933
>
> It is a mark of this young director's energy and instinct for controversy that he has within a relatively short career become an *enfant terrible* of the new German cinema. Coming of age in a country traumatised and guilt-stricken by the last war, Kloss worked in theatre, first as an actor, later as a playwright and director. Strongly influenced by Heinrich Böll and Günter Grass, his plays focus upon the individual conscience haunted by the sorrows of war, terrorism and personal betrayal. Other plays, notably *29 Marks* and *Black Friday*, explore the moral infirmities of a heartless and hypocritical society. In 1960 he made his first film, *Rosa Luxemburg*, a sensational biopic of the doomed revolutionary socialist. It won a Best Director award at the Venice Film Festival. His second feature, *Blut und Feuer* (1961), an allegory of the Hitler Youth movement, caused rioting outside cinemas. He changed direction for his next, *Three Months on*

Reichenbachstrasse (1963), a contemporary story about a sexually ambiguous young man, which some commentators have identified as veiled autobiography. Kloss, born into an artistic, well-to-do family in Munich (his mother sang opera professionally), was a child prodigy, singing and performing magic tricks from the age of four. During the Allied fire bombings he was sent to live with his grandmother in rural Bavaria. Both of his parents were killed in an air raid on the city in October 1942.

He returned to the disasters of war in *The Private Life of Hanna K* (1964), an intense study of love and betrayal which won several awards in France and was nominated for a Best Foreign Language Film Oscar. It also made a star of Sonja Zertz (b.1937), a Stuttgart-born actress whom he first directed onstage. The *New York Times* called it 'one of the most disturbing films ever made about the psychological effects of conflict'. Despite the acclaim of American critics he has so far resisted the call of Hollywood; indeed, he has never directed a film outside of Germany. At the time of going to print he was developing a film provisionally entitled *The Laudanum Waltz*. On the evidence of this handful of pictures Kloss may already claim to be one of the most gifted and idiosyncratic film-makers at work today.

At the Palais-Royal press conference back in March she had seated herself at the front, the better to study him. Behind his Lennon spectacles Reiner's eyes were pale grey, with a languid blink. He was dressed rather untidily in a blue woolly and jeans, a black Mao cap and a pair of biker boots; a scrubby beard added to the student look. The friendly, almost puckish front he presented was hard to reconcile with the sombre explorations of his country's recent past. Freya, responding to this, told him how moved she had been by the love story of *Hanna K*. Though it was the truth, she generally preferred not to throw praise around: film people tended to be conceited enough already.

But it was worth it when he smiled in reply and said: 'I shall save up that compliment and take it out later to enjoy – like a biscuit at teatime.'

Later, she made to waylay him as he was leaving the room. Reiner had never spoken at any length in public about his work or his life. Would he be prepared, she asked, to give an interview for the *Chronicle*? He looked at her as though from a long distance, and shook his head. 'Ach, I'm afraid not. My English is rather limited. Also, I fear the prospect of strangers turning out my laundry and holding it up for inspection.'

'It's your work I want to discuss, not your laundry,' said Freya.

'That's worse!' he replied. 'You would be tampering with a mechanism whose workings are not clear even to myself. That is as it should be. The artist must be always vigilant – in talking about your work, you risk losing the secret things that inspire it. Sometimes it is less important to understand than to feel.'

And on that resonant note Reiner was hustled away by his entourage.

In the library Freya packed up her notes, returned the box files to the librarian and rode the lift to editorial on the second floor. She was about to settle at her desk when she spotted across the room the stately figure of Delphine Frampton, holding forth to a couple of colleagues. Delphine, editor of the women's page, had risen through the ranks by dint of severe application and her unbiddable Anglo-French temperament. It had earned her a reputation as a bit of a dragon. Freya liked her, sensing she might be a kindred spirit, though a twenty-year age difference and Delphine's rather brusque social manner had kept Freya at arm's length. It struck her now that they really ought to talk, for Delphine was a devoted filmgoer.

Freya wandered over to her desk. Delphine lifted her chin imperiously and said, 'What is it, dear?' Her clipped tone made her sound immediately in a hurry, but Freya wasn't to be put off.

'I wonder if in your travels you've ever come across Reiner Werther Kloss?'

'Never met him, but I did enjoy his last one – *Hanna K* – awf'ly good.'

'Yes, it was,' Freya agreed, 'but he's made another one since. Have you heard of *The Laudanum Waltz*?'

'Oh ye-e-ers,' said Delphine, perking up. 'A legal dispute cropped up around its release, and then it vanished.'

'So nobody ever saw it?'

'Not as far as I know. There was a rumour that the studio tried to recut the film behind Kloss's back. He found out and took off with the negative – said he'd burn it sooner than let them ruin it.'

'Did he? Burn it?'

Delphine shrugged. 'That was the studio's theory. But there's no convincing proof he ever had it in his possession. If he did destroy it, though, it's quite a story. I mean, here's something you devote two years of your life to making – all that preparation, the writing, the shoot, the edit and so on. Then in a fit of rage you reduce it to ashes. You would really have to be quite . . .'

'Mad?'

'I was going to say "single-minded",' said Delphine. 'But yes, "mad" seems about right. I hear he's wonderful to work for, so long as you do exactly what you're told. He works very closely with his editor, Arno somebody.'

'He's here now, in London, to make a film of "The Figure in the Carpet". I'm hoping to write a story on him.'

'Is that so?' Delphine's eyes flashed with renewed interest. 'There's certainly some juice there. Are you arranging an interview?'

Freya shook her head. 'He turned me down flat when I met him in Paris. I'll get Nat Fane on the case – he's writing the script.'

'I shouldn't get too close to Herr Kloss, my dear. As well as mad, well, they say he's not averse to firearms, either.'

'What?'

'Oh, a friend of a friend told me. One of the cast – I can't remember who – was making a terrible nuisance of himself, turning up late and offending everyone left and right. Kloss put up with it only because it would have been more complicated to sack him. The last straw: after another tantrum, the man threatened to walk off the set. I think everyone would have been happy to see the back of him. My friend said that Kloss reacted quite calmly, told the actor he was very welcome to try walking off, but he should bear in mind that he had a pistol stored in his valise and wouldn't hesitate to use it. A silence fell, and the actor decided to call his bluff. Kloss got out of his chair, went to his locker and returned half a minute later with a Luger in his hand! And then showed him it was loaded.'

'Golly. What happened then?'

'They barely spoke again. But he didn't walk, and the crew didn't get another peep out of him.'

'Rather brilliant of Reiner,' said Freya.

'Wasn't it?' said Delphine, joining her stiffened middle and index fingers in imitation of a gun barrel and blowing over the top of it. 'Instructive, too. I shouldn't mind trying it myself next time I negotiate a pay rise.'

INT. CONCERT HALL — NIGHT.
CHAS *is seated in the middle of the auditorium listening to a symphony. He is on
his own, and absorbed. After some moments
he happens to look up, and the camera
tracks his gaze to a box high to his left.
He spots there* JANE *and* VEREKER, *and his
expression turns shifty; he looks away. He
hasn't seen them in a year.*

  Camera switches to JANE'S *POV in the box.
We see* CHAS *down below. Has* JANE *picked him
out too?*

INT. HALL BAR — NIGHT.
The concert interval. CHAS *is drinking at
the crowded bar. He is unaware of the
approach of* JANE *behind him.*

                    JANE
  Chas!

He turns to face her.

  I thought it was you.

                   CHAS
                 (*shyly*)
  Hello, Jane. How - how are you?

  106

JANE

I'm here with Hugh. We haven't seen you in such ages. I've missed you!

CHAS

I've been pretty busy . . .

JANE

Well, I *know*. I see your name all over the paper - even on the front page, wasn't it?

CHAS

Yes. (*He laughs modestly*.) The front of the *Middle*, as it were. They use me because I'm available - and cheap.

JANE *looks at him fondly, shaking her head at his self-depreciation.*

JANE

Hugh's just upstairs. Why don't you come and say hello?

CHAS *pulls a regretful face.*

CHAS

Oh, I'm not really . . .

JANE

What's the matter?

A beat. CHAS *is not moving.*

CHAS

To be honest, I'm a little embarrassed. That weekend at your place last year - the way he so gracefully squashed my review.

Now my name's all over the place, as you say, and I imagine Hugh Vereker just thinks - 'He's no great shakes.'

                    JANE
                 (*frowning*)
He hasn't said anything of the kind. He hardly ever discusses his work - or his reviews.

                    CHAS
Doesn't he? He's not mentioned the, er, trick?

                    JANE
What 'trick'?

                    CHAS
Oh, it's nothing - forget it.

                    JANE
Look, I don't want to force you, but it would be lovely to see you again. Will you come down to Bridges for another weekend?

                    CHAS
I'd love to be able to . . .

                    JANE
Is that a 'yes' or a 'no'?

The concert-hall bell rings, signalling the interval's end. JANE *is looking at him expectantly.*

                    CHAS
Of course it's 'yes'. I'm just snowed under at the moment - been working like a dog.

JANE

All the more reason you should have a break. I'll phone you next week with a date. You won't let me down, will you?

JANE *leans in to kiss him goodbye. She searches his face for a clue to his strange mood.* CHAS *raises his hand in farewell to her smiling retreat. As he turns back to the camera we see his face, disgruntled and self-accusing.*

INT. TURKISH BATH — NIGHT.
The steam room is almost fogged. Through the murk CHAS *steps uncertainly. He peers around.*

CHAS

George? Where the - ?

GEORGE

Over here.

CHAS *follows the voice until he makes out a seated figure, a towel around his waist.*

CHAS

I can't see a bloody thing.

He sits down and leans his head against the tiled wall. They are silent for a few moments.

GEORGE

So, this girl. She's rich, good-looking, in search of a husband. What's the problem?

CHAS

I'm not sure. She's great, you're right - it's just . . . I don't feel that much for her.

GEORGE

Chas, Chas . . . What are we going to do with you?

GEORGE *closes his eyes, head back.* CHAS *steals a sidelong glance at him.*

CHAS

How goes it with Gwendolen, by the way?

GEORGE

It was going rather well, until I told her my news.

CHAS

You have news?

GEORGE

They've asked me to be Rome correspondent - for six months.

CHAS
(*amazed*)
And you're going?

GEORGE

Next week. That's why I called you, dear boy. This is *arrivederci*. I'm in the dog-house with Gwen.

CHAS

I thought you two had an understanding . . .

GEORGE

So we did. But it's not much use when her
mother is back in the very pink of health.
Gwen won't leave her, so any immediate
prospect of marriage is kaput. And yet
she's furious with me for going.

CHAS

So it's over between you?

GEORGE

Oh no. We'll muddle through. It's only six
months, as I reminded her.

*They are silent again, each occupied with
their own thoughts.* CHAS's *face twitches
with curiosity.*

CHAS

And what of the other great prospect –
have you given it up?

GEORGE

Vereker, you mean? Not at all.

CHAS

I thought your ardour must have cooled.
We haven't talked of it for a while.

GEORGE

It's never left my mind! And who knows, a
change of scenery might be useful in the
ongoing investigation.

CHAS

I saw him the other night – Vereker. He
was with Jane at the concert.

III

GEORGE

You talked?

CHAS

No. I had an unaccountable aversion to
meeting. Ever since he told me about it
at Bridges - about the buried treasure -
I find myself reluctant to engage with
him.

GEORGE

Was he rude to you?

CHAS

No, on the contrary, he was kind. But I
have the impression that he enjoys his
secret, and he slightly despises me for
not getting anywhere near it. I tried to
explain this to Jane, but she hadn't a
clue what I was talking about. Isn't it
odd - she and Vereker have been friends
for ages, and yet he's never mentioned the
thing to her.

GEORGE

Perhaps it's not what he wants a friend
for.

CHAS

But how can *she* be so incurious about
him?

GEORGE

I dare say she's more interested in the
man than in the books. I can understand
it. A writer doesn't always want to be
surrounded by literary people.

                    CHAS
Maybe it's just writers who can't leave it
alone. Gwen, for instance.

                    GEORGE
Of course. But she hasn't cracked it either.

                    CHAS
I read *Down Deep* the other day. I was
impressed.

                    GEORGE
You should write and tell her. She loves
to hear praise.

                    CHAS
I'd have thought she was above that kind
of thing.

                    GEORGE
I've never known a writer who was. Tell
her! You could make yourself a friend for
life.

CHAS *laughs uneasily. He steals a look at*
GEORGE, *who remains quite oblivious.*

7

Billie was having a cigarette on her break when another waitress, Janet, sidled into the canteen. There was 'a bloke' at reception asking for her. From the wary look in the girl's eyes Billie knew it would be Jeff, shoulders freighted with the news of his latest setback. Since the initial agreement to take all six of his collages the gallery had negotiated it down to two. He had already lost face, as well as the promise of cash. If they reneged again she thought he might lose the will to live.

She stubbed out the cigarette and replaced her frilled cap: waiting staff were not supposed to be seen in the hotel without one. With a sinking heart she hurried down the corridor and through the residents' lounge, rehearsing phrases the while to soothe his piqued pride. When she got to reception, however, there was no sign of Jeff, and her relief began to wrestle with her guilt: perhaps he had been unable to face her and slunk off? She saw a man with his hand raised to her in greeting.

'Hello,' said Nat. 'We've met before.'

Billie blinked at him uncertainly. 'Oh, yes. With Penny, at the agency,' she said, her subconscious blanking the first time, here, when he'd caught her pilfering.

Nat looked around the lobby. 'I wonder if there's somewhere we could talk?'

She experienced a stab of panic. The thing had happened weeks ago, and he'd let her off – surely it was too late for him to reconsider? Trying to keep her voice steady she led him to a side office – more like a cupboard – where they kept stationery and a staff telephone. There were no chairs. Billie closed the door and held her breath.

Nat, sensing her nerves, offered a smile of reassurance. 'I'm sorry to parachute in like this, but I wanted a straight chat. Are you busy at the moment?'

'Well, it's always busy round here –'

'No, no, I mean "busy", as in stage work?'

'Oh. No. Nothing,' she said.

He nodded, satisfied. 'I don't want to involve Penny, not yet; better to keep it informal. There's a small part going in a film I'm writing – I've written – and I thought you'd be rather good in it.'

He enjoyed her frozen look of surprise. For a moment she seemed unable to speak, so he continued. 'It's five weeks' work. Maybe six. The film's called *Eureka*, a sort of romance–mystery thing. Reiner Werther Kloss directing. We need someone to play a rich young lady named Jane. You'd take a screen test, but I think with –'

'Yes, of course,' said Billie, feeling a lightness inflate her lungs. A film. A part in a film! She'd heard of Reiner Werther Kloss. 'But . . . you've never seen me act.'

Nat arched his eyebrows. 'That's not quite true, is it?' He patted his breast pocket, where the faint outline of his wallet was visible. He felt a delicious quiver of guilt as she blushed. 'Pardon me. But you *were* very convincing.' 'I'm sorry that I – you know. It's not something I've made a habit of.' This was true. Apart from the incident with Nat, Billie had only stolen once before, in another opportunistic moment when an American businessman had accidentally left his money clip in the hotel bar. The fold of banknotes rested there, ignored, and almost without thinking she had lifted it. The man had reported the theft to the hotel manager, an investigation was mounted and Billie, along with the rest of the staff, was questioned. But she never really felt suspected, and she had been eighty pounds to the good.

She had got away with it. She had been strapped for cash – waitressing barely paid the rent – and had depended on handouts from Nell for too long. In the days following she had gloried in her luck and bought herself a few things. It was wonderful to have money in your purse. But her peace of mind was shot. She didn't feel guilty about her victim, exactly; he didn't look like the type who would go short. But she felt guilt nonetheless, a deep-lying throb of disquiet that wouldn't leave her alone. It made her cringe to think what Nell would say if she ever found out.

She had resolved not to do it again. And until the afternoon Nat had come in and casually tossed his wallet onto the table she thought she never would. Temptation had got the better of her: had nearly plunged her into calamity. But some angel of providence had intervened. Instead of being prosecuted for theft she was now being courted for a job. If she had believed in God she would have got down on her knees and thanked Him.

Nat in the meantime was telling her about the auditions. 'We've seen a few. Isabel Duncannon was the last.'

Billie felt a sudden deflation: Isabel Duncannon was too bright a star to fail. 'She's bound to get it.'

'Not necessarily. The producers weren't sure about her, and our director was distinctly un-enamoured. So the door's still open.'

Billie squinted at him. 'I've not done any film acting before.'

'My dear girl, you seem determined to back your way into the limelight. Modesty is all well and good, but occasionally in life there comes along a gift so obvious it might as well be tied with a bow. This is one such.'

'I know, I'm sorry. It's just that it's come . . . out of the blue.'

'The best things usually do,' said Nat, taking out his card and a pen. 'There's a little rehearsal studio in Marylebone the company's using. I'll write the address here. Say, twelve thirty this Friday?'

She took the card and read it. 'Thank you. Really. Will you send me a script?'

Nat hesitated. 'Don't worry about that for the moment. They'll want a look at you, that's all. Perhaps you've got a party piece you can do.'

'Will you be there?'

'Of course,' he said, moving to open the door. 'Don't look so tragic about it; this could be your Judy Garland moment! See you Friday.'

Filming was due to start the last week of May, so they needed a decision on Isabel Duncannon quickly. Nat, Berk, two assistant producers, the cinematographer and an associate producer found themselves in agreement that Miss Duncannon was a good fit for the part. All that was required now was the OK from Reiner. He had watched her audition from behind his tinted Lennon spectacles, and at the end thanked the actress with a graciousness that Nat found somewhat disconcerting. He had never known a director to have such manners.

After she had gone they sat around the table while one of Berk's assistants ran through the production schedule. Then they listened to a report from a location manager. An hour passed before the talk turned back to Isabel Duncannon and the expected formality of hiring her. Through the gathering murmur of agreement Nat, picking up that Reiner had gone quiet, leaned in to ask him his view of the matter.

'She is very good. She has poise, and a clear voice, and of course she's very beautiful.' Reiner paused, then squinted into the distance. 'But this is a woman to admire. Not one to love. There is confidence in her – too much. I want someone who brings uncertainty to this character. Jane is young and rich, yes, but she doesn't know her own attraction. She has the humility of the self-doubter. Miss Duncannon . . .' He shook his head. 'She is not that woman.'

Berk shifted in his chair, frowning. 'Well. She's the hell of an actress, my friend.'

'That is not in dispute,' said Reiner. 'We invited the lady to this audition already knowing what she could do. I was looking for something else, something beyond the reach of technical skill. Maybe – maybe it's just an expression on a face. A look.'

A blank silence intervened. One of the producers asked him what sort of 'look' he meant. Reiner leaned back.

'Well, consider the story of a young and virtuous wife. Her husband is serving a prison sentence – not for a violent crime, just some error of judgement. Maybe he was bankrupt, or involved in a fraud. For some years she has patiently waited for him, visiting him in jail while enduring her own loneliness. In the meantime she has had to resist the advances made by other men, who know her situation. She is like Penelope waiting for the return of Odysseus. The imprisoned man is fortunate indeed to have the love of such a woman!'

Nat glanced around the table to check the effect of Reiner's story; he could almost discern a vaporous cartoon question mark floating above the heads of the assembled. Oblivious to their confusion, Reiner continued.

117

'Now, the time of the husband's release draws near. They are counting down the weeks, and the wife is excited, tidying and preparing their home for the big day. While she is clearing out an old trunk she happens to come across a box she has never seen before. She opens it, and finds there a cache of letters. What are these? She reads them, one by one, and slowly her expression changes – they are love letters written to her husband by another woman. And she instantly knows from the dates on them that this affair happened within the span of their marriage. To think: the husband that she loved and stood by for years – this man has betrayed her. Picture her face as turmoil rises within, the different emotions, of hurt and anger, yes, but also of terrible confusion. She loves him still. Imagine this agony played out. *That* is the face I am looking for.'

Berk was first to break the silence. 'But where's that in the movie?'

Reiner shrugged. 'It's not. It's a story I've invented to explain something.'

The air of bafflement was palpable. Nat felt inclined to laugh, but in admiration, not mockery. He loved the casual way Reiner had trotted out his fable. That was the moment he understood what sort of actress was required for the part of Jane. What's more, he knew where to find her.

Billie stepped off the bus at Kentish Town and crossed Fortess Road. The heat of the day was uncomfortable, but she hardly noticed. Her mother's house was a tall Victorian villa that had seen better days; the stucco and brickwork were flaky, the front windows clouded. It had been inherited from her parents, but with no money for its maintenance it looked a little forlorn. A palisade of dusty trees screened it from the street. Billie hurried up the tiled path and rang the bell.

A young denim-jacketed man with a northern accent (Kevin, she thought his name was) answered the door. He was a student at UCL, one of an ever-changing retinue of lodgers; her mother liked the company, and probably needed the rent money. Billie greeted him brightly. 'Is Nell in?'

Kevin, peering at her from beneath a lank fringe of brown hair, mumbled, 'Yeah, upstairs, I think.'

He stepped aside and she passed down the hallway, which smelled of boiled lentils and old carpets, with top notes of patchouli oil. From one of the rooms she heard singing and the plaintive strum of a guitar: someone was playing 'It Ain't Me Babe' as though it might be the end of the world. Billie climbed the staircase. The walls were covered with Nell's work – landscapes from her time at the Slade, the odd portrait, more accomplished as the years went on. Billie felt quite proud of her mother's stuff; though it made her a modest living, it had never received its due. She used a back bedroom as her studio, from which was emanating the muffled drone of a radio.

'Hi, Mum,' she said, poking her head round the door.

Nell gave a little jump and shot her a goofy grin. 'Darling – I wasn't expecting you.' She dropped a thin brush in a jar and moved her easel to make room for them both. 'Careful. Don't get paint on you.'

'I didn't mean to interrupt,' she said as they kissed each other. 'Can I have a look?'

'Oh, I was just pottering,' said Nell, who after a little coaxing showed her the picture she'd been working on. It was a landscape, with two distant figures standing at its edge, one of them puzzling over a map. 'Have you taken the afternoon off?'

'Actually, I've just handed in my notice at the hotel.'

Nell, in the middle of wiping her hands, looked up sharply. 'You haven't.'

Billie nodded. 'I had to. I've got another job.' She allowed herself a gratifying little pause. 'It's a part in a film. They called me today to say I'd got it.'

Nell's mouth dropped open in surprise, then let out a shriek of triumph. They fell into each other's arms. 'Oh, Billie! That's smashing news. But you didn't even tell me you had an audition.'

'I didn't tell anyone,' she admitted. 'I decided to keep shtum.' She had learned that it was better not to raise people's hopes: if it turned out you hadn't got it you then had to deal with their disappointment as well as your own.

Nell beamed at her. 'You're a sly one. So tell me, tell me!'

Billie recounted the story of running into Nat Fane at Penny Rolfe's office (she omitted mention of their first encounter) and how he'd called at the hotel to invite her to an audition. It was the part of a young society woman called Jane. She hadn't realised at first what a 'big' film it was to be – a young German called Reiner Werther Kloss was directing, he'd won all sorts of awards, this would be his first film in English . . .

'But, Mum, you'll never guess who's starring in it. Vere Summerhill.'

'Go on!' cried Nell. 'God, I remember swooning first time I saw him in *They Fought Them on the Beaches*. Vere Summerhill and John Mills.' Her eyes misted over.

'Maybe I could get you onto the set to meet him.'

'Ooh, imagine! Mind you, he's queer, isn't he?'

'Christ! I wasn't planning on matchmaking you.'

'And this fellow Fane – he must think you're the bee's knees. Never seen you in anything and yet seeks you out personally! What's he like?'

'Oh, lots of charm, rather a tease. Bit full of himself. He's written a lot of plays and films; won an Oscar a while back.'

Nell made a just-fancy-that face. 'So when d'you start?'

'End of this month. They all seemed very excited about it.'

'I should think so,' said Nell, who glanced at her watch. 'Are you going to stay for some dinner?'

'Well, I thought we might go out for a curry, you know, to celebrate. I mean, it's not every day you get cast in a *motion picture*, is it?'

Her mother began rubbing her hands in a little mime of thrilled anticipation, then stopped abruptly. 'Is Jeff coming?' she asked warily.

Billie rolled her eyes. 'No. He's going to some boring concert with his mate. It's just you and me tonight.'

Nell's face brightened again: her feelings were quite transparent. 'All right! I'll tidy up here first and then make meself presentable. Why don't you give the Agra a ring and see if they've got an early table?'

Nat, who rarely visited Islington, had chosen a restaurant beyond the ken, and the purse, of most of its inhabitants. Freya had heard of Carrier's, a posh new place in Camden Passage, though she had yet to dine there; she tended to go to the fish and chip shop on Upper Street. They had been meaning to get together for weeks, but Nat had fallen so far behind schedule on the *Eureka* script that even now he felt nervous about taking a night off. He kept the engine running outside Freya's house at Canonbury Square, tooting the horn in summons. She laughed on seeing the drophead Rolls.

'Look at you. Like a proper movie mogul,' she said, folding her long legs into the passenger seat. He leaned over to plant a kiss on her cheek.

'I used to dream about driving one of these,' he said, pulling out of the square. 'I couldn't imagine anything more ... *splendiferous.*'

Freya noticed passers-by staring as the car purred along the street. 'Isn't it rather expensive?'

'Put it this way: the monthly repayments alone are more than my rent. But d'you know, I can't do without it. The illusion it gives me of being protected is like no other.'

'Protected against what?'

He shrugged. 'Misfortune.'

'So you're living an illusion.'

'Aren't we all? I mean, one depends on the illusory to make life bearable. It's funny, I've often had the impression that the car is very kindly giving me a lift.'

'Well, perhaps you could ask it to park *right there*. We've arrived.'

The restaurant was small, with swagged curtains and honeyed lighting at the tables. On being seated Freya watched Nat steer his gaze about the room; it was not just for the cuisine he had made the trip. He halted in mid-surveillance. Discreetly, he dipped his head towards her and said, sotto voce, 'Don't look now, but the lady dining at the next table along . . .'

Freya, impatient of dissembling, sneaked a glance and saw a dark-haired woman of about her own age, Spanish-looking, sultry. 'She seems familiar, but – you may recall – I'm rather short-sighted.'

'Ava Gardner,' he whispered.

'Gosh. The West End really has come to Islington. She's very lovely. Are you going to say hello to her?'

'I am perfectly content with the loveliness I have in front of me,' said Nat, with a suggestive slow blink.

She smiled back at him. 'You're nice. Not everyone thinks so highly of me. I've just had a letter from Didier, the man I was . . . in Paris? He's very sore about my vanishing act. I can't really blame him.'

Nat scrutinised her. 'I'm rather eager to hear about this. Perhaps when I've secured us a drink.'

He commanded the attention of the waiter, and over a bottle of the Widow Clicquot she recounted the story of Didier and Claire and her disastrous flip-flopping between them. Nat's face as he listened was hawkish in absorption; delight danced in his eyes, and Freya privately considered the likelihood of certain details from her story resurfacing in one of his plays. He was quite ruthless about cannibalising his friends' lives, and he always professed to be baffled when anyone took offence. He had no concept of writerly discretion: for him, life was merely the uncooked dough of art.

'I'd love to have seen the look on the mother's – Odette's? – face when she caught you and Claire in flagrante.'

Freya made a shuddering noise. 'God, if looks could kill.'

Nat narrowed his eyes. 'Odette, where is thy sting?'

Freya laughed. 'I have an impression that I might be hearing that line again some day.'

'Brother *and* sister, though. You know, I rather wish I faced both ways. I have a fancy that men are more receptive to the swish of a cane; perhaps it comes from schooldays. Unfortunately I am repelled by the sight of male genitalia.'

'Count yourself lucky. It's much simpler to swing one way or the other. What happened with that girl you were seeing?'

'Naomi. In something of a *froideur* at present. Last time we met she decided to give me a piece of her mind: said I was conceited, snobbish, egocentric. Oh, and a has-been. We haven't spoken since.'

' "Has-been" is a little harsh,' said Freya, which drew a pained smile from Nat. 'And there's no one else?'

'Well, there's a young actress I'm – but no, I mustn't. I haven't the *time* for one thing. They're badgering me daily for the script.'

They hadn't finished the champagne, yet Nat had ordered another bottle to go with the starters, brandade of smoked trout for her, *fruits de mer* in aspic for him. He'd also asked for a jar of caviar on the side. Freya, who had seen the prices on the menu, hoped Nat would be paying. Nat himself, a natural spendthrift, only ever worried about money when his accountant called for a meeting.

The waiter had poured, and departed.

'Puligny,' Nat supplied, unable to stop himself giving the glass a pompous swirl and sniff. 'When you dream of France, you're really dreaming of Burgundy.'

'Delicious,' said Freya, taking a sip and wondering if that would do as a wine-note. 'This is all a bit extravagant for a Wednesday night.'

Nat stared at her. 'For you it's just a Wednesday night. For me, however . . .' He watched as her puzzled expression cleared.

'Oh, Nat, it's your birthday. I'm *so sorry*! Why didn't you remind me?'

He spread his palms in a beatific gesture of forgiveness. 'It's not a number I'm especially keen to celebrate.'

Freya went pop-eyed. 'Forty!'

'Shhh, for God's sake,' he hissed. 'I'm trying to keep it low-key. You're the only person I've seen all day.'

Freya tilted her head. 'Come on, it's not as bad as all that. I should know – I'm forty-two.'

'Yes, but you look about thirty. Some mornings I check my reflection in the mirror and wonder who put Auden's mug there in its place.'

'Nat, you're in the prime of life. How many others can say they've won an Oscar by the age of – the age you are?'

But he only sighed. 'Seven years ago, now. Since then it's been one anticlimax after another. There's a smell starting to hang around me'.

'A smell of what?'

'Of failure. That's why I need this film to be a hit, else they'll forget about me altogether.'

'Of course it'll be a hit,' said Freya, sensing the need to buck him up. 'What do you think of Herr Kloss, by the way?'

'I was rather taken with him. When we first met at lunch I

thought, Who's this dishevelled youth? But he's very self-possessed, and well mannered. Amazing English, too. He claimed it wasn't good enough to write a screenplay, but that's balls. I'm pleased to say he was also a fan of *The Hot Number* – "it hit my funny bone",' he said, in a drawling imitation of Reiner's accent.

'Yes, he told me his English wasn't up to much; it's his excuse to avoid being interviewed. But I'm going to write about him whether he likes it or not. There's something *mysterious* about Kloss.'

'Mysterious?'

Freya proceeded to recount her investigations – in particular the 'lost' film, *The Laudanum Waltz*, possibly destroyed by his own hand, and his stand-off with the film company over its editing and release. There had been rumours of previous run-ins during his time as a theatre director; it seemed that Reiner had little use for people who challenged his authority. If he didn't get his way, things would quickly begin to unravel. Entire productions had been known to come to a standstill.

'Where's he from exactly?' asked Nat.

'Oh, a spa town near Munich. Bad something.'

'Bad Vibes? Bad Karma?'

'Something like that. I gather he was quite a promising athlete.'

That nudged Nat's memory. 'Yes, he told me he played football for the local team, and would have got a trial with Bayern but for some disobliging coach.'

'What would really help me is a face-to-face. D'you think you might be able to engineer a meeting with him?'

Nat stared off uncertainly. 'I'll try, of course. I'm pretty sure Reiner won't allow a journalist onto the set. The problem is he's clocked you already – he knows you're on his case.'

'Can't be helped. Maybe you could get him round to Albany one day and I could drop in entirely by coincidence.'

They both had the chicken Kiev for the main course; Nat remarked it bore no resemblance to the dish of that name he had recently eaten in Moscow. He had been out there to a premiere of one of his early plays.

'A very congenial audience. Laughed in all the right places, too, which surprised me. But oh, the *boozing*! Vodka, vodka every-where, and not a drop undrunk. Neck or nothing with that lot. I suppose it's the only thing that gets you through those Russian winters.'

'And you'll be off again on location?'

'Yes, Sussex and the Ligurian coast, with a few days in Rome. There was talk of India – where George Corvick has his revelation – but they couldn't get the money for it.'

A mumble of voices had risen around the adjacent table. Ava Gardner and her date were just leaving, and the restaurant manager had come to bid them goodnight. The whole room seemed to be holding its breath, waiting for the perfumed presence to waft among them. As she started to move Nat, watching her intently, half rose from his chair, like an iron filing leaping to a magnet. If she had even glanced his way he would have addressed her, but her gaze didn't deviate an inch, and in a moment she was gone. He slumped back on his seat.

'I thought you were going to introduce yourself,' said Freya.

'I was,' he said, with a little wince. 'I lost my nerve. She wouldn't have known me.'

'You could have explained. Told her about your Oscar.'

But Nat's thoughts had run on. The 'has-been' barb had stuck in his skin and festered. He'd had a sudden vision of Ava greeting his name with a polite look – a blank look. It couldn't be endured. After a clenched pause he muttered, almost to himself, 'Christ, I need a hit.'

She had insisted on paying, and when the bill came she quickly smothered the shock with a look of nonchalance. Nat, with twenty years' experience of her facial tics and tells, pulled a sympathetic grimace.

'Oh dear. Why don't you let me have it?'

He extended his hand, which she slapped away in dismissal.

'Don't be silly, it's your birthday. Anyway, it's not so outrageous,' she said airily.

Nat looked at her. 'That is a lie.'

'Yes, I'm afraid it is,' she agreed, and they laughed. It was a little embarrassing that he'd raided the top end of the wine list all evening: he had been expecting to pay. As she peeled off the notes from her purse she added, 'Just think of me eating tinned soup for the next month.'

EXT. STREET — DAY.
CHAS *walking through Mayfair, his stride purposeful. As he goes we hear:*

GWEN (*v.o.*)
. . . to say how pleased I was to receive your letter, Charles. *Down Deep* was a book that cost me many sleepless nights, so to hear of its effect on you was very gratifying. You write with such insight and warmth about characters who for three years were as precious to me as a close friend . . .

EXT. FRONT STEPS OF BUILDING — DAY.
A sign announces it as 'The University Women's Club'. CHAS *enters.*

INT. DINING ROOM — DAY.
GWEN *and* CHAS *are seated at a window table. They have just been served drinks by a waiter, and face one another.* CHAS *looks round interestedly.*

GWEN
I've been a member since I came down from Cambridge. I don't see why men should have the run of every club in Mayfair.

CHAS

I'd never heard of it.

GWEN

I suppose you belong to some rather grand
place.

CHAS

No. Only thing I've ever joined is the Scouts.
And I think my membership there has lapsed.

GWEN
(*laughing*)
You should get George to put you up for
the Turf.

CHAS

I've relied too often on George's patron-
age. Have you heard from him?

GWEN

He wrote to me last week. He'd just attended
Holy Mass at St Peter's.

CHAS

You're joking.

GWEN

Oh, he's always had a little *tendresse* for
Catholicism. Didn't you know?

CHAS

George? Well, I've heard him talk about
it, but I didn't know he'd gone native.

GWEN

Do you suppose he's seeking divine
intervention?

A beat, as CHAS *considers the possibility.*

> CHAS
>
> I shouldn't think he needs it. As long as I've known him he's always got what he wanted.

> GWEN
> *(with a slow smile)*
> Has he? I wonder . . .

> CHAS
>
> Did he mention Vereker at all?

> GWEN
>
> He did, as a matter of fact. He told me he'd just pitched a book proposal to Antrobus – a study of the novels of Hugh Vereker. They commissioned it within the week.

> CHAS
> *(surprised)*
> He kept that quiet. Does that mean he's going to talk to the author?

> GWEN
>
> No. At least, not until he's unlocked the secret.

> CHAS
>
> Hmm . . . Vereker believes no one ever will.

> GWEN
>
> Then there'll be no book.

CHAS *fiddles with his cutlery. He has something to say, but seems nervous of beginning.*

                              CHAS
It's odd – you remember I went round to
Vereker's house that time to apologise for
blabbing? He said something then that was,
well, maybe the only clue he'd ever slipped
me.

                              GWEN
                        (leaning in)
Really?

                              CHAS
I confessed to him that I'd discussed his
secret with you and George. I explained
who you were, and that you were probably
going to marry one day (sorry). On hearing that he said, 'That might help them.'

                              GWEN
How? How would being married help one to
solve it any more than being single?

                              CHAS
I don't know. He said, 'We must give them
time.' That was all.

                              GWEN
What did George say about it?

                              CHAS
I didn't tell George. To be honest, until
now I'd forgotten about it.

GWEN stares at him for a few moments.

                              GWEN
Forgotten? I think he might find that hard
to believe.

CHAS *shrugs, not quite able to catch her eye.*

> CHAS
>
> You can tell him now.

A waiter arrives with their food, and the conversation is left hanging.

INT. DINING ROOM — DAY.
The remains of lunch on the table. CHAS *is lighting a cigarette for* GWEN.

> GWEN
>
> Seen anything of your friend Jane Burges?

> CHAS
>
> We ran into one another a few weeks ago. She invited me to a weekend party at her place in Sussex.

> GWEN
>
> Are you going?

CHAS *pulls an uncertain face.*

> If you did go, would you be able to bring a friend?

> CHAS
>
> You? I couldn't guarantee Vereker would be there . . .

> GWEN
>
> Do you see an ulterior motive in everything?

CHAS

Most of the time. I wouldn't think you'd want to go merely for the splendour of Jane's country seat.

GWEN

Perhaps I'd like to go just for the pleasure of your company. What would you say to that?

CHAS

I'd say you were probably teasing me. But I'll ask Jane if I might bring a friend all the same.

GWEN
                    (smiling)
You're too kind.

8

'Quiet on the set. Roll camera.'

'Turning over.'

'Speed.'

'Scene nine, take one,' said the clapper, and hit the sticks.

A loaded pause, and Reiner called 'Action'.

The first week's shooting on *Eureka* was nearly over. Billie, sweating under the arc lights, gathered herself for the last scene of the day. It had been a trying introduction. She had known that film-making involved a lot of hanging about and kicking your heels, a glacially slow pace of doing things that could test one's boredom threshold to the limit. She wouldn't have minded that; it sounded better than the dreariness of fetching and carrying all day at the hotel. But this was something different. The long stretches of inertia, the mind-numbing delays, were suddenly punctuated by bursts of activity that demanded the most intense concentration. It was like being woken from sleep at random hours of the night and asked to recite by heart a poem, over and over, a task made no easier by people interrupting and telling you to try it again. At times she felt close to tears, because the lines she thought she had learned would, under this constant barrage, dry on her tongue or else vanish from her mind altogether. She knew she must hang on and not give way, though she noticed the scowls of the assistant director when she blanked her lines again. Even Jürgen, Reiner's phlegmatic cameraman, had looked faintly puzzled at her muffing yet another cue. She really wondered if she was up to the job.

Reiner himself had been very sweet to her. Having rehearsed the first scene she was to play in, he had given her arm a little shake and said, 'You will be fine.' His voice suggested that he knew something about her that she didn't. Once filming was under way, however, Reiner was too busy with other things to be able to give her special attention. She quickly understood that in the grand mosaic of the production she was only a tile, and maybe not even that. A shard. When Julie the script girl happened to sit down next to her Billie cast an eye on her notes – the position of the furniture, the angle at which a character stood in a scene, even the length of ash on a lit cigarette. Get these details wrong and the continuity was shot. Amid so much concentrated activity, the toing and froing, who cared if Billie felt lost?

She tried to make herself agreeable to Ronnie Stiles, who was playing Chas. Most of her scenes would be with him. On set he was cocky and flirtatious, joking – almost capering – in front of every young woman he encountered. He was not at all her idea of Chas. When they shook hands he gave her a saucy little wink.

'Billie. What kinda name's that for a bird?'

'Oh, my mum was mad about Billie Holiday. It's funny, though, because I knew a girl at school called Ronnie.'

Ronnie stared at her, suspicious for a moment. Then his expression cleared. 'Oh well, at least they didn't call her *Reggie*.'

'I thought you were fab in *Mafeking*,' said Billie.

'Ta. You know I was hired to play the cockney sergeant? Then the producer had a look at me and decided I should do the major instead. They said it was the fastest promotion the British Army 'ad ever seen.'

'And you had to learn to ride and shoot.' Billie had read about it in one of the movie magazines.

'Yeah, that bit was easy. I knew horses. The 'ard bit was learning how to speak like an Old Etonian in a weekend. The rain in Spain . . .' he began with prissy enunciation.

'Well, you had me fooled. I thought you'd been born to it.'

Ronnie flicked his straw-coloured hair. 'Not bad for a kid from Stepney, was it?'

He yarned on a little more until a tall dark-haired girl in a minidress strolled by, and Ronnie's gaze followed her hungrily. 'Blimey,' he said, whistling under his breath. He winked again at Billie as he rose from his chair and left. 'See ya later.'

When Reiner finally called it a day and dismissed them, Billie felt relief surge through her. Someone suggested they go to the studio bar, so she straggled behind a bunch of them, hoping to be included. The room was already packed and smoky when she arrived; they were a gregarious lot, film people, all gabbling away like friends who hadn't seen one another in months. There was not a single other person who was on their own. Billie sidled over to the bar, trying to reorganise her features into a look of amiable ease, as if she found it natural to go solo, and indeed almost enjoyed it. The truth was that for the last two years her entire social life had centred upon Jeff. He didn't like her going to places without him. The only time she went anywhere on her own was to her mother's, whose company he couldn't abide.

On being served she wondered if somebody would invite her to join them; just a friendly glance might be all that was required. She took a sip of gin and chewed on a bitter-tasting olive. Across the room she spotted Ronnie, deep in conversation with the tall girl who'd caught his eye earlier; she supposed he wouldn't welcome an interruption. The bright twitter of the bar room was oblivious to her. Someone *must* talk to me, she thought, taking a longer swallow of gin. Perhaps I could go outside and pretend to make a call from a payphone. She was considering this option when from a large cluster of folk at the far end of the bar Vere Summerhill emerged. He was clearly on his way out, so she would have to impose herself to stop him. Her wave was sufficiently frantic to attract his notice.

'Miss Cantrip, hello.' She could tell from his automatic smile that he was reluctant to dally.

'Please, it's Billie.'

Vere, seeing that she was alone, paused a moment. 'How's your first week been?'

'Oh, you know, everyone's been friendly . . .'

'Rather overwhelming, I imagine,' he said kindly. 'Would you like a drink?'

Billie, too grateful to speak, smiled her assent. They sat at the bar. Vere, calling to the barman by name, made a little gesture whose meaning became apparent when a bottle of champagne in an ice bucket was set before them. He poured them each a glass.

'So you and I do our scenes next week,' Vere said. 'Should be fun.'

Billie nodded. 'I hope I won't let you down. I haven't covered myself in glory so far.'

'Well, you're still finding your way. It took me a long time to adapt from stage acting to the screen.' His gaze was as sad as a spaniel's, yet it had a smile in it, too. His gentleness with her was almost too much to bear. She took a moment to gather herself.

'There's such an awful lot of *waiting*,' she said presently.

'I know. But you get used to it. And you learn to develop what the French call *maîtrise de soi*: self-control. It's what makes you ready for the moments when you're on, the tension involved in them. If you don't have it in preparation you arrive at those moments distracted, or irritated. One needs to be collected.'

'Oh God,' murmured Billie.

'Don't be disheartened. Everyone's terribly pleased with you.'

'Everyone? I don't think so.'

'Reiner just told me you look wonderful in the rushes.'

Billie couldn't tell if he was making this up, but she listened as Vere explained a few tricks he'd learned over the years: how to keep your concentration, how to address the camera, how to project yourself without seeming to. *Underact*, he advised her, that was the key; if you forced yourself to keep still and use your eyes, the camera would look after the rest. This is better than having a tutor, thought Billie. Whenever Vere posed a question, he wasn't trying to catch her out or score a point off her; it felt more like he wanted to lead her, by suggestion and illustration, to her own small share of the truth.

They were still deep in conversation when Nat breezed by, looking pleased with himself. He was carrying a sheaf of printed pages in a loose folder – the latest draft of the script, he explained, which he and Reiner had been revising.

'I've just written some outstanding scenes for you two,' he declared, lighting a cigarette and blowing a jet of smoke over them.

'That merits confirmation,' said Vere drily. 'We've just been discussing the art of screen-acting. A shame if our efforts were wasted for the lack of an actual script.'

'Have no fear,' smiled Nat, his mood on an upswing. 'Some things are worth the wait. Think of *Eureka* as a rare orchid, lovingly tended in the hothouse of creative endeavour, and unique once it blooms.'

'My mum loves orchids,' said Billie. 'They're one of her favourite things to paint.'

Vere rose from his stool, and turned to Nat. 'At this point I'd make do with a bunch of daffs. Don't spend too long in the hothouse, darling – there's a danger you may wilt.' He had to turn in for the night, he said. Billie rose too, and leaning in to kiss him mumbled a few words. Vere patted her arm, then gave Nat a friendly nod in parting. When he had gone Nat took his place on the stool.

'Dear old Vere. Such a worrier.'

'You seem very good friends.'

'Of course. What you were whispering in his ear?'

Billie thought this rather nosy of him, but said, 'I just wanted to thank him. He saw me on my own and stopped to chat. He gave me some tips about acting on film.'

'Then use them. Vere's a master of underplaying – half the time he doesn't appear to be acting at all.'

Bille felt a sudden wave of exhaustion engulf her – the trials of the week were catching up – and told Nat that she ought to be on her way. He asked her how she was getting home.

'Train to Waterloo and then a bus to King's Cross.'

'I'm going east. Let me drive you.'

She politely demurred, but he brushed aside her *no, honestly* and insisted: she gave in. In the Twickenham Studios car park she did a double take on realising that the blue-black Silver Cloud, massively imposing, was his. Was she ever glad he had insisted! By the time they were coasting along the Cromwell Road the street lamps were muzzy orange lollipops against the gloaming. Nat, at the wheel, asked prying questions about her domestic arrangements: she told him a bit about her history with Jeff, careful not to sound grumpy or disaffected.

As they reached King's Cross she was mulling over a way to thank him, not just for the lift – for everything. But there seemed so very little you could give a man who drove a Rolls-Royce.

On the spur of the moment she said, 'I wonder if you'd like to, um . . .' But her nerve had failed her. She couldn't do it.

Nat glanced at her. 'What?'

'Oh, nothing, forget it . . .'

'For heaven's sake, *what*?'

'Would you like to, perhaps – if you're not busy – come for dinner one night?'

Nat's face broke into a grin. 'I thought you'd never ask.'

He had dropped her right outside the flat. The lights were on as she descended the steps, and she wondered if Jeff had heard her saying goodnight.

'Who was that?' he asked her as she let herself in.

Billie made a little grimacing smile. 'Nat Fane – you know, the writer. The one who got me the job.'

'He drives a Rolls,' he said wonderingly. 'Jesus. I thought writers were meant to be *poor*.'

'He was just telling me how expensive it is to run: more than the rent on his flat! I think he's an exception. Most writers *are* poor.'

While Jeff considered this, Billie collapsed into the armchair and kicked off her shoes. She began to massage her tired feet. He went off to the kitchen. It was stupid of her to have asked Nat to dinner; she knew she couldn't bring him here: there wasn't room, there weren't enough chairs. She also felt pretty certain that he wouldn't be Jeff's cup of tea; he would think Nat affected and full of himself, which, to a degree, he was. Yet for all that he was wonderful company; a one-off, really. She could take him to a restaurant somewhere . . . though she couldn't possibly afford the sort of places Nat frequented. He'd been telling her about a place he'd eaten at in Islington, which made her think he was more democratic in his tastes than he'd let on. Then it emerged that this restaurant charged 70/- for a set menu and that Ava Gardner had been at the next table, so she could forget about going there.

Jeff returned carrying a tray. He put down the plates and cutlery with an unceremonious clatter, opened a large bottle of pale ale and poured it into a glass.

'You want some of this?' he asked.

She shook her head. Whenever she made dinner she put out napkins and place mats and sometimes lit a candle, to make it cosy. Jeff didn't hold with that kind of thing – he thought it bourgeois and 'poncey'. At least the baked beans were good and hot. She watched him setting about his food. She had hardly seen him this week; a studio car picked her up each morning at six thirty, and she didn't get back from Twickenham until nine or ten.

'What have you been up to today?' she asked.

Jeff slowly shook his head. 'Called in at the gallery. They've put both of the collages on the wall downstairs.'

'That's good!' Billie said hopefully.

'There hasn't been a single enquiry about them.'

'But it's early days, Jeff. You can't expect instant success.'

He only scowled, head over his plate, spooning beans into his mouth. A silence followed: she wondered if she could tell him about her day, though he hadn't asked. When she had got the part she assumed he would be pleased, because it meant an end to their money worries, at least for the time being. He had congratulated her, and barely mentioned it since. She couldn't tell if this was due to a lack of curiosity, or to something more troubling. Now he looked at her suddenly.

'So, this Fane character. Is he married? Single?'

'Er, I don't know. Divorced, I think.'

'I suppose he's got you in his sights.'

'What?'

'He must be after you. Why else did he seek you out for this film?'

Billie stared at him. 'Oh, thanks. Is it that unlikely I got the part because he thought I was good?'

'You told me he'd never seen you act before.'

'I still had to do an audition – they wouldn't have hired me just on his say-so. Anyway, he's much too old for me.'

'You like an older man,' he persisted.

'Yeah, but he's like, *forty*, or something.'

Jeff, who was thirty-five, took a long swig of his beer. 'Well, there'll be loads of younger blokes sniffing around. It's a film set.'

'I'm sure I'll have to fight them off,' she said with a half-laugh. 'God, if you could have seen me in the studio bar this evening. I was there on my own for ten minutes – not a single person came up to talk to me. In the end I had to waylay Vere Summerhill. And he only stopped cos he felt sorry for me.'

'Yeah, but there's Alec Madden, and the ratty-looking one, what's-his-name – Ronnie Stiles. I notice you've got quite a few scenes with him *of a romantic nature*.'

'How d'you know that?'

'I looked at that script you left lying around.'

She stared at him in disbelief. 'You read the script? Haven't you got anything better to do?'

'So you're not denying it.'

'Denying what? Jeff, you're being paranoid. I've no interest in Ronnie Stiles, or Nat Fane, or anyone. The only thing I'm interested in is the job I was hired to do. I don't regard it as a lonely-hearts service.'

Jeff pushed his plate aside and lowered his head into his hands. In a quiet disconsolate voice he said, 'You're so naive. Surrounded all day by creeps who've got nothing else to do but ogle girls. I bet they can't wait for the scenes with you in your swimming costume –'

'For Christ's sakes, Jeff!' said Billie, rising from the table. 'What's got into you? You talk like these people have never seen a woman before. They're just blokes, professionals, doing their job. If there's anyone giving me the creeps at the moment it's *you*.'

'The fact you're getting so shrill about it only confirms what I'm thinking,' said Jeff. His self-righteousness had taken on a martyred note. Billie briefly considered firing a barb, and stopped herself; it would be better not to say anything at all. Jeff had turned his face away. She lingered for a few moments, then left the room.

In the bedroom Monty stared at her with round-eyed disapproval. He had obviously been earwigging all this time. She put *Beatles for Sale* on the Dansette, the volume turned low. It was her favourite album of theirs, and her favourite cover, the four of them in a line against a blurred autumnal backdrop; something sombre – or soulful – in those dark northern gazes. She slowly undressed and got into bed. She picked up the pages of script for the following Monday and switched on her bedside light. A long dinner-party scene was scheduled in which she would be the centre of attention; she began to read through her lines, trying out different tones of voice under her breath. She thought about her conversation with Vere in the bar, how gentle and considerate he had been. Oh, if she could only acquire a little of his self-assurance, his air of command before the camera . . .

She could hear Jeff moving around, probably having another

ale and a joint. Well, let him stew. She read on till her eyelids began to droop. Monty lay curled up at the foot of the bed, snoring quietly.

A sharp noise woke her, and she groggily checked the illuminated dial on her alarm clock. Twenty past one. She turned, expecting to find Jeff next to her, but she was alone. A narrow band of light peeped from under the bedroom door. Her inclination was to turn over and go back to sleep. It was too late and she was too tired to have another row. But she dragged herself out of bed and put on her dressing gown.

The living room was in darkness but for the shy illumination of a floor lamp. The air was sour with beer and smoke. Jeff was slumped on the sofa, an arm slung across his face. He'd finished off two bottles of pale ale and moved on to vodka; it was this bottle that had fallen on the low table and made the sudden noise. He showed no sign of having heard her come in. She tiptoed towards him.

'Jeff?'

He started on hearing her voice. His arm dropped from his face, which was bleary with drink and – could it be? – tears. Reflexively he turned away. But she could see his shoulders trembling piteously. She sat down next to him.

'What's the matter?'

He shook his head. When she reached for his hand he gave way to a wrenching sob. 'I know you're going to leave me,' he said in a choked voice.

'What? Don't be silly.'

'You will. I can tell.' It began to pour out of him. He'd been so low these last few weeks, what with the gallery messing him about over the collages, nibbling away at his confidence. The one thing that had kept him going through these lean times was Billie. He knew he could be difficult – 'a bit moody' – but she had always been there to support him: 'a rock', he called her. Only now it felt like his rock was under threat. The new job was taking her away from him. She had been so distracted these last weeks she hardly seemed to *notice* him. If it was just about the work he'd understand, but being in the company of men all day long . . .

'Don't. Don't start that again.' She leaned into him and caressed his cheek. 'I'm not going anywhere. If I've been distracted then I'm sorry. I'm new to this and it takes a lot out of you. It's intense. But it'll be over by August.'

Jeff sighed heavily. 'I wish you didn't have to.'

'But I *want* to do it. Making a go of this is important to me, just like your work's important to you.' She saw him bridle at this proposed equivalence, but she let it go. They talked on, going over it again, until Billie, fatigued by her iterations of assurance, insisted they turn in for the night. She was about to get up when Jeff grabbed her wrist and fixed her with a pleading expression.

'Look, I won't ask this again, but you have to tell me,' he said, shushing her weary protest. 'You won't go off with Nat Fane, will you?'

Billie felt her shoulders slump. She composed herself for one last effort. 'No, Jeff. I won't.'

She was moved by his neediness. She also faintly despised it. And she now considered it vital to keep quiet about inviting Nat to dinner.

EXT. BRIDGES, COUNTRY HOUSE — DAY.
A car pulls up on the drive in front. CHAS
and GWEN *get out. The front door opens and*
JANE *emerges to greet them, while a member
of her household carries off their luggage.
They disappear into the house.*

INT. DRAWING ROOM — DAY.
JANE *is pouring tea for her guests.* GWEN
and an older man, ROLLO, *sit on opposite
sofas.* CHAS *stands at the fireplace, hands
in his pockets.*

> GWEN
>
> It's a beautiful house. I gather you inher-
> ited it.

> JANE
>
> Yes, from an aunt. I was seventeen at the time.

> GWEN
>
> Gosh. What a responsibility. Was there any-
> one to help you?

> JANE
>
> Not really. My parents died when I was
> three. My aunt was my guardian. But I
> learned to cope pretty quickly.

ROLLO

And now she keeps the best table in Sussex. She's well known for it.

JANE
(*to* GWEN)
I like having friends down here. It would
be a shame to run a house like this and
not have people to fill it.

GWEN

Charles often tells me what marvellous
times he's had here. Awfully nice of you
to let me tag along with him.

CUT TO: JANE *turns a fond look on* CHAS.

JANE

He knows he's always welcome. You must show
Gwen around - the wild flowers in the
paddock are lovely at the moment.

CHAS

At your service. Are you expecting anyone
else, Jane?

JANE

A few. The Finches. Dean Drayton. And Hugh
Vereker, my dear old friend - I expect
you know him, Gwen.

GWEN

No, I don't. Though I've read him of course,
with great admiration.

JANE

Oh, then I'll be sure to place you next
to him at dinner.

CHAS *gives* GWEN *a brief knowing look while* ROLLO *asks a dull question of* JANE *about the local fishing.*

INT. CORRIDOR — LATER.
CHAS *knocks at a bedroom door, and hears a voice within, 'Come in.'*

INT. BEDROOM — DAY.
GWEN *facing a dressing-table mirror sees* CHAS *in the reflection, leaning around the door.*

> CHAS

See you in the hall - five minutes?

> GWEN
> (*addressing the mirror*)

I'll be right down.

EXT. FRONT COURTYARD — DAY.
CHAS *and* GWEN *set out for a walk around the grounds of Bridges.*

EXT. GROUNDS — DAY.
GWEN *and* CHAS *stroll round an ornamental lake.*

> CHAS
> (*in mocking imitation*)

'Keeps the best table in Sussex' . . . What a twerp!

GWEN
(*laughing*)

Jane's very beautiful, isn't she? You never said.

CHAS

Didn't I?

GWEN

No. And she's besotted with you. (*She stares at* CHAS *for a moment.*) You don't seem all that bothered.

CHAS

Jane can have her pick. There'll be someone else to tickle her fancy soon enough.

GWEN

But why not you?

CHAS

I'm sure you know the phrase 'the heart has its reasons'.

GWEN

They must be very persuasive ones for you to turn your nose up at a girl like that.

CHAS

I suppose so. (*He stops, looks at her for a moment.*) You said George had written to you. Has he made any progress - with the book, I mean?

GWEN

He's still making notes. I don't think he's anywhere nearer 'the thing', the secret.

                    CHAS

You're soon to meet the keeper of the secret.
I had a feeling Jane would invite him.

                    GWEN

You know, I've heard so much talk of Hugh
Vereker and the 'inscrutable mystery' that
I feel bound to find the man himself a
disappointment.

                    CHAS

You won't think so when you meet him. He's
quite different from his work.

                    GWEN

How so?

                    CHAS

There's a warmth in him you don't find in
the books. I had expected somebody
quite . . . remote.

                    GWEN

That makes *you* sound rather disappointed!

                    CHAS

No, no. It's just that liking him, as I
do, has rather spiked my guns. If he had
been the cold fish I'd imagined I would
have stuck to the task.

                    GWEN

Ah. So you've given up on it?

                    CHAS

I'd prefer to enjoy his company rather than
chivvy out his secret. I don't believe I
can do both.

GWEN

Charles, what a scrupulous fellow you are.

She smiles at him, and they walk on.

INT. DINING ROOM — NIGHT.
A candlelit dinner for twelve. VEREKER *at
the head of the table, between* GWEN *and*
DEAN DRAYTON. JANE *has placed herself next
to* CHAS, *who follows* GWEN's *conversation with
sidelong glances. On* CHAS's *other side,* JANE's
mousy friend MAUD.

MAUD

I seem to remember you were writing for
a newspaper when we last met.

CHAS

Indeed. The *Middle*?

MAUD

Oh yes. You told me you wrote quite a lot
of book reviews.

CHAS

And still do. You work in academia, I
think . . .

MAUD

I teach Victorian literature, with a special interest in the role of the single
woman. It's quite a fertile subject.

CHAS

I can imagine. (*He smiles politely, and
looks along the table again to* GWEN *and*
VEREKER.)

147

GWEN

I suppose you must be working on another
book.

VEREKER

Not at the moment. I've not been in the
best of health, and it becomes rather difficult to concentrate.

GWEN

I'm sorry to hear it. Are you being looked
after?

VEREKER

Well, my doctor has suggested a rest cure.
Makes me sound awfully valetudinarian,
doesn't it?

GWEN

Will you go away?

VEREKER

Yes. I've a place in Portofino. I'm not
sure it will do me much good, but who
knows?

GWEN

I hope it does. Italy is a great restora-
tive. I wonder, have you heard of a man
named George Corvick?

VEREKER

The name seems familiar, but . . .

DRAYTON

Books editor of the *Middle*, yes? Bright
chap.

GWEN

He's taken a sabbatical from the paper, to
write a book - about our esteemed novelist here.

DRAYTON

Indeed? He has a publisher?

GWEN

Antrobus. He also told me he'd recently
hit on a title for it. *The Figure in the
Carpet*.

VEREKER

Ah. Now *that* phrase I've heard before.

*He looks away for a moment, though not
down the table at* CHAS, *who's listening in
disbelief.*

George Corvick. Well, I shall look out for
his name.

GWEN

You won't be very far from him in Italy.
He lives in Rome.

VEREKER

My dear, you seem to know this man rather
well . . .

GWEN

I ought to. He's my fiancé.

JANE
(*overhearing*)

You're engaged, Gwen? How thrilling. Have
you set a date?

                            GWEN
Not yet. George is going to be in Italy
at least until September. We'll decide after
that.

Camera on CHAS, *his expression a mixture
of shock and dismay.*

INT. LOUNGE — NIGHT.
*The dinner party has broken up into groups.
Four of them play bridge.* GWEN *and others
sit by the fire talking. In the corner*
VEREKER *has come to say goodnight to* CHAS
and JANE.

                          VEREKER
Forgive me, I must retire. I seem to need
my bed earlier and earlier these days.

                           CHAS
                  (*rising from his chair*)
It's been a pleasure to see you again,
sir. I hope you enjoy your rest cure.

                          VEREKER
Thank you. I'm sorry we haven't - all well
with you?

                           CHAS
Oh yes. Still writing about books . . . and
missing the point of them.

                          VEREKER
                       (*laughing*)
You're being modest. I've seen a few of
your things in the papers and thought,
There's a man who knows what's o'clock.

                    CHAS
But I think you recall my failure where
your own work was concerned.

                   VEREKER
Well, yours and everyone else's! (*They shake
hands.*) Goodnight, Charles. (*To* JANE.) My
dear, thank you for another splendid
evening.

                    JANE
I'll see you up to your room, Hugh.

They exit, leaving CHAS *to finish his drink
alone.*

CUT TO: *A few minutes later.* GWEN *detaches
herself from the others and approaches* CHAS,
drinking in the corner.

                   GWEN
What are you doing here on your own?

                    CHAS
                 (*stiffly*)
I think I'm still in shock.

                   GWEN
Oh, from what?

                    CHAS
You're kidding. First of all, the small
matter of your being *engaged*? Why didn't
you tell me?

                   GWEN
It's not official. We have an . . . understanding.

CHAS

George never told me he was a bit engaged.

GWEN

We all have secrets. Do you tell him everything?

CHAS

Of course not. But I couldn't have resisted letting *that* slip.

GWEN

He's more discreet than you imagine.

CHAS

Hmm, and more underhand. 'The Figure in the Carpet.' I mentioned that very phrase to George months ago.

GWEN

But you're not writing a book.

CHAS

All the same, he knew it was mine. I don't go stealing things from him.

GWEN

I'm sure he just forgot.

CHAS

How convenient – for you both. 'Oh, forgot to tell poor old Chas about our engage-ment. And about nicking that line of his for my book.'

He rises from his chair and knocks back the remainder of his drink.

Nice to have friends, I must say.

CHAS *exits the room, leaving* GWEN *standing there.*

INT. BEDROOM — NIGHT.
CHAS *is asleep in bed. A knock is heard on his door. He wakes, dozing - then comes another knock. He switches on his bedside light, and the door opens to reveal* GWEN *in her dressing gown.*
   Camera angle reverses to GWEN *stepping into the bedroom.*

                    GWEN
   Do you mind if I come in?

                    CHAS
   What time is it?

                    GWEN
   I'm not sure. I wanted to apologise . . .

CUT TO: GWEN *undoes her gown and lets it fall to the floor. She is naked, back to camera.*

   . . . and make it up to you. Is that all right?

Camera fades.

9

Harry Pulver bit off the head of his baguette and began chewing it savagely. Around his neck he wore a huge white napkin, a gourmand's comfort blanket. He ate with his mouth open, so Nat could see whitish gobbets of the crab he had been forking in there as well as bits of bread and glints of his gold teeth. Harry, at the head of a long mahogany dining table, had placed Nat and Berk on either side of him. He was short and thickset, with a boxer's habit of turning his eyes rather than his neck to address you. Lights from the chandelier pinpointed tiny broken capillaries in his nose.

'Get them whatever they want to drink,' he told a lackey. It seemed he wasn't going to offer them anything to eat. Berk asked for a Coke. Nat, risking it, asked for champagne, which was brought to him without comment. On the way to the house in Seymour Place Berk had talked about Harry Pulver with a frowning and untypical obliquity that did not put Nat at his ease. He was a sound businessman, Berk insisted, and he loved movies. Without his money they wouldn't have made the budget for *Eureka*. Everything would be fine, just so long as he didn't stare at the 'piece'. Nat was quietly horrified: the man kept a gun on him! Though why should it be a surprise? As for not staring at it, didn't people like Harry wear a gun precisely to *make* people like Nat stare at it?

The dining room's long windows peered onto a higgledy-piggledy arrangement of roofs and chimneys, framed by the night sky. A faint hiss of traffic drifted upwards. On receiving a summons they had come straight from the studio.

'Where's Reiner?' asked Harry suddenly.

Berk made a clicking noise of regret. 'Back in the Fatherland – Nuremberg, as a matter of fact. Overnight trip.'

'What for?'

When Berk hesitated Nat said, 'Cup Winners' Cup Final. Bayern Munich versus Glasgow Rangers. Reiner's their number-one fan.'

Harry's thick eyebrows knitted into a frown. 'So he wastes a whole day's studio time for a football match. Does he think I can shit money?'

Berk laughed. 'He'll make the time up. I gotta tell you, though, Harry, the dailies are out of this world.'

Harry nodded, and returned to scraping out the meat from the crab shell. Nat watched him, fascinated. He could see no sign of the gun, no bulge at his shoulder or hip. What mainly puzzled him was Harry's hair, black as a raven's wing and teased into a crest over his brow, which made him look like a superannuated Teddy boy. Did he dye it, or was he wearing a wig? It was still an object of sly contemplation when Harry looked up from his plate to stare him in the eye.

'What?' he said, with a little jerk of his chin. His expression shifted from stillness to truculence in an unnerving instant.

Nat, caught mid-inspection, improvised: 'Just admiring that crustacean. I had the most wonderful crab last week at Wilton's.'

Harry rolled his tongue around to dislodge any flakes on his teeth. 'I get mine from a feller at Billingsgate. My old man used to be a porter there, back in the thirties. We was poor as you like, but we always 'ad fresh fish, and the rest: whelks, cockles, eels.'

'That so?' said Berk. 'Where we lived –'

'Then he worked in Shoreditch,' Harry continued, ignoring him, 'in a fried-fish shop round the corner from us. When I bought the place – he was dead by then, from his lungs – I named it after him. Morry. Morry's fish shop.'

'Or you could have called it Memento Morry,' said Nat before he could stop himself. Harry squinted at him, wondering if he'd heard something disrespectful. He looked at Berk for clarification.

Berk, who hadn't a clue either, returned a comradely shrug. '*Writers* . . . So, Harry, what's on your mind?'

With no more than a flick of his eyes Harry commanded the attention of another white-jacketed minion, who stepped in and took his plate and napkin away. That was a curious thing about power, thought Nat: it stayed put, it didn't move. It got others to move for you. He hadn't even stood up to greet them. After a little more grooming – brushing off invisible specks from his shirt front – Harry splayed his stubby fingers on the edge of the table, like a concert pianist about to give a recital.

'I've got a young friend,' he began, and pushed a buff envelope down the table in Berk's direction. 'As a, whatchamacallit, "sleeping partner" in this production I reckon I'm entitled to make a suggestion now and then. Have a gander.'

Berk opened the envelope and drew out a sheaf of ten-by-eights, all black-and-white portrait shots of a young woman. He leafed through them one by one, and, at a nod from Harry, passed them over to Nat. She was eager-eyed, mid-twenties, a brunette with long legs; the shots had a professional air, they had come from a studio, though the girl was no glamour model. There was something awkward and unpractised in her look. She hadn't learned how to carry herself, or to hold the camera's gaze. But she was pretty, like a nice girl from the tennis club.

'Her name's Gina. Gina Press. Started out as a dancer. Bit of a show pony, but a good sort.'

'A very fine young lady,' said Berk, glancing at Nat, who nodded in agreement. He knew what was coming, and composed his features accordingly.

'She wants to be in films,' said Harry with a little shrug. 'I'm sure you've got something she can do.'

'Can Miss, er, Press act?' asked Nat.

'A bit. Might not be Garbo, but she's a quick learner.'

After a pause Berk said, 'Thing is, Harry, we gotta pretty full complement, cast-wise. Can she do hair and make-up?'

Harry shook his head. 'When I said "in films", I mean she wants to act.'

Berk looked across the table in appeal. 'Nat?'

Nat considered for a moment. Not having finished a script yet, he could hardly object to making late changes; winging it was part of the screenwriter's job. And they weren't being asked in any case. 'I'll find a way to, um, accommodate her. We can improvise.'

Harry's mouth broke into a leer of satisfaction, like a music-hall comic who'd just got his first laugh. That's what he wanted to hear — improvise! This last word set him off on a reminiscence about his service days in Egypt during the war. Their platoon had been caught in a tight spot, German tanks apparently ready to blow them all to hell. Enter some young captain whose genius for improvisation not only got them out of their corner but gave Jerry a fright to boot. Harry deployed the salt cellar and pepper pot and ashtray as tools in his battlefield recreation, shifting them about as though he were hunkered down with the strategists at HQ . . . but Nat wasn't really listening. He was spellbound again by Harry's strange tonsorial arrangement, and how that black lick of hair managed to hold itself so stiffly upon his brow. Once or twice he sensed Berk's disapproving eye, worried that he wasn't giving Harry's war story his undivided attention.

Without warning the voice cut out. Nat was trapped again under the scalding fury of Harry's glare. Once in an evening was bad enough; twice was surely terminal.

'What are you looking at?' asked Harry in a low voice, which then jumped to a parade-ground bark. 'What? WHAT?'

Oh Christ, thought Nat, feeling something shrivel within. 'Nothing. Not . . . I was just — your story, about Egypt.' His voice sounded choked in his throat.

Harry's eyes bulged from beneath the eaves of his brow like those of a sumo wrestler about to grapple his opponent. Nat would have laughed at this image, had he not been immobile with terror. He wondered if this was the moment at which the gun would be produced. After a brooding silence Harry said, 'Last time someone looked at me like that, d'you know what I did to him?'

'Hey, Harry,' said Berk, coaxingly, 'we're all friends here, right?'

Slowly, very slowly, Harry dragged his eyes away from Nat and rested them on Berk. 'We're not friends. This is a business meeting. And next time I call one you'd better make sure the Kraut turns up. Bayern Munich? I've shit 'em.'

He shoved his chair backwards and rose to his feet. He muttered a few words to another of his crew, standing like a statue in its niche, then turned back to stare at his guests. This, Nat decided, was his way of bidding them goodnight. He stalked out of the room without another word. The minion entered and began to clear the table. Berk, straightening, indicated to Nat it was time to leave.

Outside, the late-spring evening had turned a velvety purplish-black. They walked for a few moments in silence until Berk, shaking his head, said, 'This guy . . . this is not my kinda guy.'

'Then why have anything to do with him?'

'You know why,' he said, and stopped. 'Jesus, Nat, what the hell were you – I *told* you not to stare at him.'

'I didn't mean . . . Where was the gun anyway?'

'Gun? Who said anything about a gun?'

'You did. You told me, "Don't stare at the piece." '

Berk looked aghast. 'What? I was talking about his *hair*piece. The guy wears a fucking toupee – can't you tell?'

Nat was momentarily dumbstruck. 'Well, you confused me. When I was last in New York "piece" distinctly meant a handgun. Why can't Americans just speak English? The word you were looking for is *wig*.'

Berk had closed his hands as if in prayer and pressed them against his face. 'Wig, piece, whatever the fuck you wanna call it. Why did you – didn't your mother tell you it was rude to stare?'

'I'm sure she did. I forget. *Mea culpa*.'

'You'd better keep out of his way,' said Berk, flagging down a cab. 'And you'd better write a great part for the tootsie.'

Nat chuckled. 'Right. Just so we're clear, "tootsie" is his – what? Pet chihuahua? Mother-in-law?'

'Don't kid around,' said Berk over his shoulder. 'And hurry up that goddamn script, else I'll be paying my own plane fare home.'

Reiner, back from Germany, was in a near-euphoric mood when he got to the studios on Friday. He was wearing a Bayern club jersey presented to him, apparently, by the team. They had beaten Rangers 1–0 after extra time, and he and Arno had joined 'the boys' afterwards for a party at their hotel. (Arno looked like he'd been on a week-long bender.) With the smile even wider than usual, Reiner had instructed the cast and crew to assemble in his office at lunchtime, where 'a surprise' would be awaiting them. Berk, chastened by the meeting with Harry Pulver, said that 'soccer' was all very well but they had a movie to make – could they not postpone his Bayern celebration till the weekend? But Reiner replied that his gathering had nothing to do with the Cup win.

Nat, intrigued, had bagged himself a position on one of the sofas and watched as the rest filed in: actors, cameramen, lighting assistants, grips. Sonja, still in full make-up, came and sat next to him. Then Alec Madden drifted in. It seemed they didn't know what was going on either. The room gradually became so crowded that people leaned against the wall or sat on the floor. Nat was reminded of students cramming themselves into a debating chamber, except the mood felt cheerful, relaxed; nobody was occupying buildings or pushing for a confrontation with the police. Reiner, bespectacled and unshaven, a string of beads over his football shirt, was at his most genial, encouraging people to find a space. When he spotted Vere, sombre in tweeds, he jumped out of his chair and insisted the older man take it. Only Berk, skulking in the doorway, looked ill at ease, suspicious of anything that smacked of the impromptu. Sonja leaned over to whisper in Nat's ear, 'He is possibly worried that Reiner will announce a pay rise for everyone.' Her closeness to him, and the smell of her scent – Mitsouko, he thought – were rather provoking.

When the room had settled Reiner stood before them, smiling. He said he was sorry for not organising a more comfortable assembly room, but this was a spur-of-the-moment thing so his office would have to do. 'And at least everyone will now remember where they were when they first heard this.' So saying, he called over to his sound operator, Franck, asking him if they were 'ready to go'. Franck mumbled something and raised his thumb. Only then did Nat notice that two huge speakers had been positioned on either side of the room. A sudden amplified hiss made a few of them jump and the music began to play: a dense, chugging bass-and-drum beat overlaid with whining rock guitar, then a familiar voice – in an unfamiliar hectoring style – took hold. It was clear to everyone who it was. The rock stomp gave way, for a period, to an Edwardian variety orchestra, serenading an imaginary audience; then it was back to the fuzz-guitar, the snap of the gated snare, the somewhat ranting vocal. Sonja cupped her hand over

Nat's ear again, only this time she had to speak up because the music was at full blast. 'It's their new one. Reiner told me about it. It's called *Sgt. Pepper*.'

The music relaxed after that raucous overture. The band's wide-stepping harmonies seemed to pour out of the speakers in great waves, rolling over the room with their melodic swagger. Irritated at first by their youth and good looks, Nat had affected to disdain the Beatles as just a beat combo riding a fluke. He clung to the elitist's reflexive suspicion of popular taste: whatever the masses exalted, he despised, however much he may have enjoyed it otherwise. They were too universally adored to be any good. Weren't they? His resistance, worn down over the years, broke altogether on the release of *Revolver*, which didn't sound like any pop music he'd ever heard, by anyone. He was reluctant to play the juvenile game of having 'a favourite', but even there he couldn't help himself: John, of course. He loved his sardonic nasal twang, his offhanded insolence at press conferences, the conspiratorial fervour he shared with McCartney when performing onstage, like they both had some urgent secret to communicate. He had a sense that Lennon might be a spanker.

On the other side of the room Billie looked about her. The abrasive start to the record had left her bemused; she didn't much care for it, really. It reminded her of the heavy stuff Jeff listened to, like Jimi Hendrix, with the guitars amped up to a scream. McCartney had been almost shouting to make himself heard. Now, as the songs unfolded, like flowers, she began surrendering to it; around her people had the stunned, pleasured air of concertgoers. Some lovely thing about getting better had stuck in her head – it sounded so *friendly*, somehow. Tilting her gaze she found Nat, who acknowledged her with a lift of his brow, as if to say 'This is fun', or maybe 'This is weird'. Billie had long known a new Beatles record was coming, though after the 'Strawberry Fields'/'Penny Lane' single she hardly knew what to expect. That last song, for instance, seemed to come out of nowhere – yet it was distinctly and sensationally their own. It began with John singing something terribly sad about a car crash, with lots of echo on it. Halfway through it changed, an alarm clock rang, and Paul took up the vocal – a more humdrum sort of lyric in double time with a piano behind it – before it switched back to John's echoey dreamlike ramble. And then another spiralling orchestral crescendo, up, up, climbing to the tippy-toppiest notes of the scale until the whole construction collapsed on a great concluding note

DNNNNNNNNNNNN . . .

They were all silent as the last reverb faded away. Someone began to clap, and catching the spontaneous mood the rest of them joined in. Reiner, who had been leaning back on his desk, entranced, pushed himself upright.

'Ladies and gentlemen,' he said, as the applause thinned, 'you have just been listening to the future.'

Afterwards they talked about it in the studio canteen. Nat had been enraptured, but he was struggling to articulate its effect. He wanted to know what the others had made of it.

'Friends of mine saw them years ago when they were in Hamburg,' said Sonja. 'Rough young men in leather jackets, playing rock and roll. Now they seem like composers, the way they put things together.'

'That last song was out of this world,' said Nat. 'Who'd have thought the band that sang "Love Me Do" would ever be capable of *that*?'

Billie smiled. 'I loved the middle bit, when it changed to Paul. It's like one moment he's conscious and the next he's fallen down a rabbit hole and entered somewhere – I don't know – where things don't make sense, but it doesn't matter, because they don't have to. You just have to be there, to let the experience come to you.' She made an apologetic shrug – that had probably sounded a bit fey, she thought.

Nat was staring at her, an odd look on his face. She felt herself colouring with embarrassment. But instead of making some satirical reply he said, almost dreamily, 'You're absolutely right. In fact you've just given me the most wonderful idea.'

She sensed he was quite serious. 'Oh, well . . . my pleasure,' she replied, thinking he might continue, but he was off in a reverie. Along the table she saw Vere, eating a small salad. She wasn't sure if he preferred to have his lunch alone, but instinctively she leaned towards him.

'Did you enjoy that, Vere?'

Startled, Vere looked around, blinking his way back to attention. 'You mean Reiner's little entertainment? Yes, I was rather taken by it. Talented musicians. Something of the music hall, I thought, in there. I enjoyed the oompah one very much.'

Nat looked sly. 'I had an idea you'd be a fan.'

Vere seemed to hear the insinuation. 'Well, of course. I liked them in that silly film they did, horsing around. They've grown their hair a bit since then.'

Billie turned to Sonja. 'I didn't know Reiner was so –'

'Oh, he loves them. When we've been on set in Germany he plays them all the time. They are – what is the phrase? – his good-luck charm. I remember him playing one song over and over: "Day Tripper".'

Nat nodded slowly. 'I fancy it's going to become impossible to talk about their music any more without mentioning drugs. That sense of dislocation. When Billie talked about falling down the rabbit hole just then it came to me that certain of these songs describe – in the common parlance – a trip.'

'Not an experience I'm familiar with, I'm afraid,' said Vere.

'You've never tripped?'

'Oh, I've done that,' said Vere, twinkling. 'I mean I've never fallen down a rabbit hole.'

At the end of lunch they were ambling towards the sound stage for that afternoon's scenes when Billie caught Nat at the door. She had been trying to get a private word with him all week, but now that the moment had come she felt tongue-tied.

'We were talking the other night – I asked you, do you remember . . . ?'

'You may have to remind me,' said Nat.

'About you coming to dinner?'

'Of course!'

The only thing was, she hurried on, would he mind coming instead to her mum's house in Kentish Town? Her own flat was small and grotty, not really made for entertaining, whereas her mum's would be cosy – and her sister was a *really good* cook. Nat secretly thought it a little strange, having envisaged an intimate supper à *deux* rather than a 'cosy' night *en famille*. He knew there was a boyfriend on the scene, though Billie didn't talk about him in a way that invited curiosity. Perhaps he wasn't made for entertaining, either. And her mother being there was probably a sign of encouragement, a meet-and-greet opportunity – out with the old boyfriend, in with the new.

She had surprised him. The light-fingered opportunist he had first encountered at Brown's had turned out to be a charmer. The faint vibrations of self-doubt coming off her only enhanced the allure. He had stuck his neck out when he'd suggested her for Jane – she was untried in front of a camera – but the gamble had paid off; he knew that Reiner was pleased with her. She'd repaid his faith in other ways, too, never complaining, always on time, friendly to everyone. Compared with Pandora she was a veritable paragon of humility. On previous films he hadn't hung around on set, owing to the boredom involved and the daily mortification of his screenplay being mangled in front of his eyes. It was like sausages; you didn't really want to see what went into the making of a film. With *Eureka* it was different, since the provisional – unfinished – nature of the script required him to be on hand for tinkering. Yet he'd found himself secretly enthused on arriving at the studio each day, knowing that some part of it would entail the open and entirely legitimate contemplation of Billie Cantrip. She had one of those faces, pretty at a certain angle, pretty ordinary at another. Not so much the girl next door as . . . the girl next door but one. So what? Looks weren't everything. But everybody liked to look.

The opening night of the Ossian Blackler retrospective at the Royal Academy was one of those events where the bohemian beau monde met their plutocratic counterparts head-on. You could distinguish one tribe from the other by their respective commitment to velvet or jewellery. Velvet frock coats, velvet skirts, velvet loons, velvet jackets, velvet fedoras, velvet waistcoats, velvet furbelows, velvet minis, everywhere you looked someone had it on: velvet was simply the element you moved in, the unspoken sartorial handshake of the party-going classes. Freya was wearing a slim-cut bottle-green trouser suit, in velvet, and was half wishing she'd chosen something else.

The faces and ages of the assembled were wholly disparate: blanched debby girls with kohled eyelashes, lizard-skinned old ladies with handbags to match, mop-haired Lotharios with Zapata moustaches, choleric old boys in club blazers, skinny models in frilled blouses and thigh-high boots, society matrons in black with costly bangles flashing on their wrists. They drank sparkling wine. Freya had brought along her friend Fosh, a photographer colleague from their days on the bygone magazine *Frame*. Stocky and stubbly, he carried the extra plumpness of middle age with an undefiant ease; he had been around 'beautiful people' too long to be afflicted with self-consciousness. He was surveying the room with the sceptical eye of a smudger, though it was an evening off for him.

'Same old faces, every night. You wonder what on earth they have to say to each other. Must be all of twenty-four hours since they last met. And what's this we're drinking? Crémant? Thought at least they'd break out the champagne for Ossie.'

'You've changed,' Freya said. 'Time was when you'd have loved being surrounded by dolly birds and tipping back free booze.'

'Yeah, well. Married man, now,' Fosh said with peeved pride, his eyes devouring a pair of young women on a flounce-by.

'Being married shouldn't exclude you from having fun. Or from having a good *ogle*, it would seem.'

Fosh gave her a sidelong look. 'God, you're like Lindy – never fails to catch me having a shufti at the talent.'

'That must be nice for her.'

'You can look – even if you can't touch,' he said with a note of regret.

'Talking of which, we should try and have a once-over of the paintings before it gets too crowded.'

They pushed off into the heaving sea of guests, some of them clustered around the paintings, more of them absorbed in each other's company. The Blackler oeuvre dated from 1946, when he was still at the Central School of Art; street scenes from his stamping ground of Paddington and Soho mingled with early portraits of ill-looking girlfriends and fly young men in dark suits and ties. His speciality was the nuanced notation of flesh colours, translucent and bluish in the strained years of rationing, then graduating to a more ambitious palette of greys, creams, pinks as pale as onion skins. Nudes started to proliferate in his work, though exhibited en masse Freya couldn't help noticing that as the brushwork got bolder Ossie's feeling for the person within grew coarser. His sympathy for these vulnerable forked creatures appeared to thin before her eyes.

Fosh saw them differently. In his early years Ossie had struggled to impose himself. Like many young painters he borrowed from his masters, muddling their styles. Once he had discovered his own technique, he was liberated. No longer did he feel obliged to soften the reality of the human condition – the shrunken, sagging flesh, the defeated expressions. He had scoured his work of sentimentality, refusing to compromise or to mollify. After years of uncertainty he had learned to paint as he saw.

'I'm not denying the bravura of it,' said Freya, standing before a portrait of Hetty Cavendish, a favourite model of Ossie's whom she had once known. 'I just think, along the way, he's become blind to them as *people*. Goya could be hard on his subjects, too, but he never denied them a soul. There's something too ruthless in Ossie.'

'He's got a misanthropic streak, it's true. But he's still a genius.'

'I'm afraid I disagree,' said Freya. ' "Dazzling" technique is a wonderful thing, but on its own it can't make you a genius. There has to be something else behind it.'

Fosh stared at her. 'Like what?'

'I don't know. Something vital. Maybe it's to do with feeling.'

'Oh, come on –'

Their debate was abruptly curtailed by a voice calling her name. Looking round she saw Nat approach, with a strikingly handsome woman in tow. Her face seemed familiar: she was slender-hipped, with amused blue-green eyes and a Slavic slope to the cheekbones.

'I thought you'd be here,' Nat said, leaning in to kiss Freya. He introduced his companion as Sonja Zertz, smaller than she appeared on-screen but possibly more exquisite. Sonja offered her hand and a 'hello' that sounded as if she'd rather been looking forward to this moment. Freya returned a helpless smile.

Nat, after a quick glance around, said, 'They've all come out for Ossie, haven't they? Anybody who's nobody is here.'

'That's a nice suit you've got on,' said Fosh. 'What is it?'

'Mohair and silk. My chap Doug cut it for me. I knew that velvet would be de rigueur this evening,' he explained, 'which is why I was determined to wear something else.'

'The first time I met Nat he was wearing a velvet suit,' said Freya. 'A party on the Banbury Road, let's see, 19—'

'About two hundred years ago,' Nat said, flatly dismissive.

'You were at university together?' said Sonja.

'Oggs-ford,' drawled Nat. 'Freya was at Somerville.'

'But I didn't complete my degree,' Freya added, looking at Sonja. 'Nat was the star. Did you know he used to act?'

Sonja's eyes glittered with interest. 'Really?'

Nat, a little stiffly, said, 'I'm afraid so. As a young – younger – man I fancied myself the heir to Olivier. The critics thought otherwise.'

'But you're happy to be a writer,' said Sonja coaxingly.

'It took me a while to learn that nothing makes a writer happy for very long,' he said with a mock-rueful smirk. He turned again to Freya. 'Have you been in the other room yet?'

'We were on our way.'

'Ah! Then you haven't seen it?'

She looked at him in puzzlement, which Nat took as his cue to lead them off. They made their way through the chattering throng to the next room, where he came to a halt in front of a squarish oil. As soon as Freya saw it she felt a little jolt. It was a nude, entitled *Pregnant Woman on a Bed*. The woman, raised on her elbows, lay on a grubby-looking striped mattress. The painter's position, at the foot of the bed, allowed a partial view between her long splayed legs. Shadows hung about the scene – it had a nocturnal feel – though the woman's face was clear to see.

They stared at it for some moments, until Fosh said to Freya, 'Is that *you*?'

She nodded, slowly. 'I've not seen it before. He did a sketch of me one evening – that's all I knew of it.'

'Interesting,' Nat mused. Freya could hear in his voice what he was thinking, but said nothing. 'Here's a question,' he continued. 'What is the most beautiful part of a naked woman?'

'I'd better not say,' said Fosh, sniggering.

Nat, ignoring this, looked at Freya. 'I'll tell you. It's her face.'

Sonja, nodding in agreement, said, 'So you have a child?'

'No,' said Freya with a brave smile. 'Another thing I didn't complete. It was – I had an accident.'

There was a brief embarrassed pause. Sonja, with a pained expression, put her hand to Freya's arm. 'That must have been a thing to break your heart.' The phrase was simple, something any stranger might have offered. Yet it was spoken with such feeling that Freya, to her own surprise, felt her eyes moisten.

Covering for it she said, with a laugh in her voice, 'Typical of Ossie, not to even tell me about this. D'you know, when I turned up at his studio that night he was completely naked apart from a pair of boots.'

The others looked nonplussed by this revelation. Fosh said, 'What were you thinking while he was . . . drawing you?'

'I don't quite recall. Do you ask that because I look rather vacant? I'd smoked a lot of Ossie's kif, I think.'

'The virtuosity is astonishing,' Nat said in a pontifical voice. 'No one else paints like that.'

'That's funny,' said Fosh, 'just before you arrived we were discussing that very thing. Freya thinks there's something missing in Ossie; something that stops him from being a great artist.'

To Nat's enquiring look Freya said, 'There seems to me a coldness, at least in his treatment of women. He paints their flesh without really *seeing* them. Looking at this' – she nodded to her own portrait – 'it's clear who it is. But you couldn't deduce anything from it.'

'There's not much of your personality in there,' agreed Nat, narrowing his gaze.

'Or your beauty,' said Sonja with a half-smile.

'You're trying to make me blush,' smiled Freya. 'But I never do.'

'I suppose Ossie's problem is he's had so many women they all blur into one,' said Fosh. 'Not that I'm suggesting . . .'

'There's something in that,' said Nat. 'Mauriac wrote somewhere that the more women a man knows, the more homogeneous becomes his idea of women in general.'

'Is the artist here tonight?' asked Sonja. 'I would be most interested to meet him.'

Nat, feeling a strong reluctance to let that happen, said, 'When I last spotted him he was preoccupied with a bevy of women. They never learn, you see.'

Sonja shrugged, as though it were of no importance. The four of them moved off to do a circuit of the room. Sonja, slightly in advance with Fosh, glanced back now and then. Nat, on whom very little was lost, remarked, 'I think you've made an impression.'

'Less forbidding than she appears on-screen,' said Freya.

Nat, waiting a beat, lowered his voice. 'Just *entre nous*, please satisfy my vulgar curiosity about you and the artist.'

'Oh, Nat! Ossie? Surely you know me better than that.'

'Well, with your limbs disported on that bed so provocatively, and him in the altogether, too. Hard to believe he didn't even *try*.'

'He may have made an approach. I managed to rebuff him.'

Nat gave a smile of undisguised delight. 'Ha. The retreat from mons. *Not* something Ossie's done very often, I suspect. If ever.'

A few minutes later, having caught up with Sonja and Fosh, they were preparing to make their exit when the crowd parted and the man of the evening approached.

'Ossie!' cried Nat. 'What a show. Congratulations.'

Ossie Blackler accepted this with an unsmiling nod. His dark, feral gaze took them in at once, before he focused abruptly on Freya. 'I saw you looking at it – the one of you.' No hello or welcome was offered.

'I had no idea you'd painted it,' replied Freya.

Ossie's eyes widened crazily for a moment, possibly in surprise at such a neutral response. But Freya knew better than to flatter him. Women, in his book, scored no points for pertness or charm. The silence was lengthening awkwardly.

'So what did you think?'

Freya considered for a moment. 'It's very accomplished, of course. But if I hadn't been there I'm not sure I'd have known it was me.'

It wasn't exactly what she'd thought, but some complacency in Ossie's tone had piqued her. At her side she felt Nat's nervous silent laughter. Ossie seemed to brood on her words, looking away, and Freya wondered if she had offended him. But when he spoke again it was apparent his thoughts were running elsewhere.

'I shouldn't have changed the title. It was those long legs of yours that first put me in mind of it. All the time I was painting I thought, yeah, this is the one. Then the gallery advised me to change it to *Pregnant Woman on a Bed*. I don't know why I took any notice, it's not nearly as good.'

He seemed aggrieved at the memory. Nat, with a sense of foreboding, asked, 'So . . . what was the original title?'

Ossie's expression didn't change. '*Tits on Stilts.*'

There was a shocked little pause before Freya felt herself starting to laugh.

EXT. STREET — DAY.
CHAS *walks up the steps of* MRS ERME*'s*
house and knocks at the door. GWEN *admits*
him.

INT. LIVING ROOM — DAY.
CHAS *and* GWEN *sit opposite one another drink-*
ing tea. Both have a watchful air, considering
the other.

                    CHAS
          (*pointing a finger upwards*)
     How is . . . ?

                    GWEN
     There's no need to whisper. She can't hear
     us. The doctor says she's very frail. But
     she's been this way before and recovered.

                    CHAS
     She doesn't . . . suspect?

                    GWEN
     Suspect what? Oh, you mean - *of course*
     not! Nor does anyone else, which is how
     we're going to keep it.

CUT TO: CHAS *looks rather crestfallen.*

                    CHAS
I beg your pardon. I thought you might be -

                    GWEN
Oh, Charles, don't look so hurt. I'm engaged
to be married, and there's nothing to be
done.

                    CHAS
You could end it. It's just an engagement.

                    GWEN
'Just!' I don't think you understand. George
loves me. He's been a rock while my mother
has been ill. I couldn't throw him over now.

INT. LIVING ROOM — DAY.
Later. CHAS *is reading a newspaper,* GWEN *is
at her typewriter. A knock sounds on the
front door, and* GWEN *goes to answer it.*

INT. HALLWAY — DAY.
*A postman stands on the step with a tele-
gram.* GWEN's *expression is suddenly apprehensive
as she takes it. She reads it, with shock.
The postman asks if there is a reply, and
she shakes her head. He departs.*

INT. LIVING ROOM — DAY.
GWEN *enters, looking as if she's seen a
ghost.*

                    CHAS
                 (*rising*)
What's wrong?

GWEN

It's from George. A telegram. He's got it –
he's got it.

CHAS

Vereker? What does it say?

GWEN *hands him the telegram, which he reads.*

'Eureka. Immense.' But . . . he doesn't say
what it is.

GWEN

How could he, in a telegram? He'll write it.

CHAS

But how does he know?

GWEN

That it's the real thing? I'm sure when
you see it you just *do* know.

CHAS
(*wonderingly*)
Strange that he should have discovered it
out there. I mean, in Rome, with all its
distractions . . .

GWEN

Oh, but that's the way he knew it would
come! He knew the change would do it, the
different atmosphere. All it needed was a
touch – the magic shake – and it would
fall into place.

CHAS

I see. (*He pauses.*) Do you think he'll go
to Vereker, to confirm it?

GWEN

I suppose so. But he'll write before that.
Think of what he'll have to tell me.

CHAS

About his coming home?

GWEN

Charles! I mean about Vereker - the figure
in the carpet. Though perhaps it won't go
in a letter if it's 'immense'.

CHAS

Not if it's immense *bosh*. If it won't go
in a letter then he hasn't got the thing.
Vereker impressed on me that the 'figure'
would go in a letter.

GWEN

It's a nuisance that he doesn't have a
telephone in his flat. (*She checks her
watch*.) He'll be in the library now in any
case. I'm going to send him a telegram.

GWEN *goes to the phone, then looks back at*
CHAS.

Charles, I think perhaps . . .

CHAS

Of course. I should be going anyway.

CHAS *gets up and walks to the door. She
has the telephone in her hand, waiting.
He makes to go back and kiss her, then
thinks better of it. He lifts his hand in
goodbye.*

EXT. STREET — DAY.

CHAS *watches* GWEN *through the window. She doesn't notice, being utterly absorbed in the phone call she's making. He walks on, brooding.*

10

The early-summer morning was unsteady with heat, creating a shimmer around the park. A white butterfly toppled and rose on the breezeless air. The brilliant trees seemed to vibrate with their greenness, though Nat couldn't be sure if that was just an after-effect of his trip. He'd dropped some acid in the early hours and found his vision blotching with colour, then sizzling with it. Time went into an elastic loop. He and Naomi must have listened to *Sgt. Pepper* all night, on repeat; the tunes were still jumbled in his head. Now he was coming down, and had ambled into Green Park to sit in this deckchair and watch the world go by. He was a little obsessed with tripping at the moment. Everything seemed irides-cent, saturated, electric. The tangerine-coloured scarf that Naomi had worn almost blinded him with its hot rays. When he asked her to take it off she told him she already had, which was weird.

It had turned out all right with Naomi in the end. She had come round to Albany for supper – he'd got in two dozen oysters, out of season and somewhat milky – and they'd drunk a bottle of Muscadet with them. Then they'd flopped on the sofa and had a serious talk, or as serious as you could be while smoking that much pot. It had made them both quite frisky, and before he could decide if it was a good idea or not they were tearing off each other's clothes. It was the first time they'd ever done it without the fore-play of canes or belts or whips; maybe that was why it felt like it would also be the last time. Afterwards, in a voice hoarse with smoke, she told him about a feller she'd been seeing for the last few weeks, off and on, someone who really *understood* her. Nat supposed the man would have to be very understanding indeed, should he walk into the room right now and find Naomi semi-recumbent in just her bra, him with his prick in post-coital wilt.

No, this was as it should be. They'd had some fun, some fights – some exquisite flogging – and now they would part as friends. She could have her 'feller', with his understanding ways. But where to now? Of course he had taken a shine to Billie, who perhaps returned a little *tendresse* for him. The dinner at her mother's place was coming up soon. Then his evening with Sonja at Ossie's show had stirred his loins. Yet she remained aloof, laughing off the invitation to a euphemistic 'coffee' back at his place. As for the newcomer, Gina, well, she was Harry Pulver's moll and thus strictly out of bounds. She was sexier than she'd appeared in her publicity snaps. That she was almost clueless in front of the camera surprised nobody. But she was game, popular with the unit, and sufficiently in awe of Reiner to do what she was told, or as close to it as her talent – and her slight deafness – allowed.

He and Reiner had been getting on famously since their first trip together. The two of them had met at Reiner's suite at the Connaught a couple of weeks ago to discuss the script; they'd ordered room service, and from seven till just before midnight they'd worked over most of the key scenes in the film, including a suggestion of Nat's that brought a spontaneous eruption of delight from his director. He had for days been circling George's 'eureka' scene – the moment when he finally deciphers Vereker's secret – trying to find a plausible way for this epiphany to spring out. It had come to him, he had explained, quite by chance, during that lunchtime recital of *Sgt. Pepper*. When they were talking about 'A Day in the Life' in the canteen Billie had compared it to falling down a rabbit hole and finding yourself in a place you couldn't make sense of, not immediately, but that it didn't matter because what you'd been looking for was already there. It was a matter not of finding but of *recognising*.

'And how is George able to do this? Because he's been tripping,' Nat had said.

'A Henry James acid trip,' Reiner had said, laughing madly. 'Brilliant!' He'd jumped up and kissed Nat's forehead. Then he was off and running, describing how he could shoot it, the different filters he might use, the sound design. Nat hadn't seen him this excited since Bayern had reached the final of the Cup Winners' Cup. He loved this about Reiner, not just his passion for ideas but his urgent resolve to try them out, to make them real. Even now, after a long evening, he'd begun sketching a storyboard of George's flashback – the humdrum routine of a morning as he unwittingly moves towards his revelation. He'd muttered to himself in an undertone: 'This will be so . . . fucking . . . *awesome*.'

Nat had mooched around while his host made notes and sketched. He'd smoked a cigarette and called room service for another bottle of wine. Ten minutes later Reiner had snatched the large sheet of paper from his block and flourished it before him. He'd drawn about twelve frames, rough but economical, the first of them an alarm clock ringing on a bedside table; of George getting out of bed, facing himself in the bathroom mirror, having breakfast, then noticing with a glance at the clock that he's running late. The next set of frames had him outside, in hat and coat, hurrying for a bus, going upstairs, lighting a cigarette. The penultimate frame showed his face in dreamy close-up, the last side-on, overhearing a voice behind him on the bus.

'Then the camera plunges down through the passage of George's inner ear and into his hallucinating brain. We cut to – the fire-works!' He'd made an explosive motion with his hands.

Nat had stared at the storyboard. 'So you've drawn the song. This is the middle section, McCartney's.'

'Of course it is,' Reiner had cried. 'Our own small tribute to the genius of the Beatles. And to the Master.'

The Henry James Acid Trip. It sounded like an avant-garde rock group. 'Can it be done?' he'd said doubtfully.

Reiner had smiled. 'It can. It will.'

Later, they'd dropped a tab each to celebrate their breakthrough, and while they'd waited for it to take effect Nat had asked Reiner whether he'd ever had a bad trip. Only once, he'd replied, from stuff a rent boy had sold him on the street in Munich. 'Ach, evil, worse than bad. It was a *black* trip. Everyone I met for the next four hours had heads like rats! Long sharp teeth and whiskers. I was fucking terrified, and that was even before I looked in the mirror. Oh, man. The flesh seemed to be melting off my face, like wax from a candle. Whatever you do, my friend, *never ever* buy acid on Reichenbachstrasse.' Nat, still in his wary novitiate with the drug, had assured him that he would not.

They had gone on talking for a while. Reiner had got up to put on a record, not the Beatles, something more jangly and American, the guitars had a gorgeous high chime, like silver bells. He had become aware of Reiner addressing him, in a concerned voice, and then plonking himself down next to him on the sofa. (About thirty seconds later Nat had realised that he'd asked him to sit there.) Objects had begun to blur at the edges, take on a glimmering fringe of light. The kaleidoscope had started up behind his eyes, but it wasn't scary, in fact it was beautiful: he was transfixed by it. The music, with its seductive crystal tone, flowed around the opened space within his head, a great reverberant cathedral of sound.

'Nat. Nat? Are you all right?'

He had looked at Reiner, and felt an immense wave of tenderness engulf him. He was holding his hand and nodding, yes, it was wonderful, and now the mode had changed. He was riding a magic carpet in whose weave he could discern every blissful figure, though he wasn't sure if he was saying it or thinking it, and it didn't matter either way, because Reiner understood.

Freya was writing at home one morning when the telephone rang: it was a secretary calling from the production office of a new film company named Cosenza–Pulver. She'd never heard of them. They were working on a project in London at the moment, the girl explained – a film called *Eureka*. Anyway, she'd been asked to telephone and invite her to a cast and crew party a few weeks hence. Would she like to be put on the guest list? This had to be Nat's doing, Freya realised, as she took down the time and date. There was a moment's confusion about the address, however. 'It's the *Thomas Bertram*,' said the girl. 'Is that the name of a pub?' 'No, no, not a pub – a boat. It belongs to Harold Pulver.' It transpired that this vessel would carry them down the Thames to Richmond, where they would arrive in time for dinner at a hotel. A guest of Harold Pulver! 'A pirate ship, then,' she wanted to say, but thanked the girl instead and rang off.

That evening she had her own guest for supper at Canonbury Square. Answering the doorbell she had found her father, Stephen, irresolute on the pavement. He was staring distractedly back at the road.

'Dad. Is something up?'

Stephen pointed at the navy-blue Jaguar he had just parked. 'Brand new. I'm wondering if it's safe to leave it here . . .'

'Of course it is!' she replied with an irritated laugh. Her father had lived in Chelsea for most of his life, and it amused him to regard Islington as barely more than a slum.

'Oh well. Too late now,' he smiled, entering the hall with a little shrug. He handed her a dusty bottle of Margaux, which she briefly examined.

'Looks expensive.'

'It is,' he replied. 'Should go well with the roast chicken.'

There had been no consultation as to the meal: if it was just the two of them she would always roast a chicken. She left him in the living room while she fixed them drinks in the kitchen. Stephen, now in his late sixties, had settled into a look that was half squire, half bohemian. He was dressed in a nicely cut corduroy jacket and checked shirt on top, paint-spattered twill trousers and off-white plimsolls below. His days as portrait painter of a smart London set were long gone, without regret; it had left him free to concentrate on what he preferred, parks and streets, and the river. Humming vaguely while he inspected the cards on her mantelpiece, he picked up the stiff-backed invitation to Ossian Blackler's retrospective.

'Did you go to this?' he asked her as she came through with gin and tonics.

Freya nodded. 'You?'

'Mm. Some good things there,' he said, in a puzzled way. He belonged to an older generation of artists who didn't much care for the cult of personality surrounding Ossie. In Stephen's view one was simply a painter, not a social contrarian or a political outlaw.

He looked enquiringly at her. 'Did you talk to him?'

'Briefly. He was surrounded by his admirers.'

'Of course.'

'Did you notice that picture entitled *Pregnant Woman on a Bed*?'

Stephen thought for a moment. 'I don't recall it. Why?'

'Oh, I just wondered. Nat was there and he thought all the women Ossie paints have begun to look exactly like one another.'

Stephen pondered this, seeming to sense he had been put on the spot. 'Maybe so. I can't claim Blackler's breadth of experience with women, but it's a problem for a painter if he can't differentiate one from another. To be honest, I think he paints *dogs* more tenderly than he does women.'

Later, when they were having seconds, Stephen tried to sound nonchalant as he asked, 'So how *is* Nat?' There had been rumours for years that Freya and Nat had been an item; her father evidently believed there was an untold story.

'Oh, you know Nat,' she said lightly. 'Always amusing. Always discontented. He turned forty recently– we had dinner at a fancy place in Camden Passage. Ava Gardner was at the next table.'

Stephen's eyes widened. 'Good Lord.' Another pause followed. 'Is Nat, um, involved with anyone at the moment?'

Freya had the impression that it wasn't really about Nat he wanted to know. 'I think he's been seeing someone, but it's over.'

'Right, right. So there's no urgency to settle down?' Now she knew for sure that he was fishing closer to home. She had no tolerance of coyness.

'Dad, you could just ask me, you know. I'm not seeing anyone, and I've got no plans to "settle down".'

Stephen tucked in his chin and blustered a little. 'That's not what I – I was merely wondering –'

'It's all right, I don't mind. But you have to understand, with men and me it's probably never going to work.'

He looked at her, frowning. 'Don't be silly. You just haven't met the right one.'

Could she talk openly with him? He might not yet be ready to hear the truth: that she was more likely to fall in love with a woman than with a man. Was it worth getting into, this far down the line? She looked at his lovable, lined, uncomprehending face.

'I'm not sure I'm the marrying kind.' She flashed him a rueful smile. 'How's Diana?' Diana was her stepmother – Stephen's second wife.

'She sends her love. Had to go north for a big house clearance. They wanted her help with valuing the paintings.'

'She seems to be doing a lot of that.'

'Well, they're closing down so many of the old houses nowadays. Plenty of bargains if you know where to look. Plenty of crooks, too.'

The word gave her a prompt. 'Something I meant to ask: have you ever come across Harold Pulver?'

'Harry Pulver. God . . . met him once or twice, just after the war. He supplied a lot of booze to clubs, then began buying up the clubs. I read something about him recently.'

'He broke some waiter's jaw. I mean, he's a villain, isn't he?'

'I don't think that's in much doubt. Why?'

'I'm following up a story on a German director – Reiner Werther Kloss? He's making a film here at the moment. Nat's done the script, and apparently Harold Pulver is producing. It seems such an unlikely thing for him to put his money into.'

'It may not be his own money,' said Stephen. 'Even if it is, he's probably worth a fortune from his rackets.'

'I've just been invited to a party of his – on a boat. I think Nat must have swung it for me.'

'I hope you'll be careful. Probably crawling with thugs, knowing Pulver.'

Freya laughed. 'What, you think they'll make me walk the plank? It's more likely to be crawling with actors and agents. I haven't been out on the river for such a long time.'

'Nor I. Must have been before the war.' He held up his glass to the light. 'Sorry about this claret. Quite a bit of sediment in there.'

'Hadn't noticed,' said Freya, taking a long swig before getting up to look for cigarettes. It was late. The night was so warm the kitchen sashes were still wide open. She returned with a packet of Player's, which she offered to her father.

'Now I think of it, he once did some acting himself, old Harold. Bit parts in films.'

'Maybe he's hoping for another shot at the limelight.'

Stephen gave an abrupt laugh. 'The artistic temperament – "the disease that afflicts amateurs", Chesterton called it. The tragic illusion that because you have "feeling", therefore you must be an artist.'

'Well, an illusion, maybe,' said Freya, 'but *tragic*?'

'For them, yes. The tragedy of the artistic temperament is that it cannot produce any art.'

Freya took a thoughtful drag of her cigarette. 'Well, should I meet Harold Pulver on his boat I must remember to bring that up with him.'

*

Once her father had gone, she put Coltrane on the turntable and started clearing up. She covered the remains of the chicken with a plate and put it in the fridge; it would make a soup for tomorrow. By midnight she was ready for bed when the phone rang: it was Nat, his voice unsteady and overloud against the background conversation.

'Darling, can you hear me? I wondered if you fancied coming over: we're at the Myrmidon, then it's back to my place.'

'Nat, are you stoned?'

'No, no. Pounds, shillings and pence, rather.' He had been trying to proselytise her to the wonders of LSD for weeks now. 'Come join!'

'It's late. I'm just about to turn in.'

'Oh, darling, it's a lovely night in June, you can see the stars and moon, if you want me to I'll croon –'

'Oh, please desist, you loon,' she said, cutting the doggerel short. 'Funnily enough I've just been talking about you with my dad. He wanted to know if you'd found love yet.'

'How perfectly charming of him. Can I really not tempt you?'

'Sorry, Nat. I'm beat. But thank you for arranging the other invitation – it sounds terribly exciting.'

A puzzled silence fell at the other end. 'What's that?'

'Harry Pulver's boat trip; the cast and crew party.'

'How d'you know about that?'

'A woman from the *Eureka* production office called me this morning. I assumed it was on your say-so.'

'Nothing to do with me . . . though I wish it had been!' She could now hear someone else importuning him at the other end, the background becoming foreground, and his attention was lost for a moment. When he came back his thoughts had scrambled again. 'So, darling, I wonder if you're coming over?'

'No, I'm not.'

'Well, that *is* a shame.'

'Goodnight, Nat. Go easy on the you-know-what.'

In bed, she tried to read, but her eyes kept drifting between the lines, and she had to go back whole paragraphs to pick up the thread. Another night she might have got a cab to Albany and joined Nat in his revels. Too tired now. Something else was preoccupying her. If Nat hadn't invited her to the boat party, who had?

Billie arrived outside the King's Cross studio. It was about seven in the evening and the pub opposite was filling up, drinkers standing on the pavement. Jeff had hardly used the place since they'd begun renting – the grottiness still depressed him – but Billie called in once a week just to check up. She worried about mice, and burglars, though there was really nothing there to steal but a few of Jeff's collages. A couple of times she'd stayed there late into the evening, not quite able to face his company. He'd been so morose recently it was hard to be in the flat. She made the long days of filming her excuse to avoid him.

As she ascended the grimy narrow staircase she could hear a racket from somewhere, banging and snapping; someone was building something, or mending it, perhaps. At the half-landing she realised with a start that the noises were coming from inside the studio. With a quickening heartbeat she let herself in, braced for a confrontation. The sight that greeted her was a strange one: Jeff, stripped to the waist and sweating from the exertion of destroying his latest artworks. He had torn the canvases from their frames and set about the latter with a hammer, reducing them to shards of firewood. He looked wildly around at her standing in the doorway.

'What on earth are you doing?'

He swiped his beaded face with the back of his hand. 'What does it look like? I'm getting rid of them,' he said, glaring from beneath his brow.

'Well, I can see that – *why* are you?'

For answer he leaned another large frame against the wall and stamped against it with his boot. It cracked, and he moved in with the hammer. The wood began to splinter; he took another swing, then another.

'Jeff. Jeff! Stop, please. Just – *stop*.'

He straightened, and turned an impatient look on her. When she held his gaze he finally puffed out his cheeks and let the hammer drop to the floor.

'They sent them back. The gallery. Paid me half of what they agreed, said there was no way they could sell 'em.'

Billie shook her head in sympathy. 'Well, that's rotten of them. They should have honoured their agreement. But that's no reason to destroy them. Someone else might want to see them.'

Jeff huffed out in disgust. 'You think so?'

'Yes, I do. And you have to believe it, too, or what's the point?'

'I've been asking myself that for a while now. What is the point of me going on, slaving over stuff that people just don't get?'

'But people do,' she said brightly. 'You've sold work already. Some artists take years to get theirs even seen, let alone sold.'

'Don't mention Van Gogh, for Christ's sake.'

'There are plenty of others. My mum almost starved herself before she got her break. But she always had faith in her talent.'

'Being lumped in with your mother isn't going to make me feel better,' Jeff said sullenly. He bent down and began stacking the broken frames in a pile. Then he stopped and looked sharply at her. 'What are you doing here anyway?'

'I look in every so often. It's our responsibility, as tenants.' She could have added that it had devolved on her to pay the rent on the place, so who was he to sound narked about her dropping by? But she was too tired to have a fight. In the corner stood one of his smaller collages, which she presumed was about to be broken up like the rest. She picked it up, inspecting it at arm's length. It was made from cut-up swatches of cloth and tailor's drawings. 'I like this one,' she said, hoping that to say so aloud would make it true.

Jeff stared at her for a moment, then picked up his T-shirt and shrugged it on. 'You're holding it the wrong way up,' he said, with a sad shake of his head.

'Well, I want to keep it anyway,' she said, tucking it under her arm. 'Come on, let's get a drink. That pub across the road looks nice.'

EXT. STREET — DAY.

CHAS *is walking down a London street. (Jazz plays in the background, quiet at first, then more confident.) He stops outside a bookshop where stalls of books are on display. He looks down at the titles, running his finger along the spine of one or two.*

Camera focuses upon a book with a title that almost jumps out at him. It reads, in bold letters: EUREKA. *We see the surprise on* CHAS's *face. He picks it up to inspect, and as he does so the pages of the book flutter open and a folded note of paper falls out. He goes to catch it, but a gust of wind has picked it up and shooed it beyond his grasp. He reaches again for it, but the note - now blown open to a sheet, with writing visible but not legible - has danced away down the street.* CHAS, *frowning, follows it, almost catching up before it flies off, eluding him. As he picks up his pace so does the paper. He starts dodging between pedestrians as he pursues it: the jazz score busily matches his manic efforts to grasp it. The paper continues its maddening flutter through the air,* CHAS, *now in desperation, running. We watch him barge past people, who spin round to watch him, bemused or offended. Finally, he enters* a deserted side street, his eyes still on the piece of paper. It has at last come to rest in the gutter. He stops, out of breath, and walks up to it. We see an expression of relief on his face. Got it!

Just as he bends down to pick it up the sheet of paper windmills away along the gutter, then nonchalantly plops between the bars of a drain.

Camera looks up from beneath the bars at CHAS, standing alone, disconsolate.

INT. BEDROOM — NIGHT.
We see CHAS asleep in bed. His eyes flicker open, he wakes and clicks his tongue, exasperated.

INT. KITCHEN — DAY.
CHAS, in his dressing gown, potters about making breakfast. He still looks bleary from sleep, perhaps depressed by his dream. He has just lit a cigarette when he hears the doorbell.

INT. HALLWAY — DAY.
CHAS opens the door to find GWEN on the step. She holds up a letter, her expression enigmatic.

> GWEN
From George. This morning.

CHAS stands aside to let her in.

INT. LIVING ROOM — DAY.

GWEN, *seated in an armchair, casts an appraising eye around* CHAS's *living quarters, noticing their modest, rumpled condition. It's as if a chatelaine has just dropped in on her tenant's hovel.* CHAS *enters the room carrying two mugs of tea and sets them on the table. He is still in his dressing gown.*

>   CHAS
>   What does he say?

>   GWEN
>   Vereker invited him to his house in Porto-
>   fino. I'll read it to you:

CUT TO: *A flashback of* GEORGE *in his sports car heading north from Rome along the Genoese coast.*

>   GEORGE (V.O.)
>   Of course I was tremendously excited to
>   get word from him. We'd corresponded already
>   about my book, but he'd been brief, and
>   made no offer of help. Once I'd told him
>   that I'd 'got the figure', though, he was
>   very quick to reply. Invited me to come
>   and stay at his place.

CUT TO: GEORGE *waiting, suitcase in hand, at the door of a pretty villa, being answered by a maid who smiles and admits him.*

CUT TO: *An ivy-creepered courtyard at dusk, where* GEORGE *has been shown to a table and brought refreshments by another staff member.*

GEORGE (*v.o.*)

I was told that Vereker was asleep — he always has a nap around this time — but that he would be down for dinner. I was to make myself at home. While I waited, though, I saw a nurse arrive and go upstairs. It made me wonder if the old man's 'rest cure' had really worked. Eventually he presented himself . . .

CUT TO: *A well-appointed dining room, candle-lit, windows open to the night.* VEREKER, *frail but jolly, has just entered and shaken hands with* GEORGE, *and they sit down to dinner.*

GEORGE (*v.o.*)

. . . and we talked and dined, as if we were old friends. He was so *genial*, quite a different character from how I'd imagined him. I remember Chas telling me something similar —

CUT TO: GWEN *raises her eyes to* CHAS *a moment, then bows her head again to the letter.*

GEORGE (*v.o.*)

I couldn't square the man with his books. The high ironic style didn't go with this twinkling fellow. But *that* was a puzzler for another day . . . By the time we'd finished dinner and the cigars came out my nerves were quite *taut* with anticipation — I had never been so eager to have a matter out in all my life.

CUT TO: GEORGE *talking very earnestly with* VEREKER, *who listens, smiling. Room has gone*

darker, the candles in a confessional quiver.
The camera holds on this two-shot while
GEORGE*'s v.o. continues.*

GEORGE *(v.o.)*
So, finally, I laid out my theory, iden-
tifying what I believed to be the animating
principle of his work - the figure in the
carpet. Even at the last I couldn't be
absolutely sure, but he gave me a look
when I'd finished that felt in itself like
an admission. Then he smiled, and he said,
'Well done.' I think I laughed with the
relief of it. All those hours of wondering -
and I'd got it at last!

II

The cooling system in the studio had broken down, and the atmosphere was close to swampy. Berk, his denim shirt darkening at the armpits, had been arguing with one of the engineers. He couldn't understand why nobody had bothered to fix it. 'I'm sweating like Nixon here, and these people just hang around with their thumbs up their asses.' The engineer to whom he addressed this complaint languidly examined his thumbs and walked off.

For one so arrogant Ronnie Stiles had proved rather more popular among the unit than Nat could fathom. Being good-looking lent Ronnie great confidence, and he had become susceptible to the vanity – common in his profession – of having vastly more to say than a mind that was fit to supply it. Ideas of improvisation were his speciality. Reiner responded to him with such good humour even Nat nearly missed the sarcasm beneath; but the director would have his revenge. The set was a bedroom for a love scene between Chas and Gwen. Its cramped design, already an inconvenience, now became a positive trial in the heat. Just before the camera rolled Ronnie, in bed with Sonja, moved his hand an inch above her breast. He turned with a leer to Reiner.

'How about I put me hand there?'

Reiner turned enquiringly to Sonja, resting on her elbow. She exhaled a jet of smoke. 'Not unless you want me to put this out on it,' she said, holding the glowing tip of her cigarette an inch above Ronnie's wrist. Someone sniggered in the background.

'And there is your answer, Ronald,' said Reiner. 'Camera, ready?'

So Ronnie kept his hands to himself, though he seemed to brood on his moment of thwarted invention. He was overheard at the lunch break complaining about Reiner as a 'jackbooted tyrant', and would do little goose-stepping impersonations behind his back.

In the afternoon, he was in his bedroom for a solo scene: Chas waking up in the night from his paper-chasing dream. They had just fixed the lighting to show his sleeping face in the dark when Ronnie called for a halt.

'Reiner, can I just run something by you? I don't think we're making enough of this moment.'

Reiner stared at him. 'Enough?'

'Well, I've just woken up from a nightmare, yeah? Wouldn't it look more convincing if I sat bolt upright in bed, staring into the camera?'

'No,' said Reiner.

Ronnie knitted his brow. 'Why not?'

'It is not a nightmare, merely a dream of frustration that has woken him.'

'Yeah but, this is cinema. A sudden look of fright' – he bugged his eyes – 'very dramatic.'

Reiner paused, scratched his beard. He looked over to Nat. 'Let us ask the writer. Have you ever woken from sleep in this way?'

'Never in my life,' Nat replied.

'Has anyone here done so – jumped from sleep to waking like a jack-in-the-box?'

Jürgen, the cameraman, shyly poked his head round. 'Just once. I was out camping and had accidentally set my bedding on fire.'

Reiner laughed, and fired off a few phrases of German that no one else could catch. Someone else offered the experience of waking from an attack of cramp. Reiner nodded, and said, 'Let us allow, then, that fire and – *was ist?* cramp? – may cause a sudden movement in the sleeper. Otherwise it is an invention entirely of the cinema to catapult oneself into an upright position. Ronald?'

Ronnie, stubborn to the last, argued for at least 'giving it a try'. Reiner, to general surprise, agreed. 'Let us see then your "dramatic" moment of awakening. Jürgen, place the camera over – yes, just there.'

They set up the shot. On the call of 'Action' – Reiner spoke the word softly, not in a director's bark – Ronnie raised himself upright from the pillow and, hyperventilating, stared into the lens. Nat looked at Reiner, wondering. This would be a test of his authority: to let Ronnie have his way, or to overrule him with disdain. In fact, he did neither. He exchanged a quick word with Jürgen, and then said, 'Let's try it again.'

They tried it again, and again. After the sixth take of Ronnie jerking himself forward, alarm written over his face, there was a pause. Reiner changed the angle slightly, and said, 'Again.' The sticks clacked and they did another, and on it went. By the eighteenth take Ronnie looked thoroughly fed up, and his vaunted expression of fright now undeniably absurd.

'OK,' said Reiner, nodding his satisfaction. 'Thank you, Ronald, for your patience. But before we break let's do one more, as the script has it. "We see Chas asleep in bed. His eyes flicker open, he wakes and clicks his tongue, exasperated."' He smiled on the last word. So Ronnie did the shot, waking from sleep, moving nothing but his eyes. A click of the tongue. 'Cut.' A sigh of relief could almost be heard around the room. Having checked the monitor, Reiner said to Jürgen in a voice just loud enough for Ronnie to hear: 'Print the last one.'

Billie absent-mindedly packed her groceries at the shop till. At the studio they'd had a laugh behind Ronnie's back over the nineteen takes that afternoon; someone had even sneaked a Polaroid of him pulling his woke-up-in-fright face and pinned it to the noticeboard. She had been in such a good mood, and decided to call on Vere in his dressing room.

Without really thinking about it she threw open his door and cried 'Helloooo!' Vere, seated, his head bowed as if in prayer, looked round with a start. His brow darkened with annoyance.

'Has nobody ever told you it's polite to *knock*?' he hissed.

'Oh, sorry,' she began, suddenly flustered.

He turned away, muttering to himself. 'Hardly know why I bother.'

Billie, caught on the threshold, was about to withdraw on tiptoe when Vere turned again and fixed a cold eye upon her. 'So what urgent message did you have to communicate?' His voice, usually so mellifluous, was as clipped and formal as a Kensington privet.

'Oh, er . . . I didn't – I was just –'

'If your interruption has no purpose, would you *kindly* leave me in peace?'

The shock of this was like water dashed in her face. He had never spoken to her like that before. As far as she knew he had never spoken like that to anyone. She gasped out another apology and closed the door. But it preoccupied her on the way back to Waterloo in the train, and all the way to Kentish Town on the bus. She had noticed that Vere had been a little subdued of late, which may have been why she'd called on him, hoping to restore some of the old cheer. That was a mistake. But why? What on earth had happened that he should turn on her so furiously?

At her mother's house she was relieved to find that preparations were under way. The fusty odour of ageing carpets and unwashed clothes had been masked by joss sticks, and the thump of music from upstairs had been silenced: Nell must have told her lodgers to clear off for the evening. Surfaces had been dusted. Even the spotted mirror in the hallway, which threw Billie's questioning expression back at her, had been given a cursory wipe. Downstairs, the kitchen was fragrantly fogged. Nell was tending a large pan of soup, while Tash sat at the table peeling carrots.

'Here she is – the film star!' crowed her mother, her smile showing the glint of a gold tooth. She was wearing her paint-flecked dungarees.

Billie rolled her eyes. 'Mum,' she said, half in greeting, half in reproof. Nell's ingenuous pride in her was a bit embarrassing. 'You'd better not say anything like that in front of him. I mean it.'

'Why not? He's the wotsit – scriptwriter – isn't he?'

'Yes, and that's *why* you shouldn't.'

Nell looked in appeal to Tash, who said with a smirk, 'It wouldn't look cool.'

Tash, four years older than Billie, carried herself with a worldly self-confidence her sister admired and envied. She was a lecturer at Hornsey College of Art and seemed to know more about every-thing – fashion, foreign politics, modern novels, cinema, cooking – than Billie knew about anything. She smoked roll-ups and wore a lot of black. Tonight's outfit was a paisley scoop-necked T-shirt and skirt with shiny black patent-leather boots. Only the defiant set to her mouth might have given an admirer pause. Billie wondered for a moment what Nat would make of her; Tash could be quite uppity.

'I like what you're wearing,' Billie said to her.

Tash barely glanced up. 'Yeah, just the thing for peeling carrots. So what time's your friend coming?'

'I told him half seven.'

Her mother let out a little shriek. 'I'd better get changed! Can't have him seeing me like this.' She tore off her apron and made for the door. 'Darling, keep an eye on that soup while I'm gone.'

Billie looked about the kitchen, where they would eat, and realised that here too Nell had been on a thorough spring clean. New ivory-coloured candles had been set in holders, the 'good' crockery and napkins were out, the Chianti looked a little pricier than the usual stuff. Billie gave the soup a stir and turned to her sister.

'I've not seen this house look so spick and span in years.'

Tash lifted her chin in agreement. 'He that's coming must be provided for,' she said in a prim Scottish accent, and they laughed: it was a line Billie had once spoken onstage. That Tash had remembered it was typical; she could quote reams of poetry off by heart. They talked about their week; Tash had been hard at it in the library – term had finished and she was trying to write a book.

'How are things with Jeff?'

Billie paused. 'Not so good. He's very down, you know, about his work. The gallery can't sell it.'

'Won't someone else take him on?'

She shook her head. 'Even if they did, his recent stuff's gone. I found him breaking it up with a hammer.'

Tash pulled a face. 'That doesn't sound healthy.'

'I think he's going slightly mad,' said Billie, staring off. 'He should probably do something else, but I wouldn't dare say that to him.'

Tash, listening, had gone to the stove and was putting the chicken she had sautéed into a casserole with the stock. She looked around for a moment.

'Did you get the paprika?'

Billie slapped her forehead. 'Oh drat! I knew I'd forgotten something.'

Tash said it didn't really matter, she could use curry powder instead, but Billie wouldn't hear of it. 'I'll be just a sec.'

She hurried off to a corner grocery where the man sold her a dinky jar of paprika. She was crossing Fortess Road again when she noticed a gleaming motor swing by and park just up from the house. It was Nat's Rolls, and Nat was climbing out of it, looking around with the bemused air of an explorer who had somehow fetched up on the wrong continent. His frown cleared on spotting Billie along the pavement. His clothes, a lilac shirt beneath an off-white suit, were unmistakable, and as incongruous as the car.

'How nice to see your friendly face. I have to say this neighbourhood is quite new to me,' he said, swooping down and planting a kiss on her cheek. He reeked of L'Heure Bleue.

'This is us,' said Billie, nodding at the house. As he sauntered up the path with her she remarked upon his loafers: sleek, mottled and expensive-looking.

'Alligator skin,' he supplied.

'You don't see a lot of shoes like that in Kentish Town.' Or a lot of people like you, she thought. He was carrying a couple of bottles of red wine. Billie was anxious about her guest, who she supposed never really mingled outside showbiz types; he might be easily bored by plain north Londoners. She hoped that his Rolls would be safe on the road outside. When her mother came downstairs to greet him wearing a floaty orange kaftan and vampish make-up Billie looked in alarm to Tash; but Nat stepped forward and ducked his chin to her hand in a flamboyant gesture of chivalry. Nell gave a little giggle in response. When he performed the same number on Tash she merely offered an arch smile, and turned back to the stove.

Nell made a show of being impressed by the wine Nat had brought. 'Haut-Brion,' she read from the label.

Nat, on the verge of correcting her pronunciation from 'Bryan' to 'Bree-on', checked himself, and only said, 'I think '59 is considered a good year.' He was rather tickled to find himself the Cantrip family's guest of honour, and pleased that Billie's boyfriend – Jed? – was out of the picture. Whatever the sister was cooking back there carried a promising aroma.

They started with gin and tonics, mixed by Billie with a heavy accent on the juniper. She couldn't quite get over the spectacle of

Nat Fane standing amid the clutter of her mother's living room. He was steering an interested gaze around Nell's paintings, hung in haphazard fashion and seeming, from Billie's uncertain perspective, possibly a little suburban. But Nat thought otherwise.

'These really are very accomplished. The brushwork . . . Billie tells me you were at the Slade.'

Nell smiled. 'Oh yes, ages ago. I met the girls' father there.'

'It wasn't *that* long ago, Mum,' said Tash, with quick loyalty. She turned to Nat. 'She was also a model in her spare time.'

Nat tweaked his respectful expression up a notch. She wasn't bad-looking, it was true, for an older woman. And they did say that if you wanted to know how your girlfriend would look in the future, check the mother. He sensed an opening for a compliment. 'Yes, I can see that. You have the model's poise. And you've handed on to your daughters those tremendous cheekbones.'

Nell, waggling her hand in mock dismissal, looked as if she might pass out from delight. Tash, in contrast, let out a snort of scornful mirth. Billie, still nervous, decided to put on some music. She chose something she thought would calm her mother, a selection of arias, and indeed she was soon swaying along to Handel, her eyes closed in blissful absorption.

'I heard this at Covent Garden recently,' said Nat, after a moment. 'Funny thing about opera; I can only really enjoy it when it's sung in a language I don't understand.'

'What d'you mean?' said Tash.

'Well, I have very little Italian, but the words always *sound* romantic. Translate them into English, though, and they're usually banal. Take this, for instance' – he paused at another flourish – 'I had listened for years to "Ombra mai fu" supposing it to be some magical valentine, a love ode. Imagine my disappointment on discovering that the song is in fact addressed to a *bush*.'

Nell nodded. 'Mm, that *is* disappointing.'

'Maybe with opera the meaning is in the melody,' said Billie.

'Exactly,' Nat replied. 'Opera is ridiculous enough already without having it explained in English. Whereas the composers of popular song at least understand the essential wit of our native tongue. You can hear it all the way from the music hall to *Top of the Pops*.'

'But surely in opera you have to understand the drama going on,' said Nell. 'Otherwise it's four hours of people screaming at each other – and you can get that at home.'

Nat laughed and shook his head. 'It's precisely *because* I don't understand what's going on that allows me to enjoy it. I don't care two hoots if the cast is singing in German, Dutch or Cherokee, just so long as the noise they make pleases me.'

Tash, who had nipped off to the kitchen, now returned. 'Dinner's ready.'

'Ah, two words that gladden the ear in any language,' said Nat.

Whatever nerves Billie had been fielding about their guest evaporated over the dinner table. Nat had set his charm dial to full, mixing conviviality with just the right degree of flirtatiousness. Of course he still did more talking than listening, Billie noticed, but he had manners, too. He praised Tash's chicken fricassee ('Do I taste paprika in there?') and declined to resume smoking until the others had finished. In the candlelight their faces had gone rosy with the wine. Her mother, mesmerised by Nat's fluent chatter, seemed to look younger of a sudden, and even Tash, wary of extravagant personalities, had deigned to join in the laughter.

'What's the thing you're most proud of?' asked Nell, chin cupped in her hands as she gazed across at Nat. He paused for a moment.

'I suppose I ought to say the Academy Award, or perhaps getting my first play on in the West End. But if I'm being honest, my proudest moment has nothing at all to do with my work.'

'Oh?'

'Some years ago a dear friend of mine was villainously framed by the police and put on trial, allegedly for soliciting two young men. The charge was gross indecency. I stood bail for him – noblest thing I've ever done. Maybe the *only* noble thing I've ever done.'

Billie looked agog. 'You mean Vere?'

Nat nodded. 'But I'm afraid they still sent him to prison.'

Nell's mouth had puckered in sympathy. 'Ooh, I remember that trial. We just couldn't believe it – Vere Summerhill, a *queer*! I'd been in love with him since my teens. And you're still friends now?'

'Of course. I should introduce you to him; he's almost the last civilised man in Europe, eh, Billie?'

Billie smiled and nodded, keeping her own counsel.

'How's the film going?' asked Tash. 'Have you finished the script yet?'

'Ha, you've heard! It keeps changing. But the director and I have at last settled on key elements in the story. If all goes according to plan it should surpass any Henry James adaptation you've ever seen.'

'*The Innocents* was pretty good,' said Tash combatively.

'*Eureka* will be better,' replied Nat.

The look she returned now confirmed in Nat a suspicion that had been fermenting almost from the moment he'd arrived. Billie, it seemed, had not invited him here for herself; she was preparing the way for her sister. Tash's early brittleness must have been down to nerves; she had thawed as the evening proceeded. Well, a shame about Billie; he'd had his hopes, despite the boyfriend. Yet he had to admit, of the two sisters Tash was actually the better-looking. The slope of her neck showed very alluringly in that top, and the dark eyes, smoky with kohl, were those of a sexy witch.

Returning from a visit to the loo Nat found Billie heading him off before he'd got to the kitchen. She gestured to the living room to indicate the need for a quiet word, and he followed.

'I have to ask you something,' she began. He read anxiety in her eyes, and wanted to set her mind at rest.

'I fancy I can guess what it is,' he said suavely.

Billie squinted at him. 'So you've noticed it, too?'

Her tone of concern wrong-footed him. This might not be as straightforward as he imagined. 'Perhaps you should explain.'

'I mean about *Vere*. He's been in such a strange mood lately.' She proceeded to describe their encounter at the studio and his sudden snappishness at her interruption.

'That doesn't sound like Vere at all.'

'I know. D'you think something's wrong?'

'Probably not. You know actors, my dear – a touchy tribe.'

They heard enquiring voices from the kitchen. Nat acknowledged Billie's troubled look. 'I'm sure it's nothing – we all have our rough days. But I'll have a word with him.'

Nat followed her out of the room. This was not playing out the way he'd anticipated. He wondered, not for the first time, if he was rather slow on the uptake about the lives of his friends. It had been pointed out to him that he was too absorbed in his own affairs to see what was going on elsewhere: selfishness, he supposed, might be the root of it. Freya, never reticent in holding him to account, had once observed that his engagement with people was only fully secured when he saw them as material in waiting. It was probably true. The difference was, he didn't really consider that a fault.

Back in the kitchen Nell was making coffee. Billie reminded Tash that she had a favour to ask of Nat: it transpired that she taught design at Hornsey and was in the middle of writing a book about women's clothes in cinema.

'That's a good subject,' he said. 'Which films have you been looking at?'

Tash, lighting a cigarette, said, 'All sorts, from the silents on. Lots of thirties Hollywood, comedies, women's pictures. Edith Head. Rosalind Russell in *His Girl Friday*. Grace Kelly in *Rear Window*. Deborah Kerr in *Bonjour Tristesse*. Beaton's costumes in *My Fair Lady*. You know the sort of thing.'

'Yes, I should say so. A favour, you say . . . ?'

'I wondered if the wardrobe lady on *The Hot Number* would be willing to have a chat. I mean, given how much of it is set in a ladies' fashion department.'

'I'm sure Jeanette would be delighted. I'll get you a number.'

'Thank you,' replied Tash evenly.

'See, I knew he'd help,' said Billie, with a quick smile at Nat.

They had talked past midnight, sipping coffee and smoking, when Tash said that she'd better be pushing off. She lived in a flat in Marylebone. Nat, sensing his moment, offered to give her a lift home: he happened to be driving that way.

'Don't worry, I can manage. There's a late bus.'

Nat pulled a face. 'It's really no trouble,' he said, wondering if she was playing hard to get. Billie leaned over the table to her sister.

'Tash, you must. Wait till you see his car.'

Outside, the road was quiet, the air stilled to a midsummer sultriness. They followed Nat out to where he'd parked the car.

Under the sodium glare of the street light he pulled back the hood to reveal its pale-leather interior. Nell let out an incredulous squawk and stared at Nat.

'A Roller! Is this yours?'

'Well, who else's would it be – the milkman's?' said Billie, rolling her eyes.

Nat, with a lordly chuckle, turned to Tash. 'As I said, I'm going your way.'

Arms folded across her chest, Tash seemed the least impressed of the three: he suspected that Rolls-Royce owners weren't warmly regarded at Hornsey College of Art. But with a tilt of her head she accepted his offer, and a shuffling quadrille of departure ensued. He invested his thanks and goodnight kiss to Nell with the affectionate respect of a potential son-in-law. Billie and he embraced with a familiarity sanctioned by their profession, though he held the moment a little longer to convey, he thought, a phantom wistfulness.

As the car glided down Kentish Town Road Nat kept up a lively flow of patter. It was a curious thing to him that the less demonstrative Tash was, the more beguiling she became. She was not flirtatious, nor especially friendly either, yet she paid him very close attention. She had a habit of quietly absorbing whatever he said and then pausing before she replied – and the pause grew more disconcerting, for it seemed to create a slightly fatuous echo of each remark he tossed out.

He raised a silent cheer, however, on learning that she had recently split with her boyfriend. Who cared if she was on the rebound?

Tash glanced at him. 'You married?'

'I was. To an actress, I'm afraid.'

'Watch it. My sister's an actress.'

'Oh, Billie's in every way a superior being. She's a credit to the species. And she has some fellow, I gather . . .'

'Yeah. Jeff. He's an artist – not a very good one. He's quite a bit older than Billie.'

'Ah.' It hadn't really impinged on Nat before now that he was a fair few years older than Tash. 'I don't see why the difference in age should be *calamitous.*'

'Nor do I. In their case it makes no odds anyway, Billie's more of a grown-up than Jeff will ever be. Compatibility, well . . . I think it depends on other stuff. Age is mostly irrelevant.'

'Absolutely,' murmured Nat.

'How old are you, by the way?'

'That's a very blunt question.' He had not admitted the number (the truthful number) out loud before, except to Freya, at his birthday dinner. But since Tash had just conceded that age in a romance was 'irrelevant' he felt it would become him now to do so – to be brave. He took a deep breath. 'I'm forty.'

He gave her a sidelong look, bracing himself for her sharp intake of breath or, worse, a mocking titter. But Tash merely nodded and said, 'Uh-huh.' He took that as a timely endorsement.

They had left behind Regent's Park and were turning into Baker Street. Nat fished out a packet of cigarettes from the glovebox and offered it to Tash, who took one.

'Light one for me, would you?' he said. He had played this scene several times before, himself at the wheel, the woman riding shotgun and passing a cigarette from her lips to his: a feline prelude to intimacy. Tash, however, instead of putting his cigarette in her mouth, had simply ignited it from the tip of her own, and handed it over without comment. It felt disappointing, but then Nat knew that women had their different approaches; some went all in with the eye fluttering and the hair flicking; and some, like Tash – like Freya, come to that – played a waiting game, matter-of-fact and poker-faced right up to the decisive moment.

'This is me,' said Tash, indicating the left turn into Blandford Street. Nat drew up outside her building and made a point of switching off the engine. It seemed to give the midnight street a hushed mood of anticipation. For a moment he stared dead ahead, then turned an enquiring gaze upon her. She returned a smile that didn't crease her eyes.

'So,' he began, in a tone that suggested there was a good deal more to come.

'Thanks for the lift,' she said, reaching, inconceivably, for the door handle.

Nat, with a half-laugh, said, 'Are you not going to ask me in for a nightcap?'

Tash looked at her wristwatch. 'It's rather late.'

'And yet, we have the whole night ahead of us,' he replied, in a coaxing voice.

'Well, I don't know about you, but I need my kip.'

'My dear girl,' he crooned, softly taking hold of her hand, 'you can sleep when you're dead.'

She laughed good-naturedly. 'The thing is, if I don't sleep properly, come the morning I *am* dead.'

'Then I suggest you sleep improperly,' he said, caressing her hand in his. Again, she didn't invite, but she didn't resist, either. With his free hand he patted his breast pocket. 'I have certain mind-altering substances on my person. How about we go inside and shed our . . . inhibitions?'

Now she looked at him shrewdly. 'I'm beginning to sense –'

At last, he thought.

'– that you've got this all wrong.'

'How so?'

She removed his hand from hers, politely, and paused. 'This wasn't meant to – I imagine you've been thinking tonight, *I might get a bit of a knock with the sister.*'

Nat tucked in his chin. 'I wouldn't have put it quite so crudely. But I did think I was being – perhaps – "set up".'

Tash gave out a little groan, lowering her head. 'Well, you *were*, sort of. But not with me.'

Nat was baffled. 'Then who? Billie?'

'Oh God. *No.*' She looked at him in a mingled spirit of pity and exasperation. 'With my mum.'

Nat stared at her, aghast. 'Your mother? But she's –'

'Forty-seven. Not that much older than you. You admired her cheekbones, remember?'

He couldn't speak. How in the name of all that was holy? He had been charming, as he would be to anyone's mother, and she had responded in kind. They had got on very well. But he hadn't for a moment imagined he was being groomed as her *suitor*. Now he realised the significance of that little conversation they'd just had about age. It wasn't about the gap between him and Tash: it was the one between him and Nell! Seven years was all, and still he hadn't made the connection.

He sensed Tash's gaze on him. 'Your mother – Nell – will she be expecting . . . ?'

She shook her head, with an air of defeat. 'It's all right. I'll tell her you're – "spoken for". But you might have to explain it to Billie. She was the one who got it into her head. She thought Mum was maybe, I don't know, your type.'

He was too mortified to argue. *Your type?* How could she be his type when he plainly had more in common with women who were young and lovely and unburdened by the baggage of children and divorce? He wasn't ready for a mature woman, for he wasn't yet a mature man. Was he?

Tash had opened the car door and stepped out. She must have detected something in his stricken expression, because she added, 'I'm sure it'll be soon forgotten.'

'Goodnight,' Nat managed to croak. He watched her let herself in and close the door. As he drove on through the implacable streets he felt that he'd suffered some sort of existential concussion – a flooring *coup de vieux*. He had been in the dark, and he had been shown the light. Tash and Billie loved their mother; they had only meant to help. But their contrivances had shown him for what he was – a forty-year-old man, single, self-deluding – and now he wished himself back in the dark.

INT. CHAS'S FLAT — DAY.
GWEN *and* CHAS *are looking at one another*
steadily, wondering. After a moment she
folds the letter she's just had from GEORGE
and puts it on the table between them.

> CHAS
> (*nodding at the letter*)
> So . . . how does he end?

> GWEN
> Oh. That Vereker pressed him to his chest -
> and invited him to stay there a month. He
> wants me to join him.

> CHAS
> No, I mean, what does he say about *it* -
> Vereker's secret?

> GWEN
> He said that it's 'immense', and yet it's
> simple. (*She picks up the letter to quote.*)
> 'Nothing has been more consummately done.'

> CHAS
> Yes, but *what is it*?

GWEN

You're not going to like this. He won't
spill the beans until I arrive. He wants
to see the look on my face as he tells me.

CHAS

For God's sake ... I never knew George
could be such a tease.

GWEN

I suppose he thinks - she's waited this long,
what difference will a few more days make?

CHAS

You'll go, of course?

GWEN

I don't think I can, not with the state
my mother's in - I daren't leave her.

CHAS

He'll be champing at the bit waiting to
tell you.

GWEN

It can't be helped. But you could go.

CHAS

Me?

GWEN

Why not? You're the one who told us about
it in the first place. The idea has a nice
symmetry.

CHAS

You're his fiancée. It's you he wants to
tell.

GWEN

And given that I can't be there you're the
next best thing.

CHAS

Are you sure? Things have rather changed
since George and I last spoke. If he knew
about what's been going on . . .

GWEN

But he doesn't, and you must make sure he
won't. *That* secret is in the vault - you
understand?

CHAS

Of course. All the same I feel quite a
blackguard . . .

GWEN

It's a bit late for that, isn't it? 'Blackguard.' Honestly, Charles, the things you
come out with! I'll write to George this
evening and tell him how things lie here -
and that you'll be the advance party.

She looks at her watch, and rises.

I should be going, my mother will be wondering where I am.

CHAS *rises too, and steps across the room.
He has an eager glint in his eye.*

CHAS

I thought you might . . . stay a while.

GWEN

I'm sorry. Not a good idea.

206

                    CHAS
It seemed a good idea the other night.

                    GWEN
But now I have other things on my mind.
So you'll have to excuse me.

EXT. CHAS'S DOORSTEP — DAY.
GWEN *is about to step into a taxi.*

                    GWEN
Don't look so glum. Just think - you get
to hear about Vereker's secret first-hand.
And Italy's lovely this time of year.

GWEN *waves and the taxi drives off.*

12

Freya was in the office late one afternoon when she heard her name being called. She turned to see Delphine Frampton beckoning her over with the stern hooked finger of a headmistress to a recalcitrant pupil. The large rings on her hands looked like fancy knuckledusters. Men had been known to tremble at the sight, but Freya wasn't intimidated by her brusque manner, or her menacing jewellery.

The life of the office – phones ringing, colleagues trooping by – barely seemed to impinge on Delphine once she had focused her beam. It was a kind of talent, this resistance to distraction. She would have been a useful companion during the Blitz, briskly getting on with things as the ground quaked around them. She began without preamble, 'Now, that conversation we had about Reiner Werther Kloss – have a look at this.' She handed over a press release headed by the name of a Munich arts theatre. It announced a celebration of the work of Kloss. A week-long festival of his films and several of his early plays was to be staged; discussions and lectures about the director were also scheduled.

'Rather young to be given your own festival; I mean, he's hardly Murnau,' said Delphine. 'In any event, you might find it useful as background – you're still researching that piece on him, I suppose?'

Freya nodded, and told her about the boat trip.

Delphine's gaze became beady. 'Make sure you corner him.'

'I'll certainly try. My friend Nat keeps on saying what great friends they are and how he'll get me an "audience" with him. So far nothing.'

'Then you might have to do it by yourself.'

Freya checked the dates of the tribute week. 'I've never been to Munich before,' she mused.

'Here's your chance. See where he shot *Hanna K*, talk to a few people. It won't harm you to be there while they're toasting the local hero.'

When Reiner had turned down her request for an interview it had simply encouraged her to dig further. At first she thought his disdain of the publicity circus was high-minded and principled; it was the work he cared about, as befitted a true artist, not the industry's appetite for gossip. Now she wondered if his shunning the spotlight had a different motive: maybe he had something to hide.

'You seem quite keen for me to go,' said Freya.

Delphine permitted herself a half-smile. 'Well, I think there's a story there. And I would back you to find it.'

On the Sunday following the dinner at their mother's Tash had called at Frederick Street bearing gifts: a beaded black cocktail dress and a small clutch bag in sequinned silvery blue, which flashed like a kingfisher's wings. This last was the sort of unconsidered trifle Tash regularly picked up in junk shops and antique markets; she had an eye for it.

'*God*, this is . . .' Billie said, awed by its loveliness.

'I know,' said Tash. 'The dress might be a squeeze. Just don't make any sudden movements in it.'

'Hmm, it is a little snug,' said Billie, wriggling her way in and forcing up the zip. She stood in the centre of the living room, hands on hips. 'Can you see my undies through it?'

Tash tilted her head appraisingly. 'Only if you stare quite hard. Maybe you should go without.'

Billie choked back a snigger and glanced towards the bedroom where Jeff could be heard slowly getting dressed. Tash, noticing, lowered her voice.

'How are things?' The meaning of the question was all in her eyes.

Billie in reply gave a tiny grimace and shook her head. Since the day she had found him breaking up his work with a hammer there had been a stand-off between them. Jeff seemed to have withdrawn into himself, which actually felt more disquieting than his usual recourse to tantrums. At least when they argued she could be sure of what he was thinking; now he just smoked and brooded.

She heard the kettle whistle and went out to the kitchen to make a pot of tea. On returning she found Tash reclined on the sofa, leafing through a souvenir book of Beaton's photographs from the stage production of *My Fair Lady*. Nat had lent it to Billie to pass on.

'Good of him to remember, wasn't it?' said Billie. 'He said you could keep it as long as you liked.'

Tash said, 'Thank him for me,' and dipped her head back to the book. Billie, intending to have a post-mortem on their evening, sensed a reluctance in her sister to cooperate. Nat hadn't said much the next morning, either, beyond a cursory thank-you and a pleasantry about her mother. She had hoped for a little more enthusiasm all round.

'Mum really liked him, anyway,' said Billie, as if she were picking up a previous conversation. 'Thought he was a bit full of himself, of course – but ever so entertaining.'

Tash, still horizontal on the sofa, looked up again and gave a nod. 'He is very entertaining.' Her tone was so matter-of-fact it might have been mistaken for irony. Billie waited for more, but nothing came.

'So . . . Nat didn't say anything – when he was driving you home?'

'About what?'

'About *Mum*.'

She shook her head in such a way as to indicate the matter closed. This only goaded Billie's curiosity: she didn't want to think her matchmaking venture, however unlikely, had been a complete damp squib. 'Maybe I should bring her along with me, you know, to this party.'

Tash clapped shut the book and stared at her. 'Don't do that. He's not interested in her, Billie, I'm sorry.'

'How can you tell? According to you he didn't say anything.'

'Can't you just leave it?'

'Well, I'd rather know why you're so certain.'

Tash sighed, and paused. 'He misread the whole thing. He thought he was being set up with me, not Mum.'

Billie's expression passed rapidly from startled to incredulous. 'You? But he's, like –'

'Old? Men don't think like that. They just see a girl they fancy and go after her. Doesn't matter to them if they're closer in age to the mother.'

Billie was trying to imagine how the misunderstanding came out. 'Did Nat – I mean, did he . . . ?'

'Nothing like that. He looked a bit put out when I didn't invite him in – and when I told him what you'd had in mind he looked *shocked*.'

Billie put a hand over her mouth, smothering a nervous giggle. 'I suppose it's comical, really.'

'I don't think he found it all that funny,' said Tash, who also began laughing. 'To be honest, when he arrived at Mum's I thought at first he was queer. I mean, those *clothes* . . .'

The bedroom door had opened, and Jeff, in denim jacket and jeans, stood there with the unsmiling air of a ticket inspector. He greeted Tash with a barely perceptible lift of his chin, then looked at Billie. 'Who are you talking about?' he said. It occurred to Billie that he was paranoid enough to imagine they'd been talking about him.

'Oh, just a friend,' she said lightly.

'But who?' he persisted.

'Nat Fane. The scriptwriter.'

'I know who he is,' he said. 'But what was he doing at your mum's?'

'We had him over for dinner last week. Tash cooked.'

Jeff silently absorbed this. 'Very cosy. Presumably you did that so you wouldn't have to invite me.'

Billie felt her heart sinking. This was exactly why she'd meant to keep it quiet.

'To be honest, I didn't imagine you'd want to meet him. And I *know* you wouldn't want to see my mum.'

'You might have said something. Do you not trust me?'

The unhappy answer to this, as far as Billie dared consider it, was *no*. She thought him in his present state too fragile to trust, and preferred to go behind his back rather than risk another scene. But now something else had snagged Jeff's attention: he had just noticed the cocktail dress.

'Why are you wearing that?'

Tash, alert to the tense mood, stepped in. 'It's something of mine I brought for Billie. Doesn't she look good in it?'

'Going to a party in it, by any chance?'

'I am, actually,' Billie said, tiring of his peevish tone. 'There's a cast and crew get-together next week, and I wanted something a bit glamorous. Tash has lent me this.'

'Glamorous,' Jeff said in doubting echo. 'You think so?'

'Don't you like it?' asked Billie.

'Looks tarty to me.'

Billie gasped, stunned into silence. Tash, however, wasn't one to shirk a fight. 'That's nice, Jeff. Insulting both of us at once there.'

'Just being honest,' he shrugged.

Tash shook her head, more pitying than indignant. 'And you wonder why you aren't invited to dinner. Ha! Billie, come on, let's get out of here.'

But Jeff was ahead of her, opening the door. 'Don't bother, I'm going. You can stay here and slag me off to your heart's content.' He slammed the door behind him, though not quickly enough to miss Tash's defiant 'Good. We will!'

They watched him stalk up the basement stairs and disappear. A residual sourness lingered in the room, like smoke from a fire-cracker. Billie sadly unzipped the back of the dress, mortified. She looked at Tash, who was half amused, half amazed by what she had just witnessed.

'I'm sorry about that,' said Billie quietly.

'You don't have to apologise. It's his problem, not yours.'

Billie looked away. 'He's just in a bad way. He's depressed about work – about everything – and he lashes out at people.'

'You mean he lashes out at *you*.'

'I'm just the one who's around.'

'Don't make excuses for him, Billie. He's a swine to say that. If it'd been me I'd have clocked him.'

Billie didn't say anything. If she poured it out now – told her what had been going on – she wasn't sure she could stop herself breaking down. There was pride involved, too. She and Tash were close, but she didn't want to admit that she might have wasted the last two years and more on a boyfriend her sister hadn't much liked from the start. Jeff *was* a swine, she knew it, really, yet she had kept hold of the slim possibility that things would pick up and he might revert to the person she fell in love with. But they hadn't; and he hadn't.

The city sweltered in the heat of July. Cabs prowled through Covent Garden hunting for fares. Nat, in his lightest summer suit, was already sheened in perspiration as he skipped up the steps of the Garrick Club. He carried under his arm a copy of *The Times*, which contained a news item he thought might please his host. Within the cool, musty gloom of the hall he asked the porter whether Mr Summerhill had arrived, and was directed to one of the small lounges on the upper floor. He felt the reassuring creak of the oak stairs under the thin soles of his loafers. Victorian actors and dramatists, their likenesses caught in oil, peered down from heavy gilt frames.

An arrangement had at last been made to discuss Vere's projected memoir, for which Nat would enlist as ghostwriter. An editor at the publishing house had been in touch to talk about money. Once filming on *Eureka* was done they would need to clear a little time in the diary to get started on the reminiscences. Nat had suggested that they meet at Albany, but Vere instead had proposed lunch at his club ('May as well use the place while I'm here'). He offered a little wave from the corner table where he sat, by the window.

'Nat, darling,' he said in his melodious croon. His handshake was dry and papery. He was dressed in a serge pinstripe suit, though he showed no sign of discomfort in the heat. 'I've got a gin and It on the go.'

'I'll have the same.'

Vere, with the merest lift of his eyebrows, signalled the waiter, then offered Nat a cigarette from a fancy silver case.

'I gather you're close to a finished script.'

Nat laughed at the implied rebuke. 'One final push. I fancy I'll still be handing in pages on the last day of shooting.'

Vere shook his head. 'Even when we made those absurd little thrillers at the Marlborough in the thirties it was never quite as seat-of-the-pants as it's been on this one. I wonder if Reiner can pull it all together.'

'If anyone can . . . He's a brilliant improviser, that boy. Comes from his work in the theatre.'

Vere nodded, then fixed Nat with a stare that felt strangely and unguardedly fond. Disconcerted for a second, Nat smiled back and picked up *The Times* he had brought in. Riffling through its pages he found the article. 'Here, listen to this. "The Sexual Offences Bill has received royal assent. Debate in the House yesterday blah blah . . . has decriminalised homosexual acts in private between two men who have attained the age of twenty-one." Victory at last!'

He passed the paper to Vere, who read in silence to the end; he folded it up carefully before handing it back. His expression was indecipherable.

'You must be pleased, surely?' said Nat.

Vere tweaked a smile. 'I find it amusing that even the bill's sponsors plead for homosexuals to comport themselves "quietly and with dignity" – no "public flaunting", as they put it. I've a feeling they'd prefer it if we didn't appear in public at all.'

Nat, feeling his triumphant messenger role somewhat deflated, pulled a face. 'I thought, after what you've been through, this would be a red-letter day.'

'Well, of course, but it's come rather late for me, I'm afraid. How could one really know what it meant to live if one wasn't allowed,' he sighed, 'to love?'

'But you can now,' Nat protested.

'As I said, too late for me, dear boy. Thirty, even twenty years ago, I would have danced in the street – gone in for a little *public flaunting*, even. But I've grown old. The party has started when I'm no longer able to join in.'

Nat must have looked crestfallen, for Vere leaned over to give his hand a consoling pat, and suggested they went down for a bit of lunch. The dining room had an off-season feel – a lot of members summered out of town – and they got a table straight away. As they were examining the menus Nat's eye was drawn to the signet ring glinting on Vere's pinkie. He'd seen it before.

'I don't often wear it,' Vere admitted. 'It was bequeathed to me by a great-aunt I hardly knew. I think she lived in Oswestry. She came from a time when the Summerhills were landed gentry, hence the family crest.' He held it up for a closer inspection.

Nat squinted at it. 'Very handsome. Lends you a certain distinction.'

'That implies I have been somewhat short of the quality hitherto,' said Vere with a snuffling laugh. In a moment of abstraction he revolved the ring on his finger, as though he couldn't quite believe he'd bothered putting it on. The waiter came to take their order – they both chose the sole meunière – and Vere, egged on by his guest, ordered a bottle of champagne to mark the 'great day'; Nat still hoped to make something of the occasion, despite Vere's seeming indifference. Once the waiter had poured and left the bottle with a napkin around its neck, Nat raised his glass and proposed a toast. Vere, anticipating it, shook his head.

'Let's drink to something else.'

'Very well. How about to our joint venture – the memoir?'

At this, Vere's expression changed. One could not be sure – he gave so little away – but it seemed almost a wince of apology. Had he had second thoughts about their collaboration?

'This is what I wanted to talk to you about.'

'Ah. Have you decided on someone else?' said Nat, bracing himself for another rejection: he seemed to be collecting them at the moment.

Vere fluttered his hand in dismissal of the thought. 'Not at all, darling, you're the ideal man. It's just that –' He stopped, and leaned back in his chair. 'I don't think a joint venture is feasible. What would you say to writing the book on your own?'

Nat blinked in confusion. 'But it's a memoir. *Your* memoir. I'm just the writer for hire.' He wondered now if Vere had lost interest in the project, or whether he simply couldn't face digging up the past. It might be exhausting to confront so many ghosts at once. 'What do you mean by "feasible", anyway? Are you going off somewhere?'

Vere gave a wistful half-laugh. 'In a manner of speaking.'

A dread that had stolen almost unnoticed into Nat's consciousness was starting up a tom-tom in his chest. It had first been planted there, he realised, when Vere had talked of the Sex Bill as 'too late' for him. Nat had taken that as a sixty-year-old's rueful nod to his lost virility; now he felt he had quite misapprehended the remark. He looked in appeal across the table, and Vere, holding his gaze, said quietly: 'I didn't mean to tell you like this, but in the circumstances, I'm sorry, it seems unavoidable.'

And that told him for certain. 'Oh no, Vere. No. Not you.'

Nat, to his surprise, felt tears brimming over his eyelids. He could hardly bear to listen as Vere described his last visit to Harley Street, the doctor's grave concern, the series of X-rays, the diagnosis. 'You said it was just a check-up,' he gasped, almost accusingly.

'I thought that's all it was,' replied Vere patiently. 'I'd had a scare last year and got the all-clear, remember? Well, these things have an unfortunate habit of coming back.'

A long time seemed to pass before Nat could command his voice.

'Did they say – do they know – how long?'

'Maybe six months. A year, if I'm lucky. It's in the lungs and making further inroads.'

At this point the waiter reappeared with their food, and Nat averted his tear-smudged face in embarrassment. They stared for a moment as the fish steamed on their plates.

'O my prophetic sole,' he muttered. He had to pull himself together, and a silly pun would be a start.

Vere chuckled, and filled up their glasses again. 'Here, I have a toast, if I may,' he said. 'To the end of the line. The last of the Summerhills.'

Nat looked at him, aghast. 'You can't mean . . .'

'I have one relative left in the world. A sister, lives alone down in Hampshire,' Vere said, in a strangely cheerful voice. 'She's no more likely to have an heir than I am.'

The stoical way he said this caused Nat such a pang he thought he might break down again. 'To you,' he croaked.

'To the last of the Summerhills,' Vere gently corrected him. They drank. 'And I must ask you, dear boy, not to let any of this out – not yet. On a personal level I couldn't stand the fuss. And money-wise it might damage the film, too, with the insurance and so on.'

'Will you be able to . . . finish it?'

'I should think so. I get tired, of course, and I'm not quite the ray of sunshine I'd like to be.'

It was all falling into place for Nat, who now said, 'I fear you may have been a little short with our mutual friend; Billie?'

Vere gave a wince of dismay. 'That was the day I'd heard. The poor girl got me at just the wrong moment.'

'I know she'll understand. She's got a kind heart.'

They struggled through their lunch. Nat had lost his appetite, though he drank very determinedly. Vere did little better, pushing the food around his plate before abandoning it in favour of a cigarette. They talked about the remainder of the shoot, the week's location in northern Italy and a few days in Rome. It was not ideal, given his condition, but he would make the best of it. Nat knew he would: it was the old spirit of self-sacrifice that Vere's generation had absorbed in the war. Head down and carry on. It might be sensible, Nat suggested, to slip Reiner the news on the quiet: it would enable him to arrange filming around Vere's need for rest. The latter nodded his acquiescence.

Nat was feeling rather woozy from the drink by the time they descended the club steps. On putting his arm out for Vere he felt that he himself might need propping up more than his companion did. The summer afternoon had been ticking by sedately while he'd been inside, dealing with a bombshell. He asked the porter to whistle up a cab for Vere. While they lingered on the pavement he said, 'Is there anything I can do for you – anything you need?'

Vere shook his head slowly. 'Although, please think about the book. The publishers will only give it to some dolt, otherwise.'

'I'm not sure, you know, without your . . .' He didn't want to complete the sentence for fear that it sounded like Vere was already gone.

'You'd have my papers, of course: correspondence, diaries and so forth. You're the man best qualified to write it, darling.'

'Really?'

Vere looked at him. 'You know, when I was in prison friends kept promising to come, and sometimes they made excuses or else they just didn't bother. Too scared, perhaps. All the time I was inside – I've never told anyone this – I only had two visitors. One was my lawyer. And the other was you.'

He had a distant smile on his lips as he spoke, though Nat thought he detected behind his nonchalance what it had cost him in pride to admit this. It struck him as odd that Vere hadn't ever really talked about Pentonville, though perhaps no odder than his never having asked. As the taxi pulled up to the kerb he turned to Nat with a solicitous frown.

'You'll be all right, won't you?'

That Vere, the condemned man, should be asking him such a question seemed to Nat quite the wrong way round. But his throat felt too constricted to say anything very meaningful. 'Vere,' he began, and then shook his head.

'Don't upset yourself, dear boy,' Vere said. 'I've really had the most marvellous time.' He gave Nat's arm a little pat before he climbed into the cab, which drove him away up the street.

EXT. HARBOUR, PORT OF RAPALLO — DAY.
CHAS, *in sunglasses, carrying a suitcase, walks up the ramp of a passenger ferry. The boat is filled mostly with holidaymakers in high spirits.* CHAS *is the only passenger who seems to be on his own.*

EXT. FERRY, AT SEA — DAY.
CHAS *stands against the rail of the stern, looking back at the water churning in the boat's wake. Camera switches POV to look face-on at* CHAS, *the sun glinting off his shades. He doesn't see the passenger behind him stop and do a double take. It is* JANE, *also alone.*

                    JANE
    Chas?

                    CHAS
                (surprised)
    Jane!

            They kiss one another.
    What are you doing here?

                    JANE
    Same thing as you, I imagine - going to
    Portofino. I'm visiting Hugh. Hugh Vereker.

                              CHAS
So am I. Or rather, George Corvick, who's
staying with him - he's invited me.

                              JANE
You know that Hugh's ill, then?

                              CHAS
George said something about a nurse being
there. How serious?

                              JANE
He had a stroke - just last week. His
doctor's told him to rest. I had a letter
asking me to visit.

                              CHAS
So he was well enough to write?

                              JANE
Yes, but he's quite frail. His
handwriting . . .

CHAS *can see that she's upset. He takes her
hand in a comforting way.*

                              CHAS
I'm sorry to hear it. But I'm sure he'll
be pleased to see you.

EXT. FERRY, AT SEA — DAY.
CHAS *and* JANE *are strolling along the upper
deck, amid other passengers leaning at the
rails, chatting, taking photographs.*

JANE

Why didn't you tell me you were coming? We could have made the trip together.

CHAS

It was a spur-of-the-moment thing. Gwen – whom you know, of course – had some quite important news from George. He asked her to visit him. But her mother's ill, so she suggested I come out instead.

JANE

Important news? What's happened?

CHAS
(*pausing*)
I don't exactly know. George has been researching a book about Vereker – Hugh – and seems to have discovered, well . . . something.

JANE

That's rather mysterious. Couldn't he just have told her what it was on the telephone?

CHAS

Hmm. I gather George wants to divulge it face-to-face. Sorry, I know it must sound . . .

JANE

Potty! Has he found out some scandal about Hugh?

CHAS

No, nothing like that. It's a book about his work, not his life. It's difficult to –

it goes back to that weekend at Bridges when you introduced us. I'd written that review of his book in the *Middle* -

CHAS

                    JANE
Yes, and you were rather offended by Hugh's reaction.

                    CHAS
I got over it. In any case, it seems I'd been barking up the wrong tree about his work. Everybody had, according to him. There's some trick - but no, forget it.

                    JANE
What 'trick'?

                    CHAS
Oh, it's nothing, really. Don't concern yourself, Jane, it's not that important.

                    JANE
                 (*bemused*)
It's important enough for you to come half-way across Europe!

They have stopped at a spot on their own. CHAS, *shielding his eyes, gazes out to the horizon.*

                    CHAS
Look. That must be Portofino.

CHAS *is too preoccupied to notice* JANE *looking at him in a keenly appraising way.*

222

13

The *Thomas Bertram* lolled against the landing stage as guests made their way up the boat's roped gangplank. Nat, not a keen sailor, hopped down onto the wooden deck and instantly felt himself wobble. Low sun had burned off the intruding cloud and left the sky an acrylic blue. The Thames lay spread out before them. Nat parked himself against the stern rail and accepted a gin cocktail from one of the liveried waiters strolling stiffly around. He hadn't anticipated the swank – or the size – of Harry Pulver's yacht; it stood high on the water, every fixture and fitting on it burnished to a gleam. He wore a new white suit whose own dazzle he tried to dim with his sunglasses; he could dress like a film star even if he wasn't one. He stared out to the river.

'Are you trying to look like a film star?'

He turned to find Gina Press grinning up at him. She was wearing an aggressive perfume and a close-fitting frilled green dress that barely covered the tops of her legs. A pair of heart-shaped sunglasses lent her a kind of holiday sauciness. Not for the first time Nat fell to imagining what she would look like in just her knickers.

'In this company I wouldn't dare,' said Nat, stooping to kiss her. 'You look ravishing in that, by the way.'

'Thanks! Harry doesn't like it,' she said, with a wary glance around her. She leaned in to whisper, 'Said it was so short he could see me whatsit.'

Nat, trying not to check for himself, sipped his drink. 'No pleasing some people.'

They talked about the day's trip: from Greenwich the boat would take them all the way down the river to Richmond, where they were due to arrive in time for dinner. Gina was excited by the prospect of the onboard dancing, music courtesy of Dox

Walbrook and his quartet, the American jazz outfit who had been hired to do the score for *Eureka*.

'Dancing – really?'

She looked at him. 'You don't sound all that thrilled.'

'There's a Latin saying – *nemo saltat sobrius, nisi forte insanit*. It means, no one dances sober, unless he happens to be insane.'

'Sorry?' said Gina, with an uncertain frown.

'It's just my excuse for not being a very good dancer.'

'Don't believe you!'

Nat, who really couldn't dance, replied, 'I'm sure Harry will be an energetic performer.'

Gina pulled a grimace. 'Not today. He's coming with the missus. She won't let him out of her sight.'

The mistress's lot, reflected Nat, who envied Pulver his voluptuous bit on the side and felt his gorge rise at the thought of what they got up to. He supposed Harry must be in his late fifties, had hit sixty, perhaps – old enough, in any case, to be Gina's father, rather than the lardy lump who got to bounce himself on top of her. He sighed inwardly at the injustice of it and tipped back his drink. 'A finger in every pie, and a foot in every grave,' he quoted, in an afterthought.

'Sorry?' said Gina.

'Nothing,' he smiled, 'just a line I was –'

Gina leaned towards him. 'Sorry, darling, you know I'm half deaf.' This was no exaggeration. A childhood infection had left one ear useless. She knew she ought to wear a hearing aid, but vanity forbade it. Nat had noticed her at the studio craning her neck forward, trying to catch what people were saying. She had told him once, 'If I don't hear someone for the third time, I just laugh and hope for the best.'

Though fond of her, it had not prevented him trying a wicked little experiment. They had all been drinking in the studio bar one night, and spotting Gina alone for a moment he'd approached her. She was staring abstractedly into a little compact, fixing her make-up. Goaded by desire, he said to her, quite clearly, 'I wonder whether you've got pants on this evening?'

Her eyes flicked up to meet his. 'Sorry?' Her expression was sharp, and he felt for an instant he'd blundered.

'I said, I wonder whether you've got plans on this evening?'

She had smiled innocently back at him and said that she was meeting a couple of friends in town. He knew it was a mean thing to have done, but he'd found the risk of it too exciting.

While they had been talking the last stragglers had boarded and the deck already looked a little crowded. There came a sudden jolt beneath them. The engine was stirring; the mooring ropes had been unloosed and tossed onto the stern. With a sort of unwilling-ness the *Thomas Bertram* heaved away from the landing stage. The waiters were having a hard time of it finding a way around the partygoers, who had chosen to congregate, sheeplike, on the lower deck. From out of the throng Ronnie Stiles approached in an extraordinary get-up. A high-buttoned, hectically patterned silk shirt fought for attention against a double-breasted purple blazer with gold brocade facings. His trousers were guardsman-tight with a showy silver buckle, while a knotted cravat made a foppish, foolish adornment at his neck. Nat knew he'd got it all from Mr Fish's in Mayfair: he'd bought a similar shirt there himself in a leopard-skin print a few weeks ago and hadn't yet dared wear it in public. He had felt like a forty-year-old man trying hard to be 'groovy'. Mutton dressed as leopard.

'Ahoy, me hearties!' Ronnie cawed annoyingly. He delivered a smacking kiss to Gina and gave Nat a wary masculine nod.

'Ooh, Ronnie, look at you,' cooed Gina admiringly.

'I don't think he needs further encouragement on that score,' said Nat, meaning to be droll but sounding rather catty.

'Well, it's a party, isnit? Gotta wear the clobber,' said Ronnie, giving Nat a quick once-over and then looking away, as if his own 'clobber' were beneath comment. Nat wished he'd brought some chemical refreshment. He'd been overdoing it lately. Walking into a friend's living room he had been taken aback by the spectacle of the television screen ablaze with colour, a full polychromatic assault on the eyeballs. Was he tripping? He must have been star-ing hard at it, because the friend proudly announced it was an actual colour TV – they'd come on the market a few days ago.

Meanwhile his second gin cocktail, sunk in ninety seconds, had improved the shining hour. The afternoon was taking on a lift as he watched the churning wake of the grey-brown river. On either side London slid by in an anonymous fresco of wharves and basins and sleeping barges and monstrous cranes criss-crossing the sky-line, latticed reminders that the city was building, clearing, digging, building ... He thought of Whistler's dockside sketches of old salts and mots, of Dickens on a cruise downriver for a pals' supper of whitebait and hock. It had changed, and yet it was the same. The river had been here long before London had arrived, and would remain, he supposed, long after it had gone. As they rounded the bend at Wapping the high windows of an old factory blazed in the sun.

'Nat! Over here!' His reverie was broken. He swung round to see Penny, his agent, waving to him from the upper deck. With a slight droop of his spirit he realised he would have to go to her, thus surrendering the lovely Gina to Ronnie. He flashed a parting smile, and was rewarded with a wink. Yes, she was quite some-thing, that girl. He started through the crowd, nodding here and there at faces he knew – Franck, the sound man; Alec Madden, trousers bulging as usual with that packet of his; Julie, the diligent script girl, who gave him a little wave. There were others there, mostly men in funeral suits and ties who looked like they hung about the boxing gym – Pulver's cronies, he supposed.

Penny, in one of her swirly summer kaftans, offered her cheek to be kissed. She had a glass of orange juice on the go.

'Is that all you're having?' asked Nat, with the drinker's fear of social isolation.

'This is a work trip for me, darling,' she said, with an expansive sweep of her hand. It was true: Penny's tinted glasses were owlish, but behind them her eyes were hawkish, scrutinising the scene below. 'Who's that dolly bird you were ogling?'

'Hmm? Oh, Gina – Harry Pulver's bit on the side. Was I ogling?'

'On stalks, dear.'

'Must be that dress she's wearing.'

'Dress? That's not a dress – that's a *fanny valance*.'

Nat spluttered a laugh. He'd forgotten Penny's gift for a coarse turn of phrase. They talked about the final stretch of filming. The unit was off to Italy next week for ten days, and Nat was along for the ride. Penny looked at him shrewdly.

'You've done very well. Jetting off to Italy just to kick your heels on set.'

'I'll be working. Those scenes won't write themselves.'

She snorted. 'Probably be quicker than you if they *did*.'

'Reiner likes improvising,' Nat shrugged. 'He's just had another idea about the soundtrack. Wants to use "A Day in the Life" – you know it?'

'They won't let you have that,' said Penny with unillusioned firmness.

'They've talked to Epstein.'

But Penny was shaking her head. 'Even if they license it, can you imagine the cost? I mean, Pulver's got boodle but he won't run to that.'

Nat had noted the opulent furnishings and the champagne and the seafood platters they were at that moment bringing out to tempt the guests. If anyone could afford the Beatles' copyright . . .

Penny had moved on to another subject: his next job. 'A spy thing. London and Marrakesh. Talman's producing and says that you're their first choice.'

'Pull the other one,' said Nat, not eager to speculate on how many other writers they'd sounded out before him. Penny said that he'd have to deliver a draft by the end of September.

'And that's a *real* deadline. They won't put up with any dodges. Talman's lot mean business.'

The end of September wouldn't give him much leeway. 'Not sure I can do that, to be honest.'

'Why not?'

'Vere. His memoir. I need to get started, interviewing him.'

Penny frowned sharply at him. 'But that's just a ghostwriting job. You can do it any time.'

Nat pulled a face. 'It's not as simple as that,' he began, and, wary of rousing Penny's suspicions, changed tack. 'I mean, I've promised Vere we'll get cracking.'

'Nat. Darling. We're talking about a studio picture. With stars. With serious money attached. You *can't afford* to turn this down.'

'But Vere's an old friend.'

'Vere knows the business. He'll understand. I'll tell him myself, if you like. Is he here?'

Nat shook his head. 'He's indisposed.'

He couldn't allow her to suspect Vere's condition lest she twigged his dilemma and began a campaign of persuasion. Penny was an agent to the tips of her fingers: she wouldn't accept even loyalty to a dying man as an excuse for turning down a job or a fee. He would have to bluff while he worked out a schedule for the book. If Vere could soldier on a while and help him with a few reminiscences, all might be well – he could do the screenplay in his spare time. But if his old friend were to fade as quickly as Nat had begun to fear, a hard choice faced him.

At the other end of the boat Billie was helplessly nodding away to the monologue of a studio person whose name she hadn't caught – an accountant? – and taking in barely a word. She had been so distracted with wretchedness these last few days she had come close to skipping the party altogether. In the end Nell had persuaded her to go; if she stayed she would only fret and brood over what had happened.

What had happened was terrible – almost unspeakable. Relations with Jeff had been in the deep freeze, but through an effort of will she had kept going. Now that he had withdrawn almost into silence she found herself solely responsible for any civilised interaction. During the day, when she was at the studio, he stayed in the flat and smoked in front of the telly. If she got back in time they would have a mournful little meal together before Jeff went off to the pub, alone. Few of his friends called any more. When she asked him about this he shrugged and said that he had nothing to talk about, so what was the point? In retrospect she realised that the breaking point must have been the moment she told him about her next job. Penny Rolfe had called her that week to say that an American director Berk knew wanted to audition her for a new costume drama. She had only meant to make conversation, but she knew at once from Jeff's clouded brow that she ought to have kept it to herself.

'So you'd go to America?' he asked her. Well, if they liked her enough at the screen test . . . 'How long for?' She didn't know how long exactly but guessed that it might be six to eight weeks. Jeff stared at her. They had been eating while they talked, and at this he carefully placed his knife and fork across his plate and pushed it away. Without another word he stood up and went off to the bedroom. She sat there, wondering what he was up to. After a few minutes he emerged with his jacket on and made for the door. She asked him where he was going and he stopped, with a hint of reluctance. 'I dunno,' he said. 'Just some place where you aren't.'

It was late by the time she heard him come back. She got out of bed and found him sitting on the sofa, in the dark. She asked him where he'd been; he said nothing, only shook his head. Should she put the light on? No answer. He wouldn't even look at her. She hovered in the doorway for a moment, mumbled a goodnight, and went back to bed.

She didn't know how long she had been asleep when something, a noise, woke her. Groggily she raised her head from the pillow. A shadow was standing right over her. 'Jeff?' He didn't speak or move. She reached for the bedside light and snapped it on. The sight turned her blood to ice water. Jeff stood there, his eyes fixed upon her, expressionless. In the first few seconds she wasn't sure what he held in his hand; something that glinted, maybe a torch. No, it wasn't a torch, it was a hammer, the hammer he had used to smash those collages into bits. Her first instinct was to scream, to leap up out of bed and scream for help. But then that would only provoke him into attacking her, bashing her skull until – it wouldn't take him long. She sat up, holding her breath, nerving herself to speak if only she could find her voice from inside her constricted chest. She thought it would be better not to sound terrified.

'Jeff?' she said quietly, and swallowed. 'Can you – can you put that thing down? Please?'

But Jeff didn't respond. He seemed to be in a trance. Was it drugs? she wondered. She had to think quickly or else he would crack the top of her head like a breakfast egg. 'I know you're leaving,' he said in a low monotone. 'I'm going to make sure you don't.'

She kept her voice even. 'I'm not leaving. Why would you think that? I know you've been through a lot lately. An awful lot. I've tried to help you, to support you, renting the studio

229

and – well – I've sometimes had the feeling that you didn't *want* me to help you, that maybe I was making things worse. But whatever problem there is we can get through it, Jeff, you and me.'

He was still holding the hammer, tapping it against his thigh. But then she saw that Jeff's eyelids were drooping. He swayed a little, like someone drunk, or dead tired. She asked him if he was all right, and he blinked a few times before he said, 'Yeah, I'm all right.' She took this as her cue to get up from the bed, slowly, slowly, until she was almost facing him. At least at this distance she could put up a fight – pin his arms, or knee him in the groin, maybe. Jeff took a step back, unsteady now, and when he lifted his hand he used the hammer absently to stroke his head, as though it were a brush. He seemed to have forgotten what he'd come in to do. 'I'm just going to get a glass of water,' she said, making herself sound casual. As she went around him she thought he might grab at her, but in fact he lowered himself, resigned, onto the edge of the bed.

In the kitchen she tried to calm herself and think. She opened a drawer and took out the carving knife. Then she noticed on the worktop a squat brown bottle of Nembutal, the lid off; a bottle of vodka stood next to it. How many had he taken? Did he mean to numb himself before he set about her? A few swift blows to the head, and then black out. It seemed to put a cowardly skew on his malevolence, as though he could only go through with it under the false fugue of sedation. Well, she wouldn't go without a fight, she thought, gripping the knife a little tighter. She tiptoed back towards the bedroom, bracing herself. Jeff was where she had left him, on the bed, only now he was on his back, unconscious.

She called his name, prodded him, but he didn't move. His face was slack, empty – a mask of unknowing. Quickly, she got dressed, then tore out a few clothes from her wardrobe and stuffed them in an overnight bag. At one moment Jeff stirred, muttering indecipherably, and she held her breath: if he woke now she would have to defend herself. But he subsided into sleep, and she completed her getaway preparations, levering out from a drawer a little package of banknotes she had squirrelled away. Outside, on Gray's Inn Road she hailed a cab that took her to Kentish Town. Her mother, still up, answered the door, and the moment Billie saw her face start to crease with concern she felt her eyes brimming over with tears.

The thought of the hammer had ambushed Billie with a gripping spasm of nausea. The studio person was still talking at her, only now her attention was shot. The reek of the oily river in her nostrils was overpowering, and her breaths were suddenly shallow in her lungs. She had to get to a toilet – *oh God, right now.* As politely as was possible she excused herself and hurried off; a waiter pointed her to a staircase. She felt her stomach buck like a wild horse about to throw its load. She clattered down the metal stairs into a corridor at the same time as a tall woman in a navy trouser suit approached from the other end and reached the loo door before her. There was a haughty set to the woman's expression, and Billie faltered. This was not the face of someone you could beg from.

She didn't have to beg. The woman squinted at her. 'Are you all right?' And then, 'I think you need this more urgently than I do.'

She was standing aside, and Billie gasped out her thanks as she darted through the door and slammed it shut. She just had time to flip the seat up and kneel before she heaved out a great bilious *hwaargh* into the bowl. *Oh God oh God oh God.* She groaned, aware of the raucous noise but not caring. She leaned in again and felt another lurch up her throat, but this time there was hardly anything, just a strangled trickle that brought tears to her eyes. She reached up to flush the porridgy pebble-dashing around the bowl, then rested her forehead a moment against the cool porcelain rim. That felt a little better, though her throat ached.

An enquiring knock sounded behind her and the door opened a crack. It was the woman who'd let her go in front.

'Oh dear. Anything I can do?' She stepped inside the cubicle, quite unembarrassed, and handed Billie over her shoulder a paper napkin. 'Reminds me of the war, there were always girls being sick. The only *useful* thing you could do was to hold their hair.' Her voice was sympathetic, yet it was also feathered by an unmistakable note of amusement. Billie longed to lay her head on the floor and be still for a couple of hours.

She wiped her mouth with the napkin and gingerly raised herself to her feet. The woman, towering over her, pulled a face.

'Poor thing!' she said, with a playful frown. 'I'd recommend you go straight home to bed, but unless you're a strong swimmer . . .' She looked through the little porthole window. 'We've only just passed Tower Bridge.'

Billie dabbed at her leaking eyes. She must look a mess, an impression confirmed when the woman made a wincing gesture. A dribble of sick striped Billie's black dress from shoulder to chest. Hurriedly she used the napkin to wipe it away.

'Oh God,' she muttered. 'What a fright. And today of all days.' She was an actress, she explained, and her agent planned to introduce her to people.

'Let's get you fixed up, then,' the woman said, and briskly opened her clutch bag. She handed over a compact. 'I'm Freya, by the way.'

'Billie. Thanks for being so –' But Freya batted away the sentiment, and joked that this was the longest conversation she'd had since boarding. It turned out she was an old friend of Nat Fane's.

'I've heard Nat talk about you, actually,' said Billie. 'You're the journalist, aren't you? He said –' But she stopped herself, belatedly realising that what Nat had said to her was probably in confidence: she was pretty sure he had called Freya 'the one that got away'. Freya waited while Billie did some light repairs on her face. The girl still looked fragile but the colour was coming back to her cheeks. Unfortunately there was no disguising the ghostly imprint of the vomit dribble on her dress.

'Here, take this,' she said, unloosing her patterned silk scarf and draping it around Billie's neck. It effectively camouflaged the stain. Billie felt that any more kindness from this woman would make her cry.

Her glance fell on the label. 'This is *Pucci*.'

'Yeah, and it was a present. So you'd better look after it.' She gave Billie the once-over. 'Are you ready to go up?'

Billie nodded. 'I think so.'

'All right. Wait for me while I have a wee.'

They emerged back on deck just as Dox Walbrook and his band were starting up. The slow tempo of 'My One and Only Love' sounded to Freya more like an end-of-the-evening number than a set opener, but still, the creamy cushioned tone of Walbrook's tenor sax was fine by her any time of the day. Billie was keeping close to her side, like a shy girl on the first day of term. Sunlight glittered on the Thames.

They were edging their way through a little cluster of guests when a woman detached herself and stepped in front of them. It took Freya a moment to recognise the lynx eyes and imperious cheekbones of Sonja Zertz. She was wearing a mannish, pinstriped suit with wide lapels and had slicked back her hair like a ballroom dancer of the 1930s.

'Hello again. Freya, yes?'

'I couldn't place you for a moment – your hair.'

Sonja grinned. 'It is my "Weimar gigolo" look. Ah, Billie! You two know one another?'

'We've just met,' said Freya. 'We were on the lookout for *drinks*.'

Sonja spun round and, as if she were the hostess herself, beckoned a waiter. Freya took a gin cocktail from his tray; Billie only wanted water. Sonja, shading her eyes, cast her gaze around the bright prospect of the river. 'What glorious luck to be on a boat today! The benefit of having a rich patron.'

'Where is he, by the way?' asked Billie.

'Oh, he's joining us at Chelsea, or somewhere,' said Sonja. 'I suppose he wants to make a dramatic entrance.'

'Like, walking across water?' suggested Freya.

Sonja smirked. 'I don't think Mr Pulver has much in common with Jesus.'

'Has he visited the set?'

'I've never seen him once. Reiner said that he'd had a meeting with him a few weeks ago – not *gemütlich*.'

Freya had been keeping an eye out for Reiner Werther Kloss but so far hadn't spotted him. Billie, meanwhile, was being dragooned by her agent into a huddle of studio people, leaving Freya and Sonja alone together. Freya decided to respond to the candid interest of the woman's gaze with some candour of her own.

'Am I right in thinking you invited me to this thing?'

'Of course,' replied Sonja, with a little pout. 'Is there something unusual in that?'

'Well, only in so far as I'm a complete stranger.'

'But I like complete strangers. The stranger the better.'

233

She said this with an insolent gleam that amused Freya, and slightly irritated her. Who did this one think she was – Dietrich? She asked her where in Germany she was from.

'Stuttgart. But I left years ago. I live in Munich.'

'Ah. Then perhaps you could recommend a hotel,' said Freya. 'I'm going there next week.'

It was the first time Sonja had looked surprised. 'Why?'

'A festival honouring the work of your director, as a matter of fact. Useful for the piece I'm researching.'

Sonja drew in her chin sharply. 'But you know he's here?' Freya returned a look of innocent interest, secretly hoping that Sonja might be the one to provide an entrée. At that moment a thickset, curly-haired fellow with sweat on his top lip interposed himself.

'Sonja, everything good?'

'Everything *peachy*, darling,' she said, allowing herself to be kissed. 'This is Freya. Our producer, Berk Cosenza.' The man offered her his hand, also sweaty, and a distracted nod. Sonja tipped her head at him. 'Something the matter?'

Berk made a grimace. 'Have you ever tried a "jellied eel"? Harry told me to pick up a bunch of 'em at Greenwich. Now, I can eat most anything – look at me – but I just tried a mouthful downstairs, and Jesus, it's like chewing a dead tramp's eyeball. Truly, I gagged.'

'Did you have it with liquor?' asked Freya.

'I wish I had!' he exclaimed. 'A big Scotch might have taken away that God-awful taste.'

'No, not that kind of liquor. It's a green sauce that traditionally goes with jellied eels, made from parsley and, um, stewed eel water, I think.'

Berk looked at her in horror. 'You gotta be kidding. What kind of a country is this? The stuff you put in your mouths! Harry told me it's a "great London delicacy" – wanted to serve it to his guests.'

'It's an acquired taste,' admitted Freya. 'Though I've never actually known anyone to acquire it.'

'That I can believe.' Berk called over a waiter and asked him for a large Scotch on the rocks, and smiled at Freya slyly. 'You put the idea in my head. So, you're a friend of the *legendary* Miss Zertz here?'

Freya looked at Sonja. 'You could say. I'm also a writer on the *Chronicle*.'

'She's doing a piece about Reiner,' Sonja supplied.

'Then we should get you to meet him,' said Berk, looking round.

'I've already met him, at a press conference. I asked him for an interview and he very politely turned me down.'

'Playing hard to get! He just needs some warming up.'

This promising connection was broken when one of the boat's crewmen sidled up for a private word with Berk, who excused himself. Throughout their encounter Freya had felt Sonja's gaze upon her; there was an inviting sultriness in it. The *Thomas Bertram* was now deep into tourist territory. Leaning on the rail, Freya shifted her body in slight invitation to watch the riverfront skimming by. Seen from this unaccustomed perspective the Houses of Parliament and Big Ben looked like stage-set creations, familiar and yet strangely, almost deliriously surreal. Red buses the size of Dinky Toys shimmered over Westminster Bridge. She half expected Sonja to comment on the famous sights, but instead she let the silence between them lengthen. They could hear Dox Walbrook introducing a guest singer, a woman, who laughed easily at his drawling blandishments. *Nice to be here, thank you, Dox* . . .

The saxophone crooned out an intro and the woman's attractively husky voice took up the lyric:

> *This bitter earth*
> *Well, what fruit it bears*

Sonja had joined Freya against the rail and silently offered her a cigarette, which she took. The churn of the water, the warm slanting sunlight and the music wafting down the deck held her in a magical trance of stupefaction; it was like being high, only without the springboard of drugs.

For a few seconds everyone's face went dark as the boat passed under the bridge, and the singer's voice echoed in the tunnelled gloom. Bands of light rippled on the black water below. The brief eclipse held a delicious intimacy, like the moment the lights went down before a show started. If she wants to kiss me, now would be the moment, Freya thought.

But Sonja, her face lit by the tip of her cigarette, only said, 'The Marienbad.'

'Sorry?'

'You asked about a hotel, in München. You must stay at the Marienbad. I know the manager there, he will take care of you.'

'Thanks. Remind me to write down his name.' The boat emerged again into the daylight, and the spell was broken.

'No need,' Sonja said, with one of her slow blinks. 'I'll get them to call you. Too bad I'll be away: I would have liked to show you round the place.'

'That would have been nice,' Freya replied breezily.

There was a pause before Sonja spoke again. 'May I ask you a question? You said before that you and Billie had just met. So how then did she come to be wearing your scarf? I saw it on you — no? — when you stepped on board.'

'Ah. She'd had an accident, just at the moment we met. There was a mark on her dress — the scarf helped cover it up.'

'You give away your clothes to strangers?'

'They're only clothes. And I like strangers, too. The stranger the better.'

They smiled at one another.

Dox Walbrook and his band had just taken a break as the boat came into Chelsea Harbour. The skipper and his white-jacketed crew made themselves busy lowering the gangplank and securing the boat to the landing pontoons. The waiting staff had done a once-around of the upper and lower decks, collecting glasses, plumping cushions, sprucing up the bar. For a moment Nat wondered if they were going to line up and pipe the owner aboard, but in fact Harry and his entourage — the wife, whose helmet of ash-grey hair looked as brittle as a meringue; an elderly lady who was possibly his mother; a couple of goons — stepped up the plank with relatively little ceremony. Berk performed the role of welcoming committee, though given it was Harry's boat an air of superfluous oddity was unavoidable.

Nat had introduced Freya to a pale older man named Arno, who had edited all of Kloss's films, and an actress, Gina. The latter was a vivacious young woman with a beseeching smile, though her expression would go strangely blank at times, as if she were deaf. Nat and Arno treated the girl with noticeable gallantry, though in Nat's case it might have been influenced by the brevity of her minidress. Just when Freya had begun to think that Kloss was avoiding her, without warning her quarry joined their little group. He wore a bead necklace of vaguely Eastern aspect over a plain T-shirt with jeans and monkey boots.

'Reiner, this is a dear friend of mine, Freya Wyley,' said Nat suavely. 'She's been dying to meet you.'

Reiner smiled amiably and offered her his hand. Freya said, 'Actually we've already met, after the press conference you did at the Palais-Royal in March.'

Behind his spectacles Reiner's eyes narrowed. 'Have we? I meet quite a few people . . . my apologies.' Freya couldn't tell if he was bluffing or not.

'I'm writing a piece about your work. I'll be going to Munich next Friday for the grand Kloss-fest. They must have invited you.'

'Kloss-fest,' repeated Reiner. 'I like that! Yes, Veronika Braun's an old friend of mine. She wants me to go, but ach, the timing is impossible, with the film.'

She decided to try a more provocative line. 'I wondered if you could tell me what's happened to *The Laudanum Waltz*.'

He didn't flinch. He explained that he and Arno had just settled on a final cut when the film became embroiled in a legal dispute. The studio wanted to recut certain scenes; they had resisted; the film remained in limbo. 'It's frustrating,' he said mildly. 'The film was a mess to start with, but Arno did some fantastic repair work in the editing room. He turned the whole thing around.'

They all looked at Arno, who was shyly dismissive of this tribute. 'I only helped to smooth it out. The genius is the *Regisseur* here.'

But Reiner wasn't having this. 'As Arno well knows, every film is made three times: once when it is written, once when it is shot, and once when it is edited. In my experience, the last of these is the most important. The editing governs not only the shape and rhythm of the film, it more or less determines its meaning also.'

Nat, slightly nettled, said, 'Well, I'd like to see how a film acquires its "meaning" without a writer.'

Freya, aware that they had strayed from the point, interposed. 'Do you know where the negative of *The Laudanum Waltz* might be? There's a rumour that someone burnt it.'

Did she detect the smallest twitch in Reiner's poker-faced serenity? 'I know nothing of that,' he said. 'It would grieve me to think it was gone forever.'

At that moment Berk hove into their midst, clearing the way for a squat, thickset man with small, glittering eyes and a pugilistic jaw. His short-sleeved shirt revealed muscled forearms so hirsute they almost hid the strap of his gold watch. Freya recognised Harry Pulver and his dark Presley-ish quiff from newspaper photographs. She couldn't help noticing the mood of obsequiousness that seized everyone in his orbit; everyone but herself and Reiner Werther Kloss. Even Nat stood a little straighter in his presence. Berk was gesturing towards her.

'And this is Miss Wyley, a journalist – know all about them, eh, Harry?'

Harry's chin lifted as he said, 'Which paper?'

'The *Chronicle*,' she replied.

'Never read it,' he snapped, implying that because of this it might as well not exist. 'You people are always tryin' to get one over on me. Dunno why. Some reporter said I'd been diddlin' the Revenue. Bare-faced lie. Another called me a tax exile – complete lie.'

'Ah, so you *do* read the *Chronicle*. That was one of ours.'

Harry stared at her for a moment; Freya stared back. 'They can print what they like. See if I care.'

There followed, for Harry's benefit, a verbal love-in on the subject of the *Thomas Bertram*. Berk initiated it, remarking that even in the Hamptons he'd never seen a yacht as lavish as this, while Arno enquired as to the exact dimensions and capacity of the vessel, which Harry droned out in a rich man's mixture of boastfulness and boredom. There was much oohing and aahing over its magnificence. Freya was amused to see Nat joining in the descant of praise, making a joke about Cleopatra's barge that nobody quite got. Harry ignored him, in any case; he ignored most people. Having checked on the whereabouts of his mother and his wife, he moved away without another word; Gina, catching a telepathic signal, followed close behind.

The sun had begun to dip as the boat continued westward, the scenery no longer a broken jumble of warehouses and factories but riverside villas and their orderly lawns sloping down to the bank. The pubs and cottages of suburban west London admired it from a distance, while small tugs and skiffs bobbed alongside like sightseers at a royal procession. Dox and his quartet had swung into their second set. Nat, afloat on his sixteenth gin cocktail, had observed his own rule about dancing and was now performing a slow shuffle to their cover of 'Maiden Voyage'. Slowly, other guests filled the floor, prompted by the loping, laid-back tempo; the tiny shiver of the drummer's hi-hat sounded like soda water poured over ice. A woman in a skinny-rib sweater and wide floppy hat joined him, and he smiled at her absently: over her shoulder he could see Sonja and Freya, languidly entwined in a mock waltz. How he loved watching Freya move, that tall, loose-limbed sway; he wondered if there'd ever be a time when he wasn't somewhat in love with her. Sonja, about an inch shorter, had her own provoking sexiness in the androgynous Weimar-cabaret outfit. Together they looked like girlfriend and boyfriend, the one enhancing the other, like Ginger and Fred.

The cruise might have concluded in this sun-buttered haze of drinking and dancing had it not been for an unscheduled eruption of unpleasantness. The landing stage at Richmond was in sight when Freya, retrieving a clutch bag she'd left on a bench, happened to pass an open cabin and overheard a raised voice. Harry Pulver was berating someone: a member of staff, she presumed, such was the savagery of his condescension. *Are you fucking deaf? Eh? I've just asked you a question.* She knew she ought to walk on, it was none of her business, they were about to disembark. But Freya could never resist the whiff of confrontation. She put her head round the door: there was Harry glowering not at a minion but at Gina, her face averted in mute humiliation. Neither of them noticed her until she said, 'Actually, I believe the lady *is* deaf. But there's really no need to shout at her.'

Harry almost jumped. The shock of being interrupted, let alone *told off*, was apparently so far beyond his experience as to baffle him. 'What the – who the hell d'you think you are?' His voice came out a low incredulous growl.

Freya wrinkled her nose. 'Oh, just someone who thinks a deaf person should be treated with a little more consideration. That's who.'

The girl, Gina, was eyeing her in cowed amazement, and Freya had a sudden sense that answering back to Harry Pulver was like answering back to the Queen: it simply wasn't done. Harry had half turned towards the intruder. '*Consideration?* Out of here, hoppit, you fucking – *journalist*. Now. Unless you want me to throw you out.'

Freya shook her head. 'Didn't take long for your mask to slip, did it?' She lingered a moment in the doorway. Bristling with anger, she considered broadening her field of fire to include his repellent manners, his high-handed entitlement, his bullying of a woman. But instead she made do with two words: 'Fucking *arse-hole*.' She slammed the door and walked back towards the deck. That was the problem with parting shots. The pleasure of getting the shot off was blunted by not hanging around to appreciate its effect.

Nat, who by degrees had been getting purchase on the skinny-ribbed girl, saw Freya approach from the corner of his eye. She looked furious. He felt a dread of something nameless as she made a beeline for him; he knew her so well he could have spoken her next utterance himself: 'You won't fucking believe what I've just seen.' But a sudden anxious murmuring had risen in her wake. A shadow was right behind her. Harry Pulver had caught up and was jabbing a finger in her back. 'Oi! Think you can talk to me like that?'

Nat made a point of avoiding physical violence, at least outside the bedroom. He had not been involved in a fight since Oxford, when he was occasionally assaulted on the street for wearing make-up. But an instinct – protective, romantic, he didn't know what – compelled him to place himself between Pulver's barrel-chested bulk and Freya. He heard himself saying how it wasn't really on for a fellow to menace a lady like that, though he didn't get very far with his defence before he watched, almost in slow motion, Harry's face bearing down on his own. A starburst of pain shot past his eyes as he felt his nose crumple beneath the momentum of Harry's meaty forehead. A woman's shriek pierced the air. Dazed, he staggered back, grasping the rail, while behind him he heard a scuffle break out and voices raised in protest or conciliation.

Nat found Reiner squatting at his side, muttering something in German and holding out a handkerchief, for his nose appeared to be pouring with blood. Then Freya was at his other side, her voice agonised with sympathy. 'Oh, darling, it's all down your lovely suit.' He considered, through watering eyes, his spattered white shirt. The odd thing was, with his nose throbbing and his clothes ruined, he felt his moment of madness worthwhile, if only to feel Freya's arm hugging his neck.

The incident, having shivered the timbers of the *Thomas Bertram*, was the talk of the party once they were ashore at Richmond. The guests had resumed their drinking in the garden of the Lord Raglan, overlooking the river, where dinner was to be served. Harry Pulver had been led away by his retinue and seated at a distance from the *Eureka* crew, and only Berk, mindful of the bankroll, kept up the show of fawning bonhomie for his partner.

Julie the script girl, who had once done a first-aid course, fixed up Nat's face with some help from the boat's medicine chest. His nose wasn't broken, but he still smarted with the pain; he looked a fright with the gauze and cotton wool plastering it like a racehorse's noseband. It was gratifying nevertheless to find himself the centre of attention, talked of as the man who had 'taken on' Harold Pulver in defence of a lady.

'I didn't lay a glove on him, I'm afraid,' he said to Billie, who had missed the whole thing. It amused him to float the implication that at another time he might have given his adversary a damn good biffing.

'He's a regular gallant,' said Freya fondly. 'Greater love hath no man than to take one on the nose for a friend.'

'Was he going to hit *you*?' Billie asked her, aghast.

'I think he'd have liked to.'

Ronnie Stiles, passing their table, stopped to stare. 'Ding-ding!' he called to Nat, raising his fists and performing a little duck-and-weave. 'I hear the Thomas A Becket wants ya for a bout next Saturday, mate.'

'Tell them to contact my agent,' he fired back, and got an appreciative leer from Ronnie. Christ, how little it took to become popular! He'd had more admiring looks for being nutted by that brute than he'd managed during the entire premiere of his last film. Maybe he should get poleaxed more often.

As the adrenalin started to wear off he felt a vicious throbbing not just in his nose but his whole head. Alcohol might be the remedy, only he was already up to his waist in gin from the boat. He caught Freya's eye and made a coded gesture with his fingers. With a nod she announced that she was taking Nat for a walk 'to clear his head'. On the way they happened to pass Dox Walbrook, sitting calm as a Buddha with a glass of neat Scotch. Freya decided to introduce herself.

'I loved your version of "Lazy Afternoon". Actually, I loved it all.'

Dox, eyeing her from beneath his porkpie hat, nodded courteously. 'Thank you, ma'am.'

'I'm Freya. This is Nat.'

He offered them his hand, squinting at Nat. 'Man, you musta got someone *mad*.' His Georgia accent was smoky and relaxed, like his playing.

Nat's laugh was snuffly beneath the plaster. 'Yeah. But he looks worse than I do.'

Dox twitched a smile at this bravado. Freya asked him if he'd like to join them for a smoke, and he ambled alongside them to the edge of the pub's low garden wall. Night had set on; a scimitar moon hung in the purplish sky. The Thames was an inky blue-black, gleaming here and there from the lights of small boats. Along the path the pale outline of the *Thomas Bertram* could be seen, a whale among the minnows. Freya had rolled one of her large 'prison' spliffs and lit it. She took a couple of long drags and handed it on to Dox. Soon the air around them was scented with the ropey smell of pot.

Nat, drawing the smoke deep into his lungs, felt the first hit like a mallet to his cerebral cortex. He staggered a moment, and felt Dox's quick steadying hand at his back. 'Easy, brother.' After a minute or so his balance seemed to correct itself, and his head felt pleasantly aswim.

'First time I ever smoked this stuff was with Jerry Dicks. He used to bring it back from Morocco.'

Freya nodded. 'Me too. Poor old Jerry.' She turned to Dox. 'A photographer we used to knock about with.'

Nat was frowning with the effort of recall. 'That music-hall monologue he was always doing. *I'm subject to colds and they make me quite deaf / And then I can't hear what you say / A feller once asked me if I'd have a drink / I heard that with a cold by the way . . .* How does the rest of it go?'

'I don't remember. He knew hundreds of them. He was a great performer – and smoker,' she added.

'This dude still around?' Dox asked politely.

Freya shook her head. 'They found him dead in his bed at a Brighton hotel. A couple of years ago. Never quite sure what did for him in the end – emphysema, TB, pneumonia . . .'

'God, I miss him,' muttered Nat.

Freya missed him too, but she felt it wasn't the right time to be mourning in the company of an outsider – an illustrious one at that. Instead she asked Dox about his forthcoming work on *Eureka*. It transpired that a couple of the pieces they'd played this afternoon were for the score. The talk moved on to jazz greats, then to his contemporaries, the ones he'd played with, the ones he'd have liked to play with. When she asked who, he returned a wistful look.

'Coltrane.' He had died a few weeks ago.

While they were yarning away Nat's stoned gaze surveyed the moon, the jetty, the campfire. He paused on this last. Strange to have it so near to the boats. He refocused, and saw that it was a fire all right, but with no one attending it. It seemed to be coming *from* a boat – the big one. He shut his eyes, then opened them wide again, trying to take it in. He took a few steps forward. There was no doubting it now. The *Thomas Bertram*, the eighty-footer, Harold Pulver's pride and joy, was in trouble. Flames were rippling hungrily over its deck.

He turned back to Freya and Dox, absorbed in talk. 'Er, I don't want to alarm you, but our ride home appears to be on fire.'

Freya followed his gaze. 'Oh God. We'd better raise the alarm.'

'Or we could just let it burn.'

'Don't be stupid, Nat. There might be someone on board.'

'Shit,' murmured Dox, who stared for a moment before heading towards the blaze. 'My fuckin' horn's in there!' He broke into a run.

They were fifty yards away when an explosion rocked the boat and sent debris raining across the jetty. Dox had pulled up, a hand shielding his eyes from the conflagration. In the distance they heard the droning siren of a fire engine. People had emerged from the pub to gawp. The yacht, wreathed in leaping flames, wore the mournful and magnificent aspect of a Viking funeral ship. It already looked beyond saving.

EXT. COURTYARD OF VILLA, PORTOFINO — DAY.
Crane shot of the ivy-creepered courtyard as CHAS *enters, to be greeted by* GEORGE, *looking tanned and relaxed. Jazz plays over the scene as we watch them talk.*

EXT. COURTYARD, GROUND LEVEL — DAY.
CHAS *and* GEORGE *seated at a table with drinks.* CHAS *looks rather tense and shifty.*

> GEORGE

So what news from home? How did Gwen seem to you?

> CHAS

Oh, a bit distracted. Of course she really wanted to come, but her mother –

> GEORGE

I know. Another relapse.

> CHAS

It looks quite serious . . .

> GEORGE

It always *does*. Then she's back! That woman's made more farewell appearances than Nellie Melba.

CHAS
(*lowering his voice*)
Talking of farewells, how's our patient?

GEORGE
I spoke to his doctor yesterday. He said there's not much to be done other than make him comfortable. It was quite a thing – what Hugh himself would have called a *coup de vieux.*

CHAS
Poor man. (*He pauses.*) Looks like you arrived just in time, though . . .

GEORGE
Hmm? Oh, yes, I see.

At that moment JANE *enters, looking pale and drawn. She sits at the table, sensing the mute enquiries of the men.*

JANE
He's sleeping. I managed to have a few words with him before he went off. (*To* CHAS.) He knows that you're here.

CHAS
He can speak?

JANE
No. But he understands. And he has a little notepad he writes on. The doctor thinks he may still –

CUT TO: CHAS *and* GEORGE *glance at one another. They understand that such optimism is almost certainly misplaced.*

EXT. HARBOUR CAFE — DAY.

CHAS *is drinking black coffee and smoking as* GEORGE *approaches his table. He sits down, shaking his head.*

                    GEORGE
This is going to hit her hard. She's more
like a daughter to him than a friend. How
long have they known each other?

                    CHAS
Years. 'Daughter' isn't wide of the mark.
Jane was an orphan from three. Vereker
never had any children - for obvious reasons. I dare say she'll inherit
everything.

                    GEORGE
Will she be his literary executor?

                    CHAS
I'm not sure she'd care for the job.

                    GEORGE
I wonder if I should - God, sorry. The
fellow isn't even in his grave yet.

                    CHAS
You never know, she might appreciate the
offer. Maybe I could ask her for you.

                    GEORGE
Would you do that?

                    CHAS
When there's an appropriate moment . . .

GEORGE

Quite. I wouldn't dream of bringing it up before he's -

A long beat as CHAS *shifts in his seat, waiting for his own moment.*

CHAS

I can't deny that I'm hoping for something from you in return. Gwen told me about your 'revelation'.

GEORGE

Yes . . . it was quite an experience. I should tell you that these last few months I've been hanging out with people who drop a fair amount of . . . substances.

CHAS

You mean -

GEORGE

'Turn on, tune in, drop out.' Don't get me wrong - I'm not a drug fiend! - but when in Rome . . . So I've dropped a tab occasionally.

CHAS

But what has this to do with Vereker?

GEORGE

I'll tell you.

CUT TO: *In flashback,* GEORGE *is asleep in bed. An alarm clock rings and he wakes blearily.*

GEORGE (*v.o.*)

It seemed a morning like any other. I felt
a bit hung-over from a party I'd been at
the night before.

CUT TO: GEORGE *in his dressing gown, yawn-*
ing and making coffee in his kitchen. He
lights a cigarette and skims the newspaper.
A glance at the clock on the wall tells
him he's running late.

GEORGE (*v.o.*)

I threw on some clothes and went out to
get the bus.

CUT TO: *A street in Rome,* GEORGE *hurrying*
along as a bus pulls into a stop. He steps
on - it's crowded - and takes a seat near
the back.

GEORGE (*v.o.*)

So I was sitting there, not noticing much,
when I heard this voice say something.

CHAS (*v.o.*)

In Italian?

GEORGE (*v.o.*)

Possibly. I don't remember. But the voice
triggered some brainstorm. I suppose I
must have been tripping still from the
party, only it wasn't like any trip I'd
had before. It was more like a fugue.

CUT TO: GEORGE *wandering through a field of*
summer flowers, sunbeams bouncing off the
camera lens. He is wearing the same

clothes - his office suit and tie - but his expression is beatific, serene, enraptured. A jazz piano and drum play out a seductive figure, repeating it over and over. As GEORGE *advances into the field the flowers seem to perform a woozy, languid dance in time to the music.*

> GEORGE *(v.o.)*
> Everything I'd been thinking about Vereker - his themes, his stylistic motifs, his narrative patterning - it all fell magically into place. It was like - like a fog had lifted, and I saw the work whole, as if for the first time. 'The figure in the carpet' wasn't a puzzle any more - maybe it wasn't a puzzle in the first place. I could see it right there in front of me, in all its beautiful simplicity.

CUT TO: *The present, the cafe at Portofino.*

> CHAS
> Eureka.

> GEORGE
> Precisely. The unimagined truth. Strange to think it might never have come to me without the stimulus of . . . a trip.

> CHAS
> *(after a long pause)*
> So . . .

> GEORGE
> So?

CHAS

For Christ's sake, do I have to ask? All
right. What is it - the figure in the
carpet? The *secret*.

GEORGE

Chas, come on. You think after all this
effort I'm simply going to tell everyone?

CHAS

No, not 'everyone'. *Me*. Your friend - the
person who put you on to the thing in the
first place.

GEORGE

For which I'm very grateful. And when it's
finished you will have pride of place in
the acknowledgements of my book.

CHAS

Fuck the acknowledgements! I want to know
now. I deserve to know.

GEORGE

I'm sorry, Chas. It's for the book - it's
the soul of the book. The definitive portrait of Hugh Vereker. I can't let you
peep under the curtain before it's ready.

CHAS

I came here by train and bus and ferry
for this -

GEORGE

I thought you came to pay your respects
to a dying man.

CHAS *rises from his seat, throws down some coins for his coffee.*

> CHAS
>
> I can't believe you. You must be so desperate to make your name you've forgotten what it is to be a friend.

> GEORGE
>
> I think we both know who the desperate one is, Chas.

CHAS *turns on him a look of pure scorn and walks off.* GEORGE *watches him go, then calls to the waiter.*

14

Freya had not visited Munich before, and perhaps of her own accord never would have done. It existed in the more blinkered reaches of her mind as a fanatical centre of sausage shops, beer halls and Nazism. This last was now allegedly in abeyance, though something about the city's municipal orderliness and the dry obedience of pedestrians at traffic lights seemed to give the lie to its reformed ways. She had imagined the place to feel somewhat more chastened. The reception at the Marienbad Hotel had put her on guard from the off: the manner in which the unsmiling desk clerk ran his eye down the ledger and announced that he had no record of a reservation for 'Wyley' answered to the stereotype of all she had expected from Bavarian hospitality.

This impression was almost instantly overturned by the appearance of the dapper hotel manager, Gerhard, who welcomed Freya with a graciousness befitting 'a friend of Miss Zertz'. Sonja, true to her word, had taken it upon herself to arrange the accommodation, and Freya could find no fault with the seigneurial suite he showed her to, or the view from her window down Maximilianstrasse. It seemed that Sonja really was a local heroine, to judge from the posters of the Kloss-fest she had spotted around the city – a dramatic black-and-white still of her face from *The Private Life of Hanna K.*

They had last seen one another at Richmond on the night the *Thomas Bertram* went up in flames. The good news was that there had been no casualties, aside from a crew member who had suffered minor injuries in making his escape. The copy of *The Times* she had bought at the airport carried a few column inches about the ongoing investigation. Early reports that the fire had started through an electrical fault had by now been dismissed. Police investigators examining the charred hulk of the vessel had uncovered certain 'suspect materials'. The case for arson looked incontrovertible. 'Whoever is responsible for destroying Harry Pulver's yacht,' Nat had said to her, 'should be tracked down and shaken warmly by the hand.'

She had just unpacked her bag when a knock came at the door. A waiter stood there with his trolley: on it a bottle of Krug lolling in an ice bucket. I haven't ordered this, she told him; but his English wasn't good, and she had no German. She signed for it, then phoned down to Gerhard, who explained, with a smile in his voice, that the champagne had been specifically requested for the room by Miss Zertz. She caught her expression in the room's gilt mirror, and laughed at herself.

Below, trams ghosted along the street as if on casters, their bells clanging; the scene reminded her of London twenty years ago. She read more of the paper, had a bath and then lay on the bed, smoking a small joint. An hour later the telephone on the nightstand woke her from an impromptu nap: she was still wrapped in a towel. It was reception calling to say that her guest had arrived. She had forgotten about this. The bedside clock informed her it was 6.30 p.m. She dressed quickly and went down to the lobby, where Gerhard, her new friend, conducted her to the bar. A petite, slightly nervous woman with short dark hair was waiting. She wore a zip-up black leather blouson and introduced herself as Veronika Braun, one of the festival organisers.

'I spoke with your colleague at the paper,' she reminded her. 'Miss Frampton.'

'Yes, it was Delphine who set this up,' said Freya. 'I gather you're a friend of Reiner's.'

'That's correct,' she replied matter-of-factly. There was much excitement about the festival, she went on, in an unexcited voice. There had been a good deal of interest from newspapers and the media, not just in Europe – even the *New York Times* had sent along a correspondent. The director had sent the festival a message of 'good luck' for the occasion.

'He's very disappointed that he couldn't attend in person,' said Freya.

Veronika stared at her. 'You know Reiner?'

'No. But we met at a party last week, and he said it was unfortunate he had to be in Italy for filming.'

Freya sensed a little quickening of interest in the woman now the fact of her acquaintance with Reiner was out. After a drink in the bar Veronika led the way to the theatre on Müllerstrasse where one of his early plays, *29 Marks*, was being staged. As they walked she opened up a little about her own history with Reiner: they had first met at acting school, where he had become a star student, writing and directing his own plays. She had been somewhat in awe of him, so when he abandoned the school ('he was bored by the teachers') and asked her to join a new theatre company he was setting up she didn't think twice. It was basically a handful of them to start with. Reiner chose the plays and directed while she helped with the casting and the producing; the others handled the publicity and the fund-raising. They struggled at first, barely filling the upstairs room they had turned into a theatre. But almost by force of will Reiner made it work, first with a scabrous production of *The Beggar's Opera*, then a shadow-haunted version of *Faust*, with himself in the title role.

Kloss productions became celebrated, and Reiner was for a time the wonder boy of Munich's underground theatre scene. And just when he seemed likely to break into the mainstream he gave up acting and turned to film-making. Freya heard a shiver of regret as Veronika related this, but further discussion was cut short as they arrived at the Fengler Theater, where a queue was already snaking along the street. Veronika conducted her inside and showed her to a seat near the front of the auditorium; she had to hurry off, but they would meet afterwards for dinner, if she wasn't busy. Just before the lights went down two young men, both dressed like off-duty sailors in caps and leather jackets, sidled in and settled themselves just in front of her. It took her a moment to realise that their attire was a homage to Reiner.

Gina, head back on the pillow at an angle of agonised surrender, gave out a long moan. *Thank Christ*, thought Nat, whose tongue ached from its super-extended probing. He squinted up at her from between her legs like a marksman through cross hairs. Gina's neck and face were beginning to crimson in the way he found so exciting in a woman working her way to climax. A thin shaft of afternoon light pierced the curtains and fell across the bedroom floor; voices could be heard drifting up from the hotel swimming pool, punctuated by the occasional soft splash of a dive. He felt the sweat running off his forehead and into his eyes. His tongue, could it have spoken, would have cried for mercy. Another moan came from Gina, longer, and needier.

He felt a stiffening in her haunches, and a shiver trembled the length of her. As it did, a metallic click went off just behind his shoulder. He glanced around: Sonja, in her knickers, her face partially obscured by the camera she was holding. It was the long-lensed Nikon F he'd recently acquired, the same one what's-his-face used in *Blow-Up*. She lowered it; her expression was watchful, her mouth about to crease into a smirk. She said a few words in German, which he understood from a little game they'd been playing earlier. He raised himself onto his knees and straddled Gina's waist. He had thought this bit might be tricky, but it wasn't. The recent memory of the caning each woman had dealt him sprang up, bobbing, and with the aid of a few swift strokes he came, ecstatically. He heard two further clicks go off before he sank down on top of her.

How had this happened?

They had arrived – the cast, the crew, the screenwriter – in Portofino three days ago, tired and sweaty after the drive from Genoa airport. Their hotel was perched high on the hill overlooking the bay. From his balcony he had gazed out like a Roman emperor in his summer eyrie. The stately Mediterranean wobbled and glistened, first bands of green, then of navy, then of aquamarine. On the first day Reiner went off with Ronnie and Alec Madden to rehearse the long cafe scene between Chas and George. Nat had spent the morning wandering about the chic little harbour and its warren of boutiques; he bought a pair of playboyish swimming trunks he wasn't sure he could get away with. While drinking an espresso at a bar he was distracted by the sight of a teenage girl languidly shimmying inside a hula hoop. As people stopped to watch, the girl displayed a few tricks, allowing the hoop to run up and down her body or over her shoulder, then speeding up her revolutions until it became a blur. The athletic grace and suppleness of her brown limbs mesmerised him. Nat picked up the Nikon and, pretending to focus on a spot out to sea, slyly snapped her.

His nose was still tender from the assault the previous weekend. His eyes were raccooned with bruises, so he wore his aviator sunglasses from morning till night. Someone from Harold Pulver's office had sent Nat flowers by way of an apology. In the days that followed, the story of the *Thomas Bertram* had scorched across the papers. It had taken the fire services an hour or more to get the blaze under control. The flowers had been quite unnecessary – that smouldering wreck was the compensation. True, he'd felt sorry for Dox Walbrook and his band, who'd lost all their gear. Dox himself had looked inconsolable. What nobody could work out was who might have started it. This was no casual act of vandalism, according to the police; it looked like the work of someone who knew how to set a fire. One consequence of it, which seemed to please everyone, was that Harry would not be joining them on location in Italy. He was too busy dealing with the police and the insurance people and the alibis of underworld *slags* who might have done this to him.

Nat walked back up the wooded path to the hotel and found a little gathering of his colleagues on the shaded terrace. The wardrobe lady, Caro, and Joan the make-up girl were swatting some argument around like a shuttlecock while the others half listened. The subject was a notable French couturier – Brochard – and whether he was queer or not. Nat wasn't interested in the person or the question, and sensed that the others weren't either. Sonja was sipping a daiquiri. Gina, in her Lolita sunglasses, was painting her nails. The pretty hairdresser, Helen, and an epicene youth named Aubrey, the set designer, sat slumped in cane chairs, fanning themselves. It was a beautiful slow August afternoon.

He ordered a Martini as the talk droned on. The assembly required a tincture of mischief. He thought of a little game Jimmy Erskine had once taught him: invent a bit of gossip – the more outlandish and indefensible the better – and wait to see how long it takes to boomerang back to you as fact. He cleared his throat.

'I dare say it won't matter to Arthur Brochard soon whether people think he's queer or not.'

Caro, a large, fierce lady whose monologue he had interrupted mid-flow, glared at him. 'What do you mean?'

'Oh, just that he'll have more pressing things on his mind.'

Now the others were looking at him, curious. 'Like what?'

Nat said, with practised nonchalance, 'Well, from what I've heard, Arthur is soon to become' – he lowered his voice – '*Martha*.'

There was a stunned pause, then Caro, chin retracted in an outraged expression of disbelief, said, 'That is quite the most *ridiculous* thing I've ever heard.'

Nat, expecting as much, shrugged his innocence. 'I'm only reporting what was told me, dear. Don't shoot the messenger.'

'Do you mean to say he's having a . . . ?' cooed Helen, goggle-eyed. There was a stifled titter; the others looked at one another, trying to gauge precisely the credence they ought to bestow on this bombshell.

'I believe he has begun the, um, process,' said Nat, managing to command a straight face. There followed some mutterish debate among them as to the relative difficulty of gender-swapping. Easier to go from man to woman, it was agreed, than woman to man, what with the –

'Who told you this?' Caro put in sternly. It wasn't clear to Nat if she resented his being first with the gossip or the high probability that he was spinning them a line.

'A well-connected friend of mine. He knows the surgeon.' He waited a beat, then said, 'Or rather, should I say, *she* knows the surgeon.'

Gina, whose poor hearing Nat could tell had just caught up with the story, drew in her breath sharply. 'You mean you – *no*!'

Nat nodded solemnly, enjoying himself now. He resisted their importuning him for a name, on the grounds he couldn't betray a confidence. Only Caro continued to look unimpressed. Eventually she said, to no one in particular, 'Well, you wouldn't catch me letting someone fiddle with my parts.'

'You wait until you're *arsked*, cheeky,' Nat shot back in his camp voice, and the table collapsed in mirth, apart from Caro who gave a cross little pout and fell silent. Emboldened by the shockwaves his fib had caused, Nat considered his next move. He should try the Garment Game on them.

'Anyone fancy a bit of fun?' he said with a genial grin.

He explained the rules: everyone had to count the number of clothes they were wearing and secretly note it on a piece of paper, which they would hand to the scorer. Items such as a piece of jewellery counted as one, shoes counted as one each, and so on. Everyone would take turns guessing the total number of garments worn by all present. The winner would be the one who scored the highest tally of correct guesses – which of course depended on one's skill at judging who would be wearing underpants, corsets, whatever. Caro didn't want to play, but after some persuasion she agreed to be score master.

'Is a pair of trousers one or two?' asked Helen.

'A nice distinction, my dear,' said Nat. 'Trousers, pants, *bloomers* if you will, count as one.' Pity Alec Madden isn't here, he thought – I could finally determine whether he wears a codpiece or not.

Amid much giggling they settled, each of them turning appraising glances upon their companions, quietly parsing the exact constitution of their outer – and under – wear. He watched Helen lean over to check if he was wearing socks with his loafers. They scribbled their estimates down on paper. Joan was elected to have first go, and went through her guesses with a shy glance at each of them.

'Sonja: ten. Helen: eleven. Aubrey: *really* not sure – eight? Gina: ten. Nat: ooh . . . eleven.'

They each followed. Nat occasionally challenged one of them to explain 'the accounting'. How, for instance, had Helen come to decide that Sonja was sporting only six items? Well, she began, after seeking Sonja's permission ('Don't mind at all, darling'), she had counted her jumpsuit, sunglasses, two sandals, that beaded necklace, and the vintage deco ring on her finger.

'And . . . underwear?' Nat queried.

Helen made a comic face. 'I don't think she's wearing any.'

Even Caro, who'd been sulking, gave a seagull shriek of laughter. At the end of the round she totted up how many correct guesses each had got, without revealing specifics, so that the game could continue. The estimate none of them could seem to agree on was Nat's. Gina counted off his outfit item by item on her fingers, with encouraging nods and *yeah*s from the others.

'Jacket, trousers, shirt, loafers – two, socks – two, belt, ring, wristwatch, undies?' – laughter, again – 'and those very nice sunglasses. I make that twelve.'

After Aubrey, Helen and Joan had dropped out; it left a three-way contest between Gina, Sonja and Nat. Following more revisions and inquisitive stares Nat delivered his final verdict.

'Sonja: seven, I think. *Pace* Helen's surmise of earlier, but intuition tells me that our Miss Zertz *is* wearing knickers.'

Sonja returned a gracious but non-committal nod.

'As for Gina,' he continued, 'let's go again from the top. Sun hat, sunglasses, necklace, bra, top, three rings, trousers – sorry, "palazzo pants" – sandals (two). Which by my count is eleven.'

Aubrey piped up. 'You forgot knickers!'

Nat arched his eyebrows. 'I think not. *Rien ne va plus.*'

A volley of *ooh*s and *aah*s and even *blimey*s burst forth. They all turned to the score master. Caro, having made a great ceremony of tallying the figures, announced, 'I'm afraid, ladies, that Nat here has got you both spot on, but neither of you got his. The correct answer for Nat is *thirteen.*'

'What did we miss?' asked Gina.

'I know!' Joan nearly shouted. 'Look, his hanky!' And indeed there was a silk handkerchief barely peeking above the line of his breast pocket. Nat hadn't even counted that himself, but quickly concealed his mistake. *Well, who cares?* he thought. *I've won!* Exhilarated, he stood, bowed to the table, and summoned the waiter. 'Drinks on me, I think.'

As the afternoon talked itself away the others drifted off to prepare for the evening. Nat walked Sonja and Gina across the hotel courtyard, scented with lemon trees, and up the hushed staircase. Gina was still marvelling at Nat's finesse in what he called *le déshabillage des autres.*

'You're so good at it! How did you know that I wasn't wearing undies?'

Nat chuckled. 'That was more to do with fantasising than anything.'

'Sorry?' said Gina.

'A shot in the dark, my dear,' he said, raising his voice. Sonja, a step behind them, had heard him the first time, and had a query of her own.

'I saw your look of surprise when Joan pointed at your hand-kerchief as the thirteenth item. I have a feeling that was not a thing *you* had counted.'

Nat turned to her. 'I wondered if you'd spotted that. You are a very Poirot of the parlour game!'

They had come to a halt outside his room. He produced the brass key with its shaggy tassle and unlocked his door.

'So what on your person did we miss?' pursued Sonja. 'A surgical truss, perhaps?'

Gina giggled, but Nat, feeling his luck really was in, only said, 'If you'd care to step inside I'll show you.'

They looked at one another and, in silent accord, followed him into his room. Nat pulled the curtains, leaving just a gap for the late Mediterranean light to penetrate, and invited them to help themselves from the drinks bar. He dragged open his suitcase and produced, from beneath a pile of laundered shirts, a whalebone riding crop.

'I think there must be an element of quid pro quo in this transaction.'

Gina, he realised, didn't have the faintest idea what he was talking about, but the veiled look Sonja directed at him suggested she was well up to speed. Without further ado he undid his belt buckle and shucked down his trousers, then his jockey shorts. The silver ring glinted against the dark tangle of his pubic hair. Gina goggled at it; Sonja, with characteristic coolness, took a sip of her drink and said, 'It seems to be responding again.'

Nat looked down; the pain, once engorged, would be exquisite. He carved the air with a triple swish of the crop — Zorro of the boudoir! — and held it out in invitation.

'Ladies?'

Freya, despite having no German, managed to construe most of what was going on in *29 Marks*. It was essentially a chamber piece, four characters playing out a sort of erotic quadrille, the mood crackling with a dark undercurrent of violence. A naive young woman, barely more than a girl, arrives at a stranger's apartment in the city. It seems she has been entrusted to him by friends, on the understanding he will find her a job. The man, suave and droll, welcomes her and they have a few drinks before another man turns up. It gradually becomes apparent that the girl is an unwitting plaything between them: the first man is going to pimp her to the second. This scheme is by degrees sabotaged when an older woman, who knows the pimp, shows up unexpectedly at his flat. A subtly vicious gamesmanship paves the way to a bloody denouement Freya could see coming a mile off.

Veronika was in the lobby to meet her afterwards. She was anxious that her guest had been bored or baffled by the play, but Freya laughed away the suggestion: she'd enjoyed it. The menace of the situation, she said, was highly redolent of a certain British playwright, and, the language barrier aside, she could easily get the sense of what was happening. In any case, the acting was smart enough to make it work in any language. As they were talking, two young men approached: the same ones in Reiner-tribute caps and jackets Freya had seen sneaking in before the house lights went down. Veronika introduced them as Jorge and Karl, both of them film journalists from Berlin. Karl was tall, with unkempt hair and a wispy ginger beard; Jorge was shorter and darker (his mother was Argentinian) and spoke the more confident English. Both had studied in London.

Veronika said, 'Frau Wyley – Freya – is writing a piece about Reiner.' It was odd how everyone referred to him by his first name, thought Freya, as though they knew him. 'So I'm going to show her around his neighbourhood.'

She invited them to tag along, and the four of them set out from the emptying theatre. Since the evening was warm they stopped first at an alehouse with its own *biergarten*, and sat on long wooden benches with their steins. Veronika herself had tottered from the bar with the tray, a duty Freya thought one of the men might have taken up, instead of tacitly conferring responsibility on the notional host of the evening. Jorge offered a satirical 'cheers' as they raised their tankards. Freya couldn't think of the German equivalent – was it *Gesundheit*? They swapped some quick-fire, desultory thoughts on *29 Marks*. The men dismissed it as juvenilia; Freya countered by arguing that juvenilia had its own charm, and in this instance seemed more accomplished than many a playwright's 'mature' work. But Karl, whose shrugs and winces suggested he was hard to please, squashed the argument comprehensively: 'The theatre is boring. It just took Reiner a little time to realise it.' Freya looked at him for a moment, and swallowed her retort with a mouthful of Bavarian ale.

From there they walked on to Reichenbachstrasse, the heart of Reiner's youthful stamping ground. With night descending the yellow glare of the street lamps lent it an air at once forlorn and promisingly sleazy. Women stood in doorways, arms folded, smoking. Men strolled and paused, like shoppers. 'That place,' said Veronika, pointing to a cheap hotel, 'is where Reiner went a lot. It has a bathhouse at the back.'

Freya nodded. 'I was told this might be a good street to buy drugs.'

A disbelieving silence followed. 'You mean heroin?' said Veronika under her breath.

Freya, amused by their horrified looks, said, 'Bit strong for my blood. I meant cannabis – you know, pot.'

Karl, with a laugh, said, 'No problem. We have some already.'

The moment of confusion seemed to break the ice. Veronika, visibly relieved, led them round the corner to a bustling little restaurant with checkerboard tablecloths, chalked menus and a mixed clientele: students, workers, night owls, even a few non-white faces. 'Turks,' she supplied, noticing Freya's interested survey of the room. 'Reiner has always loved this place. He comes back whenever he's in town.'

'Is this where he used to pick up men?' asked Jorge, also looking around.

'Sometimes,' Veronika shrugged, plainly not caring for the question. 'He usually came in late to eat, after he'd been working.'

They studied the menu. Freya, seeking a recommendation, was pointed to *Schweinebraten mit Knoll*. 'That sounds . . . chewy,' she said, hoping it might be something other than sausages.

'Roast pork with dumplings,' Veronika explained.

'Great. I'll have that.'

They ordered more beers, and talked about the festival programme. Jorge and Karl, keen students of Reiner Werther Kloss, had decided opinions on all aspects of the director's output. Both spoke in a proprietorial manner about him, and seemed not to require any contribution from the women. In their critical way they compared notes, offered theories, tested one another on film arcana. Whenever Freya or Veronika ventured an opinion they would silently consider it for a moment, then continue with their own proud line of pedantry.

'That was his first collaboration with Arno Drexler,' said Jorge while they were discussing *Blut und Feuer*.

'Ah, the editor? I was introduced to him,' said Freya, overhearing the name. That stopped them in their tracks. Had she been on the set of *Eureka*? 'Oh no, just on a trip down the Thames last weekend. They were all there.'

Karl, frowning at the implication, said, 'So . . . you have met Reiner?'

Freya nodded. 'Briefly. I can't claim any deep acquaintance – not like Veronika here.' This news seemed to irk them somewhat. It was one thing for Veronika to know Reiner – they were friends from way back – but for an outsider, and a mere hack at that, it amounted to professional one-upmanship.

The roast pork and dumplings were fine, in a stodgy sort of way. Freya had had her fill of beer and switched to vodka. Afterwards they dropped in on a wood-panelled bar up the street, and while Jorge and Karl played the pinball machine she prompted Veronika to talk about Reiner's early years. His parents – did she know? – had died during an Allied air raid on Munich; an entire shelter of civilians incinerated. He had surprised Veronika one evening when he stopped and pointed out the spot where it had happened. 'So he was raised by his grandmother in Bad Wörishofen. A lonely boy, it seems, though he sang in his school choir and played football.'

'My friend Nat told me he's football-mad.'

'Yes, he was star player for the local team, and was hoping for a trial with Bayern. But the manager took against him and didn't let him on the pitch.'

Veronika paused and flicked a glance at Freya, who sensed there was something more to come. 'There was a rumour,' she began cautiously, 'that he took revenge on the manager for this – what do you say? – snub.'

'Oh?'

'A few weeks after Reiner left the club there was a fire in the manager's office. It spread to the clubhouse. The whole place burned down.'

Freya looked at her. 'You don't mean he . . . ?'

Veronika shrugged. 'It was already a fire hazard, they said. But the investigation found that it had been started deliberately.'

'Did you ever ask him?'

'Years later. I thought he'd deny it, but he didn't. The police interviewed him at the time, but nothing came of it.'

A rowdy chorus of drinkers at the next table temporarily silenced them. *Schenkt ein, trinkt aus, schenkt ein, trinkt aus!* A couple of them were wearing Tyrolean felt hats with a feather in the band. Veronika offered a little dumbshow of apology. Jorge and Karl ambled back to the table, finished with their game; there followed some debate as to whether they should stay or go. *Trinkt aus! Trinkt aus! Trinkt aus!* Freya suggested they repair to her room at the Marienbad, where they wouldn't have to make themselves heard above the racket of drinking songs.

On the way back to Maximilianstrasse they passed a group of street musicians playing ragged, oompah-inflected jazz; a little crowd stood to watch. Freya stopped for a moment, reminded of something.

'You like this music?' said Karl, with an ironic twitch of his brow.

'Better than *trinkt aus* back there. I like this fairground thing – makes me think of the new Beatles album, do you know it?'

'The Beatles? Oh no. This is no way like the Beatles!'

'Well, there's a song on *Sgt. Pepper* –'

'No. Lennon and McCartney: genius. These people here: not genius.'

Freya laughed, despite her irritation at his dogmatic tone. 'I wasn't suggesting they were! But the oompah sound, and the waltz time –'

But Karl wasn't having it: her analogy was mistaken, these street players had nothing at all in common with the 'fab four'. Time was, Freya thought, when she would have given this cocky little twerp an argument. She wanted to say he should stop taking himself and his opinions so seriously and listen for a change: discussion didn't always have a right or a wrong, you could throw around a topic from one to another in a playful spirit, like an intellectual game of catch. But having to point out his pernickety dogmatism felt like too much trouble, and might look rather pernickety and dogmatic of *her* in return. Let it go.

Up in the suite she opened the long windows onto the street. Veronika looked bemused by the bottle of Krug, untouched in its bucket.

'The hotel provided this?'

'Apparently,' said Freya, 'it was sent by someone you may know. Sonja Zertz?'

Her eyes widened in surprise. 'A little, of course. You are friends, then?'

Freya shook her head as she picked off the bottle's foil cap. 'Not really. I've met her twice, that's all.'

The cork came off with a bam, and she poured them each a glass. Karl, settling on a sofa, tipped out his bag of pot onto the coffee table. Freya presumed he was going to roll a joint, but instead he took a large wine glass from the drinks trolley and crumbled pot and tobacco into it. He asked Jorge for a match, which he used to ignite the mixture. Then he stretched a piece of tinfoil across the rim of the glass and prodded some holes in the foil.

'Not a trick I've seen before,' said Freya. Karl demonstrated by inhaling the fumes through the perforated foil, and handed it on to her. She gave it a try and sucked one of the smoking holes: the hit scorched down her lungs and ricocheted madly into her brain, almost taking off the top of her scalp. 'Christ,' she croaked, and sank back onto the brocaded cushions. She had to steady herself a moment to stop the room swinging. Soon the air was curtained with the sweetish rubbery fumes of pot. Jorge, disdaining the wine glass, smoked his in a pompous meerschaum pipe that made Freya giggle; he suddenly looked about twenty years older. Veronika declined a smoke, and after finishing her drink rose to leave. She had to get up early to greet a bunch of journalists arriving for the festival.

'But if we have any spare time,' she said to Freya, 'I can show you around the streets where Reiner filmed *Hanna K.*'

266

'I'd like that,' said Freya, showing her out. 'It was nice to meet you. I enjoyed that play, and the pork dumplings.'

At the door Veronika threw a glance over Freya's shoulder: the two men sat slumped in their hallucinating haze. 'Are they . . .' she began, as if about to apologise for landing her with them. But Freya shook her head and said it wasn't a problem.

Later, getting ready for bed, she began laughing to herself. She had seen Jorge and Karl out around half past one, both red-eyed from the smoke. Her voice had gone hoarse as she said goodnight. The strength of the pot had taken them all by surprise, and indeed had almost caused a catastrophe. Having gone off to the loo, she returned to the room to find a scene of surreal comedy. Flames were dancing on the coffee table where the wine glass had fallen, tipping its embers onto a newspaper. Jorge and Karl, recumbent on the sofa, were serenely unconscious. 'Fuck!' she cried, and picking up a cushion beat down the flames as they licked around the wood. The commotion woke them, and they watched bleary-eyed as she extinguished the last of the fire. *Thanks for the help!* she thought sarcastically. Jorge had in fact stood up and hurried over to the champagne bucket, the ice now turned to water. But in his haste to return he stumbled and went flying, the bucket emptying over the carpet.

This pratfall for some reason struck Freya as the funniest thing she had ever seen. 'God, it's the Keystone Kops,' she said, and a giddiness that began in her shoulders rippled through her lungs: once she started laughing she couldn't stop. Karl dozily joined in, then Jorge too, though neither of them quite grasped the dizzying hilarity of the moment as she did. Maybe the hotel would also struggle to see the funny side of a coffee table scorched and blackened.

'I'm afraid I must turn you boys out,' she said after they had cleared up the mess a little. (The battered cushion had split, disgorging feathers over the stricken table.) She packed them off with assurances that they would meet at the festival screening of *Rosa Luxemburg* the next day.

Towards dawn she woke of a sudden, stirred by phantoms in her sleep. She could hear from down below the rattle and hiss of the first trams. Immediately she sat up and scribbled a few words down on a hotel notepad. Clarity had emerged from the muddle of a dream. She would not, after all, be staying in Munich. She would write a note of apology to Veronika, check out of the Marienbad and catch the earliest flight she could back to London. She had had her eureka moment.

INT. VILLA — DAY.
CHAS, *back to camera, at his bedroom window, opened on a view of verdant Italian
countryside, the sea glittering on the
horizon.* But CHAS *is not looking at the
scenery; he is hawkishly watching the distant figures of* JANE *and* GEORGE *as they walk
off towards town. He turns away from the
window.*

INT. VILLA — DAY.
CHAS *is sneaking along a corridor. He stops
outside a room. He senses activity below,
nurses, maids, the hum of the household.
With a furtive glance behind him he opens
the door and slips into the room.*

INT. BEDROOM — DAY.
*From the suit hanging on the door and the
books at his bedside we can tell this is
GEORGE's room.* CHAS *looks around, considering, then goes to the little desk piled
with papers. He quickly looks through them —
but what he seeks isn't there.*

INT. BEDROOM — DAY.

Another angle as CHAS scouts the room, peeking in the wardrobe, checking under the bed. In a drawer he finds a carved Moroccan box. He opens it, finds eight tiny tablets and, after a moment's hesitation, pockets them. He looks around the room, doing a slow 360-degree turn. He guesses that GEORGE will have brought notes on his book about VEREKER - but after their argument he may have taken the precaution of hiding them. CHAS stares at himself in the cheval mirror, pondering; behind his own reflection he looks at the wardrobe again. It's tall, with a fancy cornice running across its top.

INT. BEDROOM — DAY.

CHAS stands up and in a reverse angle we see him approach the wardrobe. He takes a chair and steps onto it, enabling him to sweep his hand along the top of the wardrobe. He stops, feeling something. He lifts up a leather document wallet, the size of a briefcase.

                    CHAS
              (triumphantly)
  Ha!

He steps off the chair, holding the document wallet. He tries the catch: it's locked. He looks around again, in search of a key, but he intuits that GEORGE must have it. He picks up a paper clip from the desk and folds it out. With the wire he tries to

unpick the lock, to no avail. He mutters
an expletive under his breath. The secret,
he is convinced, lies within that wallet.

He stands on the chair and returns the
wallet to its hiding place. Reluctantly he
steps back towards the door, and with
another rueful scan of the room he exits.

INT. LIVING ROOM — DAY.
CHAS *is reading on a sofa when* JANE *enters,
carrying a tray of tea things.*

                    CHAS
  George still out walking?

                    JANE
  Yes. I'm just going up to see Hugh. Will
  you come?

                    CHAS
              (*closing his book*)
  Of course. Here, give me that.

INT. STAIRCASE — DAY.
CHAS, *carrying the tray, follows* JANE *up the
stairs.*

                    CHAS
  How has he been?

                    JANE
  The doctor said he's a little better, but
  still very weak.

INT. BEDROOM — DAY.

A nurse stands as they enter, and whispers
a few words to JANE before leaving the room.
CHAS puts down the tray at the bedside.
VEREKER, head propped against a mound of
pillows, watches him silently. He looks
spectrally pale, though animation lingers
in his gaze. CHAS is clearly shocked by his
physical decline.

                    JANE
                 (brightly)
    Dear heart, how are you? A little better?
    I've brought Charles to see you. He's come
    all the way from London.

VEREKER raises a hand in greeting. He picks
up his notepad and writes a few words in
pencil. JANE takes the pad and reads.

                    JANE
    Hugh asks what you're working on at the
    moment?

                    CHAS
    Um, just the usual, sir. Reviews for the
    Middle, occasional essays . . .

CHAS looks ill at ease. JANE sets about
pouring the tea and helping the patient to
a cup.

                    CHAS
                (trying again)
    I've been rereading some of your books.
    It's strange how different they seem when
    one knows that, well —

272

CHAS *looks to* VEREKER *in the hope of some
sign. Perhaps now, in this twilight hour,
he will disclose the secret of his work.
He waits, but the old man only stares ahead.*

> CHAS
>
> I just wanted to say how much I enjoyed
> them.

CHAS *looks to* JANE, *who smiles and gives
him a nod, as if to say 'you can go now'.
He turns to* VEREKER *and gives an awkward
little bow, then leaves the room.*

INT. LIVING ROOM — DAY.
JANE *returns from* VEREKER's *room. It is now
late afternoon.* CHAS *is mooching by the
French windows, and turns an enquiring look
as she approaches.*

> JANE
>
> He's sleeping. I wish — I wish there was
> something more I could do.

> CHAS
>
> You're doing as much as any friend could.

JANE *shudders, and bows her head. When she
looks up again her face is a mask of tears.*
CHAS *walks over and puts his arms around
her, an embrace she welcomes desperately.*

> JANE
>
> Oh, Chas, I can't bear it. I feel so . . .
> helpless.

CHAS

There. You mustn't upset yourself. (*He looks at her in a searching way.*) You look done in. Sit down and I'll get you a drink.

INT. KITCHEN — DAY.
CHAS *fills two tumblers with ice, slices a lemon and pours out gin and tonic. He pauses, his expression first thoughtful, then crafty. He puts the drinks on a tray and carries them out.*

INT. LIVING ROOM — DAY.
CHAS *and* JANE *are sitting together on the sofa. They are on to a second round of drinks.* JANE *has recovered from her crying jag, and looks fondly at* CHAS.

JANE

I'm so glad you're here.

CHAS

Good . . . D'you think Hugh was pleased to see me?

JANE

I'm sure he was.

CHAS

Of course, now isn't the right time to talk about it, but somewhere down the line I suppose you'll have to make a decision about his literary executor.

JANE
(*nodding*)
Hugh and I have already talked about it.

                    CHAS
Oh . . . Does he have someone in mind?

                    JANE
He favours George, I think. I gather they
had talks together - about his work.

                    CHAS
I see.

                    JANE
You don't think that's a good idea?

                    CHAS
                 (*frowning*)
Oh, George is very capable. But I wouldn't
say he's the ideal candidate. There are
others . . . better qualified.

                    JANE
Really? Who?

                    CHAS
           (*with a modest chuckle*)
It hardly becomes me to say so, but . . .

                    JANE
You? Oh, I didn't -

                    CHAS
I think I'm pretty well placed. I know the
work inside out. Hugh seems to respect me.

                    JANE
Even though he was rude about that review
of yours?

CHAS

I don't hold that against him. Perhaps, if
the subject came up, you might –

JANE
(*doubtfully*)
If you really want me to, I will. But
he'll make up his own mind in the end.

CHAS

Of course, of course. I'd just like him
to know that, as his devoted reader and
admirer, I'm available.

JANE *takes a sip of her drink, and gives
him an earnest look. Then* CHAS *becomes
conspiratorial.*

CHAS

One other thing. Let's keep this between
us. If George finds out we've spoken about
this it will only make things awkward.

CHAS *directs a tight little smile at* JANE.

15

Midway through the shoot in Portofino two latecomers arrived, separately, at the unit's hotel. The first of them was sitting on his own in the lobby when Billie happened to be passing through one evening. Vere Summerhill, in a crumpled linen suit, hadn't noticed her, and in the circumstances Billie would rather have avoided him until they had to meet on set. They hadn't spoken since the day he had bawled her out of his dressing room. And yet the sight of him looking so fragile plucked at her heart. His face was pale, a mask of pure exhaustion.

'Vere?'

He looked up, a distance in his eyes. Then his smile came, and he struggled to his feet. 'My dear. How nice –'

'How are you?' she said, keeping her voice light. They kissed, and she could hear the effort of his breathing. 'You look rather tired.' She had stopped herself saying 'ill'.

He dipped his head in admission. 'I'm not quite the traveller I was. The plane, the drive, takes it out of an old fellow.'

'You're not old,' she said, determined to gee him up. It seemed the staff were still preparing his room, so Billie suggested they had a drink while he waited. Vere took her arm as she led the way. Since when had he been walking with a stick?

They settled on padded stools in the expensive gloom of the hotel bar. She had a Campari; Vere wanted only a tonic water. He asked her how she was liking Portofino – it was a place he'd visited in his younger days – and what the mood had been on set. He would have travelled with the rest of them had he not been obliged to arrange some personal business in London: a meeting with his solicitor, certain other duties. He was vague, and she sensed he didn't want to go into it. 'How's Nat?' he asked eventually.

'He's been the life and soul. He introduced this game – I wasn't there, I'm afraid – where you have to guess how many clothes everyone around the table is wearing. He won, easily. Do you think Nat has a bit of a thing about underwear?'

Vere smiled fondly. 'To put it mildly. He's been getting people to play that game since I first met him God knows how many years ago.' He paused, and caught her eye. 'As a matter of fact Nat and I spoke recently. He wanted me to come on the Thames trip.'

'Yes, I was sorry not to see you there,' Billie put in.

'I couldn't go, though I heard all about it, of course. Up in flames! But that wasn't what I wanted to . . .' He shifted in his seat, frowning. 'He – Nat – reminded me of a grave discourtesy I did you, a few weeks ago, I think you –'

'Oh, no, it's fine,' she said, embarrassed, but secretly glad that he had acknowledged it. Vere was shaking his head.

'No, my dear, it was *not* fine. I was rude to you, and I am very sorry for it.' He had taken a light hold of her hand. 'I can only say in my defence that I'd been, that day, distracted by a bit of bad news. But that's no excuse.'

'Bad news?' she said, leaning towards him.

'Oh, just an adverse reaction to some medicine. A nuisance. I was in a bloody mood.' Now he gave her hand a little squeeze. 'You forgive me?'

'Vere, *of course* I do. I just want to know that you're all right.'

He waved away her concern: it was nothing, a bore. The doctor had warned him he should 'take it easy' and not put himself under a strain. 'I told him, quite truthfully, that my scenes would involve merely lying in a bed; poor old Vereker breathing his last. He seemed to think I was being macabre!'

He had spoken in an amused way, yet Billie felt something ominous in his words. She wondered if he really might be ailing. But Vere had already changed the subject; having deflected her solicitude over his health he was asking her about life at home. She had a boyfriend, didn't she? Billie nodded, and sensed his curiosity. He's an artist, she said, they'd been living together for a while –

'Is he nice?' Vere suddenly asked, and when he saw her hesitate he rephrased the question: 'I mean, is he worthy of *you*?'

The tenderness of the question, and the catch in his voice, took her aback. She couldn't think of another person who might have asked her such a thing, apart from her mother, and Tash. She had to take a swig of her Campari to help blink away the salt-watering in her eyes.

'Actually I'm having a break from him at the moment. I'm back at my mum's.'

Vere looked at her, and nodded, as if to say he would not pursue it any further, and she was grateful. A few minutes later they heard voices from outside and Nat walked in with Sonja and Gina, all of them looking somewhat exhilarated. They were delighted to have Vere among them at last; Nat behaved towards him with particular warmth, Billie thought, like a son fondly reuniting with his old dad. But Vere was not slow to tease him.

'Have we a finished script yet?'

Nat returned a wry smile. 'Almost.'

'This must be the longest gestation of any literary enterprise since Casaubon was at work.'

'Who's he?' asked Billie.

'A sad scholar – in a novel,' said Vere. 'The Reverend Casaubon has spent most of his life compiling what he imagines to be his great work, "The Key to All Mythologies". Day and night he labours on it, neglecting all around him, including the young and virtuous wife who believes him to be a genius. She wants to help him, but he is beyond help. Life passes him by, love passes him by, until the fateful day his wife happens to glimpse a few pages of the monumental opus he has been scratching away at. She realises, to her horror, that Casaubon is no genius; he is in fact a deluded, dried-up, talentless old pedant. What's more, she now knows what he knows: that he will never finish it.'

'That's a sad story,' said Billie, her eyes cast down.

'Indeed. There's a warning there.'

After a pause, Sonja said, 'So what happens to this fellow?'

'What happens? Oh, he dies.' Vere chuckled and gave a tiny shrug.

Nat, who felt a pointed thrust in the story, said, 'You're right, there *is* a warning in Casaubon. But I'm writing a screenplay, not some musty old treatise nobody cares a rap about. I've got one little problem to unknot, then we should be home and dry.'

'Hooray,' cried Gina, who understood at least that note of resolve, if not much else. 'Let's have a drink, Nat. I'm parched!'

While the others chatted, Nat waited at the bar to be served. His 'little problem' was preoccupying him. It came down to this: Chas takes acid for the first time, hoping it will enable him, like George, to discern 'the figure in the carpet'. Of course one had to wonder whether anyone, in the history of scholarship, had taken acid to help solve a literary puzzle. Yet Chas by this stage is desperate enough to try anything. What the scene had to convey was the hallucinatory dazzle of his trip; it had to be something 'far out', as the hippies would say. The doors of perception would crack open fleetingly, offering a shaft of light, then close again before Chas could make sense of it. But by what *visual* means could the elusive moment be expressed?

In the meantime the barman had tilted his head enquiringly. *'Allora, signor.'* It could wait till tomorrow, Nat thought. This was cocktail hour.

Early next morning Billie got up for a swim. The sun was just peeping above the cliffs, and the pearly Mediterranean light had yet to soften, as it would later in the heat. There were not many others around the pool. A German couple were stretched on the loungers; two Italian teens were gabbing away in the corner; the pool boy was diligently dragging the blue lengths with his long-handled net. There was one other she hadn't seen before, a young man, alone, his dark suit and tanless complexion indicating his recent arrival. The *Mirror* he was absorbed in baldly announced his place of origin.

Billie, in her plum-coloured one-piece, gingerly lowered herself into the water, gasping at the shock of the cold. She swam four lengths of crawl very quickly to warm herself up. As she floated on her back she had the impression of the newcomer watching her, though it was hard to be certain given the beetle-black sunglasses shielding his eyes. The man was still going through his *Mirror*, methodically, licking a thumb to flick back each page. She turned and swam on, her thoughts immersed in the fabulous time they'd had last night at the bar, Nat being hilarious and showing off in front of her and Sonja and Gina. His charm had even drawn out

Vere from his shell. *Is he worthy of you?* That's what Vere had said to her, a question that was really a compliment. She had never been sure if he had much liked her before, if his courtesy towards her was merely a reflex of his actorly, old-world manners. She had thought him too grand to be concerned with a fledgling like herself. But that question had changed everything: it sounded like he'd meant it.

She climbed out of the pool and settled herself, dripping, on a lounger; she chose the next but one to the *Mirror* man; sociable, but keeping a distance. It was nothing to her whether he said hello or not. Closer up he looked rather fly; his suit was narrow and sharply tailored, the tie at his throat raffishly loosened. His watch, on a steel bracelet, looked expensive. His dark hair was cut close and brushed forward. He had just removed his shoes and socks and laid them side by side, a concession to the holiday mood. When he looked up he caught her staring at him.

'Didn't bring the right clobber for this,' he said with an apologetic nod to their surroundings.

Billie said, 'It's usually quite hot, you know, this time of year.'

'Yeah,' he said, 'shoulda thought. My old dad was here now he'd tie a little 'anky round his head.' He laughed, revealing very white, long teeth.

He introduced himself as Joey Meres. His accent was smartened-up cockney. Billie hoped he would take his sunglasses off so she could see his eyes – from the eyes you could tell whether it was someone you were going to like or not. When he stood up to move to the lounger next to hers she made a quick inventory of him; medium height, lean, with a sporty carriage: an athlete, perhaps? From his shirt pocket he took a pack of cigarettes – Piccadilly – and offered her one. His goldish lighter sprouted a neat bud of flame. Now as he leaned towards her she could see for the first time a pale scar curving from his cheekbone to his jaw. Had he noticed her noticing it?

She smiled quickly and said, 'So you're here on business?'

'Yeah. That's prob'ly why I didn't think to bring, you know, swimmin' cozzie. Bucket and spade.' He was looking at her appraisingly. 'What about you? No, let me guess what you do.'

Billie smiled at him. 'All right. Twenty questions.'

'Does your job involve physical exercise?'

'Yes.'

'So you have to keep fit?'

'Yes.'

'Are you a PE teacher?'

She laughed. 'No! Do I look like one?'

'Not really,' said Joey, his smile revealing incisors like a baby shark's. 'You swim like one, though.'

'You've had three questions.'

'Hmm. Does your job involve wearing clothes?'

'Doesn't everyone's job involve wearing clothes?'

'You know what I mean. Are you a model, like, for a magazine?'

'No. But that's a bit more flattering than PE teacher.'

'Do you work in *h'artistic circles*?'

'Yes.'

'Are you a costume designer?'

'No.'

'Do you work with cameras?'

'Yes.'

'Ah. Are you a photographer?'

'No.'

'No?' He squinted at her in bemusement, nodding at the little camera he could see in her beach bag. 'Coulda sworn that was it.'

''Fraid not.'

'Then . . . are you with the film crew?'

'Yes. How did you know that?'

'I'm asking the questions.' His expression turned crafty. 'Do you pretend to be someone you're not?'

'Yes!' And now they both laughed.

'Bloody actress, aren't yer?'

She spread her hands in admission. 'So how *do* you know about the film crew? Are you in the business?'

Joey looked sly. 'Not the sort you mean. I look after certain interests of a gentleman you may have heard of. Harold Pulver.'

'Oh yeah. I was at a party on his boat the other day. Do they know who's . . .'

He shook his head. 'Not yet. "The investigation continues."'

'So what are you doing here?'

'You know – keep an eye on things.'

The drowsy calm was shattered by a splash at the other end of the pool: the Italian kids were cooling off. The sun had just got a little fiercer. Joey stood up and opened the white canvas parasol, creating a billow of gloom overhead. He asked Billie if the shade was to her liking, and she nodded. His expression had turned thoughtful.

'So this film,' he began, 'what's it about?'

Billie considered for a moment. 'Well, it's a love story. Two friends fall for the same woman. She's engaged to one, but she's having an affair with the other. But what the men actually fall out over is a famous writer they both admire. There's a kind of secret involved in this writer's work that's never come out. Eventually one of them cracks the secret, but he won't tell his friend what it is.'

Joey stared at her, waiting. 'Is that it?'

'More or less.'

'What 'appens in the end?'

'I don't know, to be honest. Nobody's read the full script – it's not finished.'

He gave a *pfff* of disdain. 'Call that a story?'

'Maybe you should wait till you see it.'

'I know them sort of films. They're foreign, they come with lotsa moody shots of corridors and go on for hours. Prob'ly in black and white.'

Billie shook her head. 'Colour. And it's not so dull as all that. There's sex and drugs in it.'

'Any fights?'

She hesitated, and he laughed at his question being taken seriously. Billie's gaze was distracted by a figure approaching from the far end. She gave him a wave and Nat waved back. He had spied her a while ago, and wondered about the stranger she was talking to – possibly the hotel concierge, though as he got nearer he saw the man's sinewy paleness, and his rather cocksure stance. The suit was nicely cut, slim silhouette, no turn-ups on the trousers. You could tell it wasn't Cecil Gee or Burton. It was coming to something when even the louts could afford handmade.

'Here's someone who could explain it better than me,' said Billie.

'Explain what?' asked Nat.

'The film,' she said. 'This feller would like to know what it's about.'

Nat, cutting a glance at him, gave an exaggerated shrug and cleared his throat. 'It's "about" all manner of things: ambition, envy, competitiveness, altered states, enlightenment, despair, death. It is about secrets and the value of keeping secrets. And it is about the mysterious power of art – is the *meaning* in a work of art as important as its overall *effect*?'

Joey, his expression unreadable behind his sunglasses, turned to Billie. 'You sure this film isn't in black and white?'

Nat, stung by this insolence, was weighing up a tart riposte when Joey bared his long white teeth in a smile of savage amiability. 'Joey Meres,' he said, thrusting out his hand.

'Nat Fane,' he replied. Joey looked at him harder.

'The writer, yeah?'

'I am,' he said, his pride restored.

'You had that spot of bother with Harry. How's the nose?'

Nat, bristling again, said, 'It's fine. How do you know? Are you a friend of Harry's?'

'Not exactly. Business associate. His eyes and ears, you might say.'

Nat recoiled inwardly. The palmy bliss of his Mediterranean idyll had just felt a stiffening gust. 'Welcome aboard,' he said, trying to keep his voice steady. He listened to their chat for a few minutes before taking a strategic glance at his watch. 'Will you excuse me? There's something I've just remembered I must do.'

Nat walked off, and once out of sight around the corner he quickened his step. He made first for Gina's bedroom, where his knock received no reply. He checked the bar and the terrace garden, but she wasn't there either. He checked the main filming suite, where they had closed the set for Chas's dream sequence: two hours of Sonja 'in the nod', as Ronnie had leeringly put it. Think, think. Back in the lobby he ran into Julie the script girl, who reckoned she might be up at the tennis court. Following the sound of the ball – *thock! thock!* – Nat sweated his way up a gravel path

284

to the court, the sawing of cicadas maddening in his ear. The court's asphalt surface glowed an arsenic green. There was Gina – hair up, racket in a twin-fisted hold – locked in a tense rally with Helen, the assistant hairdresser.

He watched them for a while; when a wild shot flew over the fence and brought them to a halt, Nat called out to her. Gina, beaded with sweat, bounded over to greet him through the chain-link. The shortness of her tennis skirt, of all her skirts, irresistibly pulled Nat's gaze downwards. It was his recent and intimate proximity to the area beneath the skirt that now concerned him.

'Hello, darling,' she said, catching her breath. 'Fancy a game?'

Nat smiled tightly. 'May I have a word? Just the two of us.' He saw Helen approaching from the corner of his eye. Gina beamed, and turned to her partner.

'Helen, can we have a quick break?'

They walked round to the furthest corner of the court, the latticed fence still separating them. Gina chatted and practised her strokes as she went, plainly oblivious of any danger in the offing. Nat half listened to some funny story she wanted to tell him, then gave her a level stare.

'Do you know someone called Joey Meres?'

Gina frowned a moment. 'Joey? Of course. He's one of Harry's boys.'

'Well, he's here.'

'What, in the hotel? What's he doing here?'

'At present he's chatting up Billie by the pool. *Why* he's here – that's what worries me. What kind of work does he do for Harry?'

'Oh, you know . . . collecting debts, sorting people out, keeping Harry informed. He does a bit of everything.'

' "Sorting people out." You mean, beating them up? Putting them in hospital?'

'I do know he's been in prison.'

I'm a dead man, thought Nat. 'You realise that if Harry gets wind of what we've been up to –'

'No, no,' said Gina. 'Joey's not here to spy on you – on us.'

'I wouldn't be so sure. Film sets are notorious; everyone knows they're just mobile knocking shops.'

'Sorry?'

'Harry's sent him here for a reason, Gina.'

'Well, yeah. But not for that. Harry would never suspect *you*.'

Nat paused: her emphasis on that last word was too decided to ignore. 'Why would he not suspect me?'

Gina's gaze shifted away, and she gave her mouth a doubtful tweak. 'Same reason no one else would – he thinks you're queer.'

They were fixing the boom above Hugh Vereker's bed for the scene with Chas. The night before, Nat and Reiner had had a long discussion with Vere in his suite. They had somehow managed to keep the truth of Vere's illness a secret between them. The story presented to the unit was that he had been unwell from a gastric condition but was now recovering; nobody seemed to doubt it. The director had treated his stricken actor with a notable delicacy of feeling. Berk himself had been kept in the dark, though he had taken Nat aside on the night Vere arrived at the hotel to pour out his worries about the old man. 'Reminds me of my grandpa,' he'd muttered, 'after they'd laid him out.'

As he and Reiner had talked through the scene Vere listened intently, offering a suggestion as to how this or that line might work best. By the end of the evening they had it more or less down. Vere had drily remarked that a deathbed scene in his present state should be no great test of his talent. Nat had felt another surge of love for his old friend, who had already sacrificed himself in making the trip from London. Now he had gone one better: with death looming at his shoulder he had even found a way to make them laugh.

In the morning, he appeared on set looking dreadful. He had slept badly, it seemed, though that would hardly account for the hacking cough or the grey pallor of his skin. Nat overheard Reiner asking him if he wished to postpone the filming – they could juggle the schedule. But Vere insisted they went ahead. He was determined not to let anyone down. Ronnie Stiles, wearing the square 'librarian' spectacles that so suited him as Chas, had stolen up quietly behind Nat as they waited for the camera to roll.

'How's yer bum for love bites?' he said with a smirk.

For a heart-stopping moment Nat imagined that Ronnie had got wind of his recent adventure with Gina and Sonja, but it soon became apparent that this was merely another of his uncouth salutations.

'Fine, when I last looked,' he replied. 'Are you ready for your big scene?'

Ronnie just laughed. He had the impregnable self-confidence of the unreflective. He looked around the set, where they were still rigging the lights. Vere, in a cotton nightgown, was seated on his own, smoking.

'Gotta hand it to them make-up girls,' Ronnie said under his breath to Nat. 'Anyone lookin' at him would think he was dead already!'

The following evening the whole unit got together for dinner. Most of the Portofino sequences were done, and a skeleton crew would be leaving in a couple of days for a week's shoot in Rome. The rest of them would be going back to London. Billie felt a weird relief that it was nearly over. On the one hand she'd loved the hotel, the weather had been super and they'd had some laughs. On the other, she felt harrowed by Vere's frailty – clearly, he was far from well – and discomfited by the odd atmosphere that had trailed Joey Meres onto the set. Though she rather liked him, he was regarded with suspicion by most of the crew, who knew him to be a 'face' around London. The toothy grin, which ought to have tempered his saturnine menace, served only to compound it.

At the dinner Joey was seated next to Gina, the only one who seemed at ease in his company. Even Berk, on his other side, looked like a man who'd just noticed a scorpion in the soup tureen. But the room eventually relaxed under the influence of the wine and the occasion; their ten days at the hotel were nearly up, and the awareness of their imminent dispersal whipped up a sentimental mood. Toasts and bibulous avowals of companionship were made. Berk paid a tearful tribute to Reiner, and another, longer one to Vere, whom he called the finest British actor of the last thirty years, an accolade Nat had previously heard him apply to Olivier, Gielgud and James Mason. Vere accepted the compliment with a grave bow.

Later, one of the crew took over the piano, and Nat announced the start of party pieces. Caro kicked them off with 'Puppet on a

String'; Berk sang 'Luck Be a Lady', shaking imaginary dice in his chubby fist; Ronnie and Alec Madden did a scene from *Double Indemnity* (Ronnie, in a wig, played Barbara Stanwyck, bringing the house down); Billie sang 'Norwegian Wood' and then harmonised with Helen on 'Baby's in Black'. When Vere was begged for a turn he shook his head, and Nat, coming to his rescue, performed a little monologue Vere had made famous in one of his 1930s romances.

The surprise of the evening came late on. Nat had thought Sonja might refuse the call – for an actress she could be curiously shy of the spotlight – but when Reiner whispered something in her ear she gave a reluctant laugh and rose from the table.

'I have been asked to do this very sad song.'

She had a quiet word with the pianist before beginning. It was from a Brecht–Weill opera, she explained, about a woman who had staked her life on the love of a man, and was then betrayed. Halfway through the song Sonja stopped abruptly; up to that moment she had held herself quite still, caressing the words. When she resumed, she sang in English.

Surabaya Johnny, no one's meaner than you.
Surabaya Johnny – my God and I still love you.

At a nod from her the pianist picked up the rhythm, his choppy, bar-room chords pushing it onwards. Sonja herself seemed to have flicked some internal switch; an electric charge crackled off her. She stalked around the room, vamping, declaiming, imploring, upbraiding the mysterious 'Johnny'. As the song slowed and built to its climax she circled Joey Meres, once, twice, then grabbed his tie and leaned in to his face. Her eyes burned with accusation.

You wanted it all, Johnny,
I gave you more, Johnny.
Take that damn pipe out of your mouth, you rat.

The whole room seemed to be ravished by her performance. It was as if the song had been written not only for her, but about her. Sonja let Joey's tie drop, faced the room, and bowed. A stunned pause held for a moment. The first to start clapping was Joey, who looked tickled to death at his impromptu part in the proceedings. He rose, and with a gallant flourish took Sonja's hand and kissed it. The room went up in a roar of whistles and cheers.

Nat awoke from a dream the next morning and hauled himself out of bed. He dressed quickly, and without stopping for breakfast walked down to the harbour. He went into a gaudy little shop selling beach gear, Ambre Solaire, tourist tat, and found what he was looking for within half a minute. He hurried back to the hotel still gingerly holding on to the dream, half afraid he might jolt himself and accidentally tip the image out of his head. He and Reiner had talked about 'Chas's trip' over and over without getting anywhere. Now he snatched up a sheet of hotel notepaper and wrote it out in ten minutes.

He made his way up to the roof terrace, where they were preparing for the last day of photography. Reiner had just blocked a scene between Alec Madden and Ronnie, charting the wrangle between Chas and George over Vereker's estate. Nat suffered a little wobble of insecurity as he stepped around crew people and over a writhing sea of cables and leads. The idea had come to him in a flash, and might be the sort of thing that would wither and die under the cold scrutiny of anyone else. Except that Reiner was not like anyone else; he delighted in the odd and the unexpected, and trusted Nat as a connoisseur of the same.

He looked up at his approach. 'What's that?'

'Got it down at the harbour,' replied Nat, holding a red hula hoop, like the one he'd seen the girl playing with on his first day in Portofino. The memory of her performance had resurfaced in his sleep. 'I think I've got it – Chas's trip, part two of the Henry James acid experience. And this time we don't have to nick from the Beatles.'

EXT. A ROOF TERRACE — DAY.
A blinding sun creates a shimmer around the walls. A silhouetted figure, blurred at

first, seems to be dancing. Close-up on a woman, in a bikini, languidly revolving a hula hoop around her midriff. The sun at her back makes it difficult to identify her, but in fleeting moments the woman's face is visible: it is GWEN. She is seen from multiple angles, while a long jazz intro resolves itself into a version of 'My Favourite Things'.

Then, in flash cuts, another figure appears at the corner of the screen. A man, in a patterned shirt and white trousers, watches GWEN rolling the hoop around her. We see the reflection of the woman in the man's sunglasses. Is the man CHAS? It looks like him, but it could be a stranger who resembles CHAS. We see him edging closer to the woman, who continues her twirling, oblivious. The man, entranced by the spectacle, finally reaches out to touch her. As he does so the sun goes into eclipse, and all is dark. When the light returns the man is in a daze, wondering what has just happened: the woman is gone. Bemused, he turns to go, then spots the hula hoop lying on the ground where she stood.

He picks it up, flips it over himself as if to check something. Then he walks away, the melody of 'My Favourite Things' fading into the air.

*

Reiner filmed Sonja's twirling with multiple cameras, all running at different frame rates to capture her movement from slow to fast and back to slow. The sun, vital to the sequence, never wavered, and neither did Sonja, who did take after take, uncomplaining. The trouble had come from another direction. Reiner, inspired by a detail in Nat's script – that the man watching Gwen may or may not be Chas – decided someone else should stand in for Ronnie Stiles.

'But I'm Chas,' said Ronnie. 'He's me.'

'Ah, but, Ronnie, you must remember this is a trip, and under such an influence we are strangers to ourselves. Chas is at once himself and not himself, and to express this ambiguity we need a double – a *Doppelgänger*, you know the word?'

'No I bloody don't,' snapped Ronnie. He stood with hands on hips, glaring at Reiner. 'This ain't on. You just wanna wind me up.'

But Reiner shook his head. 'No. I want only to make this scene the best it can be.' He looked around at the others, as though calling them to witness. 'Our passion is our task.'

Ronnie, snorting at this gnomic phrase, turned on his heel and stalked off, muttering something about lawyers. Reiner, oblivious, scratched his beard and seemed to commune with himself. What he did next nobody could have predicted. Nat watched as he strolled to the edge of the terrace where Joey Meres was leaning against a wall, smoking. He still wore a dark suit, white shirt and black tie; only his aviator sunglasses suggested he might not be an undertaker. They talked in low voices for a few moments; at one point Joey plucked at his tie, as though Reiner had asked about it. He shrugged a little, apparently amused, and then followed the director back to his high chair.

'Mr Meres,' said Reiner, 'has graciously agreed to stand in for the scene.' A short ironic cheer went up, and Joey, smiling, gave his neck a quick sideways twist, like a boxer limbering up.

'S'long as I don't have to learn any lines,' said Joey.

'It is a scene entirely without dialogue. I want you only to gaze, to ravish your eyes upon this lovely creature.'

Joey shot a sidelong glance at Sonja, arms folded, in her black bikini. 'I think I can manage that.'

Reiner took another appraising look at Joey. 'It is a pity Ronnie left so suddenly. We could have borrowed his shirt. On second thoughts, perhaps what you're wearing already is the thing. No dress code for a hallucination.' He looked around at the bemused faces of his crew. 'Camera!'

It had just gone five when Reiner decided that he'd got what he wanted and called it a day. The sun was shrinking to a distant fireball on the horizon. Someone suggested a farewell drink to Portofino, and gradually they drifted away in twos and threes down to the harbour. In the crowded bar where they gathered Nat found himself chatting to Joey, his neck pink from sunburn. He was actually quite a good egg once you unpeeled the hard shell. His father had been a barber when they lived near King's Cross; his mum was a char. Joey had got a place at the local grammar school, but he'd been too keen on sport to bother with studying. Billie, overhearing, asked him where they had lived in King's Cross.

'Just off the Gray's Inn Road. Swinton Street.'

'Oh! I live on Frederick Street,' said Billie.

Joey nodded. 'Ha. We used to have fights with the kids on Frederick Street.'

'Bare-knuckle?' asked Nat, arching an eyebrow.

'We couldn't afford no gloves. Though I did some boxing in me time. That's how I got to know Harry and his mob – sparrin' down the Old Kent Road.'

Nat wondered if he'd drunk enough to dare a question – the question he'd wanted to ask Joey from the off. Sometimes you just had to plunge in. 'And your duelling scar – from Heidelberg?'

He quailed on noticing Billie widen her eyes in alarm, but Joey gave no sign of being affronted. He looked, if anything, a bit shy. 'I ain't been to Heidelberg, or to a duel.'

Sonja, who had also been listening, said, 'How then?'

Joey blew out his cheeks. ''Bout six years ago, I suppose, I was comin' up the escalator from Angel Tube, broad daylight. I saw this feller standing at the top, and thought, aye aye. But I didn't notice the one behind me. I'd just reached the top when he pulls my jacket halfway down my back – pinions my arms, right? The other one comes at me . . . all I remember is a flash of his hand and then a sort of . . . wet. It was only later I realised he'd tooled me down the cheek. I was lucky, really.'

'Lucky?' said Billie, aghast.

'Yeah, I mean, at least he knew about usin' a cut-throat. You go across the face, see, you might sever an artery.'

There was a brief appalled silence at the table. Nat swallowed and said, 'But who would have . . . and why?'

Joey squinted into the distance. 'Never sure who. Someone from a firm south of the river. One of Harry's rivals. All I remember 'bout the geezer was what he said as he walked off. "Nothing personal, mate." I never supposed it was.'

Sonja said, 'You are very philosophical.'

He took a drag of his cigarette. 'Dunno about that. Unless "an eye for an eye" is philosophical.' He laughed.

'You mean, you . . .'

'Well, you can't let a thing like that slide.'

He seemed to become abruptly aware of his audience – Nat, Sonja, Billie – staring at him, absorbing the implication. 'Maybe I shouldn'ta told you that.'

The next morning Nat woke with a crucifying hangover. They hadn't left the bar until two – he barely recalled staggering up to bed. The last thing he had done was burn his lungs on a giant spliff Reiner had handed him. As he was packing his suitcase he realised he must have left his camera at the bar: he'd been snapping away while the roistering among the crew got louder and beerier.

At the bar he found a waiter mopping the floor, and asked in his halting Italian whether a camera had been handed in the night before. Of course it hadn't. The man returned a high-shouldered shrug that mingled expansive measures of pity and resignation: '*Mi dispiace.*' His own fault; he should have been more careful. Some light-fingered local would now be enjoying the benefit of his long-lensed Nikon F. 'Thievin' wops,' remarked Ronnie Stiles on hearing of the loss. On the drive to the airport Nat wondered what the thief would make of the photographs Sonja had taken of Gina and himself in his bedroom. Pity – he'd have liked them as a memento of their stay.

Next to him on the coach sat Julie the script girl, who gave him a confidential nudge.

'You'll never believe what I've just heard,' she said, smirking. Nat inclined his head to listen.

'You know the French designer, Arthur Brochard?' she continued, dropping her voice to an undertone. 'Apparently, he's having a *sex change.*'

Nat bugged his eyes just so. 'No! Where *on earth* did you get hold of that?'

EXT. COURTYARD — DAY.
CHAS *comes down to find* JANE *with* GEORGE *and a young woman he recognises. Her suit-case indicates she has recently arrived.*

                    JANE
  Chas, this is Maud. I think you met one
  another at Bridges.

                    CHAS
  Hello. You came by the ferry?

                    MAUD
  Yes. George picked me up at the harbour.
  (*Turns to* JANE.) You look tired, darling.

                    JANE
  Oh, I'm fine. And I'm very glad to see
  you. Let me show you to your room.

JANE *and* MAUD *exit.* CHAS *and* GEORGE *are left together, looking sheepish.*

                   GEORGE
  Look, Chas . . . I'm sorry about the other
  day. I know how it must seem, but this
  book - it's consumed me.

                         CHAS
No, no, I'm the one who should be sorry.
That little outburst of mine was unforgiv-
able. I lost my head! Friends?

CHAS *extends his hand hopefully, and* GEORGE
takes it.

                         GEORGE
Friends.

A *short embarrassed silence intervenes.*

                         GEORGE
By the way, if you've got anything valu-
able here, I'd advise you to put it in
Jane's safe.

                         CHAS
What do you mean?

                         GEORGE
Well, I can't be certain, but I've a suspicion one of the maids has been rifling
through my stuff.

                         CHAS
Has something gone missing?

                         GEORGE
Nothing valuable. (*He looks around shiftily,
lowers his voice.*) I have a stash of - you
know? Someone's been at it, I'm sure.

                         CHAS
That's worrying . . .

                         GEORGE
I know. Wonder if they 'drop out' while
they're doing the housework?

                          CHAS
You'll probably be able to tell. Come back
to your room and find the bed's been used
as a trampoline . . . or they've taken down
the curtains and turned them into bell-
bottoms.

                         GEORGE
                       (*laughing*)
Yeah. If it is one of them they'd better
be careful. That stuff is really strong.

CHAS *nods,   and   glances   at   GEORGE,
appraisingly.*

INT. VEREKER'S BEDROOM — NIGHT.
CHAS *knocks at the door, and the* NURSE
answers it. He lingers on the threshold.

                          CHAS
I wondered if you needed a break. I'd be
happy to -

                         NURSE
                (*glancing at the patient*)
Well, I'm not sure . . . Perhaps for twenty
minutes?

*She nods, half grateful, and exits the room.
It is dimly lit, and* CHAS's *shadow as he
enters looms on the wall. There is something faintly predatory in his movement as
he approaches* VEREKER *and takes the seat*

at his bedside. The patient is propped up on pillows, asleep, so CHAS, *with a guilty look over his shoulder, clears his throat.*

> CHAS
>
> Mr Vereker? (*He leans in, and raises his voice.*) Hugh?

VEREKER's *eyes flicker open. For a few moments he looks disorientated, and seems not to know* CHAS. *Then his gaze focuses, and by the merest twitch of his mouth he seems to greet his visitor.*

> CHAS
>
> Good evening, sir. I've just come to say – to see how you are. Is there anything you need?

A pause, while he waits for a reply. VEREKER *makes no movement, but continues to study him.* CHAS, *nervous, looks to the door again before resuming.*

> CHAS
>
> To speak truthfully, I was hoping to ask you a great favour. I wouldn't do this in normal circumstances, but – well, I imagine you know what it is. You recall when we first met, at Jane's that weekend, you told me something about your work, about the secret that informs every line. Every word. I called it 'the figure in the carpet', do you remember? (*He stares at* VEREKER, *who remains impassive.*) I know that George has got it. To be honest, I always thought he would – he's smart. Much smarter than me. But it seems he's not going to let it

out the bag, not until he's finished his book. I've asked him, and he's refused. So I'm asking you, very humbly, if you'd . . . I'm at the end of my tether. I have to know. Can you please tell me?

CHAS *waits, uncertain. He sees on the bedside table the little notepad and pencil the old man used in communicating with JANE. He picks them up and holds them out. VEREKER stares at him, his expression watchful, narrow. Is there a hint of pity in it?*

> CHAS
Please?

Slowly, very slowly, VEREKER *lifts his hand to take the pencil.* CHAS *almost fearfully places the pad in front of him. The old man seems to gather himself, and with painful deliberation he begins. He holds the notepad up so that* CHAS *can't see what he's writing down. He seems to be sketching rather than writing.*

CHAS, *in an agony of suspense, watches him. Half a minute passes before* VEREKER *lays down the pencil. Then he turns the pad over to CHAS, who looks and reads – 'O'. That is all.* VEREKER *has inscribed a circle on the paper.*

CHAS *stares at it, baffled, then at* VEREKER.

> CHAS
What's this? I mean – what *is* this?

VEREKER *blinks at him, looks away. He is tired, and no longer interested.*

CHAS
(*holding up the paper*)
Please. Explain. What am I supposed to think?

No response from VEREKER. *Desperate now,* CHAS *leans in close.*

Why would you let him know but not me? Just tell me. Please. Tell me.

VEREKER *stares off, his face a mask.* CHAS *grabs the front of his nightshirt and confronts him, eyeball to eyeball.*

For Christ's sake, tell me. *Tell me.*

At this point the NURSE *re-enters the room, her eyes widening in shock at* CHAS'S *rough treatment of her patient. She hurries over, shooing him away.*

NURSE
What are you doing? Can't you see he's a sick man!

CHAS *backs away, shaken, suddenly alive to his own behaviour. The* NURSE *settles* VEREKER, *then shoots a dirty look at* CHAS. *After a few moments* CHAS *exits the bedroom. He still holds the piece of paper with* VEREKER'S *mysterious 'O' on it.*

16

Freya, at her desk, read through the two typescripts again. They were articles translated from German, one a report from a Munich newspaper of April 1950, about a fire that had destroyed the clubhouse of a local football team. The other was from a national paper, dated less than a year ago, about a warehouse fire at a Berlin film company. In both cases arson had been suspected. The clubhouse fire report mentioned that a youth had been taken in and questioned, before being released.

It wasn't much to go on. She made a clicking noise with her tongue and walked to the other end of the office where Delphine Frampton was on the phone. Seeing Freya she held up a finger – *wait there* – and hurried her call to an end with a curt goodbye.

Freya waved the transcripts. 'Your friend did a good job. Do thank her for me.'

Delphine nodded. 'Good old Mitch. Did you find what you were looking for?'

'Maybe. I don't know. The youth the police interviewed about the clubhouse fire was Reiner, no question. I talked to his friend Veronika, who obviously suspected him. The other thing she told me, well, it's tenuous but Reiner's parents both died in a fire during a bombing raid on Munich. A whole shelter was hit, and instead of digging out the bodies they just covered it over. No funeral, no gravestone, nothing but the brute fact of their incineration. It's bound to have affected him as a child.'

Delphine made a doubtful face. 'Tens of thousands died in fires during the war. It doesn't mean –'

'I know. It's just that fire seems to have followed Reiner about. Whenever, *wherever*, he's been crossed, something gets burned down. These two may be just coincidence. But with Harry Pulver's yacht suddenly going up, you have to wonder. I was there that night, in Richmond, and people were pouring out of the pub to watch. The cast, the crew – but not Reiner.'

'But what would he have against Pulver?'

'Well, he had just assaulted Nat. And I remember Reiner was the first to help Nat to his feet. He said something to him . . .'

'What?'

Freya shook her head. 'It was in German.'

'Perhaps along the lines of "You will be avenged. I have matches in my pocket."'

She snorted at the satirical jab, but the idea of Reiner as the culprit was not so unlikely. She had also talked to the paper's crime correspondent, who had been pursuing the story of the *Thomas Bertram*. According to the Met Police's fire expert, the perpetrator was someone who knew the layout of the boat, and had chosen the engine room as the surest location to get a blaze going. Yes, there may have been an element of opportunism – the criminal's ally – but there had been method and expertise in it, too. The problem with investigating a fire was that the evidence of intent would more often than not disappear in the conflagration. Nevertheless, Freya had enquired, might they assume that the saboteur had set fires before? Absolutely, came the reply from the crime man.

'So what are you going to do with this?' asked Delphine.

'I don't know.' Freya bit her lip. 'I have to wait for the fire service's report to come out. Maybe that will turn up something.'

She had turned to leave when Delphine called her back. She was holding up a piece of correspondence. 'I had a very stern letter from your hotel in Munich. The Marienbad? Mitch was kind enough to translate this, too. They've enclosed a bill for damages – says a coffee table was burnt and covered in feathers.'

'Oh God, I'd forgotten about that.'

She stared in surprise. 'What on earth were you doing?'

Freya laughed and shook her head. 'An accident. Some fucking fool, a film critic, actually, lit up a joint and fell asleep. I had to do some emergency firefighting with a cushion.'

'They're also charging for burns on the carpet.'

'I'll write them a cheque. That fire was a godsend, actually. I woke the next morning from a dream convinced about Reiner.'

Delphine consulted the bill. 'I'll put it through as "research expenses".'

Holding her drink in one hand and a rung on the fold-up stepladder in the other, Freya climbed through the opening and onto Albany's soot-smudged leads. A safety rail stood between her and a long drop to the tiled dormer below. Chimney pots, undisturbed since Regency days, presented a higgledy-piggledy shooting range above the blackened bricks. From this perspective the rooftops of Savile Row looked jagged and provisional, as if the street-planner had got his angles mixed up.

'I never knew about this,' she said to Nat, who had followed her through the trapdoor.

'They call it a "roof terrace",' he said, 'rather straining the definition.'

'It's a great view.'

'Mm. On a clear day you can see the permissive society from here.'

Nat was glowing from his sojourn. The whites of his eyes, which he had just shielded with his aviators, set off his Riviera tan. His mid-brown hair had gone blond in the sun.

'That's very Carnaby Street,' she said, peering at his shirt of sky blue and primrose paisley.

'D'you think? From Mr Fish. I've been worried I was too old to carry it off.'

Freya rolled her eyes. 'Don't start that again. What about the film? You must be nearly finished by now.'

'Almost. They've got a week in Rome and then it's done.'

'How's my new friend?'

'Sonja? A star at all times. Her party piece on the last night was a sensation. I had no idea she could sing! "Surabaya Johnny" – my dear, she quite brought the house down.' Nat had been cherishing a memory of Sonja, topless, camera to her eye as he writhed on the bed with Gina. Best to keep quiet about that. He took out a packet of Peter Stuyvesant and lit them one each. The sun, dipping west, pasted its last honeyed rays against the Albany brickwork.

Nat, sipping his drink, said, 'And what of *your* travels?'

'I liked Munich, from the little I saw. I met with a very nice woman who showed me around. We drank a lot of German ale and had dinner with a couple of critics who were very pleased with themselves.'

'Ah, the same the world over. I once fancied I might earn a crust that way myself. You see, I possessed the critic's most valuable weapon.'

'What's that?'

'Unerring judgement,' he replied. 'But the job wouldn't have held me. Even being right all the time becomes a bore.'

Freya smiled and blew a jet of smoke.

After a moment Nat said, 'And Reiner? Did you dig up any stories?'

'Only one. But it's a good one.' She paused before recounting the story of Reiner's revenge on his football coach, and of the fire at the Berlin warehouse. It was only a hunch, of course, but she felt certain that he had also torched Harry Pulver's yacht. Nat, whose expression had shifted from bemusement to disbelief, now put up a restraining hand.

'Hold on a minute. Are you seriously suggesting that Reiner is an arsonist?'

Freya nodded. 'That's about the size of it. In all three cases he has had motive and opportunity. His means are unclear, but –'

'Oh, Freya, really! The very idea. Where's your evidence?'

'I haven't any. But once you know about his parents dying in a fire, the idea becomes perfectly plausible. And it could be the tip of the iceberg – or the spark from the bonfire. He may have been doing this all of his life.'

Nat leaned in close, scrutinising her face. 'Let me look at your eyes. Are you on something? I fear you must be to have come up with such piffle. I grant you Reiner's an eccentric, but he's not a pyromaniac.'

'His old friend Veronika seemed to think otherwise. The problem with arson, as you might guess, is that the crime scene goes up in smoke. Unless the firefighters get to the blaze early enough it's difficult to recover – what's the phrase? – flame accelerants.'

'So you're really going to pursue this?' He suddenly sounded anxious.

'Yes, but' – she shrugged – 'with no great hope of success. Maybe we should talk about something else. What are you doing next?'

Nat made a grimace. 'My agent is furious with me. She got me a plum job, a spy thriller, and I turned it down.'

'Why?'

'I'm going to help Vere Summerhill write his memoir.' Freya's surprised look prompted him towards confession. 'Please keep this *entre nous*, but Vere . . . he's dying. Cancer, I'm afraid.'

'Oh no,' she murmured, touching his sleeve. 'Nat, I'm so sorry.'

He nodded, and blinked. 'He's been terribly brave. He looked so ill in Portofino I thought he might expire before the camera could roll. But like a trouper he did his big scene – a death scene, as a matter of fact. Probably the last thing he'll ever do.'

'But can't you do the memoir *and* the spy thriller?'

Nat shook his head. 'I thought I could. But they want the script in four weeks, and Vere is so close to . . . It had to be one or the other.'

'What a good friend you are,' Freya said, almost wonderingly.

'Tell that to Penny Rolfe. They were not the words she used when I turned down that film.' His smile, in afterthought, was pained. 'I could have used the money, too.'

In the days following, Nat mulled over Freya's startling theory about Reiner Kloss. The idea of his being a secret arsonist did not appear to him any less outlandish. Her evidence was precisely nil. This 'friend' of his Freya had talked to in Munich was either malevolent or deluded. There were always fantasists hanging around people like Reiner, stirring mischief as they strove for their own share in the myth. Even if he did have pyromaniac tendencies, it didn't follow that he'd set fire to Harry Pulver's yacht. What earthly reason might he have had to do so? No, Freya had gone way off the map on this one.

And yet, ridiculous as it was, he found he couldn't stop thinking about it. His mind drifted back to the day he had first met Reiner, at the Trat. Had he noticed a fanatical gleam in Reiner's eyes when he did his trick with the matches? No, he had not. It was just a bit of schoolboy legerdemain. But he did recall that story about his football coach not letting him play. Reiner had said something, he was sure, about getting his revenge. Nat had presumed at the time that this 'revenge' consisted in some personal achievement, rising above the coach's pettiness and maybe winning a trophy. Only now he wondered if things had taken a more material – criminal – turn. Could he have burned down a building? The police had interviewed him, so he had been considered a suspect at least.

It was still on his mind as he made his way through Soho the following Monday. Reiner was back from Rome and wanted to show Nat the best of what he had shot in Italy, prior to assembling a cut. When he arrived at the dingy editing rooms on Dean Street he found Reiner already at work with Arno. The latter was examining translucent amber strips of film that had been hung on a line like clothes pegs. They looked up as Nat sidled in.

'Ah, your timing is excellent,' said Reiner. 'Look at this.'

The TV monitor was frozen on the image of a woman, blurred and indistinct. When Reiner let the film run it resolved itself into the figure of Sonja, filmed in mid-shot from different angles that showed her twirling the hula hoop. Reiner, hunched over the editing desk, flipped a switch to slow the action. The music came in, first piano and drums, then Dox Walbrook's saxophone took up the tune of 'My Favourite Things', thoughtful at first, then more spiky and anxious as it proceeded. The rhythm of Sonja's movement found a complement in the repetitive circling riff of the sax. Nat watched, mesmerised. If it was this good to watch sober, how amazing would it be when stoned?

At the end of it Reiner turned to him. 'You like that?'

'Like it? It's the sexiest thing on film since Dorothy Malone took off her glasses in *The Big Sleep*.'

Reiner laughed. 'Cool, *na*?'

Nat went off to sit in a corner and listened while Reiner and Arno talked in German to one another, ironing out some technical glitch like a couple of boffins in the lab. He found himself studying Reiner, as if he might discern some incriminating flaw he had previously overlooked. He was dressed in his unexceptional way: biker boots, jeans, a black T-shirt with a blown-up white thumbprint on the front. Nothing about his boyish, mild-mannered demeanour suggested the smallest threat. He wore love beads, for God's sake. Freya had him all wrong: this was no psychopath.

Nevertheless, when Arno announced that he had to go out for a few minutes, leaving them together, he felt a quickening tingle of curiosity. Could there be any harm in probing a little?

Nat gave a dissembling yawn and said, 'Wonder if we'll hear anything more about that fire?'

Reiner looked vague. 'What fire? Oh, on the boat, you mean.'

'Mm. They've confirmed it was arson. The police are still investigating.' Reiner nodded, fiddling with the dials at his editing desk: he seemed to be only half listening. 'I gather there's been newspaper interest, too. Some odd speculation being batted around.'

Reiner, his attention absorbed by the monitor, merely grunted in response, so Nat decided to take a more direct approach. 'Very odd. D'you know, there's an extraordinary line of thought that's fingered *you* as a suspect.'

Now he did look round. 'Why would they suspect me?' His tone was not offended but curious.

'I have no idea,' he said, waiting a beat. Then, with a disowning laugh: 'Has fire-starting ever been a pastime of yours?'

Reiner had reverted to staring at the monitor, so Nat couldn't see his face. He muttered something to himself in German before he said, 'I like your English word "rum". This idea is very rum, isn't it?'

'I should say so. Best ignore it. I only brought it up because I thought it might amuse you.' He nodded at the monitor. 'Why don't you show me some more choice cuts?'

His request made a timely diversion. Nat pulled up a swivel chair next to Reiner's own and sat down to watch half an hour or so of unedited footage, some from Portofino, some from Rome. They were silent as Vere, tired and gaunt, went through a long take of his deathbed scene. At one point Reiner paused the film and said, 'He performed that so beautifully.' Nat, moved, could only nod his assent. Vere had played out his string to the last.

By this point Arno had returned from his errand, and Nat perceived that it was time to make himself scarce: they had work to do. He was ambling to the door when Reiner, almost absently, called him back.

'This story about me and the fire. They will print it?'

'Of course not. There isn't a shred of evidence. It would be libel.'

Reiner looked at him. 'So how do you know a newspaper is interested?'

'Oh, just something I picked up.'

'Who would tell you such a thing?'

Nat hesitated. He didn't want to land Freya in it. He made a friendly sort of grimace, as if to say he couldn't possibly remember, and hoped that would cover him. But Reiner's look was shrewd.

'Might it have been that journalist friend of yours? Tall lady, good-looking?'

Nat, alarmed at this sudden interrogative turn, began to bluff. 'Oh, you mean Freya? No, I don't think –'

'Freya Wyley. Yes, on the boat, we met.' He turned away, eyes narrowed, considering. Nat sensed that he had been indiscreet, and had foolishly stirred up trouble. But the next moment Reiner was back to his smiling self. 'She asked me for an interview, I remember. Well, why not? We could talk face-to-face about all these fires I have been lighting. Tell her she will hear from me!'

Freya wasn't sure why she had chosen Bianchi's to meet, except that she hadn't been there in a while and remembered liking the diminutive Italian maîtresse d', who now greeted her at the entrance. As she was led to a table overlooking the street she felt glad to have arrived first; it lent you a sort of strategic advantage, and perhaps a moral one, too. Through the open window came the secretive hum of night-time Soho, the honk of a car horn, shouts, laughter. The maîtresse d' had personally brought over her aperitif, as though from one friend to another. Freya smiled her thanks and took a long swallow of the Martini, dousing an unaccountable flutter in her stomach.

When Sonja arrived, ten minutes late, she was flustered with apologies, which Freya waved off.

'You're only a bit late. And whoever heard of a film star being on time?'

'But that is why I am always punctual,' she replied, taking a seat. '*Nearly* always. It is arrogance to arrive late – as though one says to the person who must wait, "My time is more valuable than yours." '

Sonja looked quite different from the last time Freya had seen her, on the boat trip. Gone was the androgynous cool, though not the glamour; this evening she wore a fitted silk dress, dark green, sleeveless. Her hair was down, which made her look younger, more girlish. A waiter had come to take her drinks order; without asking, Sonja leaned over to take a quick sip of Freya's Martini.

'I'll have one of those, thanks,' she said, and then to Freya, 'What must you think of me? Arriving late, then helping myself to your drink.'

But she said it more as a challenge than an apology, so Freya shrugged. 'I remember as a girl when my dad used to take me to restaurants I'd always have a crafty nip of his drink.'

Sonja leaned back to stare at her. 'Mm. I wonder what you were like – as a girl.'

'Oh . . . Quite bolshie, determined to have my own way. A pain in the neck. You'd probably have hated me.'

But Sonja, amusement dancing in her eyes, shook her head. 'I don't think so.'

The menus arrived, and they communed over them for a few moments. When Freya looked up again she found Sonja's gaze back on her.

'I want to know about Munich. Did you like the hotel?'

'Yes. Very, um, *gemütlich*. Though I hope I'm not in trouble with that nice manager.' She told her the story of Jorge and Karl coming back for a nightcap and accidentally setting fire to the table. A cheque for damages had been sent. 'And by the way, thank you for the Krug.'

Sonja smiled. 'It sounds like you were already well provided with intoxicants.'

'We got through a fair bit,' Freya admitted, recounting Veronika's guided tour of the bars along Reichenbachstrasse after they'd seen the production of *29 Marks*. When Sonja asked her where else she had visited during the weekend, Freya made an apologetic face.

'I had to leave at short notice. A story I was doing back here came up.'

'About Reiner?'

'No, something else.' She hadn't meant to lie, but she couldn't confide her suspicions to Sonja as readily as she had to Nat. As actress and director they were obviously close, and Freya didn't want to be seen peddling malicious rumours about a friend. Yet she couldn't help wondering how much Sonja did know. She could hardly have been deaf to gossip about him.

They both had the veal escalope, and made quick work of a bottle of Soave. Prompted by a second, and by Sonja's beguiling curiosity, Freya found her guard beginning to drop, dangerously. It amused her that Sonja was convinced there had once been a passionate affair with Nat.

'You're not the first person to have made that assumption,' she said.

'Do you mean it isn't true?' asked Sonja. 'He talks about you all the time.'

Freya laughed. 'That's nice of him. We've had our moments, Nat and I, but we've never been stupid enough to have an affair, thank God.'

'What do you mean, "our moments"?'

Always resistant to coyness, Freya shrugged and said, 'The very first night we met he invited me back to his rooms at college. I ended up, at his request, spanking him with a squash racket.'

'Ah . . .'

She detected something unsurprised in the syllable. 'You know about his habit?'

'I have had experience of it,' she replied, with a pert arching of her brow. 'Not all of the time in Italy was taken up with filming. He asked me not to tell you, so perhaps you would keep it – *was ist?* – under your hat.'

Freya, with a sense of being upstaged, said, 'I had no idea. Was it fun for you?'

Sonja seemed not to hear the edge in her voice. 'Well, I was glad to be of use. I have quite a good arm for tennis, so Nat was, I believe, satisfied.'

'But he didn't return your serve?'

'No! I don't want to be thrashed.' Then she laughed. 'I'm not as brave as you.'

Freya, wrong-footed, finished off her glass and poured another.

She didn't like the idea of them sharing bedroom secrets about her. Or a bed, come to that. She couldn't figure this woman out. So far Sonja had made all the running – inviting her on the boat trip, arranging the hotel in Munich, now dinner here in Soho – and Freya had been flattered by her overtures. More than flattered. But now? Maybe Sonja imagined there to be a weird sisterhood between them, as occasional partners in Nat's games of pain.

As the table was cleared Freya lit a cigarette, wondering if she had made a fool of herself, had misread the whole thing. Yet she hardly had time to regroup before Sonja caught her out with a new line of interrogation.

'Nat also told me about a friend of yours, the writer. Nancy?'

'What did he say?' Freya's tone sounded brittle, and guarded.

'Not much. That you were friends from Oxford, and lived together for a while in London.' She paused, waiting a beat. 'Is there something the matter?'

Freya stared back at her. 'Why do you ask?'

'Because something just changed in your face. Perhaps I have annoyed you with my prying?'

'I wonder – I wonder why you want to know. Nat's jolly entertaining, but you must understand he's not the most reliable witness, *especially* in matters of –'

'Freya, please,' said Sonja, leaning across the table to take her hand. The uneasy levity of moments before was gone. 'I ask because I'm interested. Because I like you. But if you would rather, I will stop.'

Her expression had darkened with concern, and Freya abruptly relented. 'I'm sorry. I don't mean to be so defensive. Nancy.' She took a breath. 'She was my best friend. She *is* my best friend; the only one I've ever had.'

Sonja, nonplussed, gave her a look that implored her to continue.

'We fell out, badly, some time ago – so badly I left the country. For seven years.' She went on haltingly. 'It's not worth explaining what it was about. I'm not sure that I could. When I got back we met up again – she was married by this point – and I realised, belatedly, though I think I'd known for ages, that I was in love with her.' She took another swallow of her drink. 'When she got divorced she came to live at my place, in Islington. It was only meant to be for a while, but she stayed for three years.'

'So you were –'

'No. Not like that. I'm afraid my – it was unrequited. The most painful love of all.' She smiled sadly. 'Nancy got married again, to a man I knew. I introduced them.'

Sonja paused, consolingly, before saying, 'But you still see her?'

'Not so much. She lives in the country now. We write.' She looked away for a moment, then back at Sonja. 'I've never told anyone that before.'

The murmurish ambience of the restaurant briefly filled the silence between them. Sonja produced a slim silver cigarette case and handed it to Freya, who took one. They lit up; neither of them said a word until Sonja, arms folded, squinting through the smoke, mused aloud, 'I can't speak for Nancy, but I imagine it would be rather wonderful to be loved by you.' Her eyes were bright as she signalled to a passing waiter. 'Shall we have one more drink?'

The cab dropped her home at half past midnight. Sonja had asked her back for a nightcap – she was staying at the Connaught – but Freya had declined, too tired and just sober enough to trust her instincts. 'I'm a liability this late in the evening. I might end up setting fire to your table.' But she promised to meet for dinner again before Sonja left London.

As she entered the darkened hallway at Canonbury Square she saw the outline of a letter on the mat. It had been hand-delivered, her name typewritten on the envelope. When she opened it she thought at first it was empty. Then she felt something stuck in the corner, and pulled out a small shiny square of cardboard. She switched on the hall light to take a closer look. It was, in fact, a book of matches.

INT. VEREKER'S BEDROOM — NIGHT.
The lamp at the bedside is turned low. The
mood of the room is crepuscular, sombre,
stifling. JANE, in tears, is holding VEREKER's
hand as he drifts away. In the background,
CHAS, GEORGE and MAUD are waiting for the
inevitable. A NURSE, keeping vigil next to
JANE, rises to answer a knock: the DOCTOR
enters and goes to check the patient.

Camera focuses on CHAS as he witnesses
the dying man's last moments. His expression is grave, and we read in it both a
pity for his friend JANE and a private feeling of thwartedness, because VEREKER refused
him at the last.

The DOCTOR holds the old man's wrist,
checking for a pulse. He lays it back on
the counterpane, and nods to the NURSE. She
gently puts her arms around JANE, who reg-
isters the moment with a racking sob.

                    DOCTOR
                  (softly)
     Gone, I'm afraid.

He checks his watch, nods to the others,
and leaves the room.

INT. LIVING ROOM — AFTERNOON.
CHAS *and* GEORGE *are seated opposite one another, a bottle of wine open on the coffee table. Both are smoking.*

GEORGE

I should telephone the paper. They'll want an obituary.

CHAS

Do you have something prepared?

GEORGE

No. But it shouldn't take me long. I feel like I have every word of his still in my head. What'll you do now? Stay on?

CHAS

I don't know. I'll see whether Jane wants my company.

GEORGE

You know, you could come down to Rome for a few days. There's a room at my place.

CHAS

Thanks. But I'm not sure that's - I should probably get back. I have a catastrophe of deadlines waiting for me in London.

GEORGE

Well, it was just a thought.

MAUD *enters, and sits down next to* GEORGE, *who helps her to a glass of wine.*

CHAS

How is she?

MAUD

She's being brave. Talking with the under-
takers at the moment. The funeral's set
for Friday. Apparently he insisted that he
wanted it to be private.

CHAS

They'll be sorry back in London. They would
have given him Westminster Abbey.

GEORGE

Which he would have hated. (*To* MAUD.) So
he's to be buried here as well?

MAUD

I believe there's a plot reserved for him
in the local cemetery.

GEORGE

Some corner of a foreign field ... He
always loved this place.

MAUD

Chas, Jane asked to see you in her room,
if you have a moment.

CHAS
              (*rising*)
Of course. Excuse me.

INT. CORRIDOR — AFTERNOON.
CHAS *wears a brooding expression as he goes
in search of* JANE. *Something has upset him.*

                    CHAS
              (*muttering to himself*)
'He always loved this place.' Huh. Like
you knew anything about him . . .

INT. JANE'S BEDROOM — AFTERNOON.
JANE, *her eyes bruised from crying, is sit-*
ting on a sofa making notes. She looks up
as CHAS *knocks and enters.*

                    CHAS
               (*on eggshells*)
Hey there. How are you doing?

                    JANE
Oh, you know. Whenever I stop to think
about him I just . . . I find it easier to
keep busy. I'm just putting together an
order of service for the funeral. Hugh
left instructions. Do you know this poem?

She hands CHAS *a typewritten sheet, which*
he takes.

                    CHAS
Robert Frost. Yes, I know it.

                    JANE
I thought you might. I wonder, would you
read it at the service?

                    CHAS
Of course. I'd be honoured.

He looks over, waiting for her to say more.
But JANE *only smiles at him.* CHAS *clears*
his throat.

I was wondering - you remember we had
that conversation about Hugh's estate?

                    JANE
Oh. You mean the appointment of his literary executor. As a matter of fact he
left a note. He asked for George to take
care of it.

                    CHAS
Oh. I see.

                    JANE
I'm sorry, Charles, I know you hoped he
might . . . I think his mind was already
made up.

                    CHAS
Of course. Absolutely. (*He holds up the
typed poem.*) Thank you for this. If there's
anything else I can do for you . . .

JANE *beams at him gratefully.*

INT. CORRIDOR — AFTERNOON.
CHAS *has just exited* JANE'S *room. He stands
at her closed door, lost in thought. He
nods to himself before walking away.*

INT. ITALIAN CHURCH — DAY.
*The funeral is under way. A smattering of
pious old women in black huddle in the rear
pews.* VEREKER'S *coffin stands before the
altar, where a priest is talking. We do not
hear his words above the music, which continues as the camera pans around the small*

*congregation. This is the private service
as the late author requested.*

CUT TO: CHAS *at the lectern, reciting the
Frost poem. The sound of his voice comes
in as he reads the last stanzas:*

                    CHAS
  Some have relied on what they knew,
  Others on being simply true.
  What worked for them might work for you.

  No memory of having starred
  Atones for later disregard
  Or keeps the end from being hard.

  Better to go down dignified
  With boughten friendship at your side
  Than none at all. Provide, provide!

*He leaves the lectern, bows to the priest,
and takes his seat back in the pew.*

EXT. CEMETERY — DAY.
*The coffin is lowered into the earth, the
priest intoning the prayers.* CHAS *and* GEORGE
stand either side of JANE.

EXT. CEMETERY — DAY.
The burial over, the few mourners disperse.
JANE *is seen in the background talking with
the priest.* CHAS *and* GEORGE *wander towards
the camera.*

                    GEORGE
              (*with a backward glance*)
  I've a feeling the padre was not a close
  student of Hugh's novels.

CHAS

I wonder if he'd heard of him at all.

GEORGE

Well, it was what the old man asked for.
Dying in exile, though - you fancy that?

CHAS

I don't fancy dying at all.

GEORGE
(*laughing*)

Provide, provide . . .

CHAS
(*stopping*)

What you said the other day, about me
coming with you to Rome. Does the offer
still hold?

GEORGE

Of course. But what about that 'catastrophe' of deadlines you mentioned?

CHAS

They can wait. And Jane's got Maud here
now. I think it's time to move on.

GEORGE

Right. Shall we say tomorrow morning?

CHAS *nods, and they walk on.*

17

The street lamps were gauzy orange against the gloom as Billie got out of the cab in Fortess Road. The summer was winding to an end. Trees cast long wary shadows across the pavement. On the cracked path to her mother's house plums lay where they had fallen, wizened, or nibbled by wasps. As she dragged her suitcase through the door she heard voices droning from the back room, and entered to find her mother and a couple of her lodgers watching a news report on TV: troops dropping down from a helicopter, troops stalking through jungle fauna.

Nell jumped up. 'Darling!' She flung her arms around her. 'Kevin, switch that off, will you?'

Kevin impassively obliged, nodded to Billie and left the room with his mate.

'How was Positano?' Nell asked, halfway to the kitchen. 'Tea?'

'Portofino. I'd love some'

When she returned, a steaming mug in each hand, she gave Billie a more appraising look. 'Lovely colour you've got. Nice place?'

'Mm. Pretty. One evening a few of us hired a little boat, took us round the next cove where they had a seafood place, sort of on stilts in the water. They pulled fish out of the sea and grilled them right in front of us.'

'Ooh! Beats working for a livin', doesn't it?'

Billie smiled. 'We did have to do some work. Everybody got on. There was a new feller there, too, on the production side –'

'Oh yeah?' Nell's tone was knowing.

'No, it wasn't like that. But he was nice. Friendly, y'know.'

Nell stared at her for a moment. 'Well, I don't want to spoil your mood, but I should tell you: I've seen Jeff.'

'When? Where?'

'Here! He came to the house. One night last week.'

'You let him in?'

'Not on your life. We talked on the step. Well, "talked" is putting it politely.'

Billie felt something, heavy as a slab, press down on her chest. 'What did he want?'

Nell gave a sigh of disgust. 'You can imagine. How sorry he was. How he'd never have hurt you. Said he just wanted to talk, looking over my shoulder to see if you were here. Ha. I said to him, "You're not comin' within a mile of her." '

Billie had let her head droop into her hands. 'Oh God.'

'I told you, you should have called the police. That would stop him showing up here.'

'I suppose I'll have to see him sooner or later. I have to collect my stuff.'

'You're going nowhere near him, my girl. Someone else can pick up your stuff. This is not a man you should be around: he's not right in the head.'

'How did you get rid of him?'

'Oh, he went soon enough, after he'd had a go at me. He said, "You never liked me, didja?" I said, "No I bloody didn't, and who can blame me, and if I see you round here again I'm gonna call the police." '

Billie took one of her mother's cigarettes and lit it. Jeff . . . well, she couldn't hide from him forever. It might be best to get it over with and meet him – somewhere in public, not the flat – see if they could sort things out in a civil way. They could be adult about it. Oh, but what if Jeff made a scene – broke down crying and started to beg? She wouldn't put it past him. Worse, she knew there was something in her that would pity him – she was susceptible to weakness, just like Nell used to be. Maybe it was a fault in the blood.

Billie bent down to her suitcase, clicked it open and took out a little package, which she put on the table.

'Here. A little something.'

Nell stared at it. 'For me?'

'All the way from Portofino. It's nothing much, just a thank-you for putting me up here.'

' "Putting you up"? This is your home, silly.'

'Anyway, I'm going to start looking for a place.'

But Nell was too absorbed in unwrapping the parcel to listen. From the folds of tissue paper she lifted a navy sweater and held it up, open-mouthed. She's just a child, thought Billie, half smiling.

'Ooh, feel how soft that is,' Nell squealed, eyes as bright as a bird's. 'Like cashmere or something.'

'It *is* cashmere. I thought with autumn coming on . . . it'll replace that other one with holes in the elbows.'

'I use that one for painting in,' her mother said, already clambering into it and stroking the soft fabric. 'This one'll be for posh.'

Nat swung the Rolls into Ennismore Gardens and parked in the shade of its baronial west side. Next to him sat Vere, eyes shielded by dark glasses, his breathing stertorous. He was twisting his signet ring thoughtfully. They had just had lunch with Vere's agent to finalise the contract.

'Are you all right?' asked Nat.

Vere nodded. 'But would you mind – I can't face anything more today. Let's make a start Friday, shall we?'

'Of course.'

The old man had taken off his glasses and lifted his gaze to the oracle of the rear-view mirror.

'Keep hearing that damned song everywhere. You know, the Beatles.'

'Erm . . .'

Vere hummed a few bars of 'When I'm Sixty-Four'.

'Ah.'

He turned to Nat. 'I take it rather personally. I'm sixty-three.'

Nat suppressed a little jolt of dread, and said quickly, 'Then I promise to serenade you with it on your next birthday.'

Vere looked straight ahead, and gave a tired laugh. Nat got out and walked round to open the passenger door, helping him onto the pavement.

'Don't forget this,' he said, handing him his walking stick.

'By the way, that ending you wrote, in the screenplay,' said Vere. 'Very good. Didn't see that one coming at all.'

Nat wanted to know which part he meant, but his friend had already given him a wave and turned up the steps of his building. As he drove back to Piccadilly he felt his eyes begin to smart as he thought of Vere: his next birthday was March. Nat had made his promise with conviction, but he felt in his bones there would be no occasion by then to sing anything for him.

He had parked on the Row and was walking towards Albany's back gate when a voice hailed him from across the street. 'Wotcha!' He wheeled round to see a young man whose face he took a moment to recognise. Leaning sportily against the bonnet of an open-topped silver MG was Joey Meres. He wore no jacket, offering a view of toned musculature beneath his white shirt. His tie was loosened against his collar. Quite a *handsome* brute, thought Nat.

'Ah, my favourite pugilist,' he said, crossing the road to shake hands. 'Waiting for someone?'

Joey's smile was on full-beam. 'Yeah. You, as a matter of fact.'

'Me?' said Nat, trying to keep his own smile in place. 'Well, always happy to receive visitors. Shall we?' He gestured towards Albany.

Joey made a regretful pout. 'Nice of yer, but I'm here on business. Harry wants to see you.'

'Harry? About what?'

'I've no idea, to tell the truth. Summink to do with work – maybe he's gonna ask you to write another picture.'

I doubt that very much, thought Nat.

'So I'm taking you to his place,' he said, opening the door of the MG, 'if you can spare the time.'

His invitation was friendly enough, yet Nat thought he detected something off in his manner; for once the charm felt stilted, not the natural emanation of his personality. Well, he could refuse this summons, but he didn't want to seem scared. Best to 'front up' and get it over with.

'Hop in,' said Joey, behind the wheel. He gave his neck a little twist, the boxer's shrug. Nat walked round the other side and got in. The car pulled out and turned left down Vigo Street. It was coming on for five thirty in the afternoon; the shops on Regent Street were just closing up. The traffic around them stuttered along the wide thoroughfare. Stuck momentarily behind a bus, Joey took out a packet of Piccadilly and offered one to Nat. He patted his pockets in search of matches.

'There's a lighter in the glove compartment,' said Joey. Nat, leaning forward, undid the catch. The first thing he saw there was not a lighter, but a camera. He took it out, gave a little laugh.

'Ah, the Nikon F. You copied me!'

He looked round, in time to see Joey's frozen expression. Not immediately catching on, Nat returned his attention to the camera. His first thought was that Joey had bought his model second-hand: he could see faint scratches on the bodywork. He turned it over in his hands, thinking. It was a replica of the one he had lost in Portofino, unless . . . He glanced again at Joey, who was now talking in the chummy, blustering kind of way people did when they were trying to cover a mistake.

'It's a great camera. Look after it,' Nat said, feeling for a light note.

'Yeah,' Joey said, his grin fixed, and then Nat knew: the camera was not a replica, it was his own, lifted that night not by some local pilferer but by Joey Meres. Of course. Which meant that Joey had seen the photos of Gina and himself frolicking in the bedroom. And who else would have had an eyeful by now? *Harry wants to see you.* You'd have to be a fool to diddle with the boss's mistress.

Joey had just gunned the car across Oxford Circus. He hung a left into Marylebone; Pulver's place was five minutes away, on Seymour Place. Nat had to think quickly. Replacing the camera in the glove compartment he felt around for the lighter; he found it, a brass Zippo. At the next set of traffic lights Nat flicked it open and held the flame to Joey's cigarette. As the engine dawdled, by stealthy degrees he lowered his hand to the inside door catch. Almost in one movement he pushed it open and sprang out, just missing a car that had come up on his blind side. From the corner of his eye he saw Joey throw away his cigarette and get out.

'Nat! For God's sake!' But Nat wasn't looking back – he was sprinting across the street, dodging oncoming cars that blared their horns furiously at him. He heard Joey shout, 'You can run, mate . . .'

Heart pumping furiously, Nat hit the pavement and ran in the opposite direction to which Joey had been driving – the time it took him to turn the car round would give Nat a head start. This was new. He never ran, let alone for his life. He glanced once over his shoulder to check if he was being pursued and saw nothing, but he didn't stop. Crossing back over Regent Street he looked around for a cab; there were none for hire, so he kept going. Soon, sweat was pouring off him, and he slowed to a jog to catch his breath. He had to get out of sight – Harry would soon have his crew on the case, tracking him like hounds. Those photographs, though – of all the bad luck. Who could he turn to? His first instinct was Reiner's suite at the Connaught, but of course they'd know about that. Vere? No, not in his present state. Obviously Gina was out of the question. He didn't want to think about what Harry was going to do to her.

He had turned up Great Titchfield Street, walking now, racking his agitated brain. He might have to get out of the country for a while, take cover in some undiscoverable hole and wait it out. But where? His life was in London. He couldn't live in exile, for Christ's sake. He had a sudden image of himself shuffling along a lonely esplanade, like poor old Oscar at Berneval-sur-Mer. He stared distractedly into shop windows, as if inspiration might lie there. He was about to cross over when he caught the flash of a car's silver bodywork: Joey, in his MG, was bowling right past him, so close he could see the scar on his jaw. He had his eyes on the road, thank God. Nat dodged into the embrasure of a tailor's shop, waiting, trying to calm his hammering heart. He peeked out, watching the MG shrink into the distance.

He needed to get to a telephone. Doubling back he found a small hotel round the next corner, and went over to the public phone booth, checking his pockets for change. He called Freya's home number first, without reply. Then he called her at the *Chronicle*, where someone told him that she was not at her desk. Who else? Freya's postcode reminded him that it was also Billie's, N1, a realm as vast and mysterious to him as the Amazon.

There was no listing of a Cantrip in N1. And was she there anyway? He seemed to recall Billie telling him that she'd recently moved back to her mother's – some problem with Reg, or whatever his name was. So what about the mother's place? He checked down the list and found it: *Cantrip, N. 58 Fortress Road, NW5*. He dialled and waited. On the fourth ring a woman's voice answered.

'Billie? Thank God! It's Nat. Look, I'm in an awful jam – *really* awful – and I wondered if you could help me.'

'Oh, Nat, of course. But how?'

'I'll explain when I see you. I need a place to stay. Somewhere I won't be – can't be found.'

Billie paused, thinking. 'You can stay here, if you like.' Not with the mother, thought Nat. That would be mortifying, for everyone. Billie seemed to understand his hesitation, because she then said, 'I've got a place.' She gave him an address, which he wrote down on the phone book with a shaking hand. He listened to her directions, there was a bus that would take him there, and rang off. He wondered what she'd made of this call out of the blue; he had sounded, to his own ears, slightly hysterical.

Nat had never seen the back end of King's Cross before, except in a film: *The Ladykillers*. Alec Guinness and his scary tombstone teeth, the maddening old biddy, the smudged light of Ealing's London. The reality of the place was stranger, seedier. The dossers and meths drinkers who shambled about were of a piece with the tumbledown streets, row upon row of thwarted-looking terraces and melancholy pubs. The prostitutes patrolling the area at least seemed motivated by a sense of purpose. It was only half an hour's walk to Albany, but it might as well have been the other side of the world.

As he turned into the street Billie was waiting at the door, and waved on seeing him. There was something incongruous about him, she thought; men in well-cut suits didn't tend to hang around these parts. Up close, however, he was bedraggled and sweaty, and his wan half-smile of greeting betrayed his distraction. 'Here we are,' she said, unlocking the front door and ushering him forward. Nat was briefly reminded of student houses he'd known in Oxford years ago, the clinging odour of neglect, of mangy carpets and unwashed net curtains. Billie took the staircase ahead of him. The back windows he passed on the way up offered vistas of sooty dereliction, and he listened wonderingly as Billie explained how she'd come by the place – it was meant to be a studio for the boyfriend.

On the top landing she let them into a small squarish room,

unfurnished but for an exhausted mattress and a dress rail on which a few wire coat hangers shivered. The uncurtained window peered across to the sad pub opposite. Billie could imagine what Nat was thinking.

'It's not much, I know,' she said, apologetic.

'No, no,' said Nat, not sure if he was agreeing or demurring. He was going to say 'I've been in worse', but he couldn't think where. The single comfort to be drawn was the unlikeliness of Harry Pulver's mob bothering to look for him here. 'It's fine, just what I need.'

Billie bit her lip. 'Are you going to tell me what's going on?'

He sighed, gazing out of the window. It was rather a shaming story to tell, to Billie, at any rate, who he thought regarded him with affection, maybe even respect. But he told her anyway, about the fun and games in his room with Sonja and Gina, the subsequent loss of the camera that night in the bar – then the unexpected visit just now from Joey, who'd evidently got first look at those incriminating snaps and taken them to the boss.

'But it's not like Gina's his *wife*,' protested Billie.

'No. Just his property. And he doesn't want people like me getting their paws on her.'

Billie shook her head. 'I'm disappointed in Joey.'

'Because he's a thief?'

She heard a thin note of irony in his voice, and understood. 'No, not that. I mean his being a snitch.'

'Only doing his job, I suppose. No, the blame lies with me, and my "goatish disposition".' Billie shot him a puzzled glance, to which he replied, '*Lear.*'

They were silent for a few moments. Billie opened the carrier bag she'd brought and pulled out sheets and a blanket; she knelt down and began to make up the bed. Nat told her there was no need, but she ignored him and continued.

When it was done she asked him, 'What else do you need? Money?'

'How much have you got?'

She produced her purse and pulled out two crumpled fivers. It would tide him over for a few days while he made his exit plan. At some point he would have to recover some things from Albany:

suitcase, clothes, passport, chequebook. Though how he'd manage that . . .

'I could go,' she said. 'Do they let women in there?'

Nat smiled his gratitude. 'If I write you a letter of introduction. Would you mind? This could be the saving of me.'

They talked it through. Nat would make a list of what he needed, then telephone the porter to arrange her admittance to his set; they were quite particular at Albany about who came and went. In the meantime he would have to think hard about where he might lie low.

'Ireland, maybe?' suggested Billie. 'Some little cottage on the west coast.'

Nat made a moue of distaste. 'There's the weather to consider, not to mention the people. I was thinking of Cap Ferrat. Vere's got a place there he'd let me use.'

Billie paused. 'Is Vere – he looked so terribly ill when we were in Italy.'

He could see no further use in keeping it a secret. 'I'm sorry to have to tell you, my dear, but he's not long for this world. Lung cancer.'

He watched, helpless, as her eyes glistened. She said quietly, 'He told me, at the hotel, he'd just had an adverse reaction to drugs. I – I should have known.'

'No, he would have hated for you to know. He was determined to keep going, for the film's sake as much as his own.'

'To think how he did that death scene so beautifully.'

Nat smiled sadly. 'Reiner thought he'd never seen him do better. You know, Vere once said to me, joking, "I've had such good practice at dying." He reckoned he died in at least ten of his first thirty pictures. He was always dying. I'm sure, when his moment comes, he'll do it beautifully again.'

Later that evening Nat finally got through to Freya, who came down to King's Cross to meet him. It took some persuading on her part to get him out to the pub across the road. He didn't smile when she suggested he wore a false moustache and glasses. There was hardly anyone else in there, but he insisted on sitting at a table in the corner, close to the door.

'You may regret your levity when they start dragging the Thames for my body.'

'If you're that worried why not go to the police?'

'And tell them what? Pulver's not done anything yet. But I can tell from the fact he sent Joey Meres he's got me in his sights.'

'Meres. Why do I know that name?'

Nat shrugged. 'Ex-boxer. Likes a bit of flash. A scar on his jaw from here to here.'

Freya was thoughtful for a moment. 'These photographs of you and Gina "frolicking". Do you think Sonja is in them?'

'No. Not that I remember. But the camera was lying around.'

'So you can't be sure. Gina might have taken one, in which case –'

'Oh God,' groaned Nat, cupping his hands over his mouth.

Freya stubbed out her cigarette and rose from the table. 'I'm going to call her hotel. If she is in those pictures she needs to be warned.'

From beneath his brow Nat surveyed the poky saloon. Everything came in shades of brown: the walls, the tables, the ancient advertisements, even the nicotine-stained ceiling. The barman was stolidly drying glasses and exchanging mumbled words with a couple of old boys. Nat supposed it was much like this every night, the mood of fatigue and dreariness lingering like yesterday's cigarette smoke. The cracked lino, the ugly furniture, the despondent faces . . . no wonder you got drunk here.

He tried to read Freya's expression as she returned. 'I called the desk at the Connaught,' she said. 'Sonja was meant to be there for lunch. They haven't seen her all day.'

EXT. STREET IN ROME — DAY.
GEORGE *at the wheel of his sports car amid swirling traffic, with* CHAS *in the passenger seat. Dox Walbrook's jaunty Eureka theme plays over the top.* GEORGE *looks relaxed in his adoptive city;* CHAS *has an air of bemusement.*

INT. HALLWAY — DAY.
Camera cranes down on a high-ceilinged hall, where GEORGE *checks his mailbox. He riffles through his post, pausing at one letter with a London postmark. He holds it up in front of* CHAS.

                    GEORGE
   From Gwen.

EXT. TERRACE — DAY.
GEORGE *stands on the terrace of his apartment, which overlooks the imperial skyline of Rome.*

INT. LIVING ROOM — DAY.
CHAS *is on his way through to join* GEORGE *on the terrace when he spots* GWEN's *letter,*

open on the desk. He halts, hesitating, and leans over to take a quick peek. All he sees are the words 'All my love, darling - GWEN'.

> GEORGE
> (*from outside*)
> CHAS - you coming?

CHAS *reluctantly abandons his snooping and exits the room.*

EXT. TERRACE — LATER.
CHAS *and* GEORGE *sit there, drinking.*

> GEORGE
> Anyway, she's going to come over.

> CHAS
> Gwen? What about her mother?

> GEORGE
> Mrs Erme's sister is coming to stay, to give Gwen a break.

> CHAS
> Don't worry, I'll clear out.

> GEORGE
> (*laughing*)
> Relax. You can stay as long as you like. I'm sure Gwen would like to see you.

> CHAS
> (*nervous*)
> I dare say you'd prefer to have the place to yourselves.

GEORGE

If you want to go, I can't stop you. But
there's no need.

CHAS

Thanks. So this party tonight?

GEORGE

Just people I know from the paper. Bit of
this (*mimes drinking*), bit of that (*mimes
smoking a joint*). Should be fun.

INT. AN APARTMENT — NIGHT.

A crowded party, and CHAS *stands at the
edge of things, a wallflower.* GEORGE, *in the
middle of a crowd, spots him and beckons
him over.* CHAS *nods, and gestures to say
he'll join him in a minute. He wanders off
instead to another room, where people are
slumped on couches, on the floor. The air
is thick with pot fumes. A young woman,*
MEL, *sits on her own at the window - their
eyes meet.* CHAS *goes to join her.*

CHAS

Hello there. Chas.

MEL

Hi. (*She looks around, coolly surveying the
somewhat zombified state of the partygoers.*) I hope you don't think I've got
drugs on me.

CHAS

Oh, no, that's not - not my thing. Wine's
about as strong as I go.

                         MEL
Look at these people . . .

                    CHAS
Yeah. Like the last days of Rome.

                    MEL
               (smiling at him)
Funny. I'm Mel, by the way. So who do you
know here?

                    CHAS
Hardly anyone. I came with a friend -
George Corvick.

                    MEL
I know George.

                    CHAS
We've just got back from a . . . trip.
Portofino.

                    MEL
How lovely!

                    CHAS
Yes. It was.

                    MEL
You don't sound like you enjoyed it much.

                    CHAS
Um, it wasn't a holiday. We were there
for - someone we knew. He'd been quite ill.

                    MEL
You mean . . . ?

                    CHAS
Yeah. He died.

                    MEL
Oh, God. I'm so sorry.

                    CHAS
No, no. He was old, and he'd had a good
life. A writer.

                    MEL
Oh. Was he famous?

                    CHAS
Yes. Hugh Vereker.

                    MEL
               (*blankly*)
Vereker . . .

                    CHAS
You've not heard of him?

                    MEL
I'm afraid not. Sorry!

CHAS*'s face is a picture of bewilderment
and incredulity. But he manages to return
a weak smile.*

EXT. STREET — NIGHT.
CHAS *and* GEORGE *walking home.*

                    GEORGE
She's a nice girl, Mel. You seemed to be
getting on.

CHAS

Hmm. I wish I hadn't mentioned Vereker.
Can you believe she'd never heard of him?

GEORGE

So what? Many haven't.

CHAS

It was disappointing.

GEORGE

So she's not a bookworm. Maybe she's passionate about other things like - I dunno - macramé
or ju-jitsu.

CHAS

I'm sure she's very nice. But I couldn't
be serious about someone who'd never heard
of a writer like Vereker.

GEORGE

Oh, Chas. That's madness!

CHAS

Easy for you to say. You're engaged to a
woman who knows about books - writes them
in fact.

GEORGE

Not every woman I've known has been a
bluestocking. Besides, you could have introduced her to the work. Trained her up.
You've read *Pygmalion*.

They have reached the front gate of GEORGE'*s
building.*

INT. LIVING ROOM — NIGHT.
GEORGE *brings in a jug of water and two glasses, sets them down on the coffee table.*

> GEORGE
> Sure you're on for this?

CHAS *nods.* GEORGE *hands him a tab of LSD. They take one each.*

> CHAS
> How will I know when it - ?

> GEORGE
> Don't worry. You'll be there before you know it.

CHAS *watches* GEORGE *get up and put a record on his stereo. It's another version of the Eureka theme, slow and sultry, with lots of echo and a woman's voice calling in the background. Camera gradually zooms in on* CHAS*'s eyes, narrowing on the 'O' of his iris. The picture suddenly switches to* CHAS, *seen from behind, opening a door and entering into blackness - a vanishing point. The music continues, slurring, echoing around the same three-note figure.*

CUT TO: *The same apartment,* CHAS *seeming to wake up from sleep to find* GWEN *sitting opposite. He looks about, wondering where* GEORGE *is.*

> CHAS
> What are you doing here?

> GWEN
> That's not very friendly.

CHAS

Where's George?

GWEN

You knew I was coming. You asked me here.

CHAS

He'd kill me if he found out about this.

GWEN
(looking shifty)
He's in the next room. I think he's upset.

CHAS

No, that's not right. You wrote to him –
I saw your letter.

GWEN

He'd kill us if he knew I'd told you.

CHAS

I can't blame him.

GWEN

You like a good snoop, don't you? He knows
you went through his room.

CHAS

Told me what? You mean about Vereker - the
figure?

GWEN

Of course. This is what you've wanted from
the start.

The sound of a cough interrupts them. They
look across the room to where GEORGE stands.

336

                    GEORGE
Did you suppose I'd never find out?

                    GWEN
It was my fault, really. I was lonely.

                    CHAS
That's not very friendly.

GEORGE *throws a hula hoop across the room.*
GWEN *catches it.*

                    GEORGE
Go on then . . .

The room, the walls, begin to blur. GWEN,
*fringed in light, walks through the same
door* CHAS *came through.*

                    CHAS
Wait, wait a minute - is this it? Is this
the figure?

EXT. A ROOF TERRACE — DAY.
*A blinding sun creates a shimmer around
the walls. A silhouetted figure, blurred at
first, seems to be dancing. Close-up on a
woman, in a bikini, languidly revolving a
hula hoop around her midriff. The spangled
sunlight at her back makes it difficult to
identify her, but in fleeting moments the
woman's face is visible: it is* GWEN.

18

The porter at Albany tipped his hat on hearing her name. 'Mr Fane telephoned to say you'd be coming. You have the key to his set?'

Billie nodded. Conducting her through the rope-walk and thence into a stone-flagged courtyard the man was too discreet to ask why Mr Fane couldn't pick up his own stuff; instead he yarned a little Albany lore, worn smooth by use like old coins. He led her up a staircase to Nat's rooms, and told her to call at the lodge when she was finished. 'Mr Fane was very particular about my seeing you into a cab.' Again, he gave no sign of being curious about these instructions. She thanked him, and let herself into the apartment.

She had a list, written in Nat's flamboyant cursive, of what he called 'needful things', though she couldn't resist taking a snoop around the place first. It had the manicured look of an apartment you might see in *Queen* magazine or a Sunday supplement. The rooms were elegant and large, as she'd expected, with corniced ceilings and rippled windowpanes that seemed to have survived from the last century. A connoisseurial mixture of paintings and photographs adorned the walls. A few of the portraits were, inescapably, of Nat himself. In the kitchen she poured herself a gin and tonic, which she sipped on her way around his office, retrieving from his desk 'chequebook, diary, passport, fountain pen (the Montblanc, please)'. She put these and other items in an old leather briefcase.

It was odd, picking off someone's possessions in their absence, like an authorised burglar. Billie was suddenly reminded of their first encounter at Brown's. If she hadn't tried to filch his wallet that day she wouldn't be here now. In the bathroom she found his 'grooming case', though she wondered if a silver monogrammed hairbrush was absolutely necessary to his arrangements in exile. Directed to the mirrored cabinet she found the bottle of L'Heure Bleue, his razor, brushes. On the hook of the bathroom door hung a dressing gown in mustard yellow, the only ugly thing of his she'd ever seen. The idea that even Nat could have a lapse of taste was comforting. On entering the bedroom she jumped at the sight of the polar bear rug; for just a second the black eyes and open jaw seemed to belong to a living creature. The room resembled a stage set – Molière, perhaps – with swagged curtains, gilt mirrors, a bust on the mantelpiece and a four-poster with a scrolled head-board. For some reason she sensed Nat's influence here, his aura of ownership, the strongest. There was a ghostly impression, a dent, on the right-hand pillow. He'd asked her to pack whichever books were on his bedside table: *The Scenic Art* by Henry James, *Enemies of Promise*, and a hardback novel, *Disciples*, by someone called Nancy Holdaway. From a cupboard she pulled out a large suitcase, the old-fashioned sort with brass catches and travel labels striping the sides.

She opened a huge built-in wardrobe and started pulling out clothes. His only directive was 'shirts etc', so she improvised: a few of Turnbull & Asser's finest, a pair of corduroys, a linen jacket. The first surprise came when she opened what she assumed to be an underwear drawer. There *was* underwear – all of it women's. Black embroidered bras, scalloped bras, half-cup bras, silk cami-soles, slips, garter belts, black and white stockings, Victorian corsets, bikini pants, a motley of lacy underthings in red and black and flesh. Starkest of all, in this rainbow jumble, a plain pair of white cotton knickers – the innocent at the party. Billie's mind reeled: had Nat assumed she wouldn't look, or did he not care? Were these keepsakes donated, or stolen, or purchased? Was he a mail-order obsessive compiling a trophy collection? There was another possibility: he had worn them himself, as costumes in some private theatre of erotic fancy. She felt a bump of nausea in her stomach, not from disgust but from the sudden vertiginous excitement of accidental intimacy. She steadied herself, took a breath, and looked up to the top shelf.

She knew she was violating an unspoken trust, but her curiosity was now a runaway horse. Taking a chair to stand on she peered into the dark recess above. She touched the hard edges of a wooden box, and carefully took it down, half dreading what she might find. Flipping back the lid she boggled at a collection of canes, whips, crops, sticks, rackets. And masks! Masks to suit a house-breaker or highwayman, and carnival masks with witchy noses and pumpkin grins. An adult's dressing-up box; but from where did the thrill derive? Without thinking she took up a Pierrot mask and put it on, eyeing herself in the wardrobe's inlaid mirror. She picked up a cane and bent it like a sadistic schoolmaster, emitting a low snarl. She giggled, feeling nothing, and returned them to the box.

She had filled the suitcase and was about to close up the ward-robe when she saw, half hidden behind the rack of shoes, a verdigris-coloured metal box – the sort the staff kept at the hotel for petty cash. She picked it up by its thin handle and pulled it out. Locked, of course, but after the secrets disgorged elsewhere this had to be worth investigating. She began to hunt for the key in the desk drawers, in the bedside table, in the kitchen. The couple of keys she uncovered didn't fit. Sighing, she prepared to give up the search when her eye fell on the ring of keys Nat had given her, discarded for the moment on the dining table. She hadn't noticed the little subsidiary key beneath the Banham that had let her into the place. With a quickening jolt of trespass she inserted it into the lock, which she knew would turn half an instant before it did.

The porter had handed her into the cab with the same obliging blankness as before. She watched Piccadilly flash by, Nat's suitcase wedged into the corner seat opposite. She had cleared all trace of her brief trawl through his rooms, even washing up the glass she had used for the gin and tonic. She closed her eyes and returned to the night back in June when they'd had Nat to dinner at Fortress Road. God, to think she had tried to set him up with her *mum* – the anguish of humiliation she might have caused.

She was still trying to blink from her eyes the imprint of what she had found in the metal box: photos, a stash of them, some sleek with expertise, others just staged Victorian smut. They were variations on a theme: a woman, partly undressed, with a coy smile and her backside bared to a man, who was usually masked and holding a cane or whip. Then there were the Polaroids, in colour, explicit and unsentimental. She couldn't understand the pleasure to be had from gazing at close-ups of an anus, its pink puckered 'O' gaping at the lens. What strangers we are to one another, she thought. The Nat she knew was suave, droll, a generous friend and an invaluable patron. To think he might have shopped her, justifiably, to the police; instead he had given her the break of her life. Of course he was also known to be a bit of a devil, as evidenced in that weird game of guess-the-underwear he'd initiated at the hotel in Italy. With artists and writers outlandishness was part of the deal. But a sadomasochistic pervert?

The taxi was turning into Gray's Inn Road as she emerged from her troubled reverie. On a whim she asked the driver to stop at Frederick Street, where she could quickly collect a few things of her own. She was taking a risk – Jeff might be at home, though on a warm morning like this she thought he would be out. Having asked the man to wait she fished out her house keys and hurried down the steps to let herself in. Her relief at his absence was mingled with a sadness that it should be this way: the day he had moved in here had felt so brimful of hope. She surveyed the living room and its tidal scum of smeared dishes, loaded ashtrays, discarded newspapers; carelessness was another of the artist's privileges. An urge to clean up chafed at her, but she resisted. In the bedroom she emptied out a drawer and filled a bag with her jewellery, make-up, some perfume. She cleared another drawer of her underwear, rather ordinary-looking, even frumpy, after what she'd found at Nat's place. She hesitated over her stack of albums. It seemed too painful to extricate these tokens of her youth, the songs she'd listened to, over and over, when she was falling for Jeff. She stared at the sleeve of *Beatles for Sale* for a few moments, then put it back with the others.

She was back in the living room when a shadow descended the steps and a key scratched in the lock. Jeff stood in the doorway, immobilised with shock. He wore jeans and a T-shirt emblazoned with the name of a band she'd never heard of. His beard looked thicker.

'Billie,' he said, as though trying the name for size. 'What's going on?' A glance at the two carrier bags at her side answered his question.

'Just picking up a few things,' she said, her voice low. 'How have you been?'

He ignored that. 'Did your mum tell you I'd been round?'

'Yeah. She was all for calling the police.'

Jeff scowled, as if he might have expected such an injustice. 'You know I'd never hurt you. I can't even remember doing . . . whatever it was she said.'

'Well, you were standing over me, holding a hammer. With murder in your eyes.' She looked at him now; she felt a thin quiver of fear, still, but overriding it was pity. He seemed reduced, his presence somehow a caricature of what he had once been.

'I'd never hurt you,' he repeated.

'I'm not going to give you the chance,' she said, picking up the bags. She made to leave, and he took a step in front of her. 'Jeff. Please. You're not going to stop me.'

'Can't we just talk? You've not even heard me out.'

She sighed at that. 'I stuck with you for a long time. I know things were hard, but it meant I always had to tiptoe around you, worrying that I'd say the wrong thing, put you in a mood. It was exhausting.'

'But it's not like –'

'I can't do it any more. Whatever I used to feel, it's gone.'

'Billie.' His tone was pleading.

'I've got a taxi waiting up there. Sorry.'

When she made for the door she half expected him to make a lunge for her, but he didn't. Her foot was on the steps when she heard him say, 'Go on, then. Back to mother.'

But she realised it was beyond him to provoke her. At the top step she turned and said, 'Bye, Jeff.'

Back in the taxi she was overcome by a trembling, the sort you felt after stepping off the roller coaster at a fairground. The jelly-legs, the galloping heartbeat. It was relief, and something else – a certainty that she had made the break, and needn't ever put herself through it again. She asked the cabbie to drive around for a few minutes while she collected herself. The double discombobulation of Nat's wardrobe and Jeff's appearance was quite enough for one morning.

She paid off the driver and stood outside the studio flat for a moment, the suitcase and bags at her feet. The street was so tucked away it surprised her to see another car pull up shortly after the taxi's departure. It was a silver sports car, from which two men got out. One of them was so tall it was a wonder he could have folded himself into such a dainty-looking motor. The driver, she realised, was someone already known to her.

'Carry yer luggage, miss?' Joey Meres stood there, smiling, though it was a smile as thin as a prison shank.

Billie instinctively picked up the bags for herself. 'Joey. What are you doing here?'

Joey's grin turned rueful. 'I think you know what. We've been behind you all the way from Piccadilly.' He looked up at the house. 'Funny to be back 'ere. My old manor.'

'So you've been looking for me?' asked Billie, despairing of her own bluff.

'Come on, Billie. We know he's here. Either you let us in or Valentine' – he nodded at his enormous slab-cheeked companion – 'will take that door off the hinges.'

With the graciousness of a hotel porter Joey took the suitcase off her and nodded encouragingly at the door. Helpless, she let them in. At a nod from Joey, Valentine remained in the hallway, his face blank as granite. Billie led the way up, a sick feeling in her stomach. At the half-landing she stopped and turned.

'Please don't do anything to him,' she said, beseeching him with her eyes.

'I don't intend to. I'm just here to collect him. Harry wants a word.'

'Joey, honestly –'

He shushed her. 'Don't upset yourself. He'll be all right.'

She couldn't tell if he said this to appease her or if he really meant to spare Nat. He jerked his chin in a mute command to proceed. She took the final flight of stairs, and with a tap she entered the room. Nat stood against the far wall, grim-faced, smoking like a man about to be blindfolded.

'Nat, I'm sorry,' she said, a moment before Joey crossed the threshold behind her.

'It's all right,' said Nat. 'I saw the car outside.'

'There he is, Speedy Gonzales!' cried Joey. 'Nat, I couldn't see you for dust yesterday. What was that about?'

'I felt a sudden reluctance to accept Mr Pulver's hospitality.'

'That's as may be, but he insists, I'm afraid.'

Nat nodded slowly, and flicked his eyes to Billie. 'Please don't involve her. She was just trying to help.'

Joey scowled, seemingly offended. 'Why would I? It's *you* I came for.'

Trying to keep her voice level, Billie said, 'What'll happen to him?'

Nobody spoke for a moment, then Joey said, 'He'll most likely get a smacked arse.' The irony in his tone was unmistakable.

Nat cut a glance at Billie, wondering if she understood, but Billie's face was a mask. Joey wagged his head: time to go. 'Here's your suitcase,' he said, holding it for Nat to take. 'Plannin' a holiday?'

They made their way back down the stairs. Nat was calculating the odds of giving Joey the slip again when he saw, in the hallway, a hulking brute whose gaze carried nothing of curiosity or kindness.

'This is Valentine,' said Joey. 'Don't be deceived by his bulk: he's very quick on his feet.'

Valentine gave no sign of having heard this testimonial. He briefly stared at Nat, and opened the door onto the street. As they filed out, Nat caught Billie's eye and said, under his breath, 'Tell Reiner.' She watched them get into the open-topped car, Joey at the wheel, Nat in the back with Valentine, proprietorial, like a bodyguard.

'Joey,' she called, but he had already switched on the engine, and when he did look at her he only winked, friendly but, in the circumstances, ambiguous. He pulled out from the kerb and drove off.

At the house on Seymour Place Nat was led up the stairs, past the long dining room where he and Berk had endured an uncomfortable hour with Pulver back in June. That was the occasion Harry had asked them − told them − to create a part in the film for his 'young friend' Gina. Nat had done him that courtesy. And like many a good deed it had now come back to bite him.

Today's 'meeting' was in a room halfway to being modernised. Leather armchairs and mirrored glass fittings had been awkwardly pressed into the old shell of a lounge, its net curtains and hunting prints still clinging to a pre-war idea of genteel respectability. On a sofa in the corner sat Sonja, pale but defiant, and next to her Gina, her head bowed. They had been in the room some moments before she looked up, revealing a livid black eye. Harry himself sat at the bar eating a steak, a sullen glaze on his face; it lightened noticeably on Joey's entrance, Nat and his huge escort in tow. The only others present were a barman, and a black Labrador snoozing in his basket. Gina was looking away, so Nat twitched a reassuring smile at Sonja. But he felt only a horrible tightening in his gut.

Joey strolled over to whisper in Harry's ear; the latter, putting down his knife and fork, stared at Nat while he listened. Something had been decided. Harry was wearing a fawn-coloured shirt with a pinstriped waistcoat and suit trousers. He got down from his stool at the bar and swaggered over to Nat.

'Heard you were planning to leave the country,' he said, so close to Nat that he got a noseful of his meaty breath. 'Joey here's like a terrier after a rat. He woulda run yer down sooner or later.'

Nat, keeping his voice level, said, 'Well, I'm here now. I'd be grateful if we could get this over with.'

Harry pulled his chin back, frowning. 'D'you hear this one?' he said to Joey. 'We're keeping him from his business.'

Joey shook his head. 'Whatever that is . . .'

'I never knew writers were such *twerps*, did you? I mean, the trouble he's caused. As for the other stuff he's been up to . . .' He shook his head disbelievingly.

'Problem is,' said Joey, 'if you give someone a hiding, you gotta be sure they understand it's a punishment. This feller – he's that weird he might enjoy it.'

Harry nodded, brooding on this philosophical conundrum. He padded over to the basket where the Labrador was curled, and picked up the dog's chain. He rolled up his shirtsleeves and wound the strap around his fist. 'All the same,' he conceded, 'I think it's worth putting to the test. He's only ever had it from the ladies before.'

Right up to the last moment Nat thought Pulver would hold

off. To start beating him in front of the others was surely too grotesque, like a deranged Roman emperor whimsically turning on one of his consuls. So when he felt a sharp lash across his thighs he nearly jumped in surprise. The dog lead got tangled around him, so that Harry had to tug it free. He took a few steps back to adjust his range, and swung again, connecting this time with Nat's backside. It stung, of course, but Nat was determined to give him no encouragement: he would take it, and hope that the humiliation might be deflected upon his tormentor. Another blow, and another, came down. Gina in the corner gasped out, 'Harry, don't,' though fear choked any conviction in her voice. Joey, arms folded, watched impassively for the first ten or twelve thwacks, then stepped back to open a window; the smell of sweat had pinched the air.

Catching his breath, Harry growled, 'Are you enjoying this?'

Nat, pain singing around his body, only stared at him. Goaded by his silence, Harry repeated the question. '*I said*' – thwack – '*are you enjoying this?*' – thwack. 'Say it,' he snarled, and swung again. 'Say it!'

Nat had still not replied when a low voice interrupted. 'Stop. Stop it now.'

Sonja had stood up and interposed herself between them. Loathing seemed to crackle off her like static. 'You think you're a big man, being able to hurt him, but you're not. People despise you.'

Harry Pulver had gone pale. He was winding himself up to reply when she added, with majestic disdain, 'A pig, that is what you are. A pig in a wig.'

I wish you hadn't said that, Nat thought, just before Harry's free hand swiped her hard across the face. Sonja's head rocked back; the air seemed to tense with the raw sound of flesh against flesh. When she brushed her hair away her expression wasn't cowed or even surprised: it was scornful. Calmly, she spat in Harry's face. Time stilled for a moment. The room had tipped from its axis.

Harry wiped off the spittle, dropped the dog lead and, with an animal speed, grabbed Sonja by the throat. 'You fucking . . .' he breathed, at a loss to describe her. He looked round to the bar where he'd left his food to go cold. A steak knife glinted on the counter and he snatched it up. Nat, his reactions blunted to an underwater sluggishness, saw what was about to happen and cried out – he had no idea what he said, and it made no difference. The bright steel flashed before he even moved, and the air was pierced by a scream, Gina's – her keening went on and on while they looked at Sonja, at a stagger, her trembling hands leaking blood as they covered her split face. Suffering Christ, thought Nat, struggling not to be sick. He had seen stage blood many times before, but it never looked or smelled like the real thing, great dark gouts of it, running down her arms, dripping on the carpet.

Joey got to her just as she fainted, and he carried her over to the couch. He took out a white handkerchief from his breast pocket to press against Sonja's face. 'Gina, shut up and help me,' he snapped. 'Keep that pressed to her.'

He came back up the room to Harry, who seemed immobilised by what he'd just done. Joey stared him in the face.

'What the fuck? She's a *woman*.'

But Harry, breathing heavily, couldn't summon the will to speak. His skin was as pale and shiny as lard. Joey turned instead to Valentine and grunted an order; when Nat looked back some minutes later both Harry and the man-mountain were gone. Shirt front spattered crimson, Joey took over staunching the wound from the sobbing Gina. Sonja had come round, her moans piteous to the ear. It was decided among them to take her to Paddington, the nearest hospital.

As they drove, Gina nursing Sonja in the back, Joey kept up a nervous stream of instructions to Nat: once she was in surgery he should call Berk, he'd take care of the insurance people; keep the press out, no way did they want a story about Harry attacking a woman, he was already under a cloud after that incident with the waiter. He should also break it to Reiner, though God knows how he'd react –

Nat, finding his voice at last, said, 'I imagine he'll want to kill him.'

Joey seemed to hear something more than a figure of speech. 'Reiner?'

'He's a creature of passions. A friend of mine thinks . . . but I dare say Harry's got protection enough.' He looked askance at Joey, who didn't seem to notice, or else ignored it. His mind seemed to be running in other directions, for he now dropped his voice to a near-whisper.

'What's the name of that actor who had the accident? Smashed his face?'

'Clift, you mean?' Nat frowned, wondering how anyone could have forgotten him so quickly.

'Has he acted much since?'

'No. And never will. He died last year.'

Joey took this in with an absent grimace. Arriving at the hospital Gina, her anguish at last under a semblance of control, helped Sonja towards casualty. Joey, watching them go, shook his head. 'She's gonna spend the rest of her life trying to keep her face in profile.'

Nat was on the verge of deploring the heartlessness of this remark when he realised that Joey was simply speaking from experience. He'd known what it was to live with damage on display. 'It was only meant to put the frighteners on yer,' he said to Nat. As an expression of remorse it was inadequate, but it would have to do. A moment later he left and Nat was alone.

Freya, who'd been out most of the afternoon, got the call at her desk. She arrived at the hospital a couple of hours after Sonja had come out of surgery. They had put twenty-one stitches in her left cheek.

Nat was waiting for her as she came down the corridor.

'How is she?'

'Sleeping, in her room. She was in a terrible state – her face – but the surgeon seemed to know what he was doing.'

'Can I see her?'

Nat shook his head. They were not allowing visitors this evening. He told Freya this to save her from the truth. In her room, minutes before, Sonja had asked him, begged him, to make sure that Freya wasn't admitted: she couldn't bear to be seen like this. Nat didn't know what to say; either she was deep in denial or else she didn't realise that the injury was of a nature to make her permanently 'like this'. The only visitor she did allow was Reiner, who stayed for half an hour. When he emerged, they had talked briefly about what had happened. Nat recounted the fateful moment in a low, halting voice, forlornly aware of his own helplessness. He berated himself for not having acted more quickly in Sonja's defence, but the whole thing had passed in the blink of an eye; even Joey, with his speed of reaction, had been unable to prevent it. Reiner had listened in his phlegmatic way, betraying no sign of rage or even of dismay. Nat felt that he could have been describing a scene from a film. Before leaving Reiner asked him if he knew where Pulver had gone; Nat shook his head – truthfully, he didn't know – though Joey had probably advised him to lie low.

Freya could hardly admit to herself the mixture of dread and longing she felt about seeing Sonja, and wouldn't confess it to Nat. That face, she thought, that lovely face. Blinking her image away she said, 'I'll come back tomorrow, then.'

Nat pulled a demurring expression. 'I wouldn't. Wait until she calls you. She'll need time to compose herself.'

Her narrowly searching look made him wonder if she'd guessed, but she didn't press him. As they came out to the forecourt, Freya asked him about Reiner. With the film in the can the director wouldn't be in London much longer. Nat said, 'He told me he'd be in touch with you.'

'Well . . . I did get this through the door a week ago.' Freya showed him the book of matches, and the unmarked envelope it came in. She squinted at him. 'Do you still think he had nothing to do with that fire?'

INT. BEDROOM — MORNING.
Darkness. CHAS *opens his eyes. From his POV
we see* GEORGE *upside down. The camera flips
round to show that* CHAS *is on his back
looking up. The picture corrects itself and*
GEORGE *stands there holding a glass of orange
juice.*

                    GEORGE
    Morning. Here.

He hands him the glass, which CHAS *groggily
takes. He looks around, utterly disoriented
from the night before. We watch him puzzling, trying to put together the fragmented
episodes of his acid trip. Something seems
to click in his expression because he looks
up suddenly at* GEORGE, *who stares at him
levelly.*

                    GEORGE
    Are you all right?

                    CHAS
    Nnh? Oh . . . yeah. What time is it?

                    GEORGE
    Eight, just gone. That was quite an
    evening.

CHAS *sits up, slowly rubs his forehead. He looks terrible.* GEORGE *watches him.*

> CHAS
>
> I feel wiped out. Last night, did I - did I say anything?

> GEORGE
>
> Like what?

> CHAS
>
> I dunno. I was talking with - was Gwen here?

> GEORGE
>
> No. Though at times I did wonder who it was you were talking to. Or thought you were talking to.

> CHAS
> *(shifty)*
>
> It beats me.

> GEORGE
> *(checking his watch)*
>
> I need to go to the post office. Antrobus has forwarded some research material for the book. Obituaries, press tributes, you know.

> CHAS
>
> How's the book going, by the way?

> GEORGE
>
> So-so. But they've brought the deadline forward. There's been a revival of inter-est in Hugh since . . .

> CHAS
> *(after a careful pause)*
> Will you need some help?

> GEORGE
> Chas . . . (*He laughs.*) I think I'll be
> fine on my own.

> CHAS
> Well, if not, I'm available.

> GEORGE
> Coming for a drive?

INT. HALLWAY OF APARTMENT — MORNING.
*They descend the stairs and walk through
the hallway when* CHAS *notices something
leaning against the wall. It is a red hula
hoop. He picks it up.*

> CHAS
> Is this yours?

> GEORGE
> Mine? No. Some kid's. There's always a few
> of them playing around here.

> CHAS
> So you've never seen it before?

> GEORGE
> No. Why - have you?

CHAS *stares at it in confusion for some
moments. He shakes his head and leans it
back against the wall. They exit the
building.*

EXT. STREET — MORNING.
Rome's traffic buzzes around GEORGE's *car.*
The car's hood is down. When they stop at
a traffic light, CHAS *looks round to see*
another open-topped car, with a very pretty
woman at the wheel. She's chatting and
laughing with a man – her boyfriend? – in
the passenger seat. The wheel, and the
woman's hands resting on it, seems to revolve
at an abnormal speed. CHAS *looks freaked*
out. Eventually the lights change, and she
drives off.

EXT. STREET — MORNING.
The traffic has thickened. GEORGE *has noticed*
CHAS's *absorption in the woman.*

                    GEORGE
  The look on your face.

                    CHAS
  I think I'm still tripping from last night.

                    GEORGE
  Oh yeah. Something you said . . . 'He'd kill
  me if he found out about this.' Sounded
  a bit desperate. I remember it now.

                    CHAS
  I said that?

                    GEORGE
  Your very words.

CUT TO: *Overhead shot of the car, which has*
sped up.

CUT TO: *Rear shot of* CHAS *and* GEORGE.

                    CHAS
Are you in a hurry or something?

                    GEORGE
No. It's funny, cos nearly the first thing
you asked me about this morning was Gwen.
Why would that be?

                    CHAS
I've no idea.

                    GEORGE
Really? You see, things come out when
you're tripping - things you might be want-
ing to conceal. I think the person - well,
the figment - you were arguing with last
night was Gwen.

                    CHAS
Why would I be arguing with Gwen?

                    GEORGE
That's what I was about to ask you. You
feared that someone would kill you if he
found out about 'this' -

                    CHAS
George, slow down -

                    GEORGE
I have a fancy that the someone is . . .
me. And what would prompt me to try and
kill you?

                    CHAS
I've no idea what you're talking about.

354

CUT TO: *Camera foregrounds* CHAS's *profile, while* GEORGE *looks round at him. The car is speeding dangerously.* CHAS *is the first to realise that the car has jumped a red light. In the background we see traffic heading crosswise towards them.*

                    CHAS
   Jesus, the lights! Fuck -

GEORGE *turns his head just as a truck ploughs full-tilt into the driver's side, knocking them sideways. A hideous screech of metal and glass. The screen whites out.*

19

September had nearly passed when Freya happened on an item in a film journal speculating on the prospects of the just-completed *Eureka*. It had run into post-production trouble, mostly related to reshoots involving leading actress Sonja Zertz, who had been unavailable following what the magazine described as a 'minor accident'. The real story had been buried. There was also a financial hole to fill after the sudden withdrawal of its main backer, Harold Pulver, now believed to be living in southern Spain. Berk Cosenza, the producer, was still hopeful that the film would be ready for its premiere at next year's Cannes festival. Reiner was reportedly back in Berlin scouting locations for his next venture. Freya's efforts to secure an interview with him had failed. Her only consolation was that no one else had got one either.

Sonja had also returned home to Germany. Freya had tried to see her after she left the hospital and moved back to her room at the Connaught – in vain. In the end she had had to ask Nat to pass on a letter, which he duly did: 'I put it in her hand,' he said. It was a brief message, though as sincere a thing as she had ever written. She had waited, fretting, hoping, then telling herself it didn't matter either way. There was no reply. Two weeks later Nat called to tell her Sonja was gone.

'Don't think badly of her,' he said. 'It would be devastating for anyone, but for an actress . . . She'll never make another film.'

The midday post had arrived at the *Chronicle*, and Freya leafed through it indifferently. One item gave her pause: an invoice, ancient, flimsy, mildewed with spots. The letterhead, in a stolid Victorian typeface, announced it as coming from the office of the Imperial Hat Co. The copperplate hand had dated it to August 1890, and had jotted down the fabric of the hat and its measurements. On the reverse was something else, six words typed in Courier:

```
ashes  to  ashes,  dust  to  dust
```

The ink on these words looked fresh. She puzzled over it for some moments, and turned back to the Victorian side. No customer name or address had been inscribed. The company apparently had a royal warrant, and was located at Bathurst House, Spitalfields, London. She checked the company in a telephone directory and found nothing. She rang Companies House, where a voice informed her that the Imperial Hat Co. had gone out of business in 1955. The invoice could have been found anywhere, in a ledger, or an antique shop, or a hat.

Later that afternoon she caught sight of Fosh across the newsroom, feet up on his desk, lobbing screwed-up balls of paper into an office bin.

'Busy day?' she said.

'I honestly don't know how I manage,' he said with a grin, launching another missile.

'Get your camera. I might have something for us.'

She had to bluff a bit while Fosh drove her there. At first she had been inclined to toss the invoice away; but anonymous messages, and natural intuition, had a habit of nagging away. She needed to make sure, and had spun him a line about receiving a tip-off. Bowler-hatted City gents were already flocking the streets and descending to the Tube by the time they reached the edges of Spitalfields. They parked on a cobbled terrace of derelict shops and houses, their windows cracked or blinded by chipboard. It was always a wonder to her that the City should exist cheek by jowl with this pauperised neighbourhood. They found a gated passageway leading to a courtyard, also cobbled, where a tall brick warehouse occupied three sides. A peeling faded fascia was still legible across a doorway. IMPERIAL HAT CO. Rusting grilles barred the windows, and a chained padlock looped the handles of its double doors.

Fosh, camera slung over his shoulder, looked about the courtyard unimpressed. 'You sure this is the right address?'

Freya nodded, and wandered to the far corner where wooden garage doors indicated another entrance. She tried a painted metal latch, expecting it to be locked; instead it gave a gratifying click, and she pulled the door open. Dust swarmed everywhere as she picked her way through the cavernous gloom; behind her she heard Fosh close the door and begin to nose around. The building was divided into a series of long rooms, still occupied by workers' tables and benches. All was disuse and neglect. The walls, leprous with damp, at intervals displayed advertising boards and posters for the Imperial Hat Co., even a certificate of merit from a guild-hall. It hadn't helped in the end, any more than that royal warrant had done. In what had once been an office she found heaps of discarded letters and invoices, of a sort her anonymous corres-pondent might have helped himself to. They could hear the soft scratching of mice beneath floorboards.

'What are we meant to be looking for?' asked Fosh.

Freya hesitated. 'A film can, possibly.'

They walked right around the shell of a factory that had once resounded to the presses and punches and steamers of the hatter's trade. Their footsteps crunched on grit. There was really nothing here but shadows and dust. The end of the building brought them to the open doorway of another garage, the replica of its neigh-bour opposite. She tried an ancient light switch, as dead as everything else. Behind her she heard Fosh sigh.

'Well, unless you're going to do a piece on the decline of the hat I think we should get out of here.'

She took the shallow steps down anyway. Through the murk she approached the outline of something – a car, or rather the shape of a car, swaddled in a grimy canvas shroud. Without paus-ing to think why she took hold of the canvas's edge and tugged it. As it slid off she gave a violent start. Through the clouded passenger window she could see someone in the driver's seat.

'Oh fuck. Fuck,' she cried in fear, hand to her mouth. In an instant Fosh was at her side. He fumbled for a match, lit it, and a feeble illumination flared against the glass.

Straining his gaze he said, 'I think it might be a dummy. It's just . . . black.'

They stared at one another for a moment. Swallowing her

terror, Freya tried the car door, which was locked. They would have to try the other side – the driver's. 'Wait there,' Fosh said, and she felt glad now to have obeyed her hunch in bringing him along. She watched him make his faltering way around the car, hesitating before he took the door handle. It opened, and Fosh reared back with a cry.

'Jesus.'

'What is it?' Freya called.

For the moment Fosh didn't speak. He had crooked his forearm against his nose and mouth. She came round to join him, dreading whatever it was he had found. 'It's not nice,' came his muffled voice, warning her. She smelled it before she realised what it was: a corpse, seated upright against the wheel. It had been burnt to blackness, beyond recognition. She felt her stomach lurch, once, and waited for the nausea to pass. Then she forced herself to take another look.

Dust to dust, she thought.

Nat took turns with Reiner and Gina in keeping Sonja company while she recuperated in her hotel room. He had expected family to descend on her, and was chastened to learn (or else had forgotten) that she had lost both parents, her father in the war, her mother a few years later. There was a brother, from whom she was long estranged. Nat thought he understood now why she and Reiner were so close.

After her determination to keep Freya away, it surprised him when, on the day before he drove her to the airport, Sonja allowed one other visitor to her room. Billie had brought flowers, and a heart thumping with dread. She tried her best not to stare at the bandages that mummified half of Sonja's face. She stayed no more than twenty minutes, fearing to tire the patient, and when she leaned in to kiss her goodbye she felt a tiny flinch beneath the gauzy mask. Outside in the corridor Nat, who had tactfully withdrawn himself, offered Billie a handkerchief to dab her brimming eyes.

'She seemed so calm,' Billie choked out under her breath.

Nat nodded: the calm of resignation, he supposed. He took her down for a drink at the hotel bar. Billie sensed that he wanted to talk about what had happened that day.

'I keep thinking I ought to have done something. But at the time I was half dazed from Pulver's assault on me.' It was what he had kept telling himself, yet spoken aloud his excuses sounded inadequate; cowardly, even. It keened away at him, like a radio set jabbering from a nearby window. He wanted to close his ears, but he couldn't.

'You can't blame yourself,' said Billie. 'If anyone should have stopped him it was Joey. What was *he* doing?'

'I think he was as shocked as anyone. Just didn't see it coming.'

Billie stirred her drink thoughtfully. 'At least you're safe from him now. I read in the paper that he's hiding out somewhere in Spain.'

Nat gave a small conceding pout. 'To think I was about to drag myself off into exile. Not that a few weeks – months – at Vere's place would have been a hardship.'

'How is he, by the way? Vere, I mean.'

He looked away. ' "*When sorrows come, they come not single spies, but in battalions.*" I've had a couple of sessions with him talking about the memoir, but he gets tired so quickly and I don't want to press him.'

'I'm sure he's being brave,' murmured Billie.

'Yes. I'd hoped they might have a cut of the film to show him before he . . . before it's too late.' He traced his finger absently on the shiny surface of the bar. 'Just one more damn thing I can't help.'

The case of the corpse in the car quickly gained notoriety. It mingled the macabre and the mysterious to a near-perfect degree. The police's efforts to identify the charred 'driver' had stalled, though an autopsy established that the victim – male, probably in his forties or fifties – had been drugged before being set on fire. Early speculation that it was a tramp who had accidentally immolated himself was dismissed. Forensics revealed that the corpse had been strapped into the car post-mortem. The killers apparently wanted him to be found, though why they had tipped off the journalist in question, not a crime reporter, prompted more bafflement.

In the weeks following, by coincidence, a Missing Persons file had been opened on Harold Pulver, not lying low in his Spanish bolt-hole after all. His family, unnerved, had eventually reported his disappearance to the police, and a bright spark at the Met had posited a link between the vanished businessman and the Corpse in the Car. An examination of dental records soon established that they were one and the same. Someone had got to Harry Pulver at last. Inevitably the list of suspects would be long: he had spent his life making enemies. The police hauled in associates, rivals, debtors, former cronies for questioning; all protested their innocence. The joke went that in the London underworld it would be easier to discount the slags who *hadn't* wanted him dead. The police could make no headway. Leads petered out. The crime scene had been miserly with clues.

Freya had her own theory as to the perpetrator, one which could have set investigators on a different track. Analysis of the antique invoice would have yielded fingerprints, perhaps, so too the book of matches posted through her door. Instead, she had decided to keep them to herself, and told the police that her tip-off about the corpse had come from an anonymous phone call. Her motives were complicated. She sensed that if she did go public about 'her' suspect a reprisal would not be slow in coming. The killer had shown himself to be resourceful and decisive. Yet something else stopped her; the book of matches felt like a tip of the hat as much as a threat, an admission that she had guessed him right. Without ever speaking they had made a secret pledge to one another, her safety for his freedom. They would have to tread carefully around their collusion – both were at risk from its disclosure. But why would she have wanted Harold Pulver's nemesis brought to book anyway? He had deserved his fate, just as Sonja deserved the veil of privacy she had cast over hers.

The Pulver story was still going when she arrived one mild October day for lunch at Bianchi's. She hadn't been back since she and Sonja had met there in the summer. It seemed to her now a haunted place, and she wasn't sure why she had decided to return. Looking about the room at the other diners she felt for a moment that something of significance to herself, some warning, might be gleaned from the talk that rose and echoed against the walls. The very air seemed alive with omens. The little maîtresse d' who greeted her was, as usual, a model of unobtrusive graciousness: perhaps she had come back for her.

Freya had arrived early, and remembered being nervous while she waited the previous time. Just as she began to give herself a talking-to she looked up and Nancy was coming towards her, the smile at full-beam.

'Darling,' she said, leaning in to her embrace. Nancy's russet hair was shorter, with a touch of grey, though her figure remained adolescently gawky. Her green eyes, always remarkable to her, were framed today by the disconcerting novelty of a pair of wire-framed glasses.

'You've got yourself writer's spectacles,' said Freya, covering her surprise.

Nancy made an uncertain grimace. 'Not too grannyish, are they?'

'No. Lennonish, I'd say.'

She looked relieved. They sat down, and Freya signalled a waiter for drinks. She and Nancy could go without seeing each another for months but once together would instantly slip into familiarity. Today she felt something new, an inescapable sense that she had missed Nancy more than Nancy would ever miss her. She quickly dismissed the thought.

'You look well. Have you had a holiday?'

'A week in Florence, staying with Kay,' said Freya. 'She was asking after you. Reads every book. In fact, remind me, I've got a copy of *Disciples* I want you to sign for her.'

'Oh, I will, I will. Kay! She must be –'

'Seventy-six. Going a bit deaf, but sharp as a tack otherwise. And still makes those flooring Negronis.'

Nancy shook her head, wonderingly. 'I'm surprised you've had time for a holiday. Your name seems to be in the paper every day. Are you their crime correspondent now?'

Freya laughed. 'No, but I sometimes feel like one. There's been more interest in the corpse story than in anything I've ever written.'

'People love a mystery.'

'True. Nat's delighted about it, of course – he says Pulver's

362

involvement will give *Eureka* the greatest publicity boost it could ever hope for.'

'How is Nat?'

'Thriving. He's started a new play. He wrote something for me, actually, I must show you it.' She reached into her handbag and pulled out a folded sheet of A4. 'Lines composed for my birthday.'

She handed it over for Nancy, who read it aloud.

MY FAVOURITE THINGS

(with apologies to Oscar Hammerstein II)

Freya and Nancy and ice-cold Martinis
Albany rooftops and smoked-salmon blinis
Dead easy work for the money it brings
These are a few of my favourite things

Punts on the Cherwell and open-top Rollers
Beatles for Sale *and slow left-arm bowlers*
Lysergic acid and holiday flings
These are a few of my favourite things

Cream-coloured stockings and blue velvet jackets
Young women's buttocks and firm tennis rackets
Wild nights and love bites and silver cock rings
These are a few of my favourite things

Girls in black undies and well-composed dramas
Krug in a bucket and satin pyjamas
Thwack of the cane and the twang of bedsprings
These are a few of my favourite things

When the prick wilts
When the whip stings
When I'm feeling blue
I simply remember my favourite things
And the best of them is <u>you</u>!

Nancy looked over to Freya, and they both burst out laughing.

'I like the way it starts off quite innocently, then gets filthier as it goes along.'

'Yeah. He told me he got halfway through and thought *fuck it* – let's have some fun! I'd love to hear Julie Andrews sing this, wouldn't you? Especially the bit about cock rings.'

Their pasta had arrived, and they toasted their reunion with a bottle of Gavi.

'How's your new one going?' asked Freya.

'Oh, all right. Another tale of heartache in the Home Counties. To judge from the reviews of *Disciples* it seems literary London has had enough of me and my middle-class concerns.'

'Literary London can get stuffed,' said Freya crisply. 'Your books just get better and better.'

'Spoken like a true friend,' smiled Nancy.

'It's got nothing to do with being a true friend. I read a lot of novels, so I'm qualified to judge, and hardly any of them can do what you do. Nat says the same.'

'Well, that's nice. I suppose people must always have something to patronise,' she added mildly. 'I don't mind. It's quite funny, really, to see even the place you set a story attacked as "decadent and marginal". I mean – Henley-on-Thames!'

The lightness with which she spoke was not, Freya knew, a put-on. Ever since she had known her Nancy had the quiet assurance of a writer indifferent to trends. She gossiped about better-known contemporaries, but she didn't envy them. She noticed the condescension of the reviews, but she didn't brood on them. She cared only about the quality of her writing; the rest was noise.

Mollified by the wine and the charm of the company Freya felt able to broach a subject she had always found prickly. She couldn't help resenting Nancy's husband for taking her away from London, despite the inconvenient evidence that Nancy had settled to life in Oxfordshire very contentedly.

'How's Adam?' she said, adjusting her tone to an acceptable level of curiosity.

'He's fine,' replied Nancy. 'He's just had some good news, actually.' A fleeting movement of her face spoke warningly to Freya that the news might not be of unequivocal delight.

364

'Really?'

Nancy nodded, but couldn't quite hold her eye. 'Yes, he's just got a teaching appointment. At Princeton.'

Freya felt a sudden chill. 'Princeton? You mean, New Jersey?'

Yes, that Princeton, it was a very exciting opportunity for him, she explained, and it came with a great deal of prestige in a department –

'So you're going with him?' Freya wasn't interested in departments or their prestige; she wanted this out, now.

'Oh, Freya. Of course I'm going with him.'

'I see.' She had felt an ominous vibration the moment she'd arrived, and here it was: her best friend's 'good news'. 'So how long would this be for?'

Nancy hesitated, and Freya took a breath to hold down the panic. 'I'm not sure – two years, possibly three.'

'Three years!' she almost wailed. 'You can't. Oh God. I felt something awful was about to happen but I'd never have guessed *this.*'

Nancy kept silent, knowing, and fearing, the greater vehemence she might provoke by offering an argument. In the early days of their friendship Freya had called the shots, and Nancy had happily followed. Through Oxford and the years of sharing a flat in Bloomsbury her leadership had been irresistible, until one day it wasn't. Freya had outgrown the extreme reactions of her youth, had learned to curb her volatile temper, but nothing had shaken her conviction that she knew best – and could bend people to her will.

'Nance, please, you can't be serious. Not for three years.'

'You make it sound like I'm going to prison.'

'To me that's what it feels like. Except that you're choosing it.'

'You can always visit.'

'What, you in prison? I don't want to visit. I want you to be here, where I can see you any time.'

Nancy smiled at her sadly. There was a pause before she said, 'I can't not go.'

Freya had stopped eating and pushed her plate aside. She took out a cigarette and lit it. It was as she had thought: *She doesn't need me like I need her.* They had been through a lot together. She had done awful things to Nancy in the early days, things that still caused her a spasm of shame. There had been seven years when they didn't speak at all, so bitter was the fallout. Then there was that moment a few years ago when her feelings for Nancy had turned the whole thing upside down. Their friendship had survived it all, and they'd probably get through this, too. Except Freya knew that she would never be the priority in her life again. She took a long drag of her cigarette. Her silence might have been interpreted as a sulk, but she didn't feel like being 'nice' about it.

Nancy, always conciliatory, decided to steer the talk elsewhere.

'That actress you told me about in your last letter – Sonja? – have you kept in touch?'

'No.'

'Oh . . . I finally got to see, on your recommendation, *The Private Life of Hanna K.* She's wonderful in it, really.'

'Yeah. She was.'

Nancy paused, hoping for more. 'I thought – I gathered – well, things looked quite promising. The boat trip, and what have you.'

Freya shrugged, and waited a beat. 'Another of my failures. We'd been getting on pretty well until . . . something terrible happened.' She recounted the circumstances of Pulver's vicious reprisals, on Nat, then on Sonja. As she spoke she felt the horror bearing down on her with renewed force; she could almost feel Sonja's scream pierce her, almost see the blood fountaining down her cheek. Nancy listened in appalled silence; the colour seemed to drain from her face. Freya told her that the story was not to be repeated. The press, thank God, had never got hold of it. Sonja's agent had announced simply that she was ill and had taken a temporary retirement from movies.

'I wanted to visit her in hospital, but she wouldn't – I kept asking. She's back in Munich now.'

'Oh, Freya, I'm so sorry. Were you close?'

'We might have been. I thought there was something.' She looked away, feeling some obstruction in her throat, and drank a mouthful of wine to clear it. Whenever friends asked about her love life she would joke and say that she was a hopeless case – always with the pleasurable anticipation of being contradicted. She liked to pretend she was romantically doomed. Lately, though, she was wary of saying things like 'I'm too old and tired to love', for the melancholy reason that she was starting to believe it. She could no longer muster the irony to make her life sound amusing.

When she looked up, Nancy's gaze was on her. 'Think how she must feel, though. Sonja. It must be so hard to go from being an object of passion to an object of pity, especially for someone whose face has been so adored.'

'I wouldn't have pitied her,' said Freya, indignant. 'I'd have made her realise – but what's the point? It would never have worked anyway.'

'You can't be sure of that,' Nancy said gently, and though Freya scowled she felt secretly grateful to her for not agreeing. In the next instant it occurred to her that Nancy had spoken of pity just to provoke her response. She stared at her friend, absorbing the details of her face, her eyes, the slope of her neck, as if she might memorise them.

'God. What will I do without you?' She had meant to keep her tone light, but a sadness tugged at the edge.

'I'll be coming back, you ninny,' she said, taking her hand across the table. 'You know that, don't you?'

Freya nodded, though for the moment she couldn't speak. Couldn't see, either, for the tears blinding her eyes.

Title Card: SIX MONTHS LATER

INT. CHURCH — MORNING.
*A memorial service is in progress. Music
plays. At the lectern* GWEN *is speaking.
Camera draws back to focus upon the audience packing the pews. Towards the front
we see* CHAS, *seated next to* JANE. *All are
dressed in black.*
  Music fades out as GWEN's *voice fades in.*

GWEN
. . . He was of course a brilliant news-
paperman, and a formidable critic. He has
left behind a book, soon to be published;
he should have lived to write many more.
But his greatest success was not in his
attainments; it was in himself, in the way
he was - to all of us - that funny and
kind and most trustworthy friend. The ache
of his absence will dwindle, in time. The
memory of his presence, I hope, will never
fade.

CUT TO: *Reverse shot of* GWEN *leaving the
lectern and returning to the front pew.
This is the cue for* CHAS *to rise from his
seat and take her place before the*

audience. *He approaches the altar with a heavy limp, and a walking stick. At the lectern he composes himself and takes out a folded piece of paper from his jacket.*

CUT TO: *Camera faces* CHAS.

> CHAS
>
> George Corvick was my editor and mentor. He was also my best friend . . .

Music fades back in as the camera locks on CHAS, *his upright bearing a model of grave dignity as he bids the departed farewell. But we may dimly discern something else in his expression - the remorse of a disappointed man.*

INT. RECEPTION ROOM — DAY.
Public room of a London hotel, where drinks are being served to guests from the memorial service. Amid the crowd GWEN, *who's on the arm of her friend* DEAN DRAYTON, *spots* CHAS. *She detaches herself and approaches him.*

> GWEN
>
> Sorry not to have seen you till now. Dean and I have been away -

> CHAS
>
> Yes, I heard. My congratulations.

> GWEN
>
> Thank you. You look . . . much better.

CHAS
(*ruefully*)
Walking again is good. I know how lucky
I was to — When's the happy day?

GWEN
Sometime next year. I've been too busy
with George's book to plan the wedding.

CHAS
I've been wondering about that. I see
Antrobus has given it a new title.

GWEN
Well, it couldn't be called *The Figure in
the Carpet* any longer.

CHAS
You mean . . . ?

GWEN
George hadn't dealt with it - there are
notes, nothing specific. It's not half the
book it should have been - literally.

CHAS
I had a feeling he might have confided in
you . . . what it was.

GWEN
The secret? No. I asked him, of course,
but he refused. He wanted it to be his
'Poirot' moment, revealing the solution at
the end of the book.

CHAS
He did have a sense of the dramatic.

370

GWEN

But not the timing. With both of them gone, it's lost forever. (*She looks over his shoulder at* JANE, *across the room.*) Talking of timing, are you and Jane planning an announcement?

CHAS

Oh, you mean - marriage?

GWEN

Of course.

CHAS
            (*with a significant look*)
There's only one woman I've ever thought of proposing to.

GWEN
            (*gently*)
Charles . . . It wouldn't have worked. You know that.

CHAS *stares across the room at* DEAN DRAYTON, *then turns back to* GWEN.

CHAS
            (*shaking his head*)
It makes me wonder, all the same . . .

GWEN

What?

CHAS

Well, George I could understand. He was a catch. But Dean Drayton? What's he got that I haven't?

CHAS *and* GWEN *stare at each other for a few moments. Then* CHAS *sees* JANE *beckoning him from a scrum of people.*

> CHAS
>
> Take care of yourself, Gwen.

CHAS *walks away into the crowd.*

EXT. JANE'S TOWN HOUSE IN CHELSEA — DAY.

INT. BEDROOM — DAY.
CHAS *is getting dressed. He's absently putting on a tie and gazing out of the window. He stops, lost in thought.*

CUT TO: JANE, *entering the room, catches him unawares. She stares for some moments.*

> JANE
>
> Darling?

> CHAS
>> (*startled*)
> Sorry . . . miles away.

JANE *crosses the room, puts her arms around him. She looks at him with concern.*

> JANE
>
> You looked so terribly sad just then.

> CHAS
>> (*smiling, holding her*)
> I can't think why. I've got everything I want.

CHAS *breaks from their embrace, distracted by something outside the window. Camera changes to his POV, overlooking the street. A huge removals van has just pulled up at her front door.*

> CHAS
> (*pointing down*)
> Not trying to move me out already, are you?

> JANE
> (*giggling*)
> Silly. It's just some of Hugh's old things – furniture and so on. Been in storage since he died. I thought I'd choose a few pieces and put the rest up for auction.

JANE *leaves the bedroom.* CHAS *continues dressing.*

EXT. HOUSE — DAY.
CHAS *leaves* JANE'S *house, dodging out of the way of overalled men carrying in boxes.*

INT. CLUB ROOM — AFTERNOON.
CHAS *sits in the bar of a gentlemen's club, reading a newspaper. A waiter has just brought him a drink.*

CUT TO: *A man entering the bar sees* CHAS. *It is* GWEN'S *fiancé* DEAN DRAYTON.

> DRAYTON
> It's Pallingham, isn't it?

CHAS

Yes. Drayton.

He rises to shake hands.

DRAYTON

I didn't know you were a member here.

CHAS

Recently enrolled. My wife encouraged me.

DRAYTON

Ah yes. Gwen was talking about Jane only
the other day.

CHAS *invites him to sit down.*

CHAS

In what regard?

DRAYTON

Well, you know Gwen has been editing
George's book about Vereker. Last week she
came across a note in George's hand, a
reminder to himself to chase a box of
papers Vereker had promised to give him.
But it now seems those papers never showed
up - they weren't in George's study, nor
were they among the papers Jane handed
over when he became literary executor. So
Gwen's rather keen to ask her if everything from the estate has been released.
She thinks there's a load of papers out
there relating to a 'secret project' of
Vereker's.

CHAS

Secret project?

374

DRAYTON

Gwen wouldn't explain it to me. All she
said was these papers would provide some
clue or other to his work.

CUT TO: CHAS *is staring at him as if he
has seen - or heard - a ghost. He seems
unable to speak.*

DRAYTON

Sorry, have I said something wrong?

CHAS

No. No. You say that Gwen told you this
last week?

DRAYTON

Yes, she's been madly busy, else she would
have written to Jane. Of course there may
be no telling where the papers have gone.

CHAS, *suddenly pale, rises from his chair.*

CHAS

I'm so sorry, would you excuse me? There's
an urgent bit of business I've just remembered I must attend to.

CHAS *leaves* DRAYTON, *puzzled, in the bar.*

EXT. STREET — DAY.
CHAS *emerges from the club on Pall Mall
and looks wildly around for a taxi. Seeing
none, he begins to run.*

CUT TO: CHAS *sprinting through St James's
Square, then on to Piccadilly. He sees a
bus bound for Chelsea and jumps on the back.*

CUT TO: CHAS *on the bus, his face a picture of anxiety. He looks about, as if baffled at his fellow passengers' complete unconcern.*

CUT TO: CHAS *dashing through the gracious terraces of Chelsea, arriving at* JANE's *house panting, out of breath.*

INT. LIVING ROOM — DAY.
CHAS *bursts in to find* JANE *examining a vintage cabinet, plainly from the estate of* VEREKER. *She looks up in alarm at his pale, sweating face.*

> JANE
> Darling, what's the matter?

CUT TO: CHAS *has noticed something outside in the garden. A bonfire.*

EXT. GARDEN — DAY.
He dashes out to find one of JANE's *gardeners tending a brazier piled high with papers, which he prods in a bored, unnoticing way.* CHAS *stops, aghast.*

> CHAS
> What are you doing?

> GARDENER
> Mrs Pallingham wanted this stuff burnt, papers and so on –

> CHAS
> Oh no. No. No. No. For God's sake . . .

CHAS *tries to grab a handful of burning paper, but it's already charred to a crisp.*

CUT TO: JANE *comes up behind him, looking worried. She signals for the gardener to withdraw.* CHAS *stands there immobile, like a man watching his hopes go up in smoke.*

                    JANE
Darling, what's going on?

                    CHAS
The papers you found. What were they?

                    JANE
Oh, I didn't look at them. They were so old. But the little cabinet they were stored in is exquisite - it's a cherrywood thing, with a roundel embossed on its frame. I thought we might put it - Chas?

CUT TO: CHAS *is looking dead ahead, his eyes streaming. The smoke from the bonfire drifts right across him.* JANE *looks on in distress.*

                    JANE
Chas. What is it? Please tell me.

                    CHAS
It's nothing. It isn't . . . anything.

                    JANE
But you're *crying* . . .

                    CHAS
It's from the smoke. I'll be fine. Just - just give me a minute, will you?

JANE *continues to stare at him anxiously, then turns back towards the house.*

CUT TO: *The camera slowly pulls away and up, looking down on* CHAS *in front of the fire, a man alone. Charred fragments whirl up through the air, disappearing.*

FADE OUT.

CREDITS.

20

Vere Summerhill died at a hospice in Chelsea one morning in October. Nat had been at his bedside the night before, but arrived too late for the last moments. He had visited most days towards the end, reading to him, sharing *The Times* crossword, reminiscing. (He had kept notes.) The *Chronicle*, at Freya's instigation, had asked Nat to write a personal tribute. Its final paragraph ran:

> Vere Summerhill died as he had lived, with fortitude, nonchalance and wry good humour. He would joke that he had 'died' many times before, up on the screen; the cinema-going public had seen their idol take his leave of the world so often – as a fighter pilot, cavalier, cowboy, infantry officer – that we came to think of him as indestructible. His final role, as the writer Hugh Vereker in the forthcoming *Eureka*, may come to be judged one of his greatest. Summerhill was already dying while filming continued, and it is the mark of the man that his illness remained a secret from the rest of the cast. He preferred to keep his colleagues cheerful, and to do his suffering in private. As an actor he will be remembered for his poise – that unflappable heroic calm under pressure – and for his voice, whose fluid musical lilt he seemed to control like a virtuoso clarinettist. The right notes were always at his command. It is hard, grievously hard, to think of that voice stilled forever.

Nat drove down to a quiet village in Hampshire to meet Celia Summerhill, Vere's sister. She was three years younger, a spinster, bird-like and bright-eyed. At certain moments, in a sideways look or an inflection of her voice, he caught the disconcerting ghost of his old friend. The funeral was private, attended by a few friends from her choir. Vere was buried in a corner of the churchyard, next to a plot Celia had reserved for herself. She would be the last of the Summerhills. Back at her house she had brought out an old scrapbook of her brother's early career, newspaper cuttings of the matinee idol, and later the flying ace. Nat couldn't help noticing that the record stopped just before Vere's trial and imprisonment for homosexual offences. One might have assumed that he had died fifteen years ago.

Some weeks later he attended a memorial service at St Paul's, the actors' church, in Covent Garden. There were readings from MacNeice's *Autumn Journal*, Tennyson, and *A Shropshire Lad*. During the adagio of Finzi's Concerto for Clarinet and Strings, Nat felt his eyes grow hot with tears; he remembered Vere playing it on his old gramophone at Ennismore Gardens. The church was full, though he spotted few of his famous contemporaries from the London days; the notoriety of his prison sentence had made him as much of a pariah as Wilde had been in his day. One who had stayed loyal was Edie Greenlaw, a grande dame of the stage who had known Vere since the 1920s. At the conclusion of the service she sang 'When I Grow Too Old to Dream' in a quavering alto.

At the reception afterwards Nat searched her out.

'My dear,' he said, placing a reverent kiss on her sunken powdered cheek, 'that voice of yours would be the envy of a nightingale.'

Edie drawled, 'Oh, you're very kind, darling, though that's always been Evelyn's song, you know.'

'Not any more. Vere would have been thrilled.'

He saw her eyes moisten behind the squashed spiders of her caked lashes. 'Dear, dear man. The times we had! Did you ever see us in *Antony and Cleopatra*?'

'I think I was in short trousers at the time,' said Nat, with an apologetic wince.

'Of course. I forget what a child you are. Well, we were always larking around, trying to outdo each other. It became a little contest between us as to who could get the audience going. If it looked like I was winning Vere would contrive to whisper something and make me fluff my line: one night during my death scene I heard him mutter, "I fear that asp has just contracted food poisoning." The cast were in fits.'

'I must apply to you for more in that vein for his biography. I'm thinking of calling it *The Last English Martyr*.'

'Quite right too,' said Edie.

'At the end he asked me if there was anything I wanted – he gave me this,' said Nat, holding up Vere's signet ring on his pinkie. It still felt unfamiliar on his hand.

'He was so terribly handsome, wasn't he? If he hadn't – well, I seem to have had a rapport with queer men my whole life. At Jimmy Erskine's I was usually the only woman present. He said he liked me for being the one person ruder than he was.'

'I wonder what Jimmy would make of things today, now Parliament has passed the sex bill.'

Edie narrowed her eyes. 'I imagine he'd be disappointed. Half the fun for Jimmy was the risk. He loved to think he was getting away with it.'

Nat nodded. 'Yes, unlike Vere, who led a life of almost blameless privacy and then got fitted up by the police. I'm not sure he was ever the same after Pentonville.'

'It might have been worse for him. I'll always remember that photograph of you shielding the poor man on the steps of the Old Bailey during the trial. You were like Robbie Ross, raising his hat as Oscar walked the gauntlet at the Bankruptcy Court; "men have gone to heaven for smaller things than that".'

He held Edie's gaze for a moment. 'That might be the nicest thing anyone's ever said to me. I wonder, once I've got a draft completed, would you write a little foreword on Vere? After all, you knew him longer than anyone.'

Edie's mouth puckered with doubt. 'Oh, darling, I don't know . . .'

He took the old woman's hand and raised it to his lips. 'Please. It would mean so much. Think of it as a final gift to Vere.'

After a pause she said, 'We-e-ell, I could possibly . . .' My God, Nat thought, if there were an Olympics for wheedling I'd have the podium to myself.

A feline gleam pricked her eye. 'There'd be a *fee*, I dare say?'

Nat smiled: expert wheedler he may be, but Edie was no fool. 'I'll have the agent send you a contract.'

Freya was at home one Saturday morning when a knock came at the door. She opened it to find a woman whose face she recognised but couldn't immediately place.

'Hello,' said her caller, hopefully.

A second passed, and the clouds parted. 'It's Billie, isn't it?'

Billie smiled in relief. 'You remember. The boat trip —'

'I wasn't sure for a moment. You've done something to your hair.'

She nodded: she had gone blonde for a play they were just rehearsing. Freya (thinking the colour didn't quite suit her) invited her to come in. Billie followed her down the hallway, admiring the paintings and drawings on the wall. She looked around the bookshelves, inspecting this and that, while Freya went off to the kitchen to make them tea.

'Nat gave me your address. I hope you don't mind me dropping by,' Billie said as her host returned to the room. 'I've actually been wandering around the neighbourhood this morning. I'm looking for a place to rent.'

'Ah. I think you were living in Kentish Town when we last met.'

'Yes, still am, with my mum,' Billie said, pleased, for some reason, that Freya had remembered. 'Though before that I rented a place not far from here, in King's Cross. So I know Islington a bit.'

'It's not a bad place to live. Lots of actors and writers have moved here. It's quite cheap, and near enough to the West End.' She paused before saying, 'So you're back to the stage . . .'

'Yeah. I mean, *Eureka* was quite an experience, but —'

'I hope we'll get to see it one day.'

Billie returned a dubious expression. 'That'll depend on the lawyers, and the money. I saw you on the telly, by the way, when they announced that Pulver was dead. How did you manage to find him?'

'A fluke. I got a phone call tipping me off.' It didn't sound very convincing to her own ears, but the police had believed it, and she

382

wasn't about to spill the beans now. She sensed that Billie was troubled by something. 'What's on your mind?' she asked.

'Well, I know he had lots of enemies – Pulver, I mean – but when I read about what had happened I wondered if it was someone involved in the film. In revenge for . . .'

Freya shrugged. 'It's possible, of course. But we'll probably never know.' She leaned over for her cigarettes and offered Billie one. They smoked for a while and talked about the play she was starring in. It was a black comedy by a 'challenging' new playwright, a pretender to Nat's throne.

'I haven't told him about my being cast yet. D'you think he'll be upset?'

Freya laughed. 'Nat'll get over it. I'm sure it's a good play, and you've got a living to earn.'

They were finishing the tea when Billie reached into her handbag and took out a brown-paper package. She looked worried as she handed it to Freya.

'I've been meaning to give this to you.' Mystified, Freya opened it and pulled out a scarf, silk, patterned, by Pucci. 'You remember you lent me your scarf that day on the boat?'

'Yes . . . but this isn't mine,' said Freya, puzzled.

'I know, I'm sorry. I was going to return it, but' – she hesitated, recalling the awkward moment – 'something happened. When Sonja was still in London I visited her –'

'She saw you?' said Freya, surprised, and secretly hurt.

'Yes, we talked; not for long. Before I left she saw that I was wearing your scarf, I don't know how she knew it was yours, but she did. Anyway, she leaned over and held it for a moment, and then said, "May I have it?" I didn't know what to say, so . . .'

'You gave it to her.'

Billie nodded. 'She was sitting there and I – I didn't have the heart to say no.' She had spent the last few weeks scouring the shops for a replacement, but she could never find an exact match. 'And I remembered when you lent it to me you said to look after it, cos it was a present.'

Freya, distracted, shook her head. She considered the new scarf in silence. Billie, accusing herself, wondered if Freya was annoyed. She had done her a good turn that day, looking after her when she'd been sick on the boat and then lending the scarf to cover up the puke stain. She ought to have acknowledged her kindness by returning the thing at the earliest opportunity.

'I'm really sorry,' she began, unable to bear the silence. But Freya, to her amazement, had turned a smile on her.

'It's fine, honestly. I'm glad Sonja has it. Though I don't understand why she wanted it.'

Billie, relieved at last, said, 'Well, it *was* beautiful.'

'Yes, I suppose it was. But look' – she wrapped the new scarf gaily about her neck – 'this one's just as nice.'

They had another cigarette and talked on for a while. Billie wanted to know more about Freya's father, whether he was still in London – she'd admired his work long before she'd ever met Freya. So did her mum, Nell; she was a painter too, though nothing like as distinguished as Stephen Wyley, of course. As a matter of fact she had a new exhibition on in a couple of weeks. Would she care to bring her dad to the private view?

Just as Billie was leaving, Freya asked her, out of nowhere, if she happened to have Sonja's address in Munich. She thought she might write to her. Or maybe just book a flight and go there.

Nat was seated at a large lunch party he had never meant to attend among people he neither knew nor cared for. The sixty-odd guests were dining on duck à l'orange; he favoured the sustenance of gin and tonics. It was an occasion sponsored by a nabob of the arts who wished to debate a vital question about something Nat had already forgotten. A steady hum of conversation dominated the room. Across from him sat a Cabinet minister, flanked by a popular magazine writer and a society diarist.

He was there only because it was preferable to sitting at his desk staring at a blank page in the typewriter. He had fallen behind with the Vere biography. Thinking so much about his late friend had plunged him into melancholy. Death, or its spectre, hovered in his vision like Macbeth's dagger. He had been doing the maths. If he was to die, like Vere, at sixty-three, that would afford him only another twenty-three years; allow three and a half years for a play to be written, rehearsed and staged, he could perhaps count on completing six (and a bit) until his allotted span was up.

Knowing his own habits of dilatoriness and procrastination an estimate of five years per play was more realistic, which would mean four (and a bit) by the time he was sixty-three. Of course he might make it to McCartney's fabled sixty-four, or beyond, there was no telling, but what if some debilitating illness slowed him down, or dammed up his inspiration, or unfitted him for writing altogether?

The magazine columnist, a well-turned-out lady with spectacles on a chain and a voice that resounded unpleasantly on the ear, had just concluded a monologue fully as boring as the one that had preceded it. She looked around their table with a satisfied air, offering a narrow gap for another guest to dart in between and seize the conversational baton. As no one had the presence of mind to do so, the lady simply turned to her nearest neighbour and barked, apropos of nothing, 'And when did you last read Huxley's *Those Barren Leaves*?'

Nat managed to smother his snort of laughter behind a fake cough, unremarked by all except the young woman next to him. Her mock-prim expression nearly set him off again.

'Naughty,' she whispered, to which he replied with a smiling grimace of contrition. He had barely registered her up to this moment, and realised his first impression had been mistaken. The mousy girl he had dismissed on sight was actually dark-haired, with interesting brown eyes and a smile that revealed a row of geometrically neat teeth. He fleetingly imagined them sinking into his neck.

'Sorry, I didn't catch your . . .'

'Gwen,' she said, still keeping her voice low. It transpired she was a junior aide to the minister at the table. 'You're gulping down that gin like it's medicine.'

'Because that's exactly what it is,' he replied. 'I'm trying to numb my senses to the stentorian drone hard by us. Unsuccessfully, so far.'

She sniggered, and he felt himself being charmed. The same loud voice cut across them like an air-raid siren.

'Christ,' he muttered. 'If Lady Catherine de Bourgh here keeps this up you're going to have to stop me sticking a fork in her rear.'

Gwen looked across the table. 'Lady Catherine de Bourgh,' she murmured, without irony. 'I didn't know that was her name.'

Nat stared at her disbelievingly. For a moment he considered explaining that Lady Catherine was in fact – but no; he couldn't do it. He had spent his whole life among people to whom he could name-drop fictional characters as though they were personal acquaintances, and would receive a knowing smile in reply. It was a mark of their intelligence, almost of their civilised good manners. He was too set in his ways, too much of a snob, to strike up friendships with people who hadn't read *Pride and Prejudice*, no matter how pleasing the face or attractive the manner.

He looked around, and leaned in to whisper: 'I'm just going to sneak off to the gents.'

Gwen narrowed her eyes. 'No you're not. You're going to sneak off out of here and not come back.'

He laughed: shrewder than he thought. 'You'll get along fine without me.'

'Go on then. Abandon me to my cruel fate.'

He caught in her tone the merest feathering of regret. She had lifted her gaze back to the table, and he contemplated her in profile. She would be all right. She was young. She was a junior aide, for God's sake! But still, it was possible he may have misjudged her.

As he rose to leave he bent his head to hers. 'I'll be in the lobby in five minutes, if you'd care to join.'

The ambiguous glance she returned was maddening. If she wasn't interested then why had she pretended otherwise? He had been here before. Freya had once told him, as only she would dare, that his romantic outlook was 'basically adolescent'. On meeting a new woman he would raise his hopes immediately and vertiginously; he would idealise her, consider her a paragon of womanhood, a mate for life. The ensuing weeks he would spend mapping out the enchanted path to bliss, before his critical sense was reawoken – a misplaced word, a disagreeable laugh, even an unconscious movement of the face that betrayed some ignorance or imperfection. The cooling off would begin, her flaws gradually shifting from regrettable to unpardonable; soon he was mentally packing up to leave. And yet . . . surely the *Pride and Prejudice* gaffe was a fault of youth, one he could correct in a gentle and tolerant way instead of regarding it as a case for dismissal?

He stood in the lobby, checking his watch. The five minutes were up. He felt somewhat affronted by her non-appearance. Another minute he would give her; she had perhaps been detained by the minister, or had dithered over her pretext for scarpering. Outside he could see the London traffic, hear its subdued thunder through the glass doors. God, it was lonely out there.

A feeling of cold certainty engulfed him. She wasn't coming. He pushed through the doors and descended the steps. The afternoon light held a champagne brightness. He had thought of calling Freya, but she had gone off somewhere at short notice. Back to Albany, and the desk, for him. However sick he was of his own company, the solitude of his self, it had to be faced. The writer was a free man, but he was alone; no one else could do the job for you. So lost was he in these musings that he only became aware of the footsteps when they were right behind him.

'Hey!' came Gwen's narked voice. 'You told me you'd *wait*.'

He stopped and considered her. 'I'd given up hope.'

In the daylight the brown of her eyes was astonishing; they held a liquid brilliance, the colour of old sherry. 'I didn't realise you were a stickler for punctuality.'

Stickler. He liked that. She had fallen into step with him. He didn't really know where he was going, but he felt glad to have her at his side, her heels ticking along the pavement. Their arms brushed against one another. It took him a moment to realise that he had started whistling.

From *A New Compendium of Film and Film-makers* (seventh edition, 2016)

EUREKA (1968 UK/US, 111 min)

So many stories have accumulated around this movie – of reckless drug-taking, financial scandal, plagiarism, walkouts, reshoots, a notable swansong, a notorious murder – that it's hard to comprehend how muted was its first appearance at Cannes in May 1968. Its British release that autumn followed suit. Not many people saw it; even fewer understood it. But like Hockney's *A Bigger Splash* – another coolly enigmatic product of the time – the ripples of its influence have been deeper and stealthier as the years go by. *Eureka* is at heart an artistic conundrum, yet its tone is as brisk and varied as life itself: sprightly, sexy, witty, lyrical, creepy, elegiac. Reiner Werther Kloss harmonises these moods without diminishing either the elusiveness of its mystery or the yearning of its romance.

Chas Pallingham is the story's protagonist and dupe. A chance meeting with a revered elderly novelist, Vereker, sets him off on a quest: what is the unsuspected secret, 'the figure in the carpet', that informs Vereker's entire body of work? He is soon joined in this task by his friend and editor George and George's fiancée Gwen, herself a writer and an obscure object of desire to the moony Chas. The search for meaning transports them from swinging London to genteel weekends in a Sussex mansion and thence to the sybaritic embrace of Portofino and Rome. 'Our doubt is our passion and our passion is our task'; though in the unfolding of this *folie à trois* we are never sure if Chas's passion is more concerned with literary exegesis or romantic possession.

The film comes from a Henry James short story, 'The Figure in The Carpet', adapted freely – some might say with diabolical liberty – by Nathaniel Fane. It is no small feat to have carved out a script from the lapidary grandeur of those Jamesian sentences, though Fane's twists on the source material are violent enough to leave purists suffering whiplash: torque of the devil, indeed. His flagrant steal from the Beatles' 'A Day in the Life' for George's revelatory trip nearly brought a lawsuit from Apple Records. Yet its mood of sultry unease holds up, thanks to the hazed photography of Jürgen Haffner and the fugue-like jazz score by Dox Walbrook, whose edgy version of 'My Favourite Things' beautifully complements the famous hula-hoop sequence. One may safely predict that this will be the only psychedelic Henry James adaptation ever to reach the screen.

Both writer and director were rumoured to be so fogged by LSD during the shoot that it's a wonder anything of coherence emerged at all: Arno Drexler's sleek editing may have been instrumental in sorting order from chaos. Yet Kloss confirms here what a brilliant director of actors he is, especially with Billie Cantrip (on her debut) as Jane and his former muse Sonja Zertz (pre-road accident) as the cold and queenly Gwen. Ronnie Stiles, with his stiff carriage and stuffy language, is dead on as Chas. Note, in one of her few screen roles, Gina Press, before she became a much-loved face of children's TV in the 1970s and 80s.

It was also Vere Summerhill's final curtain. Clearly ailing at the time, he managed to be at once light and grave as the fading writer who whips his young acolyte to a frenzy of competitive chagrin. His fine, oboe-like voice haunts the film.

Some have felt cheated by the non-revelation of the finale. The mystery that has seduced and tantalised us turns out to have an 'O' at its centre: the circle of life, or a mocking zero? There's no telling, and the film would be an inferior thing if it did. 'Pay attention, but stop short of explanation,' a composer once wrote. *Eureka*, cupped inside its bubble of charm, seems only surface and intrigue, but beneath this lies a knotty question about the value of art. Can its pleasure be separated from its meaning? In other words, can we enjoy a piece of art without having to 'get it'? Nearly five decades on, this film at least offers a sly affirmative.

Acknowledgements

My thanks to Dan Franklin, Rachel Cugnoni, Ana Fletcher, Michal Shavit, Suzanne Dean, Joe Pickering, Victoria Murray-Browne, Richard Cable, Katherine Fry, Anna Webber, Seren Adams.

Also to Carmen Callil, Simon Hopkinson and, as ever, to my friend and editor Doug Taylor.

The following were invaluable to me in writing this novel: *Kenneth Tynan Letters* and *The Diaries of Kenneth Tynan*; David Thomson's *Biographical Dictionary of Film*; Len Deighton's *London Dossier*; *The Orton Diaries*; and Ian MacDonald's *Revolution in the Head*, not just a wonderful book about the Beatles but a vital one about the sixties.

I am lucky to have in Rachel Cooke a true companion and a great reader.